I0712271

THE ROSE IN THE SHADOWS

A House of Hyrax Novel

Arcadia Rayne

THE ROSE IN THE SHADOWS

A House of Hyrax Novel

Arcadia Rayne

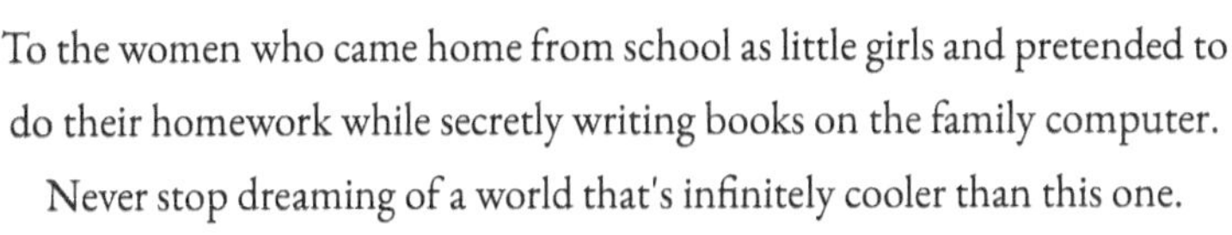

To the women who came home from school as little girls and pretended to do their homework while secretly writing books on the family computer. Never stop dreaming of a world that's infinitely cooler than this one.

CONTENT WARNING

Please note this is an Adult/New Adult fantasy novel written for a mature reader.

This story includes scenes of sexual content, violence, memory loss, physical abuse, threats of physical/sexual harm, sexual harassment, and adult language. Further, this novel includes depictions of grief and addiction that may be upsetting to some readers. Please read at your own discretion.

Your mental health matters.

Characters

- Theadora - (THAY-uh-dor-ah)

- Clayton - (CLAY-tun)

- Iris - (EYE-ris)

- Lorelai - (LOHR-uh-lie)

- Kent - (kent)

- Rankor - (RANGK-or)

- Camilla - (kuh-MEEL-ah)

- Nessira – (ness-EER-uh)

- Geia – (GUY-uh)

- King Vyncent - (VIN-sent)

- President Jonan - (Yoh-nahn)

- King Ledger - (LEJ-er)

- Alina - (uh-LEE-nuh)

- Caldrius – (KAL-dree-us)

Gods

- Crolun, The First God - (KROH-luhn)

- Ciclopia, Goddess of Beasts – (Sih-kloh-pee-uh)

- Hyrax, God of the Dead - (HIGH-racks)

- Zion, King of the Gods - (ZYE-uhn)

- Herea, Goddess of Women - (HER-ay-uh)

- Palaemon, God of the Water & Oceans - (puh-LAY-mon)

- Delia, Goddess of Pregnancy & Children - (DEE-lee-uh)

- Harmonia, Goddess of Peace - (har-MOH-nee-uh)

- Hypatia, Goddess of the Earth - (hi-PAY-shuh)

- Arto, God of Violence – (AHR-toh)

- Athene, Goddess of Wisdom – (Uh-TEE-nee)

- Pasnia, Goddess of Madness – (PAHZ-nee-uh)

- Asclepian, God of Medicine – (as-KLEE-pee-an)

- Angerelia, Goddess of Love – (an-jer-EE-lee-uh)

Places

- Athenia - (ah-THEE-nee-uh)

- Republic of Inanis - (in-AN-is)

- Promissa - (PRUH-miss-uh)

- Tenebris - (TEN-eh-bris)

- Gelumont - (GEL-uh-mont)

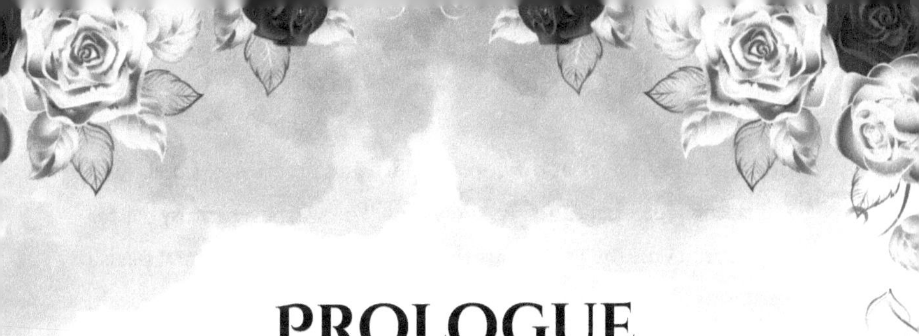

PROLOGUE

IRIS

The pink gown Iris had commissioned for the day was ridiculously extravagant, which only made her love it that much more. She had spared no expense in preparing her ensemble for the Athenian Peace celebration. She had piled her hair, pink today, elaborately onto her head and filled her bath with sparkling powder so that her dark skin was reflective under the sunlight. If she had to attend this cursed celebration, she might as well look fabulous while doing so.

It had been six years since the Great Battle that had marked the end of the Descendant War, the war that had swept the world and claimed millions. Six years since her uncle, the king of their country, Athenia, met with other world leaders and agreed to finally end the strife.

The palace had been abuzz all morning preparing for the celebration. It was one of the few events that the Royal Council welcomed the townspeople into the castle. The servants had spent the morning decorating the grounds while the kitchen had worked to prepare a feast. Now, with only a short amount of time before the festivities officially kicked off, Iris could see the Sirens warming up their instruments and the Elementals beginning to practice their magic tricks from her window.

She fucking hated this celebration.

Iris sighed as a knock at the door sounded and her friends, Lorelai and Camilla, entered her suite slowly, knowingly. This was never an easy day for her. It was not only the anniversary that marked the end of the war, but also the anniversary of the battle that had taken her aunt's life and, as a result, caused her own parents to flee the country. She hardly felt like celebrating that.

"We should go outside soon," Lorelai advised her, smoothing down the skirts of her pale blue gown. "We don't have to stay for long."

Iris loved it when Lorelai wore blue. It made her shining red hair seem even more fiery against her light skin. She suspected Lorelai knew that Iris felt that way, though. She suspected Lorelai had worn the gown on purpose, hoping it would brighten Iris' day. It did.

Camilla, on the other hand, dressed for no one but herself and now wore a low-cut emerald gown with long sleeves and a high slit. It would be a cold day in the Underworld before Camilla wore anything that could be deemed as conservative. She was beautiful, and by the Gods she knew it. She always had.

After flicking her long black hair over her shoulder, Camilla handed Iris the cloak hung by the door. "I certainly won't be staying out there long. Spending my evening with villagers is less than ideal."

Iris wanted to roll her eyes at Camilla as she buttoned the cloak over her dress. She knew the girl meant no harm, not really, not deep down, but as she went to acknowledge the comment, her eyes locked on the vase of flowers next to her bed. The water was... moving - slightly at first, then more violently as the ground under her feet trembled. The girls grasped onto walls and furniture for balance as the vase and other priceless objects began crashing to the floor.

Then, everything stilled.

"What in all of creation was that?" Camilla barked, sounding more irritated than afraid.

Lorelai opened her mouth to speak, but the sound of a splitting crack cut off her words as it echoed throughout the room. Frowning, Iris turned back towards her windows. Moments ago, the people had crowded the courtyard, getting ready for the celebration. Now, they fled.

Something was wrong.

Iris lifted the heavy skirts of her gown, which she liked a bit less now that there appeared to be an emergency to take care of. As she made her way to the door, she grasped onto Lorelai's hand.

"Stay here," she commanded. Iris needed to focus, and she would never be able to manage that if she had to worry about Lorelai.

Iris' suite wasn't far from the entrance of the castle, but by the time she arrived at the steps of the palace, violence had already filled the air. Shuddering, Iris felt momentarily as if she had been transported through time—as if she was sixteen years old again on the night of the Great Battle.

Through the fleeing townspeople, she was just able to make out the image of a woman.

She was entirely undressed, pale skin catching the sunlight, but she seemed unbothered or even entirely unaware of her immodesty. As she stood tall, the bridge underneath her quaked and rumbled, threatening to crack at any minute and crumble down entirely. Suddenly, a guttural scream tore free of her throat. Her blonde hair flew wildly as she threw back her head, unleashing a wave of magic that sent carts and carriages crashing around the townspeople.

Iris couldn't draw her eyes away from the stranger. The woman had a kind of unassuming beauty, Iris thought. If you passed her on the road, you might risk overlooking her, but a second glance could steal your heart entirely. Yet, even with her body on full display, Iris' attention was still drawn to her face, where dark lashes shrouded her vibrant blue eyes, and her subtle jawline stressed delicate pale lips.

"Who is she?" Clay, the Crown Prince of Athenia, shouted, as he rushed towards Iris from inside the palace. A sheen of sweat was already glistening on his brow.

Iris only shook her head up at him, unable to bring herself to speak. She had seen violence before, the Gods knew that, but to see it *here* again, in her home, shook her to her very core. Iris was brave; she'd been in so many dangerous situations that she'd lost count of them entirely. And yet in that moment, her fear met her memories, and together they held her in an iron grasp.

A man on the street ran towards the mystery woman, likely attempting to tackle her. The mortals might have deemed it brave, but Iris knew better. A human was useless in a fight against a Descendant. Descendants lived with the blood of the Gods in their bodies. It made them stronger, faster, and *better*.

The woman turned on him inhumanly, raising her palm high. Pushed by an invisible force, he flew through the air. When he landed on a carriage twenty feet back, the impact caused it to cave in completely. He fell, blood soaking the ground, and he didn't stand again.

"By the Gods," Iris cried. "*What* is she?"

Air Elementals could manipulate wind, Iris reasoned, but typically their abilities were restrained to brief gusts. They didn't have this kind of power. The stranger screamed again, and a blast of magic flew out, lifting the carriage off the ground and throwing it into the town across the bridge. Blood-red wine splattered across the sky as it landed on the barrels brought in for the celebration.

"Clay, she's going to hurt someone else!" Iris screamed, turning her attention once more toward her cousin. He needed to do something, and fast.

He grabbed her shoulders firmly, eyes shining bright and purposeful. She recognized that look. She suspected she might be the only one who would ever be able to notice the moments when Clay's true emotions leaked through the mask of control he typically donned. And now she could see the fear that was struggling to break out of him. Like Iris, this moment brought back painful memories for him, too.

"I need Kent. Have you seen him?" Clay yelled, searching for their friend.

Iris shook her head. She hadn't seen him since their breakfast earlier in the morning.

Soldiers marched from the castle, forming a military procession, but with nothing more than a wave of her palm, she pushed back ten at a time as they approached her.

Iris retreated towards the castle just as Kent burst forward from within. He shouted to Clay, and silent communication passed between them. As an officer himself, Kent had fought alongside Clay in the Great War. Their easy rapport didn't come from their experience on the battlefield, though; it was the years of lifelong friendship that allowed the two men to collaborate effortlessly. It truly was something special to watch the way they worked in tandem with one another. Together, they circled the woman.

Iris watched as her eyes flickered quickly, half open and half hanging closed. She was standing and yet not entirely conscious.

She's not in control of herself, Iris realized suddenly, recognizing that expression.

When Iris was a child, when her own powers had just started manifesting, she would often lose control of them. Aspects of her appearance would shift rapidly, leaving Iris exhausted and struggling to even stay standing. The woman swayed on the bridge, wild and untamed magic pouring out of her, and Iris knew she was looking at a fellow Descendant whose power was overwhelming her.

"Clay!" Iris yelled. If this woman wasn't intentionally doing this then she didn't deserve to be harmed, only subdued.

It all moved too quickly though. Clay charged at the stranger darting underneath her flying hands. She was soundless as she fought him, slipping out of his grasp time and time again effortlessly. As she lifted her arms to lash out at him with her power, he opened his mouth wide, breathing dragonfire in an angry storm. The flames snaked up her wrists and arms, but she did not scream or flinch. She hardly even noticed.

Kent's eyes widened as the woman fought on with little sign of pain, but he did not falter in his job. Clay continued to battle her, to distract her, as Kent set his eyes upon her, planted his feet, and began to sing. He started softly at first, stringing together a simple melody, but his voice grew more commanding with each moment that passed. As the magic washed over her, her head snapped violently towards Kent. She lurched towards him, but Clay grabbed her tight and held her in place until Kent's voice finally calmed her, and her body eventually stilled. She fell heavily into Clay who swung her effortlessly into his arms and began making his way back to the castle.

Quickly, Iris unbuttoned the cloak she wore and rushed to throw the fabric over the girls body. Clay hardly slowed as she did. Without another word, he stalked into the palace, leaving Iris and Kent standing frozen on the steps.

"What will happen to her?" Iris whispered.

Kent shook his head, running a hand over his face. "I'm not sure. The Dragon won't take kindly to her attacking the castle. Especially not on today of all days."

No, Iris didn't think that man *could* be kind regardless of the day. And yet, as she walked back into the palace with Kent at her side, she couldn't get the image of the woman swaying helplessly on the bridge out of her head. Iris wasn't entirely sure what had just happened, but her gut told her that not all was as it seemed.

CHAPTER ONE

"**S**top worrying, she'll be asleep for quite some time still. The sleeping potion they gave her was *strong*."

The sound of a womans laughter reverberated through my scalp, sending shockwaves of pain into my temple and the back of my neck. I tried to open my eyes, but the violent agony forced them closed once more with a wave so intense it threatened to knock me unconscious again.

"Did you see her out there? I've never witnessed anything like that!"

I didn't recognize the voice that hovered over my head, talking in an exaggerated whisper.

"Rayna, be quiet! Nurse Kira will kill us if we wake her up before the guard comes."

I wanted to call out to them. I needed to. I needed to tell them I was, in fact, awake and in pain, but my body protested.

Rayna scoffed. "Live a little, Theadora; it's not every day you get to see an Athenian traitor."

Where am I? I wondered, trying to trace back my memories.

"Ok, we saw her, so let's go. Please," Theadora pleaded, her voice tense.

"Fine, but only because I promised Samson I'd meet him in his suite in twenty minutes."

"You're going to his suite? You cannot."

"I have before and I will again. The things that man does with his hands are downright godly."

Rayna giggled again, and the sound of their footsteps echoed once more. Before I could find the strength to call out to them, I heard the sound of a door clicking shut and their steps faded into the distance.

Forcing in a deep breath, I took a mental stock of my body. I wiggled my toes and rolled my ankles. All seemed to be functional. I shifted my neck slightly, trying to ignore the stab of pain in my temples as I did so. With another breath, I focused my attention on my shoulders and elbows. They felt heavy, but otherwise unharmed. Finally, I wiggled my fingers, noticing the start of a nagging itch spreading up my hands and wrists.

Something was on me, scratching tender skin. As I focused on it, the itch grew to my forearms and elbows. It prickled until it became so unbearable that it actually... hurt.

No, *it burned.*

I shifted my arms once more and lost myself entirely to the scorching pain. My skin was burning. *I* was burning.

My eyes flew open and with a sudden gasp, I stared down at my body as if it were foreign. Someone had tied a thin, uncomfortable gown too loosely around my shoulders, and my waist and legs were strapped to a bed with leather bindings. My hands and arms, still screaming in pain, were bandaged with leaves and a pale yellow paste. I nearly gagged on the lurid smell of it.

The bed sat against the wall in an otherwise empty room. Pale white tiles covered the walls and floors that were otherwise devoid of decoration, sparing a small stool in the corner of the room. Two candles burned near the door, letting in a slight glow of light, but the space lacked any windows to the outside world. The door itself was glass, allowing me to look out. Or rather, allowing others to look in on me. But no one hovered outside. I could only see a long hall dimly lit and trailing into darkness.

"Help!" I croaked, voice raw and tired. "Can anyone hear me?"

I struggled against the restraints, but they refused to budge even an inch and though my arms were free, the pain of my injuries kept me from being able to move them above my sides. I threw back my head in frustration as minutes turned to hours.

Until finally, after what felt like a lifetime of isolation, a nurse clicked open the door and walked inside. I jerked my head towards her, taking in the image of a small woman, wearing a simple white dress and apron with graying hair tucked back neatly. Her small square shoes hit the floor with a thud at each step.

"Why am I here?" I struggled to sit up against the straps holding me down.

"Quiet!"

I clamped my mouth shut, teeth snapping together loudly. She approached me without hesitation, pulling at the leaves on my arms and glancing at the inflamed skin underneath. My arms were covered in bruises and blistered flesh that nearly turned my stomach in the second that I looked at it before jerking my head away.

"Does it hurt?" She asked, nodding towards my arms.

"Yes," I whispered, flinching as she poked aggressively at the tender skin.

Without responding, she pressed each of her palms flat against my arms and I watched as she took a deep breath in and closed her eyes. Slowly, the air in the room stilled. Frozen, I stared as a golden glow erupted from her fingertips and spread across my wounded flesh. Warmth covered my arms and I flinched, instinctively, but she squeezed down, locking me into place under her vice-like grasp.

"Stop!" I cried out. "What are you doing?"

The glow from her fingers spread over my wounded skin, and the pain eased after a moment. The stomach-turning burn of my crisped flesh was erased from every place the light touched me.

"What are you?" I gasped.

She peered up at me through dark lashes with irritation. "Try not to move. The skin will still need a bit more time to heal completely."

Her shoes hit the floor once more as she retreated back into the seemingly unending hall outside of my room. It was all I could do to stop myself from crying as she faded from view and all that was left were shadows. She didn't even tell me her name.

Time passed. I wasn't sure how much.

The sound of booming footsteps pounding through the door woke me from an otherwise dreamless sleep. Soldiers, ten in all, marched forward in dark vests and trousers. I wasn't quite sure what to be more afraid of, the fact that they looked ready for battle or that their eyes were trained on me alone. Then, as if practiced, they formed around me, surrounding the corners of my bed and the room door. No one spoke. For a moment, we were all still.

And that's when he came in.

Even while terrified and strapped to a bed, my body couldn't help but respond to him. Under his carefully tailored black tunic and leather trousers, I could make out the signs of firm muscle. He stood tall, broad shoulders pulled back as he strode into the room confidently. His sandy hair was perfectly combed back away from his clean-shaven face and remarkably sharp jaw-line.

It wasn't hard to acknowledge that he was attractive, but attractive men weren't always trustworthy.

As he pulled the stool from the corner of my room and sat it by the foot of my bed, choosing to prop a leg upon it than to sit, his stormy grey eyes met mine and there was no kindness to be found in his gaze. I couldn't fight the catch in my breath as that gaze travelled down my body before crawling back to my face.

"Well?" He finally asked expectantly, linking his hands together and leaning forward on his knees. "Care to explain what your plans were on that bridge?"

What bridge?

"This will be much easier if you cooperate," he growled after I failed to respond.

"I don't know what you're talking about."

"I will get answers from you before this day is over." He paused expectantly, waiting for me to agree to play a game I didn't seem to know the rules of. "Let's start with your name."

"My name?" I echoed, immediately feeling stupid.

"I won't ask again!" He snapped.

His voice sounded like death and pain, and the room had somehow heated to a nearly unbearable temperature with him in it. And yet, as terrifying as he was, it wasn't his interrogation or the ten guards who stood with weapons at the ready that made my body erupt into trembles.

It was the fact that as hard as I searched for an answer, no name came to my mind.

How could I not know my own name?

His eyes narrowed at me. "How about this? For every question you refuse to answer, I'll burn another part of your body until nothing is left of you but ash."

To prove his point, he grasped onto my wrist suddenly, ripping away the leaf and exposing a patch of still-healing skin. Without breaking eye contact, he raised a brow and jammed his thumb into the blistering wound.

The pain was instant and nearly blinding as I pulled my arm away and the motion tore the fragile skin. Swallowing my sharp whimper, I blinked through the tears to glare up at him.

"Theadora," I grunted through a locked jaw, grasping onto the first name that came into my mind and claiming it as my own.

"Now, we're getting somewhere," he remarked with a self-satisfied smile that sent my blood boiling. "You, of course, know who I am."

Arrogant, wasn't he?

"And I assume you know exactly the power that I have. Athenia does not take kindly to attacks during a time of peace."

"I don't know what you're talking about!"

He moved impossibly fast. In an instant he was at my side, bent over me with hands thrown on either side of my head until all I could see were his eyes and all I could smell was his cinnamon and burnt oak scent rolling over me in waves.

"You put the lives of hundreds of *my* people at risk on that bridge, Theadora, and you will tell me why!"

Heart frozen, my gaze locked on his hands. Like my nurse, his coloring began to change. But where her fingertips had exploded in a comforting light, his did something... different.

As he spoke, the veins in each hand darkened, mutating into something sinister, leaving his fingers and hands as dark as midnight. Golden scales erupted violently from the skin and the nails on each of his hands grew into *talons* that sliced effortlessly through the cotton pillow my head rested on.

I wasn't able to swallow the scream that burst from the deepest parts of me.

"Clayton Vail, you're going to give the girl a heart attack!"

I didn't dare look away from him to see the woman who had entered the room.

His eyes. They were blazing, sparkling with shimmers of light that grew in intensity until the only color that remained was a glowing bright golden. *Unnaturally* golden.

How was that possible?

We stared at each other for a moment, both breathing heavily. Then, slowly, the light in his eyes dimmed, and they settled back to their dull gray haze. He looked away first to the stranger at the door, and I quickly focused back on his hands. He was quick to fold them behind his back, but I caught sight of them as he did. There was only tanned skin, as if I had somehow imagined the whole thing.

"Iris, you don't need to be here." He sighed, turning to her.

She was a beautiful girl, albeit a bit extravagant. Her pastel pink hair hung to her shoulders in tight curls and was pulled back from her face with a flower crown. Shades of gold and sapphire decorated the lids above her dark eyes, and she wore a long gown falling towards the floor in waves of rose-hued taffeta. Her caramel skin was doused in sparkling pink and blue glitter that caught the light in the room as she walked towards me.

"Call it moral support." She smiled at him and winked. "So, who do we have here?"

She addressed me directly, stepping forward to the side of my bed with a smile. With her head tilted, she looked down at me, and one of her cheeks dimpled as she tried, and failed, to hide a grin.

"Theadora," I mumbled, repeating the stolen name that had become my own with a glance towards the man.

Clayton, I reminded myself. That's what she had called him.

"I see," she noted. "Well, Thea, everyone is dying to know how you ended up on that bridge!"

Clayton sneered at her. "Nice choice of words."

She only grinned back fondly at him over her shoulder. As she turned her attention back to me, her wide eyes sparkled with amusement.

"What bridge do you keep talking about?" I questioned.

"What bridge?" Clayton repeated, brows raised and voice thick with incredulity. "The bridge you shook so violently it will take weeks to repair! The bridge you stood on when you attacked my people and killed someone. Am I ringing any bells?"

I froze, breath caught in my throat. No. That couldn't be true.

And yet, if it were true, then maybe all of this chaos since I woke actually... made sense.

Of course that's why I was strapped to this ridiculous bed in this painfully empty room. I had hurt someone. They had somehow subdued me and locked me up here so I couldn't hurt anyone else.

But why couldn't I remember any of this?

"I don't think I wanted to hurt anyone," I mused, unsure if I was speaking more to myself or him.

"You certainly did," he replied.

"You don't understand!" I cried, struggling against the restraints. The guards around me responded at once, each stepping forward and brandishing their weapons. I froze, raising my now fully healed hands up in surrender. The loose gown fell gently over my shoulder, but I didn't dare to try to move it back into place.

"I don't know anything about a bridge, who you are, or even where I am. I remember waking up, and that is *all* I remember!"

Clayton wrapped his hands against the railing at the foot of my bed again, but his skin did not mutate this time. I was grateful for that, at least.

"Exactly how naïve do you think I am?"

"How should I know the answer to that question when *I don't know you.*"

With a swift motion, he ripped the stool off the floor and threw it across the room. I flinched as it hit the wall with a crash and splintered into pieces before falling to the ground.

"I will find out the truth whether you want to tell me or not! So, I suggest you do so now while I'm being kind in my interrogation tactics."

"Clayton, stop!" Iris gasped suddenly as she looked down at me with an emotion I couldn't quite identify.

"Problem, Iris?" He scolded, huffing with frustration.

Throwing a glare at him over her shoulder, she strode towards me suddenly, heels clicking on the floor.

"I won't speak to your naïvety," Iris called to him, "But I might question how observant you are!"

Her nails grazed my skin as she pulled the thin fabric of my gown further down my shoulder. I flinched away from her forcefully and the guards stepped forward once more, weapons at the ready.

"Doesn't this seem odd to you?" She questioned, voice sharp and eyes locked on my chest.

The guards must have been well-trained because while each of their eyes seemed to widen in surprise their hands did not waver until Clayton mumbled for them to be at ease and took a few tentative steps forward. He didn't speak, but I saw his jaw working as he glanced over me.

A flush of unease peppered my cheeks as I strained my neck to see what had captured everyone's attention. I could just make out the dark tattoo, in the shape of a weapon of some sort, inked into the skin on my left breastbone. It had one long shaft stretching up and branching into two jagged spear-like ends.

I shifted again, desperate to see more of it. "Is that a-"

"It's a bident," Iris told me, her voice quiet and tense. "The symbol of House Hyrax, God of the Dead. That tattoo is the Mark of Hyrax."

Wordlessly, Clayton ran his fingertips over the Mark, leaving pebbled flesh in his wake. I shivered just as he cursed under his breath.

"The Dragon will want to know," Iris said softly behind him.

He was quiet for a moment, staring intensely down at me while his lips pursed. Dampness covered the top of my brow and I wondered numbly how it had possibly grown so warm in the room.

"You truly don't remember anything before you woke up?" He asked, his voice low enough for only me to hear.

I nodded, too unsure of anything to speak aloud.

He bowed his head, and for a moment, he seemed to almost deflate. It was just a split second really, but long enough for me to see concern and tension hidden under his anger. There for a moment and gone in the next. When he finally looked up, his mask had returned and he once again looked powerful and in control, seemingly unaware I had witnessed his momentary crack in composure. With a wave of his hand, he beckoned a guard to come forward.

"Have the nurses remove her bandages and relocate her to the palace cells until we can call an emergency Council meeting," he commanded.

"Yes, your grace." The guard nodded.

Iris pursed her lips when he mentioned transferring me to the cells, but she didn't speak up. Perhaps that was a battle she knew she couldn't win.

He looked towards me once more, not at me necessarily. Rather his attention stayed on the Mark on my chest. "She can't wear that to the Council."

"I'll get her some clothes." Iris volunteered, speaking up for me as if I wasn't there.

"Good," he muttered. "Nothing elaborate, Iris. Regardless of what's on her chest, the Kingdom still views her as a threat. We don't need anyone to see her dressed like you. For now."

For now?

Iris nodded her agreement, and Clayton turned to leave, his guards following behind.

"I do hope you're telling the truth," he called to me from the door before finally exiting.

And without him and his overwhelming presence, the room suddenly seemed larger and easier to breathe in. Iris and I were silent for a moment, both seeming to need time to adjust to the space without Clayton in it.

"What is happening?" I whispered.

After flicking her colorful hair over her shoulder, she leaned down to pat my knee affectionately. "Don't you worry. We'll get this figured out."

"Iris, that's your name?"

Giggling, she hiked her skirts up to her thighs and tossed herself onto the foot of my bed, leaning carelessly over my legs. "Yes, I'm Iris, pleasure to make your acquaintance. Clayton, who just left, is my cousin. Sorry he was being a bit of a bully."

Her eyes widened slightly as the words escaped her mouth and her mouth tightened for a moment before quirking in a soft, nervous smile.

"Don't tell anyone I said it. His father would consider it treasonous for me to be calling the Crown prince names, even if it is all in good fun."

Ignoring the large majority of her words, I grasped onto her hand. "You have to help me get out of here."

"Unfortunately, my dear, I can only do so much." She sighed, glancing over her nails. "You caused quite a scene on that bridge. I *can* get you a proper dress, though, and we'll clear all this up in no time."

"At least tell me what's happening!" I called out to her as she stood and began to retreat. "Please, I don't understand any of this."

She paused at the door, just as Clayton had, and nodded. When she spoke again, her voice was as serious as it had been when she noticed the Mark stamped across my chest. "I will. I promise. I'll explain as much as possible when I return, but I have to get you a dress. We can't be late for the Council, or it's both of our necks on the line. You'll have to trust me for now."

With that, she left me alone with nothing but my anxieties for company. There was some consolation in the solitude this time, though, because for some reason I did, in fact, trust her. Maybe it was because she had talked to me like a person instead of a criminal. Perhaps it was because her colorful ensemble made her look more like a child than an adult. Whatever the reason was, though, I did trust that if she said she was coming back for me, then she would be returning.

CHAPTER TWO

I t wasn't long before three armed guards came to retrieve me and escort me to my cell. It was a tiny little room with a single bed and a foul-smelling chamberpot that clearly hadn't been cleaned in some time. And though it was smaller than the infirmary room they had trapped me in earlier, the cell at least offered a small window which I was grateful for.

A little natural light was just what I needed to remind me that there *was* a world outside. And maybe I wouldn't stay trapped in here forever.

A thick glass wall separated my cell from the hall outside. When I hovered by that glass and craned my neck until a cramp threatened to form, I could just barely make out two additional cells down the corridor, along with a small staircase leading to a thick steel door. I could only assume that the door led to freedom. And while most of the guards retreated down the hall, one stayed posted outside my cell.

Resigning myself to being trapped for now, I flopped onto the bed, content to peer out the window. Through the musty glass, I watched the clouds moving slowly through the vibrant blue sky. I watched them float through the air and wished more than anything that I could simply fly out of this hell to join them.

Iris wasted no time in returning to me. Like earlier, I could hear her coming long before she arrived. Her heels echoed throughout the chamber, as did her voice, as she issued countless greetings to those she passed. By the time I heard the door above the stairs creak open, I had already rushed to my feet, eager to see her again.

She stepped forward, arms filled with dark fabric and worn boots. Her lips pursed as she glanced at me with a tilted head from behind the glass wall.

"I should have brought some rouge or something," she mumbled, almost to herself. "You look like a ghost."

Wordlessly, the guard held out his hand, and the glass rippled. It shook briefly before disappearing entirely, allowing her to enter my space. I stared at her wide-eyed. That couldn't be possible.

Tsking, she grinned at me. "As if that's the strangest thing you've seen today. Now come, I had to guess your size, but I think I did fairly well."

She grabbed my wrist and pulled me toward her, shoving the bundle of black fabric into my hands and looking at me expectantly. Instinctively, my eyes flickered to the guard standing only feet away with eyes bearing into my soul. After an awkward momentary silence, Iris followed my gaze and giggled.

"McCarther, do take up your post again," she chastised. "You've seen enough of this poor girl."

He grunted but left nonetheless. She had brought me a plain dress, just as Clayton had instructed. It was a deep black woolen fabric with no jewels or embellishments. The long sleeves were loose, and the gown fell neatly to the ground without any frills or pleats. There was nothing truly noteworthy about its design, spare its neckline. It was cut low, exposing the flesh on my breastbone and, by default, laying out my tattoo for the world to see.

"Turn," she commanded, and she began lacing up my bodice.

After tying the corset, she directed her focus towards my hair. Her fingers worked quickly, tying back my long blonde locks in elaborate braids to keep them out of my face. Determined to bring color to my cheeks despite the lack of rouge, she took it upon herself to squeeze them tightly with her thumb and forefinger. The sharp pressure made me bite down on my lower lip but I didn't bother to protest.

"You'll be presented in front of the Council," she said, voice low, eyes darting out to ensure the guards weren't overhearing.

Gratitude overwhelmed me. She had remembered her promise.

"Council?" I questioned.

Her eyes flashed again to the corridor outside my cell, and she pushed me back further against the wall. She handed me the boots, and I set about tying their many laces.

"What Council?" I whispered, now suddenly conscious of my volume.

She kept her head close to mine, bowing down to help tie my other shoe.

"The Council of the High Houses. Each House of a High God has a representative on it, all except for House Hyrax right now. They're the governing body of Athenia, but the Dragon has the final say on all matters, including your case."

Dragon. Clayton had mentioned the Dragon. "The Dragon, that's Clay's father, isn't it?"

She nodded. "Yes. Only address him if he asks you a direct question. And only address him as 'your majesty.' He'll likely bring in a Truthseeker for the interrogation."

I shook my head, frowning, as my fingers finished the final loop on my boots. I could hear the guard outside coming closer. We were running out of time for her to explain much more.

"Truthseeker? What does that mean?"

"From House Herea, of course," she explained, voice betraying her surprise that I didn't already know this information. "The Descendants of the Goddess Herea."

The door above the stairs let out its signature squeal as it opened. We were out of time. I could hear the boots of guards beginning to pass through. Sighing, she pulled me to my feet and ran her hands down the fabric on my shoulders, smoothing it into place. I grabbed onto her hand, gripping tightly.

"What do you mean they're Descendants of a Goddess?" I demanded in a clipped and hushed tone.

"We're all descended from the Gods," she replied as if that much should be obvious. "If the powers don't give it away, the Marks will. We're all born with them, symbolizing our ancestors."

She tapped her fingers against the tattoo that lay on my collarbone. The tattoo she had deemed the Mark of Hyrax.

Wait. I wasn't -

I couldn't be the Descendant of a God.

I didn't have time to question her further before the guards entered my cell and began pulling me out. Iris followed us, holding onto my hand for as long as she could, her face a mask of confusion and concern. Then, as I was pushed toward the stairs by the guards, I finally let go of her, catching the sight of a small black apple etched into the skin of her wrist - a tattoo quite similar to mine.

We're all descended from the Gods.

The guards surrounded me, close enough to be a silent threat, but dispersed enough for the prying eyes lining each side of the hall to glare at me as we walked by. I imagine they wanted that. They wanted people to know they were punishing me for what happened on the bridge.

Even if *I* didn't know what that was. Even if I didn't know what I was being punished for.

I couldn't help but gawk at the palace decor as they rushed me through the winding passageways. I struggled to appreciate it the way I wanted to, but what I could see was positively awe-inspiring. Massive arches extended nearly twenty feet high, their stark white walls embellished with elaborate golden sculptures and finishings. Crystal chandeliers hung from the ceiling, sending sparkles of colored light onto us. A fresh garden of roses, tulips, and perfectly manicured shrubbery was visible through the towering windows.

As we went, it got harder to ignore the courtiers who watched me. I tried to focus on the splendor of the decor over their chatter, but blocking it out completely was impossible.

"I heard she's a Promissan spy."

"I saw the Crown Prince leaving the infirmary looking quite shocked."

"They'll need to execute her, of course. It's the only way to send a message of strength to whoever sent her."

My stomach lurched. Could that truly happen? Would they really kill me? How could they sentence me to death for a crime I didn't even remember committing?

Finally, we paused at a large rotunda in front of massive wooden doors with ornate carvings. Looking up, I stared at the mural painted on the ceiling. Nearly a dozen figures sat on a bed of pillows, all seeming to stare directly at me. In the center sat a broad man with full hair and a long white beard. In his hand, he grasped an enormous sword. He was the most commanding presence in the painting by far, seeming nearly alive because of how his eyes followed my movements, eyes that glowed with the same bronze light I had recognized in Clayton earlier.

"Keep moving!" A guard yelled behind me, giving me a swift shove in the back.

I fell forward, thrown out of my haze, and stumbled directly into the large chamber through the open doors. The difference between this room and the halls outside it was jarring. The palace outside exuded a sense of lightness and beauty, whereas this space could only be described as ominous. Without a single window, the only light came from candles hanging on sizeable wrought-iron chandeliers. The walls were made entirely of dark bricks, and the floor beneath me was dusty and beaten down as if it was comprised of nothing more than dirt that had been stepped on so many times it had hardened completely.

With a resounding thud, the doors shut behind me, and the guard pushed me again until I fell into the center of the room. Behind me were seats lifted into risers. Few people sat in them; those that did wore sparkling and intricate gowns and suits. Iris found herself a seat there, sitting close to the front. She gave me a small thumbs-up and beckoned me to turn and face the five arched balconies above me.

A bell sounded over the room, and a hush fell over the crowd behind me. Above, four figures stepped into their respective chambers and took their seats. I recognized Clayton standing behind the man seated at an awning marked for House Zion. That had to be his father. Like Clayton, he was an impossibly large man. His gray hair contrasted with his muscular arms, which were noticeable under the fitted black jacket. He did not speak at first, choosing instead to lounge back and look me over appraisingly. The remaining members of the Council all seemed to lean away from him subconsciously, as if they were afraid of him somehow entering their own enclosed spaces.

"I hereby call this Council Meeting of the High Houses of Athenia to order. May we rule with honor and dignity and please the Gods that bore us," he called out in a bored but firm voice, his eyes never leaving me.

"Praise Gods," echoed the surrounding room.

The Dragon cleared his throat. "As the reigning Dragon of House Zion and King of Athenia, I recognize Gregory Handel of House Herea, Rosalia Blackmore of House Delia, and Clara Reid of House Palaemon, and I pay my respects to the Virgin Goddess Harmonia. May she look upon this Council with pride."

"Praise Harmonia," chanted the crowd in a uniform tone that set the hair on the back of my neck on edge.

Clayton stepped forward from behind his father, handing him a packet of parchment. The Dragon took it silently, looking over it quickly before glancing back at me with irritation.

"I'm told you go by the name Theadora?" The Dragon asked me.

His expression had a certain amount of calculation, as if he knew exactly what I would say and how I would say it. From the curl of his lip to the squint of his eye, he looked positively murderous. He was almost exactly what you'd imagine a Dragon in human form to look like. Ruthless and uncaring.

"Yes," I said softly before remembering Iris' advice. "Your majesty."

"The Crown Prince informs me you have no memory of any events that preceded your waking in my infirmary; is that correct?"

I nodded, and felt the weight of unease settle over me. Judging based on the glares I received from the Council members and the hushed gasp from the risers behind me, questions in this room demanded a verbal response.

He grunted. "I must inform you that lying to any member of this Council within this chamber is punishable by death. Do you still wish to stand by that statement?"

Fear bubbled within me, but no fresh memories rose to the occasion, despite how much I wished they would. No one wanted to understand this situation more than I did, but my mind simply refused to cooperate. "I remember nothing."

With pursed lips that betrayed just the slightest hint of a smirk, he nodded silently and took a quill pen from beside him, signing his name formally on the papers. As his pen left the page, a sudden and unnatural weight settled over me, spreading over my legs first, then stretching over my fingertips and arms. The force with which it held me was suffocating, far worse than the bindings from the infirmary bed. I wanted to shriek out, but even my mouth somehow remained locked shut. I couldn't move. Someone, or something, was holding me in place.

The Dragon beckoned to the doors, which were swiftly opened at his command, and a woman crossed the threshold into the chamber with a comfortable ease. She was tall with long auburn hair and her pale blue ball gown seemed to complement her fair complexion. She strode to the center of the room, curtsied low to the ground before the Dragon, and then nodded in acknowledgment to the other Council members.

"Your majesty, Council members, I am honored to offer my services to you today." She greeted them before turning her green eyes to me. "I've been told you understand little of what is happening."

As she turned her attention to me, relaxation spread happily throughout my body, calming my frantic anxieties just as quickly as that foreign weight had settled over me moments ago.

It's her power! A voice within me yelled.

I opened my eyes in a flash.

"My name is Lorelai Pelland." Her bell-like voice called to me. "I'm what you call a Truthseeker from House Herea. Truthseekers can elicit the truth from people. Does that make sense so far?"

Her magic was hypnotizing. In an instant, her voice was the only thing I could hear. Her eyes were the only thing I could see. Lorelai Pelland was the only person in the room and the only person in the world who mattered. I could only nod at her, unable to turn my attention away.

"Good." She smiled. "We'll start small at first. I want you to know that it might be rather painful if you try to resist or lie, so try your best to cooperate. Now, I've told you my name. What is yours?"

"I don't know," I suddenly blurted out, the words erupting before I could even think it through. "Clayton was scaring me, so I said it was Theadora, but I don't actually remember my name."

Lorelai paused and glanced behind her at the Dragon. That momentary look away was all it took for her power to lose control over me temporarily, and I slumped forward, breathing heavily as my head cleared from its fog.

The Dragon was silent but nodded for her to continue. As soon as our eyes locked, I found myself ensnared in her spell again, losing the brief respite. There was only Lorelai Pelland.

"Can I call you Thea?" She asked me.

I nodded.

"Good. Thea, I'm twenty-two. How old are you?"

"I don't know," I repeated.

She frowned and shifted, grasping my shoulders and looking deeply into my eyes. Her grip on my mind somehow strengthened, surrounding me to near suffocation.

"Thea, I heard you met my friends Clay and Iris. Do you have any friends?"

Every repetition of my newly declared name sent me spiraling even further. My mouth wasn't my own, and neither were my thoughts. She was everywhere, all around me, and somehow inside me. She took up every little space. I ground my teeth so hard together I was sure they would crack, but as I struggled against her, my vision swam with blinding pain.

"I warned you not to fight, Thea. Now, tell me. Do you have any friends?"

"I think Iris wants to be my friend," I spit out, strained. Some part of me could hear snickering in the corner, but I could barely register it.

Lorelai grasped my arms tighter, her fingers digging uncomfortably into the tender flesh. "Thea, why did you attack the castle this morning?"

"I don't know," I whined.

Her magic surged around me like a vice, holding my mind into place so she could crush into it. Thousands of magical fingers poked into me. Pain exploded so violently that all I could do was whimper against it. It tore me apart from the inside out. Had the magic not been holding me into place, I was sure I would have convulsed right there on the ground from the force of it.

"I don't know!" I screamed helplessly.

Lorelai ripped her hands back from me suddenly, turning away. I fell back, landing hard on the ground, a cold sweat spreading over my brow. My stomach lurched, and it was all I could do to lean forward in time to retch onto the floor instead of my lap. I couldn't even bring myself to feel embarrassed. Every inch of me stung as I trembled helplessly on the ground. Lorelai handed me a small handkerchief, apologizing under her breath. I met her eyes as I took it and watched as she wiped her hand quickly under her nose as a tiny red droplet escaped.

No one in the room had moved during the assault. Each Council member looked more disinterested than the last, in fact. Clayton was the only one who had seemed to pay attention, having stepped forward slightly.

"Well?" The Dragon demanded.

"There's nothing," she murmured, her voice notably weaker.

"She's lying?" Rosalia asked from House Delia's seat.

"No," Lorelai mumbled. Then, breathing deeply, she cleared her throat and spoke clearly. "There was nothing. As in, no memories. No childhood, no school, nothing. I'm sorry, but I can't help you. She's telling the truth."

The chamber erupted. Each voice of concern rose higher than the last. Some protested that they should still execute me while others argued on my behalf. Still more criticized Lorelai and her abilities. Finally, Lorelai, still subtly wiping blood from her nose, left me alone in the center of the room as she retreated to a seat next to Iris. Part of me wanted to collapse under the pain that still throbbed in my head, but I met Clayton's eyes from across the room. They were golden, glowing brightly. Gently, he nodded up, and the implication was clear. Lifting my skirts from underneath me, I stood.

"Order!" The Dragon commanded. "Miss Pelland, was there any reason to suspect she might be a danger to us?"

Lorelai's hands were shaking, and she grasped them together tightly. "No, Your Majesty."

He nodded and turned his attention to me, running a hand over his thick beard as he contemplated his next action. "There is still the matter of where you came from. A girl from a dead House doesn't just come from nowhere."

"If I may, Your Majesty," called a voice from the crowd. An older gentleman, well past the prime of his life, stood from the risers behind me. His clothes were simple but refined, and his face showed the lines of a full life underneath a head of white hair. The Dragon nodded at him.

"The Council acknowledges Hansel Long, patriarch of House Athene and the Royal Tutor. What insight can you provide us with, Hansel?"

"Well, I have been speculating," he mused, stepping out of the risers onto the Council floor. "You see, the last documented member of House Hyrax was Zacharia Moore, a general killed in the early days of the Great War. Zacharia was known for celebrating war victories with particular vigor. It's entirely possible he fathered a child we did not know about. Perhaps the girl has lived among the mortals, not getting proper training for her abilities. And without proper practice and guidance, it's entirely possible that what we saw on the bridge was her magic literally exploding out of her. Further, it's possible that such an event created a trauma so great that it could have caused some rather extensive amnesia."

"Zacharia Moore was a Necromancer," Gregory of House Herea noted. "We only have historical evidence of Necromancers and Mediums descending from the God of the Dead. There's no evidence of any being born with the telekinetic abilities she showed."

Hansel chuckled softly under his breath and smiled at the Council. "And how lucky are we to see the new evolution of our Great Gods' powers among us! Praise Gods!"

"Praise Gods!" echoed the room.

The Dragon raised a single arm, and silence settled over the room again as he looked down at me thoughtfully. I tried not to show how badly I was still trembling. We briefly held each other's gaze until, finally, he stood, and the other Council members rose with him.

"How lucky we are, indeed," he mused cryptically. "We welcome Theadora, of House Hyrax, to our court. A band of guards will leave for town to investigate any additional insights into her origins. For now, I will take responsibility for the girl and welcome her as a guest of my household. Until I am sure there is no risk to my people, she will be kept under guard while she is assimilated into our court, educated in our customs, and trained to master her abilities. If Hansel's speculation is true, and the girl is not a risk, Athenia will proudly celebrate the lost daughter of House Hyrax and the revival of a once-dead House.

"Praise Gods!" chanted the court. "Praise Hyrax."

"This meeting is hereby adjourned. The guards may escort her to the Royal Apartments," the Dragon concluded, looking at me with darkened eyes before turning and exiting his chamber.

He did not hide his emotions well, I noted. It was all too clear that he did not trust me.

I wasn't sure if I blamed him.

CHAPTER THREE

Once the Dragon announced the meeting was over, people were quick to take their leave. Their eyes lingered on me as they filtered out of the dimly-lit chamber, and I could feel their curiosity fall over me in steady waves. I, however, stayed glued to my spot in the center of the room, too shocked by the day's events to think about where I should move next.

Where else was there for me to go?

Numbly, I repeated the name Zachariah Moore over and over in my head, desperate to spark some memory that would make sense of this, but none came. Certainly, someone had to know who I was! Someone had to have raised me. Someone had known who I was before those powers supposedly burst out of me on that bridge. Maybe I had siblings or a mother who would show up at the palace doors ready and able to give my life some sort of meaning and identity.

A touch on my arm pulled me out of my spiraling thoughts, and I turned to face Iris. Her smile was gentle as she hugged me quickly and patted my back fondly.

"So, you think I want to be your friend, huh?" she teased, linking her arm through mine and leading me out of the hall's center. I caught a glance of Clayton standing on the now-empty balcony where his father had presided. His eyes were dark and unreadable, but he followed our movements as we left, his gaze burning my back even as I turned away from him.

At the door, Iris nodded politely to a guard who stood waiting for us. He bowed formally and turned on his heels, leading us through the spiraling of palace corridors at a ferocious pace. There were faces at nearly every turn. At least some had the decency to hide their whispers behind paper fans or innocently raised hands; others were blatant with their speculations. Iris rambled on and on, maybe to keep me from thinking about it, but it didn't work - their whispers echoed in my mind.

"She's rather pretty. She'll make quite a splash at court."

"I still don't think we can trust her."

"It would be just like the Promissans to send a spy in right under our noses."

"House Hyrax is extinct, though. Could Promissa have been lying about their recent census?"

"Iris?" I called, stopping her mid-sentence. She had been going on about how I would need new dresses and all the designs she had in mind. It was hardly my preferred conversation topic, not when there were so many other pressing things to discuss.

"What is it?" She asked, brows pulling together as she frowned.

"What are Promissans?"

Those around us quieted for a moment, apparently shocked by my use of the phrase, but they quickly resumed their gossip more intensely than ever before. Somehow, it seemed, I had said something wrong.

She sighed, rolling her neck as if my question stressed her. The guard in front of us snorted but kept marching forward, twisting us into another long passage. This one had paintings hung on each wall. They were whimsically designed family trees mapping out the lineages of the Council Houses. My attention lingered on the tree for House Hyrax, which quite clearly ended with Zachariah Moore. Would they soon etch my stolen name there?

In this hall, we walked alone. There were no prying eyes or overly in-trigued courts people. I suspected our destination was not an area typically available to the usual guests of the palace halls. Certainly, I would be kept far away from anyone else, far away from where I could cause harm. Each step we took brought us closer and closer to whatever new cage waited for me.

"They're not a what; they're a who," Iris pointed out, her voice short. "We were at war with Promissa for many decades and only signed the Peace Treaty a few years ago. The war had... many casualties and bred much bad blood between our two nations. So the people of Athenia still have some biases against the Promissans, understandably."

"They think I'm one of them," I noted, not even bothering to frame it like a question. I already knew the answer and the insinuation that lay under the assumption was clear.

Traitor. Spy. Murderer.

Iris paused, momentarily pulling on my arm to stop me in the hall. The guard stayed and waited for us but stood at attention to not give the impression of listening in on us. I knew better. I knew he hung on to every word and would no doubt report to the Dragon everything that was said.

"You aren't, though," she whispered. "Right?"

Surely that was the question burning on everyone's minds, but coming from her the accusation didn't feel like an attack. So I answered honestly.

"Not that I know of."

She nodded softly, and her eyes fell to the ground momentarily. When she looked up at me again, just seconds later, her composure had returned, and any hint of upset was quickly gone. She tugged my arm into hers again and began marching forward, setting a pace that was nearly difficult to keep up with.

"So, this is Dimitri," she announced, beckoning to the guard behind us, who only huffed in response. "He'll be your official guardian. You'll have other guards periodically, but Dimitri will be primarily in charge of your care. So he should be able to assist if you have questions or needs."

She made it seem like he was my employee rather than my keeper, even though he was obviously here to keep a watchful eye on me and be prepared to protect everyone else from me in the event that I did turn out to be a spy.

Which I really didn't think I was.

Dimitri was a tall man, but not overly muscular. He wore a black sweater and thick trousers, the ends of which were tucked into large boots that echoed in the halls as we walked. A large broadsword was tucked into the waistband of his industrial belt and a second blade, impossibly larger than the first, was strapped over his shoulder. His face was stern, wrinkled from years of intense grimaces, and the mask of a black beard covered his chin, matching his thick hair

"Nice to meet you, Dimitri," I mumbled.

"The pleasure is mine, my lady."

I turned to Iris, eyebrows raised in a silent question. With a mischievous sparkle to her eye, she only giggled back at me.

"Regardless of where you came from, my dear, you are the last known survivor of House Hyrax. That makes you the matriarch of a Royal Council family. And a Princess."

"Princess?" I scoffed, nearly stopping in our tracks.

"It's a title more than anything. Each Council member is referred to as a Prince or Princess of their family line for formality's sake. You, my dear, are the Hyraxian Princess. None of the Council members will actually ascend to the throne, though."

"Clayton will." I realized, beginning to piece things together. "He's the Crown Prince."

She gave me a sideways wink. "Look at that. You'll ace your Descendant History lessons in no time."

I shrugged, head spinning. No wonder the palace was already alight with gossip. I was either a long-lost princess brought back to resurrect an otherwise dead House, or I was a royal traitor sent from an enemy country. Were the situation reversed, I'd gossip about me too.

"Now, there will be other people to help you, too, of course, besides Dimitri, I mean. You'll need to practice with those powers of yours to avoid another outburst, and of course, I'll arrange for a visit with my personal seamstress. Any of the palace servants will be happy to oblige you. No doubt word of the Dragon welcoming you into court as a guest of his household will already have spread."

No doubt.

Dimitri stopped in front of us, marking the end of our journey. We stood at the conclusion of the hall in front of sweeping white wooden doors with elaborate golden handles that almost dripped to the floor in finery. Carved into each door was the same etching of an oversized spear sparking into two prongs—a bident on each door to match the one now tingling on my chest.

"My lady." Dimitri cleared his throat. "These are the apartments for the Council member of House Hyrax. They're yours now."

Iris smiled and nodded, encouraging me to step forward, place my hands on each of the heavy wooden doors, and push.

As they creaked open and the beauty of the room washed over me, I could only gasp.

We entered an opening parlor with armchairs decorated in polished fabrics and covered with plush pillows and blankets. End tables of hand-carved wood sat on each end of the armchairs, and sparkling crystal chandeliers hung from above. Through the parlor, I entered the bedchamber.

The floors were smooth, made of fine wood, and a white carpet with golden stitching of leaves and vinery covered the room underneath the oversized bed. A towering mound of thick pillows nearly hid the ornate, golden headboard behind them. The duvet was lush and pristinely white, decorated with patterns that perfectly matched the carpet beneath it. Heavy curtains had been pulled back from the windows that stretched wide to display the gardens outside the palace. A dozen freshly cut red roses sat on each end table adjoining the bed, and a small ottoman in the most exemplary contemporary upholstery sat at the foot.

Iris watched as I admired the room and ran my fingers across the bedding. She was patient, allowing me to circle the bedchamber before offering me a grin and grasping my hand. Then, she led me into the spacious, and notably empty, walk-in closet, with an abundance of room for clothes and shoes. She wasted no time there, promising we would fill it before yanking me into the bathroom.

A chandelier larger than any other in the suite hung above the oversized marble tub. The tub was cylindrical, with pillars stretching up and curtains for privacy. White towels, marked with the bident of Hyrax, hung from the walls beneath the impossibly clear mirror of the vanity. A double-sink countertop offered an array of skincare and perfumes for me to choose from.

I admired the space momentarily before even the bathroom became too much to accept. Wordlessly, I stumbled back into the parlor where we had entered and fell onto the chaise in a heap. Dimitri had not followed us into the apartments, choosing instead to stand guard outside the doors, and I was grateful for the privacy. I certainly did not want many people to see the state of shock I was in. Who knew how people would perceive my reaction?

I should feel grateful for all this, but I only felt... confused.

How could I be in a prison cell one moment and told I was the keeper of such luxury the next?

What had I even done to deserve any of this?

"Iris, this doesn't make any sense," I whispered. "I know the Dragon doesn't trust me. Why would he give me all of this?"

She sighed and sat across from me, smoothing out the skirts of her gown as she did. "Anything the Dragon does, he does out of political motivation. If it's true that you are just an innocent in all of this, and he imprisoned the last known member of a royal household, that's grounds for war. Promissa, or any other country for that matter, could, and likely would, come to fight for your honor. Everyone in the world will want your allegiance because you're the last of your line. And if that wasn't motivation enough, the Dragon will want you to fully balance the Council here in Athenia."

"I don't know the first thing about your Council!" I protested.

"No, you don't, and you don't need to for now. All you really need to know is that the international community would respect a complete Council. With you in that role, it would be much more difficult for anyone to pull us into a war again. The Dragon wants that. He'll want to secure you as a citizen of Athenia, specifically because you're the last Descendant of Hyrax."

That all might be true, but my gut still told me I couldn't trust that I was safe here in this palace.

"You're right about the Dragon not trusting you," she admitted, folding her hands in her lap. "But that can change with time. And so, until it does, Dimitri and everyone else in this palace will watch you."

I pursed my lips, laughing softly as I started understanding what she seemed too afraid to say directly. I'd been so blinded by the suite's finery that I allowed myself to be fooled by the state of the situation. These rooms *weren't* a kindness from the Dragon at all.

"I never really left the prison." I realized. "He only moved me to a finer cell."

She was still for a moment, her eyes darkening, but eventually, she nodded and offered me a small smile. There was pity in her smile. I tried to ignore that.

We sat quietly until she finally stood and cleared her throat. "Well, I best be on my way for now. I'll return with some things to fill your closet in the morning."

"Iris, that's not necessary-"

"Oh, hush!" She chastised, patting my hand. "Now, you've had a long day, and I do not doubt another one will await you tomorrow. So try to get some rest tonight."

I promised her I would, and she left. As the doors swung shut behind her and the characteristic sound of a lock falling into place sounded, I sighed. Those doors wouldn't open again tonight. I was stuck here in these over-elaborate rooms. A prisoner in luxury, but a prisoner, nonetheless.

I sat in that parlor for what felt like hours, replaying the day's events over and over. The time to request food came and passed, but I couldn't even consider eating. Finally, when hues of orange and purple from the setting sun filled the room, I moved to sit on the bed, sinking into its feathered mattress heavily. As I undid the laces of my boots, I stared out the windows, watching as darkness fell over the land.

I didn't lay back into the sheets until long after shadows had covered the fields. The bed was comfortable; I couldn't deny that. So, I tucked myself under the covers and folded into the mound of pillows. Even so, sleep wouldn't come.

I finally woke in the morning to pounding on the door, having only managed to eventually drift to sleep as the sun started cresting over the gardens again.

"Theadora, please do not tell me you are still asleep in there." I heard Iris calling. "Don't make me have Dimitri knock down this ancient and historic door."

"I'm coming, Iris!" I hollered, stumbling through the bedroom.

I opened the door just as her fist was poised to knock once more. She had gowns of all different colors and fabrics piled high in her arms. Lorelai, the Truthseeker from the Council meeting, stood behind her, offering a small, apologetic smile. With them was a more petite, older woman with graying hair and a stern expression.

"Little Miss," the stranger huffed, pushing past the two girls and into the room briskly. "I don't quite care what family you come from. It is quite rude to keep people waiting."

How could I have kept people waiting when I wasn't aware they were coming?

The woman set down her bags in the parlor, not bothering to introduce herself before beginning to pull out measuring tapes, threads, and needles. I glanced towards Iris in confusion, and she only rolled her eyes at me, prancing into the room impatiently with a disapproving sigh and shake of the head. As a last resort, I turned to Lorelai, my frustration clear.

"This is Ruthie," Lorelai explained. "What she lacks in manners, she makes up for in quality work. She's the finest seamstress from here to the Great Lake. She'll be designing some gowns for you."

"It is nearly ten!" Iris chastised, hands on her hips. "Please, don't tell me you're just waking up!"

"I had a bit of a day yesterday," I reminded her, closing the door grumpily behind them.

Iris ignored the excuse and began going through her gowns, placing them in piles around us. She looked startlingly different today; her pink hair was now a bright ginger, cut close to her chin with fraying bangs. Her ballgown was yellow, made of a subtle lace that gave the illusion of petaled flowers growing atop her dark skin. She evaluated the colors that suited me while Ruthie measured my bust and muttered softly to herself.

"Is this really necessary?" I asked, eyeing an elaborately beaded gown with crystals and sparkling fabric. It was all a bit gaudy for my tastes. Just a few simple dresses would do. And I certainly didn't need enough to fill the entire closet.

"It's quite necessary!" Iris insisted. "You, my dear, are the most eligible bachelorette in the kingdom, and I intend to make sure you steal every young suitor's heart."

"She's not a doll to dress up, Iris," Lorelai said softly, smiling as she folded herself into one of the armchairs.

Ruthie ripped up my arms, measuring down the length of each. She was silent as she worked, eyeing my body shape as she moved. I could practically see her mind alight with creativity as she imagined the finery she would craft for me. Sighing, I threw my head back and submitted to it all. How much say in the matter did I really have anyway? I was stuck in this palace one way or another, whether that was captive as a prisoner or displayed as a princess. Still, my eyes betrayed me as I scowled at a glittering monstrosity of a ballgown in Iris' hands. She only winked back at me.

"I wanted to apologize to you," Lorelai called from behind me, clearing her throat to get my attention. "About the Council meeting, I mean. I understand that process can be... uncomfortable."

I grimaced. Uncomfortable was a word for it.

"You did what your king asked of you." I shrugged. "I can't begrudge you for that."

She nodded. "Still, I pushed you harder than I've ever done before. You were very strong."

Just then, a knock at the door echoed. It was a commanding sound, knuckles pounding out fiercely against the wooden frame. Ruthie jumped in surprise, cursing at losing her place in the measurements. Our guest didn't wait to be invited, holding off only long enough for us to be aware of his presence before the door opened and Clayton walked in.

His tunic was darker today, but finely tailored with velvet trim and a golden cloak. Leather trousers, which left very little to the imagination, were tucked into polished boots. His hair was as perfectly combed as the day before, and his mood was just as grim. Guards didn't follow him, but I could feel their presence outside my doors. He acknowledged the others first, nodding at Lorelai and Ruthie and walking to kiss Iris on the cheek before finally meeting my gaze.

I couldn't remember for sure, but I doubted that I'd ever seen eyes as intense as Clayton Vail's.

Slowly, purposefully, I dropped my gaze, bowing my head slightly in an acknowledging nod. He waited for a moment before he finally did the same.

"Clay." Iris greeted him with a warm smile that spoke to their familiarity. "To what do we owe the pleasure, cousin?"

He cleared his throat, folding his arms firmly across his chest and standing tall. "I'm here on business, I'm afraid. I'll have to steal our new princess from you ladies this afternoon."

Instinctively, I glanced at Iris, who had become my go-to source for information, but her face was just as confused as mine. Ruthie huffed behind us, forcing her materials back into her case.

"Why, that is just like you, Royals," she grumbled. "Always so busy, so many places to be. You drag me out here only to run off before the work is done."

I frowned, watching as she hobbled towards the door and glared at me over her shoulder. I scoffed slightly as she pressed herself past me. How she blamed me for rushing her out was beyond me. After all, I hadn't brought her here, and I certainly had made no afternoon arrangements with Clayton. Still, she muttered curses to herself about wasted time and energy before remarking how lucky I was that she had a good eye for size and detail. Iris sighed and pinched the bridge between her nose.

"I assure you, you will be paid handsomely for your endeavors," Clayton promised Ruthie, eyes sparkling with amusement.

She grumbled as she left, but only the Gods could have understood what she said.

"I better go after her," Lorelai sighed, standing and hurrying towards the door. "I still need to convince her to make me something for the Peace Ball."

Lorelai grabbed my hand as she passed by, giving me a slight squeeze and an encouraging smile as she left. It was a small gesture, but I returned her pressure. Neither Lorelai nor I enjoyed what happened in the Council chamber, but it had somehow bonded us. She understood what she put me through, and I understood the position the Dragon had placed her in. Neither of us had a say in the matter, and thus, I had made one more friend.

As I turned my attention back to Clayton, I sighed audibly. His attention on me was overbearing, despite the fact that his expression didn't betray an ounce of his emotions or thoughts. For a moment, he reminded me of the portraits of Zion I had seen, commanding and authoritative. He seemed every inch the warrior he descended from, even as he stood here in his fine clothing and palace.

I folded my hands behind my back and looked at him expectantly, knowing better than to speak out of turn.

"We owe the Kingdom an explanation for what happened on the bridge," he told me, his words firm and clipped. "This afternoon, we will hold a court meeting where the Dragon will present you to the public. We'll need you to assure them of your motives in our country."

"My motives?" I questioned.

He smirked. "To complete the Council, of course."

I chewed my lip nervously. "Shouldn't you confirm that's what I want?"

Clayton's stormy eyes darkened as he looked down at me. "Frankly, what you want, Miss Moore, is of no consequence to me. We're allowing you to walk through this castle, stay in these rooms, and continue breathing air. So you will do as the crown tells you to."

"Of course," I muttered, ignoring the shiver of discomfort that settled in my stomach.

I probably should have expected this after what Iris had told me the night before. The Dragon wanted to show that he had the last Descendant of Hyrax and would have the only complete Council as soon as possible. I was officially a figurehead in his political game. It didn't matter if he trusted me; he didn't need to. Not really.

"I don't know what happened on the bridge," I reminded him. "How can I give an explanation to anyone?"

"There's no need to worry about that," he assured me. "A speech has already been provided for you."

Not just a girl to parade around then, a puppet.

Clayton took stock of the dresses around us, gazing over each one quickly with a calculating expression. Iris followed his eyes as he scanned over each gown, but she was silent, choosing not to offer her opinion. Her silence left me uneasy. For Iris not to offer her opinion on the dresses meant this meeting was such an official matter that not even she, the Crown Prince's beloved cousin, was important enough to contribute her thoughts.

Clayton's gaze landed on the glittering mess I had disapproved of the moment I saw it. Of course, that's the one he would choose.

"That one," he announced to Iris, pointing towards it. "Get her ready. I'll be back to collect her this afternoon."

I frowned once more, but Iris only nodded at him as he began to take his leave, only to stop shortly at the door.

He sighed. "I need her to look impressive. Promissa is watching."

"Yes, your grace," Iris said, bowing slightly. I could only stare in astonishment. How quickly their relationship turned when official business was at hand.

When she turned to gather up the dress I had been ordered to play princess in, she didn't meet my gaze.

Hours later, I stood being primped and poked by the ladies assigned to help me. I had to bite my cheek to hold back my frustration when I looked at my reflection. The ballgown was ostentatious at best, atrocious in truth. The neckline stretched across my chest, exposing my collarbone and the Mark of Hyrax. Undoubtedly, the Dragon and his son would be pleased with that fact—another way to show off their new pet.

It took two servants to help tie the corset, one to hold me steady and one to yank the ties so tight I was sure I would faint from loss of oxygen. They'd strapped three-inch heeled shoes onto my feet to keep me from tripping on the long skirts as I walked, but they just made me feel even more uneasy on my feet. There was no guarantee that I wouldn't end up on the floor the second I tried to walk without help. The gown stretched out nearly four feet behind me in folds and ripples of tulle. Loose sleeves hung from my shoulders to the ground.

The gown's silhouette was enough to make me cringe, but the embellishments were the worst. As I moved, the black fabric would shift and begin to shimmer under the light. Swirling appliques covered nearly every inch with colors of silver and navy blue. It was a contradiction in every way. It was dark and yet beautiful. Delicate in its details yet bold in its completion.

Iris had looked at it on me and decreed it was the perfect dress for the last Descendant of Hyrax, God of the Dead.

I hated it.

And if the dress wasn't enough, Iris and the ladies set to work on my hair and face. They first tied my golden hair away from my face in elaborate curls and braids before filling it with flowers and a crown of silver ivy leaves. Then they darkened my eyelids and splattered rouge on my cheeks. Iris lined my lips in shades of peach with a delicate hand, her face stern and her eyes unseeing.

"You'll need to do something about that sour face," she remarked quietly, wiping her hands and dismissing the ladies. They bowed and exited the room silently.

"I don't know what you mean," I lied, my lips still pursed in frustration.

She tossed the towel carelessly and grabbed my hands so suddenly that I almost jumped away. "Thea."

She said the new nickname so desperately that my stomach somersaulted with concern.

"We all have roles to play. And right now, yours is to do what they tell you. So please, just smile, stand tall, and read the damn speech."

I was quiet for a moment as her eyes implored me for submission.

"Or what?" I whispered.

She didn't have time to answer before Dimitri opened the door and announced it was time for us to leave.

CHAPTER FOUR

I ris hadn't been permitted to accompany us, so Dimitri and I walked silently through the palace halls to where Clayton waited for me. The castle was suspiciously quiet. I scanned each hall and passage we walked, but no soul was in sight. No court ladies were fanning themselves as they glanced over at each other, no men were standing and speaking about politics and war. No one whispered about me or my heritage. The only sound echoing around us was the click of my heels against the marble floor.

"They're required to attend palace briefings," Dimitri said softly beside me, seeming to understand where my thoughts were. "Everyone will wait for you in the gardens."

"Great," I whispered, the thought accidentally escaping my mouth.

He cleared his throat as we climbed an elaborate spiral staircase decorated with the emblems of Zion. This floor must be reserved for the Dragon, I realized as my fingers dared to slide against a banister carved to look like scales.

"Stand tall, my lady," Dimitri suggested. "You slouch when you walk, like a child. Today you must be unafraid. Today, you must carry with you the strength of your God."

"Hyrax?" I asked, peering at him from the corner of my eye.

Dimitri's gaze was fixed firmly ahead, his hands folded behind him. "Of course, my lady."

Clayton waited for us at the top of the stairs. He thanked Dimitri, and the larger man stepped behind us. Clayton took appraisal of me slowly, his gaze trailing from head to toe, leaving a trail of awareness across my skin.

"Should I spin for you?" I mumbled under my breath.

Clayton's eyes flashed golden, and I was reminded of the hideous transformation I had seen in the hospital just a day earlier. His jaw twitched in irritation, but the glow from his eyes faded within a moment. I silently breathed a sigh of relief, regretting my words. The last thing I needed right now was to evoke the anger of a prince who didn't seem to like me much.

"Stand up straight," he ordered, echoing Dimitri's advice. Then, wordlessly, he wrapped my hand into his arm. His steps forward were purposeful, and he nearly dragged me across the marble hall. Each inch closer to the golden door at the end of the chamber, and the threat of what lay behind it, had my legs feeling heavy and my head feeling light.

"You are about to be entering the chambers of the Dragon. It is a great honor, and you would do well to mind your tongue. You will curtsy upon greeting the Dragon and his Queen. You will address them as Majesty. Upon greeting the members of the Council, you will bow your head in respect. Iris gave you the speech?"

"Yes," I mumbled. The notes on it had been sent to my rooms earlier in the day, and I had begrudgingly memorized them. They were thankfully short, but boastful nonetheless. Leave it to a bunch of Royals to claim an attack I didn't remember was a blessing from the Gods.

"Yes, what?" Clayton barked, his arm stiffening against mine.

I bit down on my lip hard enough to draw blood in my attempt not to flinch away from him.

"Yes, your grace," I amended.

Iris had also reviewed the basics of palace etiquette while dressing me. The Dragon and his Queen were majesties, Clayton - as the Dragon's child - was referred to as grace, and the members of the Council were to be greeted as lords and ladies. One should speak only when spoken to in the presence of the Dragon, and a curtsy should be done by sweeping one leg behind the other and bending the knees outwardly. She had made me practice for nearly an hour until I reached the perfect angles. But, of course, that was before they dressed me up in a gown with its own gravitational pull. Surely, the weight of this thing would leave me stumbling before the day was done.

"I recognize this must feel foreign to you," he admitted, his voice ever so gentler than before. After a moment the harsh mask of indifference settled over his features once more, though. "But when you step onto that terrace, you are no longer the girl on the bridge. You become a representative of this country, and more than just *your* life will depend on how you present yourself. Do keep that in mind."

"How can I be a representative of a government that holds me captive?" I wondered aloud, words escaping before I could realize they were better kept in my mind.

He moved faster than I would have thought possible. He halted us and grabbed onto my forearm with such force that I wouldn't have been surprised to see bruises forming.

"You killed a man," he reminded me, ice in his voice. "And yet you dare to stand here upset at your situation. Shall I remind you that you're wearing the finest gown in the kingdom while his family mourns tonight?"

Each word slapped against me, and he did little to soften their blow.

"I don't want the dress," I whispered, flashes of a family in tears filling my mind.

Clayton laughed darkly, still unwilling to release my arm. "You want to feel sorry for yourself because you killed that man? *Thousands* just like him died in the Great War, and thousands more will again if Promissa senses weakness on our shores. I couldn't care less if you don't like the fucking dress. Throwing rouge on your cheeks and shoving you into a gown keeps my people safe. So just do as you're told."

With that, he pushed open the heavy door, and we entered the foyer of the Dragon's private chambers. It was an expansive space with oversized couches and plush armchairs. There was a small bar to our left with a cart of undoubtedly the finest liquor in the kingdom. The amber liquid in the crystal decanter was already dwindling despite the early hour. The lavish doors leading out to a terrace flooded the room with light and a feast of fresh fruits and meats waited for us atop the long dining table at the room's far end. My stomach growled for it, but I held myself back.

Around the room, I recognized the Council members from the day before. Iris had briefed me on them, too, before I left. Rosalia Blackmore of House Delia had her caramel hair slicked back into a tight ponytail. Her gown was bright red to highlight her dark skin tone. They had kept her makeup simple, with little more than a splash of color on her cheeks. Clara Reid of House Palaemon chatted with her quietly in the corner. Clara was an older woman, past her prime from the looks of it. Her hair had long ago grayed, and she wore it close to her chin. Rather than a gown, she donned a long blue tunic over simple leggings and leather slippers. As their conversation went on, Rosalia signaled for Clara to sit, and a servant brought a chair.

Gregory Handel of House Herea had been glancing out onto the terrace, but his eyes flashed toward us as we entered. He was a simple man with nothing entirely eye-catching about him. His brunette hair was cut close to the scalp, and his eyebrows were notably bushy. His tunic was well-tailored, but did nothing to hide his frame's dreadful thinness. Still, he stood tall as we entered, tightening his hand on his emptied glass.

"She's here," he announced to the women, who glanced up silently from their conversation.

The three of them stared, and for a moment, I felt two feet tall.

I don't belong here.

"Bow," Clayton whispered to me, and I did as I was told, bowing my head to each of them silently. They notably did not return the favor.

I supposed they could dress me up as much as they wanted, but I wasn't truly a Council member. Not yet, at least. Perhaps not ever. So, while everyone around the castle might show me feigned respect, the people in this room owed me none.

Truthfully, no one in this kingdom owed me their respect. I hadn't earned it.

"Well, she's quite pretty," Clara remarked, her voice unnaturally chipper, given the general feeling in the room. She didn't notice when Gregory rolled his eyes.

"Yes," he murmured. "Maybe the kingdom will be so captivated by her beauty that they'll forget what she's done."

I gasped softly, somehow surprised by his brutal honesty, and felt Clayton shift his weight beside me. I instinctively looked toward him, unsure of why I needed his reaction to judge the situation before me, but just knowing that I did. His eyes were flecked with gold. They flashed momentarily, but it was enough for me to notice that he was just as uncomfortable as I was.

"Gregory." Clayton's voice was tight, his greeting unkind.

Gregory was silent as he hinged at the waist and bowed to his prince. Rosalia stood and did the same while Clara dipped her head low, remaining seated. I may not get their respect, but Clayton certainly did.

The Dragon came in suddenly from a back hall with the Queen trailing silently behind him. Briefly, I wondered where that dark hall led to. Just how big was this damn castle? How many rooms belonged to the Dragon alone? He carried sheets of paper in his hands and looked over them silently as he sat at the head of the table and began picking at the food. He didn't acknowledge us, but Clayton pulled me low into a curtsy as everyone in the room around us did the same.

"Your majesties," they echoed in a chorus around us. I mumbled out the greeting shortly afterward, kicking myself for my delay.

The Queen was a small woman, shorter than me, with a delicate frame. Her features were exquisite, with a small nose and high well-defined cheek-bones. She was notably younger than the King, perhaps only a year or so older than myself, and certainly not old enough to be Clayton's mother. Her dark hair had been tied at the nape of her neck, but tendrils escaped and fell in waves around her face. A simple golden crown sat atop her head.

Her gown was also simple, little more than a floor-length white shift, but she had been draped with a cape that fell to the floor around her. It caught the light strangely, and I realized it was crafted from leather patches to mirror dragon scales. They were golden, wrapping around her throat and falling over her shoulders, where they faded to ivory patches down to her feet. On her hands were elaborate bracelets of diamonds that wrapped around her wrists and fingers. Incorporated into the bracelets were golden carvings of dragons that rested on the tops of each of her hands. They were stunning pieces, I could admit, but my stomach flipped at how it all seemed to mark her as *his.*

She sat silently beside the Dragon and folded her hands into her lap. Her eyes focused on those jeweled bracelets, and she didn't look up again.

"You all may proceed to the terrace," the Dragon ordered. "Theadora and I will be out in a moment."

Rosalia, Gregory, and Clara all stood and exited through the large wood-paneled doors that led out onto the terrace. A single glance from the Dragon sent the servants scurrying away as well. Clayton however, stiffened and remained by my side. His father peered over the top of his papers at him.

"That includes you, Clayton."

Clayton hesitated, only for a moment, before bowing slightly, giving me a single warning glance as he made his way out onto the terrace. The Queen dared to glance up at her husband, who nodded at her, and she, too, bowed and took her leave.

A chill settled over me as the door closed behind them and shut me in with the Dragon. He wore finer clothes than yesterday - a long black coat that fell to his knees, with golden embellishments on the collar, wrists, and lapels. A golden sash was draped over him, decorated with medals and ribbons. His crown was larger than the Queen's, filled with rubies and diamonds. It rested on his head perfectly, not daring to shift as he moved.

"Sit," he barked, still not deeming to look at me.

It took a moment for me to convince my legs to move, but I stumbled towards him. The Queen had left her chair pulled out, but I thought better than to take the place directly next to him and instead sat a few seats farther. I desperately tried to tuck my swarming gown underneath me but had little luck and struggled in my attempt to sit comfortably.

We were silent for a time before he finally sat down his papers and looked up appraisingly at me. The skin on my chest burned as his eyes lingered on my Mark.

"I didn't get the best look at you yesterday, but it would appear the rumors are true. You are quite beautiful," he noted, his words clipped.

"Thank you."

He snorted. "I did not mean it as a compliment, my dear. It's a fact that simply makes my job easier. This would be much more difficult if you were... less endowed."

I shifted uncomfortably as he lowered his eyes suggestively toward my chest.

"You know your responsibility?" He asked me.

I nodded. "Yes, your majesty."

He humphed, standing and taking a moment to push the massive wooden chair into the table behind him. Then, he leaned forward onto the back of the seat, resting on his elbows and meeting my gaze straight on.

"Theadora, would you consider yourself much of a performer?"

"I don't believe I've ever needed to pretend, your majesty."

"Well then, let's hope you're a natural. You see, I'm expecting the performance of a lifetime. I'm expecting you to step onto that terrace, to meet the gaze of every one of my citizens, and to convince the world that you are as well-educated and well-behaved as any Council member should be. I expect you to comfort my people and inspire envy in my enemies. Theadora, I want every woman in the world to wish they were you and every man to wish he had you. You will be kind and inspiring. You will be demure and alluring. And you will stand as if you have a power that is second only to my own."

No pressure, I thought wildly.

"Those are a great many expectations." I kept my voice calm, polite even, and I did not flinch as he crossed the distance between us and let down his hand to me. His skin was rough as I begrudgingly placed my hand in his and allowed him to pull me to my feet.

"You wouldn't want to let me down, would you?" He asked, leaning far too close so that he could whisper in my ear. His voice dripped with silent threats. "After all, I understand you've made friends in this castle. People have championed you. If you were to disappoint your King, I may have to evaluate their place at this court."

A vision of Iris flashed before me—the image of her grabbing my hands desperately as she pleaded with me to play along with this ruse. I wasn't the only pawn in this game, I realized. He would use me to manipulate Promissa, and he would use Iris to manipulate me.

And he could do it, too. I had no doubt. He was a King. If he wanted someone to be punished, they would be. So what choice did I have other than to go onto that terrace and say the words that had been written for me?

So if an actress was what I needed to be, then I was about to put on a show.

He chuckled softly as he tucked my arm into his own and led me onto the veranda.

C ounting the number of eyes that stared up at me was impossible. The Dragon deposited me to stand next to Clayton and the Queen to the left of the balcony. Across from us, the three Council members stood proudly, each resting their hands behind their backs. The Dragon stood at a wooden podium which was adorned with a red sash and a golden emblem of a giant dragon with outstretched wings, surrounded by five delicately embroidered stars. Matching banners hung down from the palace above us. Wreaths of flowers and ivy had been expertly wrapped around the white wooden railings of the terrace, sending an overwhelming number of floral scents around me. Trumpets had played, and the crowd cheered as the Dragon began to speak.

"People of Athenia, may the Gods shine down fondly upon you," he called to them, raising his arms high in greeting.

"Praise Gods!" The crowd shouted at their King.

He was quiet for a moment, resting his hands on the edges of the podium. Then he looked at me with a small smile. That grin of pride spread as he let his gaze linger on me before returning to his audience.

I might be playing a role today, I thought suddenly. *But I am not the only one.*

"Praise the Gods indeed," he agreed. "The Gods have truly blessed us on this day. Our season's crops are the most bountiful in many decades, and we will celebrate six years of peace very soon. It is a great time for our beautiful country. And yet, even as our blessings seem immeasurable, the Gods have continued showing their love for Athenia by returning our long-lost daughter to us."

He paused, sweeping his hand out toward me, and as if on cue, the people erupted in applause. As before, Clayton quietly commanded me to curtsy, whispering the court protocols to follow in a hushed tone that only I could hear. I dropped one leg behind the other and bowed.

"Theadora Moore, the last daughter of Hyrax, has joined us in an admittedly unsettling way. She has lived alone for years, abandoned as an infant following her father's death. She had only the company of a single mortal woman who could not train her in our histories or even alert her to the existence of her own God-given powers. But our God's blessings will not be silenced! And on that bridge, we saw the birth of a truly magnificent display of their might."

Magnificent was one word for it. As was violent, uncontrollable, dangerous...

"My people, my friends, it is my greatest joy to introduce you to your newest sister, Theadora Moore of House Hyrax."

He walked towards me, taking hold of my hand and bowing slightly to kiss the knuckles. I didn't need Clayton to tell me to curtsy again as he did. The Dragon gave me a dark look, squeezed my hand, and pushed me towards the podium. Remembering my orders, I moved my shoulders back and stood tall.

Thankfully, I didn't trip.

As I stared at the audience, the sun's light was nearly blinding from the podium. I couldn't distinguish any features from the people I looked down at. I couldn't tell who was Descendant or mortal. I couldn't distinguish the delicate gowns and silks of the courts' people from the more simple outfits of the villagers. But I *could* feel their eyes, and my breath caught in my throat. I was on display for the world.

You've made friends in this castle.

The Dragon's threat echoed in my mind, and I took a deep breath to steady myself. I let the memorized words of their prewritten speech flow through me.

"My name is Theadora Moore, and it is with great humility and by the grace of my Gods and my King that I stand before you today. As the Dragon has told you all, we understand my father was Zachariah Moore, a necromancer of House Hyrax. Zachariah was a valiant fighter in the Great War and died before even learning of my existence. I was raised in a small cottage near the western forests without knowing my birthright. However, with age, I grew curious about the world outside those woods and made my way here."

The crowd was silent, hanging on to my every word. The Council had created the story, pieced it together with strings of unconfirmed possibilities. They had thought it was best not to show uncertainty. They proposed that having a beast we understood was better than admitting we were in the dark. I wasn't surprised. From what little I had learned in my few days at court, I knew they wouldn't want to show anything other than strength to Promissa. After all, this little meeting wasn't simply for the benefit of Athenian citizens. It was a direct message to the Kingdom of Promissa.

Try to challenge us now, it spoke, when we're the country the Gods chose to bless. As if Hyrax himself had purposefully placed me directly onto that bridge of Athenia.

"I am the last of my line," I admitted. "The last Descendant of the great God Hyrax. I have been blessed with the power of my God and the ancestors that came before me. It is with great sorrow that I, too, mourn the loss of our Athenian brother on the bridge. But we must all take comfort in the Gods, who know the divine plan for us all. Our brother's death, while it might pain us, was rightful in the eyes of the Gods. Today, he rests peacefully with my forefather in the Underworld. And today, we must all take joy in the return of House Hyrax to the court."

What beautiful lies they were. As if we could simply blame the Gods for the death of a man. As if his death was a small, inconsequential price to pay for the line of Hyrax.

Whoever had written my speech was surely proud of themselves. They must have thought hard about how to comfort the mourning people of Athenia while still projecting strength and pride to Promissa.

"It is my intent to ascend to my rightful place as a Council member in this court. I hereby swear fealty to the Kingdom of Athenia and my rightful ruler, our gracious Dragon. I will begin my preparations to take my place at his side and look forward to the opportunity to repopulate my people in this glorious land. The Gods have chosen Athenia as their blessed kingdom, and together, we cannot be defeated."

The Dragon continued the meeting, boasting promises of strength and superiority, but I struggled to pay attention. The weight of my own words was nearly suffocating me. I might be new to palace life, but I wasn't an idiot. I just stood on a stage and told the world I was swearing myself to serve Athenia, which likely had earned me enemies across the globe.

Out of the corner of my eyesight, I met Clayton's gaze. His stormy eyes were hard to read, but they flickered golden momentarily, and he glanced away. Something in those eyes, though, told me he was thinking the same thing.

The Dragon ended the meeting with a prayer to the Gods, and suddenly we were all shuffling back into his chambers. He was immediately surrounded by palace workers who offered him new reports and asked for signatures. The other Council members lingered by him, listening intently but not daring to speak. The Queen's ladies quickly came to her, serving her wine and chatting quietly. Servants dashed to the terrace to clean away the decorations.

The room was such a mess of activity that I wondered if I was as invisible as I felt while I pressed myself into a corner of the space.

It wasn't long before Clayton found me like that, shoved against the curtains of the windows, chewing on my lip, and watching the room from afar. He said his goodbyes to the servant he'd been talking to and approached me swiftly, his steps purposeful.

"The curtains are sheer," he reminded me. "Crawling into them won't hide you."

"Somehow, I don't think there's anywhere I could hide. Not when the entirety of the world now knows my name."

He looked away, his face clouded. "Perhaps not. Come, I'll escort you to your rooms."

My prison was more apt.

Still, I took his extended hand and let him tuck my arm into his own. The crowd parted for us, nodding at Clayton as we passed. He led us quickly out of the room, and I felt relieved when the door closed heavily behind us.

We were quiet for most of the walk back to the halls of House Hyrax. I hardly knew what to say to him.

"You will need to start training," he told me finally.

"For what, exactly?"

We started down the staircase, and I pulled my arm from his. Here, I could pretend I needed to grasp the banister for support, but I was simply tired of being led around for the day. I needed a moment to stand on my own.

Even if that was admittedly challenging in these shoes.

"Before ascending to your Council seat, you must prove yourself. You'll need to show a mastery of studies, magical control, and physical strength. All Council members do."

"Do you?" I questioned. I kept my voice appropriately polite but couldn't help but wonder if our future king had to earn his power or if it was simply handed to him.

He stiffened, pausing at the edge of the staircase. "The trials I go through are very different, Miss Moore, but do not make the mistake of assuming they are easy."

I stopped, my skirts sweeping dramatically as I turned back to where he had planted his feet. The halls outside the stairwell were empty, making us the only two in sight. I didn't have a guard, I realized. And neither did he. That's why he had left in such a hurry. He had been escaping his own jailers.

"You'll be prepared for the trials," he continued, crossing his arms over his chest. "We can start with your powers, since you've already proven how unsteady those are."

I shivered involuntarily.

"I'll have someone get you in the morning to begin."

"What if I don't want any part of these powers?" I asked softly.

"You simply don't have a choice in that, Miss Moore," he replied, voice firm. "Even if you were to leave this castle tonight, you wouldn't be able to leave those powers behind. They're as much a part of you as your arms or legs. So you best learn to control them before you hurt someone else."

Frustration washed over me at the sound of suspicion in his voice. I didn't *want* to hurt anyone else. Hadn't I proven that today? I'd worn the ridiculous dress and read the speech word for word. And yet, despite the fact that I had done everything that was requested of me, he still looked at me with the same fury he had in the infirmary.

"As you command, your grace."

I lowered myself into a curtsy as Dimitri appeared at my side to walk me the rest of the way home. I knew he could sense my distress, but he didn't ask me what had happened. So, I didn't ask him how he had magically known the precise second I would be alone and needing a chaperone. I wouldn't be truly alone again for a long time, if ever. Not when I was the Dragon's new favorite play toy.

Once I safely made my way back to those enormous white doors and overly charming apartments, I locked myself inside and nearly ripped the monstrosity of a gown apart as I tried to get it off me by myself. It puddled on the floor in a heap of sparkling black fabric, with runs in the tulle from my nails digging into it. Disgusted, I kicked it across the foyer and threw myself dramatically into the bed, tears already springing to life.

Half an hour later, there was a soft tap at the door from two ladies in simple gowns with their hair tied back. No doubt, they had been sent to help me out of that now ruined dress. They took one look at the shreds of the gown and me crying, naked, in bed, and wordlessly set to work. The dress was picked up and taken out of sight, and they shuffled me into a steaming bath filled with bubbles and rose petals.

"What are your names?" I asked them as I sunk into the warm release of the water.

"I am Nessira," said the taller one. She had fair skin and kind eyes.

Her counterpart was younger than us both, perhaps only sixteen. Her blue eyes sparkled with life and excitement as she glanced wildly around my room and took in the extravagance of it all. I was almost jealous of how thrilling it was to her.

"I am Geia, my lady." She curtsied low to me, dropping her eyes to the ground. I laughed darkly at the sight of it.

"Please never curtsy to me again," I told her. "I hardly deserve it, nor do I desire it."

Nessira took hold of a wooden comb and began undoing the twists and braids in my hair. It hurt, but I didn't protest. I wanted it combed out and loose around my shoulders more than I wanted to avoid the pain of brushing through tangles.

"We have been stationed as your personal ladies-in-waiting," Nessira explained. "Please do not hesitate to call on us. It's our job to help care for you."

I shuddered at the words.

I don't belong here.

Nessira, impossibly perceptive, noticed when I began shivering. And before the salty tears could fall from my eyes once more, she ordered Geia to bring warm towels. The young girl was off in a rush, promising to find the softest, warmest towel in all the palace.

"Do not cry, my lady," Nessira whispered as my cheeks dampened. "This court will challenge you, but you can never let them see you cry. Strength is sometimes noticed, but weakness is never forgotten."

She combed through my hair gently after that, careful not to pull or tug. And when her work was done, she lit a candle with a wave of her hand and promised to give me a moment while she went to fetch my dinner from the kitchens.

"Nessira," I called after her as she started to close the bathroom door behind her. "Thank you."

She gave me a soft, knowing smile, bowed her head, and left me to my thoughts. Alone, I let my head fall momentarily under the water. I waited until I was desperate to breathe again before finally returning to the world above.

CHAPTER FIVE

Nessira and Geia woke me before dawn the following day, alerting me that the Crown Prince had arranged for me to begin my training as soon as the sun crested in the east. Of course he had. Gods forbid he allow me the freedom to sleep in.

The girls were relatively silent as they helped me bathe and prepare. Nessira took the lead, often guiding the younger girl on what she should do next. I wondered if Geia had ever worked in a position like this before. Probably not, judging by how every new task seemed more exciting than the last to her. Nessira folded my hair into a single neat braid down my back. There were no extra flowers or pins, and when Geia had laid my clothes for the day on the bed, I was pleasantly surprised to see that it was not a gaudy gown.

"Would you like help dressing today, my lady?" Geia asked, her bell-like voice eager to please.

"I think I should be able to manage this alone." I smiled, glancing at the thick cotton pants and form-fitting top. The coat they left me was of thick protective fabric. I ran my fingers over its roughness and wondered what I would need protection from.

Nessira cleared her throat, calling for my attention. "We have been instructed to inform you of your invitation to the birthnight celebration of Queen Valentina. You are expected to be in attendance this evening."

I sighed, my stomach filling with nervous tingles. I wasn't particularly excited to be spending another evening under the Dragon's watchful eyes, but it was clear I had little choice in the matter.

"Your gowns have not yet arrived," Nessira continued. "But Lorelai Pelland of House Herea has allowed you to use her collection. Would you like us to select something for you while you are training?"

Geia's eyes sparkled as eagerness rolled off of her in waves. Her joy was simply infectious. And right now, the possibility of exploring the closets of a high-powered court lady was bringing her an enormous amount of pleasure. Who was I to deny that?

"I think Geia might have an eye for palace fashions, perhaps she could pick out something for me?"

The girl squealed her excitement, earning her a stern look of disapproval from Nessira. Then, collecting herself, she curtsied low and promised to bring something that would meet my expectations. Together, they began to take their leave so I could dress.

"Geia?" I called after her. "Something simple! Nothing like yesterday."

Her face momentarily flashed in disappointment, as if she had already been daydreaming about the most wonderfully grand gown possible, but she knew better than to protest. So she shook the disappointment away and assured me she would do her best to suit my taste, and closed the door behind her.

I dressed quickly, slipping into the pants and buttoning the coat around myself. The final accessories were knee-high lace-up boots of tough new leather. I silently wished Nessira and Geia had stayed to help as I struggled to fit my feet into the unmoving soles. I had just finished lacing them when Dimitri knocked on the door, alerting it was time to go.

I glanced in the mirror quickly before exiting. Over my shoulders, I could see the sun rising over the palace gardens, sending out shades of pink and tangerine across my room. At least like this, dressed in clothes I could move in with my hair out of my face, I didn't feel like I was looking at a stranger. I may not have known entirely who I was yet, but at least the girl who stared back looked like one I wouldn't mind getting to know.

Any hopes that this trainer of mine would have compassion for me disappeared as I looked at her outside the palace. At nearly a foot taller than me, she was the largest woman I had ever seen. She had dressed in similar clothing, leather pants and knee-high boots with a thick coat. She wore her dark hair loose, with a simple braid tying back half of it. Across her waist, she wore a belt of knives, three resting on each hip.

"So, you're the little thing causing all the trouble," she noted from where she sat perched on the stone wall separating the palace from its gardens. I watched as she quickly sliced through an apple with one of those blades designed to kill. She shoved the fragments in her mouth while she peered down at me.

"I'm Ryla," she told me, hopping down from the wall and landing effortlessly on the ground, not a foot from me. I did my best not to flinch as she paced in a circle around me.

"I'm one of the Palace trainers, and I'll be working to get your telekinetic abilities under control."

A scar ran down the left side of her face, from above her brow down to her lips. She smirked as she noticed the direction of my gaze, and I looked away quickly, somewhat ashamed of my brazen staring.

"Let's go," she ordered, giving me a shove from behind. Begrudgingly, I started marching forward.

"Go where?"

"You think I'm going to let an untrained telekinetic who nearly wrecked an entire bridge practice her powers near the Dragon's castle?" She laughed; the sound was rich with exasperation. "We've got a five-mile hike over the nearest mountain ahead. I hope you've broken in those boots."

I hadn't.

When we reached a clearing at the top of the mountain, my legs were screaming in agony, and I was sure my feet were bleeding. I rested my weight against a wide oak and fought the urge to buckle over while I caught my breath. Whatever my life had been like before I showed up at the palace, it certainly hadn't involved exercise.

A sudden pain hit my heart as I wondered momentarily what that life *had* been like. Did I lack stamina because I once had the luxury of being well-cared for? Was there a family out there feeling the same pain in their heart as they wondered where I was?

Ryla's soft laughter pulled me out of my thoughts.

"What?" I demanded between breaths.

"I thought a thin little thing like you would have complained more on the hike up."

A snippy remark flashed through my mind but froze on my tongue as the hint of admiration in her voice registered. So, I just nodded and straightened my posture.

"So, what now?" I asked.

She rummaged through the pack she had brought up with her and held out a single apple in her palm. My stomach called out for it, and I quickly covered my gut in embarrassment. I hadn't realized how hungry I had been, but the sight of that shining fruit reminded me that Nessira and Geia hadn't brought me breakfast that morning. From the sparkle in Ryla's eyes and the slight turn up in the corner of her mouth, I had a feeling that hadn't been an accident.

"Here," she offered, feigning sweetness.

I narrowed my eyes at her.

She openly grinned then, as if proud I had passed her first test. She wrapped her fingers around the apple and placed it on the ground before her.

"You move that apple without moving your body, and it's yours."

"I don't know how," I protested.

"You knew how to on the bridge."

She leaned back and waved a hand towards the apple in a silent invitation to try. This was ridiculous. How could she expect me to magically move that fruit when I had no memory of ever using magic in the first place?

After a few moments of silence, she pulled a second apple from her pack and bit into it, chewing slowly. My stomach raged in protest as she laughed and chucked the apple core into the tree behind me, announcing she would wait all day if that's what it took for me to move the apple.

Grinding my teeth, I focused on the fruit and where it sat on the dirt. It was a small thing, hardly the size of a full bridge filled with people and carriages. I *had* moved that. Or so they told me. I had shaken the entirety of it. I had ended a life.

And yet, the apple didn't budge.

I tried to imagine it moving. I envisioned it floating up into the sky before Ryla's face. I imagined her expression as that apple flew and landed in my waiting hand. I could almost hear the thud as it connected with my open palm. But when I snapped out of the daydream, my hand was empty, and the apple sat motionless, five feet away.

I growled in frustration.

We stayed like that for nearly two hours. The sun, which had only been dawning as I left my apartments at the palace, came to hang high in the sky above us. Sweat beaded on my forehead, and I ripped my hand against my brow angrily. Ryla was silent but kept herself well-fed. I watched bitterly as she threw back two more apples, a loaf of bread, and even a small pastry that smelled of cinnamon. I nearly screamed when she sighed, pulled out a jar of brown liquor, and started drinking deeply.

Move, damn it, I mentally cried at the apple. But if that apple was listening, it simply wasn't in the mood to move.

I was so focused on that stupid apple that I hardly noticed when Ryla had shifted her weight and reached down to her belt. I didn't see her hand wrap around one of those deadly blades and pull it out. It wasn't until that dagger had already flown by my head, nicking my ear as it passed, that I even drew my gaze from the apple. My hand instinctively flew to my ripped skin as I stared at where that blade had implanted itself in the oak wood behind me.

"What in all of creation was that for?" I demanded, voice raised.

She was at my side almost instantaneously, wrapping her calloused fingers around the handle of that dagger and ripping it from the bark.

"Magic is tied to our emotions and physical states," she explained. "Until you learn to connect with your power and control it, you'll need to find what can evoke it. Hunger and frustration aren't doing it."

My stomach sounded out in agreement with her. She rolled her eyes at the sound and held the blade close to my face. I flinched back away from it.

"Neither is fear," she announced, spinning on her heels to return to her seated position.

I wiped the tear that escaped while she turned her back to me. We continued on like that for hours until my head throbbed in pain from hunger and concentration, and we were both ready to shout. By the time we finally started our trek down the mountain, I was greedily savoring each bite of that apple. But I suspected the only real reason she let me cross the distance between us and pick it off the ground was that she didn't want to carry me back to the palace if I fainted on the way down.

On my first day as a Descendant, I'd nearly murdered a slew of people. On my second, I'd inspired a nation. On the third, I'd failed to do even the most basic task.

CHAPTER SIX

R yla may have been harsh in her teaching methods, but the Royal Tutor Hansel was positively devilish. After a bath, Dimitri escorted me to the royal library to study mythology with Hansel. Most of my lesson had comprised of being cursed at for not even knowing the basics of history.

It was hardly my fault that in my memory loss I had also forgotten any formal education I may or may not have had.

He tossed a book heavily onto the table in front of me and instructed me to read aloud.

"Athenia is governed by a Royal Council consisting of the Descendants of the High Gods," I intoned. "There are six known High Gods: twin brothers Zion and Hyrax, sisters Herea and Delia, the God Palaemon, and the Goddess Harmonia. Careful preservation of historical texts has helped us understand the High Gods' rise to power."

Hansel nodded, beginning to pace. As I slowed my reading and reached for the glass of water across the table, his arm lashed out and smacked the back of my head. I rubbed it with irritation and he only barked for me to continue.

"It is said that there were once only two realms: the Upper and Under-worlds. The God Crolun created the Mortal Realm, in which we reside. Crolun was the most powerful of all gods and father to the twins, Zion and Hyrax. As Crolun aged, he grew increasingly paranoid and worried that the other Gods would overthrow him. He imprisoned those he viewed as enemies, torturing them for amusement. Zion and Hyrax knew they could not allow their father to continue leading the realms. They joined forces with Herea, Delia, Palaemon, and Harmonia. Together, the six killed Crolun and split his power evenly between them.

"Zion, who was born first, demanded that he should be named King of the Gods over his brother Hyrax, and the other High Gods agreed. Hyrax was enraged and demanded that he be given equal dominion over the realms. Zion, eager to outsmart his brother, agreed and drafted a contract. Within his contract, though, he specified the Gods would only hold dominion over the original realms, leaving the Mortal realm untouched. Thus, Zion took power over the Upperworld, home of the Gods, and Hyrax took control of the Underworld, home of the dead. It is believed that this is the start of the rivalry between the two Gods."

I frowned. Sounded to me that the start of the rivalry was Hyrax being betrayed by someone he had considered family.

"However, Zion had already fathered children in the Mortal Realm," I read on. "And so, he maintained control over the realm indirectly through his sons. When Hyrax learned of this, he rose from the Underworld to lay siege on the Mortal Realm and so started the First War of the Gods. Many mortals, specifically those descended from Zion, were killed in the war, but ultimately, Zion's forces defeated Hyrax, and he returned to the Underworld."

"Problem?" Hansel questioned when I stopped reading and began flipping eagerly through the pages.

"It says he started the First War of the Gods. Was there a second?"

Just then, a knock sounded, and Nessira entered the library, announcing it was time to begin my preparations for the Queen's Birth Night Celebration. I fought the urge to groan. The Gods only knew what waited for me at that party.

"There was," Hansel told me, as he took the book from me and folded it into the shelf behind me. "But that is a story we will learn on another day."

CHAPTER SEVEN

Geia eyed me suspiciously as she folded towels in the corner of the room while Nessira finished the buttons on the back of my dress. She kept her head bowed, but I caught the flicker of her eyes floating up to the gown occasionally.

"Are you sure that this dress is to your liking?" She asked me timidly.

She had brought me three options from Lorelai's closet, all dramatically different from the glimmering dark fabric I'd been wearing the night before. Her first option had been an orangish ballgown with off-the-shoulder cap sleeves decorated in tiny petals. The second had been a lovely lilac color, but I took one look at the sparkling gems filling the bodice and turned it away.

The dress I had picked was the simplest by far. Made of ivory chiffon, it had no delicate decorations besides a sheer panel of lace across my midriff and two panels of fabric dripping off my shoulders. The dress cut low across my back, exposing my shoulder blades and spine, but was modest enough over my breasts to prevent me from feeling uncomfortable with being on display. Geia had stiffened when I chose it, arguing that the others were more in fashion and that this might look out of place at such a formal event, but that had only convinced me further. I asked Nessira to help me into it and did not miss the flicker of amusement as she set about securing it.

"This dress is perfect, Geia," I promised her. "It's precisely to my liking."

"Geia, fetch the diamond clips for Lady Moore's hair," Nessira instructed, her voice stern as she began folding my hair into braids and curls. I stiffened at the command, and her fingers slowed.

"Actually," she amended. "Go to the garden and fetch me some Baby's Breath flowers."

This seemed to push Geia over the edge, and she couldn't help but gasp aloud. "You're going to put flowers in her hair?"

Nessira sighed impatiently. "Oh, go now, girl. And while you're out there, try to remember what is and isn't appropriate to say in the presence of your lady."

Geia flushed and quickly curtsied before running from the room. I could feel the embarrassment flowing off of her as I chewed contemplatively on my lip. Nessira watched her leave before returning to my hair, undoing the elaborate twists she had already started.

"You and Geia can speak freely in front of me, I won't be angry."

Nessira was quiet, her strained breathing echoing throughout the bathroom. For a moment, I thought she might not respond, so I turned my attention back to the floor, content to get lost in my thoughts.

"I know," she confessed after a moment. "But Geia is young, and not all the ladies she will serve will feel the same. So, she needs to learn to indulge their... eccentricities."

Nessira's voice was soft and haunted, as if she spoke from experience. I didn't press her on the issue, though. I had been prodded myself too much lately. So, I let her style my hair, and when Geia returned with the flowers, I smiled at the young girl warmly, as if I could silently communicate that she faced no reprimands here. Geia blushed once more and dipped her head in thanks.

Once I had fully dressed, Dimitri escorted me to the Grand Hall of the palace for the celebration. As we arrived, he stood by my side and I could have sworn I heard him chuckle as I gaped openly at the room.

"The Grand Hall typically impresses those seeing it for the first time," he told me. I glanced at him from the corner of my eye.

"I can see why."

The ballroom was sprawling, decorated with the same white marble and gold finishings of the rest of the palace, and yet it was finer. Impossibly so. The windows on the far wall faced the gardens, giving exquisite views of all the roses, poppies, and other flowers. From the far window, I could see the patch of Baby's Breath from which Geia had collected my hair accessories. The flowers weren't just outside, though. The entire space had been filled with yellow tulips. Distantly, I heard Dimitri telling me they were the Queen's favorite.

Still, it wasn't the flowers, the glistening chandeliers, or the tables with fine silk cloths that caught my attention. It was the people.

Geia's hesitation at my outfit suddenly made sense.

All around me, women floated in their finest gowns. Each one I saw was more elaborate than the last. Some dresses were adorned with crystals and beads, and others had the same shimmering fabric as the dress I wore to the court briefing. And the women themselves - well, they too were decorated. Their eyelids were shimmering or colored dark. Rouge covered their cheeks, and their lips were painted. Most wore their hair up in elaborate twists and braids decorated with all forms of diamonds and pearls. Those who left their hair down had ensured that it was immaculately pinned and curled to perfection.

I looked positively plain next to them all.

My dress was simple, and my hair was in loose waves around my face, with only a few strands tucked back to hold the flowers. My love for my ladies-in-waiting grew tenfold in that moment. Nessira had known my chosen wardrobe wouldn't fit in, but she had allowed it, knowing it would make me more comfortable.

Not even Zion himself, King of the Gods, could have stopped the grin of gratitude that spread across my face.

Dimitri excused himself, and I went to stand by one of the little tables next to the feast spread. I wasn't particularly hungry, but the position put me in the ballroom's corner and allowed me to watch the people of the court. The hall danced with life around me. Watching the court members interact was like watching animals in mating season. Each man competed to stick his chest out the furthest while the ladies gossiped and sent wandering glances. Several of their eyes followed the Crown Prince as he made his way to my table.

"Lady Moore," he greeted me, dipping his eyes slightly. He had also worn finer clothes tonight, trading in the dark tunics he typically donned for an ivory jacket sealed with golden buttons. A scarlet sash had been draped across his chest, clipped together with the Athenian insignia - the dragon surrounded with five stars.

I curtsied. "Your grace."

His eyes narrowed, "You look-"

"Simple?" I interrupted almost too happily.

"Beautiful." He sighed. "You look beautiful."

My stomach flipped in surprise at the compliment and I felt an embarrassed flush flood my cheeks

"Why was I invited to this?" I asked him, changing the subject.

I couldn't imagine the Queen had personally invited me to her celebration, considering we had never been formally introduced. So, obviously there was some ulterior motive for requiring my attendance.

Couples had already populated the dance floor, their feet following elaborate steps I didn't know as music spread through the air. Clayton came to stand by me, folding his hands and leaning onto the table, mirroring my stance. For a moment, we were quiet before he shifted his weight to look at me fully.

"You're a member of this court," he reminded me.

"So the Dragon wants to show me off again?"

He laughed darkly. "You should be thrilled to celebrate your Queen's Birth Night."

I wasn't thrilled to be there, though. It was impossible to enjoy myself when I could feel the eyes and judgments of the room weighing down upon me. No, it all left me feeling a bit unsure of myself. Was I expected to dance or mingle tonight? Or would they frown at me for appearing joyful just days after the incident on the bridge?

"Behave tonight," Clayton warned me, his voice low and harsh, even as he sent a sparkling grin at a flock of ladies across the room. I marveled at the ease of it. How simple it was for him to give a sideways grin and melt the hearts of half the women in the room even as he issued threats to me. I laughed under my breath, and he raised his eyebrows questioningly.

"You and your father are so similar," I pondered.

He stiffened suddenly, standing at full attention. Golden light shined through his eyes with such a sudden fierceness that I faltered back a step away from him.

"I am *nothing* like my father," he told me.

Before I could respond or even recover from the sudden intensity of his anger, a familiar squealing filled the air. Iris latched onto me, grabbing me by the shoulders and holding me at arm's length to examine my dress, with Lorelai close behind her.

"You look stunning!" Iris declared approvingly, shoving my shoulders to spin me around in a circle for them.

I glanced at Clayton as I spun, but his fury had quickly disappeared. All that remained was that mask of astounding arrogance once more as he leaned casually against the table and watched us, one eyebrow raised. I refused to look at him again, focusing on Iris and Lorelai instead.

"It surprised me when your lady-in-waiting took that one," Lorelai admitted. "But it does suit you."

"Suit her? Why, it's the next court trend!" Iris declared gleefully. "Mark my words, by tomorrow, all these women will have their hair down! Oh Gods, *the flowers!* How positively quaint!"

Her fingers were gentle as they brushed over the white petals braided loosely into my hair.

"Come!" Iris demanded. "There are some people I want you to meet."

She grabbed my hand fiercely, dragging me through the ballroom, stopping only to grasp onto two glasses of champagne. She clinked her glass against mine before downing it in its entirety. Clayton sighed dramatically from behind us, and Lorelai only giggled.

"One glass down, and we're only an hour in," Lorelai noted.

Iris winked mischievously. "How many did you bet?"

Lorelai shrugged. "It's cheating to tell."

"Six!" A baritone voice rang out.

Before I knew it, a colossal man had gathered Iris into his arms and lifted her off the ground, spinning swiftly. He was taller than any of us, with arms the size of my head. Iris screeched in joy when she recognized who had grabbed her. A few court people glanced at us suspiciously, but the pair hardly seemed to mind.

"Rankor, what are you doing here?" She screamed in excitement.

He put her down and turned his attention to Lorelai, whom he also swept into a bear hug. She smiled softly at him.

"Not that we're complaining," Lorelai said to him, placing a hand affectionately on his arm. "It's good to see you back in one piece!"

The man shrugged. "What can I say? I needed to go find myself."

"And did you?" Clayton asked, exchanging a manly hug with the new guest.

"Perhaps not." Rankor grinned wolfishly at his prince. "But I found Elena, Lenori, and many other lovely new friends along the way."

Iris smacked his arm. "You're disgusting."

He winked at her suggestively. "Hey, anytime you want to find out how disgusting I truly am, love, you can let me know."

She stuck out her tongue at him, but his attention had already turned to me. I tried not to flinch as he gave me a careful once-over. Like me, Rankor hadn't exactly dressed up for the party. His pants were of the same tough fabric I had worn in the morning and tucked into worn leather boots, still slick with mud, as if he had come right from the mountains into the palace. He wore his shirt unbuttoned low, exposing the tops of sculpted pectoral muscles. His brown hair was longer than most kept theirs at court, falling in curls around his ears and neck, flecked with golden highlights.

"I'm Theadora," I offered, extending my hand.

He grinned, bringing my hand to his lips. "Oh my dear, I've been in the wilderness for damn near a year, and even I heard of who you were."

I couldn't hide my shiver. Not from his attention, but from the reminder of my notoriety. The fame that the Dragon had forced upon me. The status that all at once felt unnecessary and undeserved.

"Rankor is a Brawn from House Arto," Iris explained. "You couldn't tell by talking to him, but he's one of the most respected generals in the Athenian army and was on leave for the past year."

"Brawn?" I questioned.

Rankor winked. "I'm really strong."

"When did you get back?" Iris asked.

"This morning. I had planned to be back for the Peace Celebration, but I got a bit distracted foraging new... lands and such."

"Do give it a rest, Rankor," sounded an oddly familiar voice.

Two new guests joined us. Like most of the Descendants I had met, the man was beautiful, with dark skin and eyes. He bowed slightly to me and gave Clayton a formal bow as he approached. Clayton clapped him on the back fondly.

Trailing behind him was the most gorgeous woman I had ever seen. She had thick, long, dark hair tied back in a sleek ponytail behind her. Her eyes, already arguably perfect, were lined in kohl, and her full lips were painted a shade of red that stood out sharply against her tawny skin. Her black lace gown hung low over her chest and hugged her hips before flaring onto the floor around her.

"So," she drawled, looking me over with raised eyebrows and pursed lips. "You're the one we're all supposed to be excited about."

"Camilla," Clayton chastised, his voice low in warning.

"What?" She drew out the word in a sing-song tease.

"Tonight is not the night for your antics," he told her authoritatively.

"My antics? Clay, dear, you, of all people, know I only bite when I'm asked to."

I nearly choked on my champagne as she ran a finger down his arm with a certain air of... familiarity.

Rankor snickered under his breath as I dabbed my mouth with a napkin and Camilla shot me a victorious grin. Quietly, he warned her to be friendly as I turned to sit my empty glass on the tray of a server and worked to control my blush.

"Don't mind her," the dark-skinned man told me, taking space next to Clayton. "I wish I had a better excuse, but she can just be a bitch sometimes."

She scoffed, focusing her green eyes on me. "Perhaps, but I'm a bitch who can control my powers, at least. Can you say the same?"

My stomach dropped, uncomfortable with the reminder of the day on the bridge and my failures since. Camilla grinned and flicked her long hair over her shoulder haughtily.

"Nothing to say?" she teased. "Or can you only speak when the Dragon tells you what to say?"

Iris stepped forward, wrapping her hand through Camilla's arm. She shot me an apologetic glance as she redirected the woman to a table where Rankor and Lorelai stood.

"Sorry about her," Clayton apologized on her behalf. "She's insufferable on most days, but I swear there's a good person underneath the attitude."

"I heard that!" She called, though her tone betrayed that she had found no particular offense in the statement.

Turning away from me, Clayton began chatting with the stranger. They prattled on about some sports game or something. Their words were meaningless to me, but the stranger's voice seemed to echo in my head.

I knew that voice.

"Do I know you?" I blurted out to him, unable to stop myself.

He frowned as if embarrassed and shrugged. "You could say we met that day on the bridge. My name's Kent; I'm a Siren from House Palaemon. Sirens are gifted with the ability to slow heart rates with our songs. I helped Clay incapacitate you that day."

He shifted uncomfortably, unwilling to meet my eyes, but what could he possibly have to feel embarrassed or upset about? If the stories I'd been told were true, I had been entirely out of control, and he stopped me. He was positively a hero.

Clayton caught my line of sight and tilted his head at me in a slight shrug and the realization hit me suddenly: this was about politics.

Kent felt embarrassed to have used his powers against a possible Council member—the last Council member of House Hyrax, at that. Under normal circumstances, I suspected the action would be treasonous. Nothing about my arrival to this court had been normal, though.

"Thank you," I whispered to Kent.

Clayton didn't even try to hide his surprise at my words, but I continued on nonetheless.

"I'm not ignorant of the significance of that day, nor my actions. Even if I can't remember them, I take responsibility for what I did. And I'm grateful you helped stop me before I hurt anyone else."

We were all quiet for a moment before Kent bowed his head at me again and resumed his conversation with Clayton. I kept my eyes on the dancefloor, watching couples swirl effortlessly about, but I still felt the weight of Clayton's attention on me until Iris shoved a second glass of champagne into my hand and commanded us all to the dance floor.

I joined her reluctantly, hovering by her side and content to watch those around us. For a time, I even watched the Dragon and the Queen, who sat side by side presiding over the party but who didn't speak a word to each other.

As I finished that glass of champagne, I spoke freely with Lorelai and Kent as they told me stories about their childhood in the palace. By my third, I was dancing across the floor with Rankor and Iris, each laughing and trying to outdo the other. By the fourth glass of champagne, my feet were tingling and my thoughts were in a pleasant fog. Finally, I returned to that table in the back of the room, watching Kent and Rankor pass Lorelai, Camilla, and Iris between them with an ease that could only have come from years of friendship. I smiled from afar at them.

They were all so familiar with one another. More like siblings than friends.

As I watched them, longing blossomed within me. Was it possible Zachariah had fathered other children? And what of my mother? Was she still alive? Was she looking for me? Had I found myself on that bridge after an argument with her or had she encouraged me to make my way to the castle?

"Careful. Someone might see you tonight and suspect you're actually enjoying yourself," Clayton told me, sneaking up from behind. He smirked when I jumped slightly in surprise.

"I can admit that tonight wasn't *terrible.*"

"Yes, well, Iris can liven up a party all on her own. Put her *and* Rankor in a room together, and staying miserable for too long is impossible."

I grinned, watching them compete in what had to be a contest to see who could discover the most embarrassing dance move possible. I couldn't stop myself from giggling at the sight of it.

Clayton shook his head at me but gave a crooked smile. "Come on, if you're actually laughing, I know you've had too much champagne. Let me take you home."

I was hardly interested in a private stroll back to my rooms with Clayton, but I certainly had had too much to drink. My head felt too light, like it might slide off my body at any moment. A yawn escaped me suddenly, and I struggled to cover my mouth. The thought of sinking into that heavenly mattress was overwhelmingly tempting.

So, I let him fold my arm into his and followed his lead out of the ballroom. He caught Iris' eye as we left, and she waved enthusiastically at us from the dance floor. I felt the Dragon's gaze on me while we moved through the ballroom, but I found myself focusing on the Queen. She was the last thing I saw before stepping into the hall.

She hadn't moved from her throne all night. Not even once. Even though it was a celebration in her honor, she had sat apart, deigning only to look out the windows onto the garden as the sun had set.

"The Queen didn't seem to enjoy her party."

Clayton stiffened. "You'll find her highness is rather subdued in all manners of her life."

"She's not your mother," I blurted. It was obvious, of course, but it still felt wrong to say aloud.

"No, she's not," he agreed shortly. He spoke with clipped words, making his meaning clear. He would not be discussing that topic any further.

Instead, Clayton spoke quietly about some details of the artwork on the palace walls and about the history of the Gods. Some of their images I recognized from my initial history lessons with Hansel. Hyrax was absent, though. I had yet to see the likeness of my ancestor.

"Do you know how to waltz?" He asked me suddenly as we reached my door.

"Why?"

He raised an eyebrow. "The Peace Ball is in a few weeks. It's an annual celebration to mark the anniversary of peace after the Great War. Delegations from Promissa and other countries will be in attendance."

"Ah." I nodded, understanding. "And it is to be my grand debut to the world?"

His lips twitched slightly in what might have been a smile if he ever allowed himself to grin.

"I suppose," he conceded. "Perhaps you might prefer to think of it as the world's debut to you. It's a chance for you to meet some of our allies. People who might become part of your life one day."

People who might become part of my life one day. If that future looked anything like my present, I wasn't sure I wanted to embrace it. I had spent the past few days being shuffled from one mandatory engagement to the next, reading scripted words, and being constantly reminded to 'behave'.

"And what life is that?" I challenged him, alcohol taking over the better of my senses. "The one where I'm locked away in this room until you decide to display me to your next party guests?"

He stiffened, his face grimacing.

"I am your Crown Prince, Thea. You must mind your tone.".

I rolled my eyes as my anger mixed with a wave of shame. "So you say. But you're hardly *my* Prince. And the thing is, I don't even blame you. I destroyed that bridge. You *should* lock me up in this room and throw away the key!"

I threw the door open, pushed into the foyer, and dramatically threw myself onto one of the plush couches. Maturity had apparently left me after the final glass of champagne.

"But that's the thing," I continued. "You're not just locking me up, you're using me. You're treating me like a doll to dress up and parade around. And my reward for good behavior is that maybe one day I'll be able to sit on a Council I don't want to be on and live the rest of my life in a castle I don't want to stay in."

He hovered by the door, hands clasped behind his straight back. He was a picture of princely decorum, not daring to travel farther than appropriate into my rooms even though I was shouting loud enough that Hyrax himself might have heard me. I almost laughed out loud.

"Oh, do come in your grace," I teased.

His eyes flashed golden, but he stepped in, closing the door quickly behind him.

"You've had too much to drink. I will forgive your disrespect because of it, but we have customs, Thea. I am the Crown Prince of Athenia from House Zion, and you must show me respect."

I sighed, throwing my head back against the couch, wincing as I hit the wooden backboard. I was still rubbing the back of my head when a hiccup escaped me suddenly. Clayton sighed dramatically, pinching the bridge of his nose. I couldn't help but giggle once more. He wasn't wrong; I had too much to drink. I wouldn't be this bold otherwise, and I suspected I might come to regret some of this boldness in the morning.

"You didn't answer my question," he reminded me.

"What was that again?"

"The waltz. Do you know how to dance the waltz?"

I raised a brow, mimicking his characteristic expression as if to silently respond: *Do you think I know how to waltz?*

"Get up," he commanded, lowering a hand to me.

I let him pull me to my feet, trying not to flinch as he settled a hand on my back and adjusted my arm above his. His fingertips grazed the skin under my shoulder blade that was left bare under the low cut of my dress. His touch was warm, and I was acutely aware of it as he pulled me close to him and pressed my body to his. And yet, for as painfully aware of him as I was, Clayton's face was a mask of calm and purpose, as if his only thought was to teach me this dance and move on with his life.

"You'll follow my lead. When I step forward, you step back. When I go right, you go left. If you feel pressure here," a small press down onto my shoulder blade. "Be ready to spin."

He gave me no warning before launching forward and beginning the dance. I stumbled at first, his arm serving as the only thing to keep me steady. He spun us into a simple box step repeatedly, ignoring the first time I stepped on his foot and pursing his lips the second time I did it.

"I'm miserable at this."

"You are," he agreed, pressing down on my shoulder and releasing me, allowing me to twirl.

It was possibly the most ungraceful twirl ever done. He only rolled his eyes at me before pulling me back in.

We went on like that for a few minutes, completing enough box steps for me to master the feel of the movement and avoid stepping on him. My twirls were still awkward, though, and I nearly dragged us both into the ground when he attempted to dip me. His eyes flickered gold for only a moment.

"Practice," he ordered, releasing my hand and resuming his princely posture again. "I imagine you'll receive invitations to quite a few dances at the Peace Ball."

"Wonderful." I snorted. "Is that all for tonight?"

That was probably another breach of court custom to dismiss my Crown Prince like so, but my head had been spinning long before he ever pulled me off that couch, and every glance of my bed out of my peripheral had me screaming to lie down. I looked at it longingly before turning back to Clayton, expecting to see golden eyes staring back at me, but they were as stormy gray as ever.

"I imagine Iris will offer you company in the coming days. Your schedule will also include plenty of training with Ryla until you get a semblance of control over your powers."

I winced. So nothing was a secret around this castle, then? I wondered exactly how many people knew about my earlier failure on the mountain.

"But if you find yourself with some downtime," he continued. "I'll instruct Dimitri to allow for walks in the palace gardens. They're lovely this time of year."

He didn't give me a moment to collect my thoughts and even register the olive branch extended to me before he turned on his heels to leave. I stared after him for a moment, in shock, before rushing to the door myself.

"Clayton!" I called.

He turned, eyebrow raised.

"Has there been any word from the guards who went into town looking for my family?"

The air between us thickened as my stomach catapulted while I waited for his answer. When his gaze darkened in pity, my despair became overwhelming. I fought against the tears that threatened to fall.

"Not as of now," he told me.

Sighing unhappily, I nodded and prepared to bid him goodnight, only for him to step forward towards me once more.

"I'll keep looking, though." His words were heavy and meaningful.

We stood quietly for a moment.

"Thank you, Clay."

I closed the door between us, stumbled through the room, and fell onto the bed heavily. I didn't even bother to remove my gown or untangle my hair before I allowed myself to drift to sleep.

I *was underground, deep underground. Walls of cavernous rock stretched above me, sealing me in a tomb of darkness. And thoughthe world around me was shrouded in shadows, I could still see. Torches, nailed into the rock of the walls, provided enough dim lighting for me to make out my surroundings. The air was frosty and still. The silence left me feeling on edge.*

Water stretched out in front of me, perfectly still. I dipped my bare toe into it, surprised by the resistance I met. My foot touched down on the water's surface the same way I might step onto a sheet of glass. Impossibly, I didn't sink. I tested my weight, balancing on the water entirely. After it supported my weight for a full minute, I dared a step forward. Then another. I inched onto the river step by step, walking on the water as easily as I had stood on the ground moments before. Mist surrounded me, kissing my skin and blowing the skirts of my ivory gown.

Then the water shifted and my attention snapped to a man in a long wooden boat, who moved through the water slowly with each dip of his paddle. He wore long black robes with a hood pulled so low over his head that I couldn't make out his face. I shivered as he turned his head swiftly toward me. For a moment, we only looked at each other. Then, slowly, he bowed and continued his trek through the water.

I tried to follow him, stamping on the water, but each step grew more strained as if I were being pulled down. I felt stiff fingers wrap around my ankle abruptly, and I yelped, straining to see into the darkness of the water beneath me. Had I imagined it?

"Hello?" I called, searching for the man who had somehow disappeared into the darkness.

When I finally stepped onto land once more, I stumbled into another cavern. The walls were shrinking in on me.

"Is anyone here?" I cried.

The caverns opened with a rush of chilled wind. I stood in front of a giant iron gate, locked tight. The Mark on my chest burned as I looked at it, and I clutched my tattoo in surprise. I had only a moment to notice that I wasn't alone before the giant beast approached me.

It was a mammoth of a creature, standing high above me with dark black fur and three heads, each barking down at me. Their teeth were razor sharp, each one the size of my head. Slowly, the middle head dipped low, meeting me at eye level before running a tongue over its teeth. I felt his breath on me, blowing the hair back from my face. He snarled once, the sound of it ripping through my core and knocking me from my feet.

I screamed.

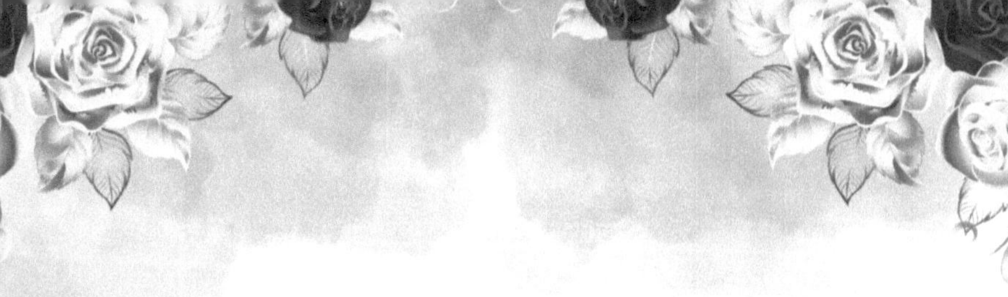

CHAPTER EIGHT

I woke to Nessira shaking me violently. She hovered over me, one knee propped onto my bed, her eyes wide in concern.

"What is it?" I gasped, barely aware of the fresh tears on my cheek.

Geia stood in the corner of my room, her hand pressed to her mouth in shock. Her fingers shook slightly.

"You were screaming, my lady," Nessira told me, her voice low.

She pulled away from me, brushing her hands over herself to smooth her skirt. I sat up slowly, my head and body aching from the night before. A wave of nausea flooded through me, and I shuddered.

"Bad dream," I muttered, frowning upon seeing my training clothes folded on the end of the bed. The last thing I wanted to do at that moment was climb another mountain.

Geia noticed my hesitancy and hurried into the foyer, quickly bringing back a tray with breakfast and a tall glass of brown juice. I looked down at it suspiciously, and Nessira tsked at me.

"It's for your stomach," she told me. "Trainer Ryla is expecting you within the hour, so eat up. Geia has already prepared your bath for you."

I grimaced as I sniffed the brown juice, but chugged it down nonetheless. It was *vile.* I gagged helplessly at the muddy texture, but it did, in fact, help my stomach. Before I knew it, I was out of bed and hurried into the bath.

The day went by ever so slowly. Ryla dragged me back over that mountain to test whether pain could evoke my powers. She started by whacking my arms and the back of my knees, then even escalated so far as to slice down my forearm with one of her blades. I had screamed at the sudden agony but was powerless to move the dagger from her grasp.

So hunger, anger, fear, and pain were all ruled out as potential triggers.

Finding the emotional catalyst for my power was starting to feel impossible.

After declaring the day to be another failure, she deposited me in the palace infirmary, where a nurse of House Asclepian, the God of medicine, healed my wounds. The process had been painful, more-so than even getting the wound in the first place, but it was truly marvelous.

Iris came to my room later that afternoon, nursing a headache and not bothering to hide the dark circles under her eyes. She curled into my bed and filled me in on the rest of the party. Highlights included Rankor winning the title of worst dancer and Iris sneaking away with both a male and female Descendant from House Angerelia. We sat gossiping together through the afternoon until Lorelai, Rankor, Camilla, and Kent joined us for dinner in my sitting room, where we all sat talking until the early morning hours.

My days at the palace all began to fall into a similar routine which, for the most part, wasn't *too* bad. I actually enjoyed my history lessons with Hansel. The old man could be a grouch, sure, but the history felt so fantastical that, at times, it was like reading stories. Stories of Gods who accomplished impossible feats and gifted their children with just a fraction of that glory.

Every so often, Hansel would take a break from criticizing me to pause and slowly nod. Those nods told me I was doing well. I was learning at an acceptable pace. And while I didn't know why I felt such a burning need to succeed in this role the Dragon had forced on me, I appreciated those nods.

I wasn't, however, finding the same success with my powers.

Each day, I got more desperate to find the trigger to draw out my magic, but I went home feeling entirely hopeless each afternoon. Ryla was getting frustrated with me. She forced me to run laps over the mountain until I was ready to fall over from exhaustion, but there was no magic. She made me read sorrowful stories that made me weep openly, but still there was no magic. She took me to see live plays that evoked excitement and passion, but *still* there was no magic.

"Is it normal for it to take this long?" I asked her one day after she had provided me with unsolvable mathematics problems to inspire embarrassment.

"No girl, usually children master their trigger before they're even walking! Using magic is as natural as moving an arm. You are simply failing at the most basic of tasks."

That certainly had inspired embarrassment.

My visits with Iris and Lorelai provided me with some joy to make up for that frustration, though. I didn't quite know what their jobs at court consisted of, but I suspected watching over me had become one of Iris' responsibilities. On the days when they were busy, Dimitri accompanied me to the palace gardens as Clay had promised he would. I would walk between the rows of roses, often just stopping to stare at the castle in frustration or look out on the mountains in longing. I didn't even know what I was longing for, though. After all, I still didn't know if there was a home waiting for me outside of the castle grounds.

There had been no updates regarding my life prior to court.

In the evenings, my foyer would fill with Iris, Lorelai, Camilla, Kent, and Rankor, and we would all eat our dinners together. It often frustrated Nessira to have extra mouths to wait on, but Geia seemed thrilled to be around them, listening in on their gossip. Most nights, I just watched them all interact. They all had an easiness among them, the kind that lifelong friends always seemed to have with one another. Iris had told me they had grown up here in the palace together. They'd trained together, and mastered their powers together, and now, though many of them were free to leave the castle, they stayed here together. They were a family.

Rankor was the most boisterous of the group, always telling larger-than-life stories from the past year that he'd spent exploring Athenia. Kent listened to him readily, often asking questions about the towns he saw or the cultures of the people he encountered. Kent hungered for knowledge in all forms, I had noticed. He often had a book in tow and never the same one for over two days in a row. Iris was even more exuberant around them, while Lorelai was pleasantly sweet, always allowing the others to talk before telling them how her day had gone. Camilla was typically quiet, frowning as if she had somewhere better to be. When she did speak, she chatted freely with the rest of the group, but hardly bothered to look at or acknowledge me.

I wasn't quite sure what I had done to piss her off, but each day she grew to be more insufferable than the last. I tolerated her presence, and I suspected she tolerated mine, because of the others. Their friendship was worth her attitude.

I didn't know what exactly I had done to earn their company each night, but I was grateful for it, nonetheless. My blossoming relationships with each of them added a much-needed dose of excitement to my life. And I did very obviously seem to need a family.

I was growing incredibly impatient with waiting for the Dragon to deliver news about the investigation into my background. It had been nearly a month since the incident on the bridge. A month and there was no more information about who I was than musings and suspicions. Nothing certain.

On the few occasions I had seen Clay, typically only when we happened to pass each other in the halls, he promised me he was still looking into it, but each day that passed left me less willing to trust those promises.

Someone had to know something.

So either they weren't looking hard enough, or they just weren't telling me what they had found.

Either way, it left me without the answers I desperately needed.

And so, one month after my arrival to court, I found myself wondering if perhaps it was time for me to become a bit more involved in that investigation. Perhaps it was time for me to go seeking some answers myself.

"What's got you so distracted?"

I jumped, letting out a shrill squeal as Iris rounded the corner into my bedroom, looking over me suspiciously. I'd been so lost in my thoughts I hadn't even heard Dimitri welcome her into the suite. Even as I joined her to sit at the foot of my bed, I found myself distracted by thoughts of escape.

"Nothing," I muttered.

She smacked my arm as she rolled her eyes. "You're a terrible liar."

That's true, I was. But did I have to lie to her? Iris had been nothing but kind to me, a true sister in every way. She had taught me everything I needed to know about court, introduced me to her circle of friends, and stood by me without ever doubting me as so many others had. If I could trust anyone, it was her, and yet, she was the Dragon's niece and Clay's cousin. So I couldn't be positive that anything I confided in her wouldn't be reported back to them.

But I had decided to trust Iris on my first day in this castle, and she had given me no reason to regret that choice.

"I want to get out of this castle, Iris," I confessed.

She laughed and lounged back on the bed, jade hair falling wildly around her shoulders. "It's a bit late for a walk in the gardens."

"I don't want to go to the gardens."

She frowned. "I don't understand."

I stood, crossing my arms over my chest as I took to pacing the room. Pacing had become a new habit of mine, brought on by too many hours alone in this room with nothing to do but wonder about my past and fear my future.

"I want to go into town," I told her. "I want to find someone who knows something about who I am and where I come from."

"The Dragon will let you know when he learns something," she told me, voice thick with what I suspected was pity.

"Then why hasn't he?" I questioned, throwing up my arms in frustration as I paused my pacing to look out the window longingly once more. "It's ridiculous to think that *nothing* has been learned over the past month. Someone had to have raised me; someone must have loved me at some point. So, where are they?"

Iris was quiet. I didn't turn back to look at her, afraid I would see the telltale signs on her face that she was going to tell me that what I was asking for was impossible. Perhaps I had made a mistake in trying to ask for her help in this. Maybe I had misjudged how much she valued our friendship above her duty to family and country.

"This is really bothering you, isn't it?" she asked me after a moment, voice low and caring.

I nodded, throat too thick with emotion to speak.

She was at my side in an instant, sighing as she grabbed my hand and pulled me into the bathroom. As we passed the closet, she drew out the plain black gown she'd initially given me to wear on my first day at court during the Council interrogation.

"Put this on," she instructed as she sat on the edge of the bathtub and rolled her neck. "Has anyone told you the details of my role within this court?"

I ris was a spy. She'd explained the details as she'd helped me dress in plain clothing and changed into a simpler ensemble herself. Her voice had gotten more serious than I'd ever heard it before as she told the stories of the criminal enterprises she'd infiltrated within Athenia and across the world. I would have never pictured my light-hearted friend doing such serious, deadly work, but as she spoke, I realized this version of her was not one I'd met before.

Turns out Clayton Vail wasn't the only one to don a mask from time to time.

She pointed me to the mirror, and her magic washed over me in a cloud, smelling like chamomile and basil. And what it touched, it *changed*. Long blonde hair darkened to the deepest shade of raven. Pale skin tanned. Thick lips thinned. The Mark on my chest slowly faded.

I stared at the unblemished skin of my collarbone, feeling oddly... on edge without that Mark.

"It won't last for long," she told me. "But it will keep you disguised while we do this. It's unlikely you'd be recognized, but the last thing we need is the Dragon knowing you're in town questioning people."

"Or that you're helping me."

Her appearance changed into that of a smaller brunette woman.

"Come," she commanded, and she guided me to the windows. "We'll need to climb out. There's a small ledge outside your windows. Enough that you'll just be able to walk on the balls of your feet. Move surely, but take your time. Not far from your window is a terrace on the floor below. It's attached to another suite that is thankfully empty right now. I'll get us into that suite, and from there, we should be able to walk through the palace and then into the village."

"How do you know all this?"

"I'm always aware of my surroundings." She shrugged.

I frowned. I had always considered myself observant, but perhaps not.

Waves of nerves filled me in a steady rhythm as she opened the window and let in a blast of frosty evening air. She didn't stop to ask me if I was sure about this or ready. She simply tossed her legs out, one at a time, and disappeared.

No time for second-guessing, I told myself as I followed her lead.

She hadn't been kidding about that ledge being narrow. It was barely wide enough for me to fit onto it, even when I stood on just my toes. I grasped desperately to the edge of my window as I found my footing. I knew I needed to move, and quickly before someone below saw me, but the only handholds available were the small cracks between the stones of the palace exterior. And though I knew it was a bad idea, I couldn't stop myself from looking down over the twenty-foot fall to the ground. A single glance was enough for me to regret this entire plan.

What was I thinking?

I wasn't a spy like Iris or an accomplished military general like Kent or Rankor. I was *barely* a Descendant at all. Truth be told, I was a miserable excuse for a royal who couldn't even call up my own powers. What hope did I have of scaling the side of a castle and living to tell the tale?

"Focus, Thea!" Iris hissed, already on the terrace below. By the Gods, how did she do that so quickly? "Stop looking down. Just breathe and inch along. You're going to be fine."

It was hard to trust that I was going to be fine when my muscles had locked, and dizziness was settling over me. As a gust of wind blew past me, my fingers clutched the windowsill tighter, so tight that I felt the tips of my nails begin to crack under the pressure.

"Breathe!" Iris reminded me in a stressed whisper.

I forced myself to inhale, bracing against another draft of wind. The air itself was frigid, but I hardly noticed as I focused on loosening my grasp on the window. I exhaled and moved my right hand to clasp onto one of the cracks between the stones. I inhaled and moved my right foot an inch down the ledge. I exhaled and moved my left hand. I inhaled and moved my left foot.

Exhale. Move. Inhale. Move.

"Keep going," Iris coaxed. "You're doing a great job."

Exhale. Move. Inhale. Move.

The process was slow-moving, but eventually, I was able to inch myself along the wall far enough to jump the small distance to the terrace down below. I jolted from the jarring impact, releasing very un-ladylike curses under my breath as I stumbled onto my knees.

"I sure hope your plan for getting back into the castle is easier than this," I muttered as I accepted the hand Iris offered down to help me.

She only giggled, pulled a pin from her hair, and set about picking the locks. In only a moment's time, the lock clicked into place, and she pushed the door open with a self-satisfied grin. Gods, how in all of creation did she do that so quickly?

Iris gripped my hand and pulled me through the room so quickly I hardly noticed my own surroundings. By the time we exited into the halls of the East Wing of the castle, most of the court was already winding down and heading to bed for tonight. With Iris' magic disguising us, no one bothered to pay us much mind as we walked casually through the halls and right out the front door of the palace.

While the Lords and Ladies of Court may have been winding down for the evening, the village outside still sparked with life. The sun had already set, but a small market still lined the dirt streets through the houses as farmers and artisans sought to barter off the last of their goods for the day. People interacted happily with each other, swapping stories and gossip while a band at the far end of the market played. Iris remained focused as we walked, scanning over the area with a calculating expression. As two children ran past us, tossing a small ball between them, I stepped closer to her.

"We don't have long," she reminded me. "We can't risk Dimitri or one of your ladies noticing you're missing."

"I don't have much of a plan."

She nodded as if she had been expecting that and gestured to a small cart where an older woman was selling fabrics of a variety of colors. Iris pulled me towards the cart and began looking over the material as if she planned to make a purchase herself.

"You lookin' for somethin' specific, dearie?" the woman asked.

Iris smiled. "Our lady favors teal. We need to be makin' her something for the ball."

I bristled, surprised by how effortlessly she adopted the woman's accent. There was no way I could do that. Did she expect me to do that?

The woman pulled out a roll of shimmering blue taffeta. "You like this?"

"It's pretty." Iris nodded and pulled some coins from the purse on her hip. "Bet you're making quite a coin with that party comin' up."

"Moreso than usual this year."

Iris raised her brows. "I'm not surprised. What with that new Hyraxian girl and all."

The woman snorted. "If you can call her that."

My stomach dropped, and I stepped towards her. I knew I should stay quiet, should let Iris take the lead, but there was an undertone in the woman's words I didn't understand. One that I needed to understand. "You doubt she's a Descendant of Hyrax?"

The woman looked over at me suspiciously, obviously noting the ways my speech didn't blend in with the rest of the townfolk, and Iris kicked my ankle as if to remind me I should let her do the talking.

"It's not that," the woman amended, as she took the coins Iris extended towards her. "I saw her myself on that bridge and at the castle d'other day. She got that Mark alright. It's that story I don't trust."

"Why not?" Iris pressed, keeping her voice light, and her eyes focused on the fabric.

"That Zachariah fellow was no stranger to these parts. Spent quite a bit of his time and coin down at Madame Stefania's."

Iris stilled. It was a small movement, almost unnoticeable, and yet it was enough to tell me she'd heard something important. She nodded her thanks to the woman, gripped my hand, and started pulling me in the opposite direction. I struggled to keep pace with her, barely keeping my grasp on the blue fabric she tossed at me.

"Who's Madame Stefania?" I questioned, which earned me some disapproving glances from the townsfolk we passed as we walked.

Iris grimaced. "You're about to find out. And I don't think you're going to like it."

She didn't explain any further before stopping so suddenly in front of a shabby wooden building that I ran into her back. Music and laughter escaped through the door that swung open and closed as various young couples walked in and out of the establishment. The shutters were all drawn, hiding what was happening inside, but it wasn't hard to make out the sound of moaning from the upper floors.

Dear Gods.

I'd overheard some of the ladies at court talking about places like this. Places where men and women alike could come to get their *needs* fulfilled.

I flushed the color of the roses on my bedside table.

Iris had brought me to a brothel. Seemingly unaffected by it, she tore the fabric from my hands, tossed it in the mud beside the door, mussed her hair, and pulled down the front of her dress until her breasts looked as if they were ready to bust out. Amazingly, I smelt the scent of her magic in the air once more and watched as her chest grew until she was impressively better endowed. Catching sight of my shocked open mouth, she winked and nodded to my own dress. And while part of me wanted to protest, a bigger part of me wanted to know what secrets that woman had known about Zachariah. So I followed her lead and stuck close to her as she pushed open the door and walked inside.

The room we entered wasn't particularly large. To my left was a long wooden bar where a burly man was pouring liquor for some of the guests. Stairs to the right led to the upper floors, and in the back corner of the room, several men stood at tables, talking and smoking. Much of the space was a sitting area where people laughed and chatted with each other on three worn olive couches.

All in all, everything seemed... appropriate. At first glance, all anyone appeared to be doing was talking, and some naïve part of me momentarily wondered if I had been wrong. Perhaps this wasn't one of those establishments the ladies at court talked about.

But then, as I looked a bit more closely, it became easy enough to discern that Madame Stefania's was meant for something *more.*

On the stairs, a thin woman wearing a tight midnight blue dress with a slit cut nearly to the very tip of her pelvic bone was tugging on the hand of another woman. They laughed as they went up, a male following quickly behind them. In the room's corner, on one couch that hid in the shadows, a couple pressed close together. The man had buried his face into her neck while her hand stretched into the top of his trousers. At the table where a group of men were engaged in cards, a woman in red sat on the lap of the gentleman at the head of the table. He was focused on his cards, puffing smoke from the cigar dangling from his mouth, but as her eyes closed and her head fell back against his chest, I noticed his other hand was deep between her thighs.

I bit my lip and turned away, suddenly desperate to hide my flaming cheeks.

I wasn't sure if I was more uncomfortable because they were engaging in such behavior publicly or because watching them made me feel oddly... curious.

I couldn't remember if I had ever been touched in that way. Had I left behind a lover with my memories?

Iris, remarkably, didn't seem to be phased by any of it. She approached the barkeep confidently, demanding to speak to Madame Stefania.

"Stefania's not here," he answered suspiciously. "What you be needin'?"

"We're from the city of Alepolis," she lied. "Just came into town. Old client of mine said he used to find girls here, said Stefania was the woman to talk to about a job."

"Name of your client?" he questioned, pouring her a drink and passing one to me as well.

"Zachariah Moore."

A woman two seats over from us began laughing. She was about my age, with chestnut hair and large brown eyes. Her expression was confident, and her gown was practically sheer. She leaned against the bar with the ease of someone who had spent quite a long time in this room.

"I doubt that," the woman said to us.

"You knew Zachariah?" Iris asked.

The woman nodded. "Came here often, he did. Wasn't particularly interested in folks like you, though. Tended to prefer the company of men a bit more than ladies like yourselves."

That... was possible, I supposed. If Zachariah was my father, though, then he had to have enjoyed the company of a woman at least once.

It was either that, or the Dragon had been wrong and he simply wasn't my father.

Just then, shouting sounded across the room as a heated conversation between two men in the space's corner turned violent. One threw a punch while the other tossed a table carelessly into the wall. The legs of it splintered in the crash.

"There they go again," the barkeep complained, wiping his hands on a towel. "Stefania will be here tomorrow. You can come back then if you're still looking for work."

Iris and I left just as he began to break up the fight.

CHAPTER NINE

Sneaking back into my room *had* been easier than sneaking out. We arrived back at the castle just as Dimitri was trading posts with another guard. Iris, in her magically disguised form, feigned a fall at the end of the hallway. Both guards tried to help her up while she cried theatrically, and I slipped right past them and back into my suite.

I bathed as quickly as I could, eager to wash the stench of the night off of me, but knew that sleep would be impossible. Too much had happened that had given me too much to think about.

The fact that Zachariah preferred male partners didn't necessarily mean that he wasn't my father. After all, it only really took one night of passion to create a child. It did make it all seem a bit more unlikely, though. Could I really trust that Zachariah, who favored male partners overall, randomly fathered me and left me in the care of a mortal woman who hid my powers from me? And even if that had happened, I still had no additional information about my mother. Was she alive? Or had she failed to come looking for me because something had happened to her?

I needed to remember what happened to me before I ended up on that bridge.

Frustrated and overwhelmed by it all, I spent most of the night pacing and tossing over the possibilities in my mind. Occasionally, I dozed off for twenty or thirty minutes at a time, only to wake suddenly once more as a fresh wave of uncertainty washed over me.

And then, as the light of morning filtered into my room, the sound of a card sliding under the door startled me. I approached it cautiously, sighing audibly as I picked it up and read the message.

The Dragon has requested your presence at dinner this evening. I've sent Nessira something for you to wear. -Clayton Vail, Crown Prince of Athenia

Did they know I had escaped last night?

Or was this just a casual dinner?

Was anything with the Dragon casual? Nothing about any of my interactions with Clay or his father made me suspect it would be. So an evening spent in their company was unlikely to be very enjoyable.

In frustration, I threw myself down on the bed and didn't bother to look up when Nessira and Geia entered my room. Nessira quickly tucked the gown away in the closet before I could see it, which told me all I needed to know about it. The evening would be another occasion in which they would expect me to play the long-lost princess. A role that would undoubtedly involve some awfully gaudy gown. I bit my lip as Nessira and Geia began preparing me. They, thankfully, didn't notice that I'd bit down hard enough to draw blood.

"When will the dresses we commissioned for me be ready?" I asked them. Once I finally had my own clothes, maybe I wouldn't have to keep wearing the fashions everyone else chose for me.

"Later today, my lady," Geia promised me. "I checked on them personally this morning. They'll be delivered in no time."

In truth, the gown Clay had sent for me wasn't *as* atrocious as the last one he had picked, but it was still far from my personal preferences. Its high neck felt like a collar closing in on me whenever I moved. It cinched at my waist and fell around me in golden waves of shimmering fabric. I was a sunbeam personified, impossible to miss. And even though the dress covered my chest and throat, the sheer fabric still allowed my Mark of Hyrax to remain visible.

Nessira styled my hair classically. She folded golden clips of ivy leaves into it and pulled it carefully into a knot at the nape of my neck.

"Is this entirely necessary just for a dinner?" I questioned as she painted my eyelids golden.

"It's for show more than anything," she whispered, as if she was afraid of being caught talking so casually. "Both a show of your status as a Council member and the status of whom you'll be dining with."

"I'm not a Council member yet."

Her eyes glittered with poorly hidden humor. "Not yet, my lady. Not quite yet."

I had imagined dining with the Dragon would come with a bit more preamble. I wasn't sure what *exactly* I had expected, perhaps some fanfare or grand announcement of my arrival as I entered the Dragons' rooms, but all I got was a grumpy servant quickly ushering me in as Dimitri and I arrived.

The Dragon, the Queen, and Clay all sat at the large dining table, giving off the impression that I was late even though I was sure I had arrived on time. A feast of nuts, berries, and meats was overflowing on the table, but the three picked at it. The resemblance between Clay and his father was startling as they sat next to each other in their immaculate royal suits. With her delicate features and almond eyes, the difference between the men and the Queen was obvious.

"Theadora!" The Dragon called as I entered. "Do have a seat!"

I bowed slightly, choosing the open seat next to the Queen. She didn't raise her eyes from her plate as I sat next to her.

"Thank you for the invitation, your majesty."

The Dragon chuckled, extending a finger at me as he looked towards Clay. "Look at that; she's learning manners in no time."

I bristled at the insult but knew better than to speak out of turn.

You just have to get through this dinner, I reminded myself.

The meal proceeded with little to note. Servants laid out the courses in front of us in perfect timing, and I ate in silence. Clay and his father prattled on about trade deals and infrastructure plans while the Queen continued staring down at her plate. I couldn't help but wonder about her. Had she always been like this, or was it her marriage that made her act like she wished to disappear entirely? Even now, during a private dinner, she wore those dragon hand chains on her wrists like a constant reminder that she belonged to him.

I spent most of the night staring out the window at that balcony where I had pledged myself to Athenia, and thereby to the Dragon, only a few weeks prior. A declaration with consequences I was currently dealing with.

"So, Theadora," the Dragon huffed as they brought our desserts out.

It was a chocolate cake. A beautifully decorated, perfectly proportioned chocolate cake with strawberry jam and cream on the side. It seemed inappropriate to dive into it while the Dragon was speaking to me. But then, it also seemed inappropriate to start a conversation right when dessert was brought out.

"I'm sure you know the Peace Ball is only in a few more short days."

I had forgotten about the Peace Ball, actually. Thankfully, I'd had enough good sense to ask Iris how much dancing would actually be involved after Clay had attempted to teach me to waltz weeks ago, and she'd had Rankor show me all the popular routines. So at least in that regard, I wouldn't be making a total fool of myself.

"I cannot express how thrilled we are to celebrate your arrival in Athenia at this year's Peace Ball," the Dragon continued. "Our war with Promissa was quite costly, as I'm sure you've gathered."

Clay shifted in his seat uncomfortably. With his eyes on his untouched plate and a single hand clutched in a fist, I'd never seen him look more like a boy. Carefully, I glanced at the Queen, who was clearly too young to be his mother.

I suddenly understood just how costly the war had been for him.

"Yes, majesty. Though I doubt I'll ever truly understand the full impacts of it."

The Dragon huffed as he smashed his fork into his dessert. "Although you haven't officially ascended to the Council, your role in our kingdom is significant, nonetheless. Many eyes will be on you as a representative of our country."

His eyes found mine, and I forced myself not to shiver with their burning intensity. Like Clay's often did, they glowed golden, though it was a darker, stormier color. They shone with the same passion as when he had threatened me that day before the press briefing. His message was obvious.

"I'm aware of my responsibilities," I told him, pleased with the steadiness of my own voice.

"Very well."

I tried not to sigh in relief as his attention shifted back to his plate. He had cleared it in no time and was already beckoning for the servants to take away his plates and pour his after-dinner scotch. I picked at my dessert, but my appetite had suddenly abandoned me, and I ended up sending it out half-eaten.

"So, Clayton tells me you've begun preparing for the trials to ascend to the Council. It's more a formality than anything in your case, but we must try to go through the proper procedures."

The Dragon droned on; his monotonous voice was the only thing standing in the way of my swift escape to shed this gown and step into a warm bath. I was sure Nessira was already waiting for me to commiserate on a terrible evening. Geia would be so excited by the prospect of gossip that she would likely be willing to sneak into the palace kitchens to steal some of the little chocolates that were saved for special occasions.

"And there is, of course, the matter of your upcoming marriage," the Dragon continued, capturing my attention suddenly.

I stilled. "My marriage?"

"Yes, I've begun considering the prospects. There's a Promissan Fire Elemental I'm currently discussing contracts with. He has some distant relation to a necromancer from House Hyrax. We're currently investigating if he could be a suitable match."

"Shouldn't that be something I decide?" I asked softly before I could stop the words from escaping.

The Dragon cleared his throat aggressively, and Clay shifted his weight. His eyes bore into mine with a silent warning.

"I just mean..." I clarified. "I hardly feel ready for a marriage, and I'm not particularly interested in an arranged marriage."

The Dragon took a deep, measured breath, as his eyes slowly began to glow. "You don't have the luxury of choosing your marriage. Producing an heir with enough genetic ties to be predominantly descended from Hyrax might pose a challenge, considering you're the last. You'll need to start the process of repopulating sooner rather than later."

"Repopulating?" My stomach locked in a sudden and uncomfortable churn.

"Miss Moore," Clay warned, his voice low and as steady as his father's.

This was... ridiculous. I had only been in this castle for a short time, only known the Dragon for a matter of weeks. How could anyone expect me to agree to him planning out the rest of my life without allowing me the freedom to make those decisions myself?

"The ultimate choice of husband is yours, of course," Clay interjected, sensing my thoughts. "And there are no laws subjecting you to stay in the marriage if it turns abusive or otherwise harmful."

Well then, at least I could be grateful for the fact my safety was prioritized higher than my womb!

Every fiber of my being pushed me to fight back against them. I wanted, more than anything, to push out my chair, refuse to agree to these terms, and storm out of the room. I wanted to remind them that, as a woman, I deserved to be treated as more than just common breeding stock.

But I was talking to a king.

And in my few short weeks at court, I'd already learned that declining the King simply would not be tolerated.

"You're the head of a Council family," the Dragon reminded me, his irritation becoming evident. "You have obligations to fulfill and customs to follow."

I knew that, of course. My responsibilities to the Council and to the House of Hyrax had been a constant weight on me since I woke in the infirmary. Not a day had gone by without someone reminding me exactly what obligations I had to fulfill because of the Mark on my chest. And yet, all I could think about in that moment was how badly I didn't want any of those responsibilities.

I didn't want to be on his Council or stay in this palace for the rest of my life. I didn't want to read his pre-written speeches or give fake smiles at his parties. But above all that, I didn't want to sign over control of what and *who* I did with my own body, simply because of a tattoo on my chest.

I hadn't even been able to summon my powers!

If it wasn't for that damned tattoo branding me as important, none of this would be happening.

The Dragon had made up his mind on this matter. That was clear from the set of his jaw and the firmness of his shoulders. Fighting back would only complicate my life at court further. But maybe, with more time, I could reason with him. Surely, there was a reasonable man hidden underneath the anger and dominance.

"Perhaps then," I appealed. "Since I'm not a Council member yet, we can table any conversations on my marriage prospects until that fact changes."

The Dragon stood suddenly, and the sound of his heavy chair against the floor released an angry screech. His fingers shifted into talons as his palms slammed down onto the table, and I hoped my face didn't expose the rush of my fear.

I had gone too far.

The Dragon wasn't a reasonable man.

I'd seen Clay begin to transform that day in the hospital, but watching the Dragon begin to take his beast form was something else entirely. The entire room seemed to shrink as his presence in it grew tenfold. Firm green scales climbed up his arms. His eyes darkened around fiery, golden iris'. The air tightened as a wave of heat rushed from him.

When he finally spoke again, his voice was low, laced with malice and a slight beastly growl.

"Do not mistake my invitation here for kindness, Theadora," he warned. "You are in no place to question me or my decisions. Do not think that your little friends or strolls in the garden mean that your crimes are forgiven. Our shaky international relations and that Mark on your chest are the *only* reasons I didn't end your life the second you walked into *my* kingdom."

His words were a weight, pressing me into my seat with a reminder of the remarkable power he constantly held within him. The power that he would not hesitate to use against me the second I gave him a reason. My stomach railed against me as I silently watched as scales climbed up his arms until even the skin around his neck rippled and turned green.

I had once asked Iris about Clay's transformation that day in the hospital. She told me that all Dragons of House Zion had aspects of their beast, but only the most powerful could fully transform and shed their human skin entirely. She hadn't elaborated further, but I feared I was about to find out just how far the Dragon could change.

I was too consumed by the weight of the Dragon's fury to even notice the scrape against the floor as Clay stood and came to my side, placing himself slightly between myself and the Dragon. It was only when I felt his fingers against my shoulder as he wrapped his hand around the back of my chair that I noticed his presence.

His position was no accident. He was prepared to throw me out of that chair and away from his father, if necessary.

"Perhaps it would be best for Theadora and I to take our leave for the evening."

"Sit down, boy!" The Dragon bellowed. "You leave when I command it!"

Clay sighed, his fingers flexing once on the back of my chair, but he did not sit. For a moment, we were all frozen in our spots. Not even the servants, balancing food on trays or beginning to pour drinks, dared to move or even breathe. We were all waiting for the Dragon to declare what would happen next.

"Am I understood, Miss Moore?" He growled. His chest heaved as he worked to contain the beast struggling to take form.

Clay grasped my shoulder, giving a tight squeeze, a silent push toward the only answer I could give.

"Yes," I breathed, tucking my shaking hands under my bottom so he couldn't see them.

"Yes, what?"

I bit down on my lip with the rush of a sudden tingling through my arms and fingers. The feeling of it flooded over me, trickling down my arms and legs and dancing across the back of my neck. The shock nearly made me forget about my current situation entirely, but the increasing pressure of Clay's hand on my shoulder shook through me, pulling me back into the room.

"Yes, your majesty." I breathed.

He smirked, his eyes narrowing triumphantly. Then, too slowly, the scales settled back into his skin, and he straightened his jacket.

"Get out, both of you."

Clay pulled out my chair without hesitation, but I was already on my feet. I didn't need him to show me out of the room, but I knew he followed me as I hiked up the skirts of my gown and ran down the hallway, fleeing the Dragons' suites while my skin still burned from the sensation of each and every one of my nerves bursting.

CHAPTER TEN

Clay wasn't far behind me as I sped through the palace in a discomforting haze. Even though I ran as fast as I could, my legs strong after my many trips over the mountain with Ryla, he caught me in no time, grabbing my hand and pulling me into an unknown room with enough force to leave my arm stinging from the uncomfortable pull.

I didn't have the strength to fight him, though. All I could think about, all I could *feel,* was the movement under my skin. The feeling of sparks traveling from the center of my stomach out through my arms and legs into my fingers and toes.

Something was very, very wrong with me.

Had I been poisoned? Had the Dragon lied about wanting to keep me alive and invite me to dinner only to do away with me?

Surely, I was dying.

That's what this felt like.

Every nerve in my body was screaming for release. I was going to explode.

The cold air on my skin was sudden as Clay pulled us onto a dark terrace. I lurched forward, leaning over the railing, desperate to have more cool air wash over me. My breath came in a rush, short heaves in and out as the electric feeling continued pooling inside of me. The garden trees shook, and the stone veranda under my feet vibrated. I hardly felt Clay as he pulled me up over the ledge and grabbed my face, pulling me to look at him.

"Breathe, Thea," he commanded. "You need to try and breathe. Putting on a display of how uncontrollable your powers are right now will help no one."

He took my hand and pressed it against his chest so that I could feel his heart beating and his chest rising with his own deep breaths in and out. My eyes never broke away from his as I followed his lead, breathing in his cinnamon and oak scent until the discomfort and pressure in me began to ease and the world around us began to still.

We stood like that, pressed too closely, my hand on his chest and his on my face, for too long. Until, finally, he nodded, let go of my hand, and took a step back.

On my own, a deep shudder escaped from the deepest part of me.

"*That* was my powers?" I whispered, incredulous.

He laughed darkly. "Congratulations, you've finally been able to summon them."

I wrapped my arms around myself, suddenly cold.

"It was... overwhelming," I tried to explain. "It felt like my skin was crawling. I didn't expect it to be so *painful.*"

Clay turned to look at me slowly, and his face was free of his regular mask of arrogant confidence and command. He no longer looked like the angry, commanding prince I'd interacted with so far. He just looked... tired.

Sighing, he ran a hand over his face and hair, pulling it out of its normally tousled perfection.

"It's like that sometimes," he told me. "Especially when you first start calling on it. The magic is always there, under the surface, waiting to be released. For those of us who are more powerful than others, it can be much more difficult to contain at times."

"And when you go too long without releasing it?"

He laughed softly and raised an eyebrow in a smirk that left me slightly off balance.

"Can't say I've ever tried to go too long without a release," he insinuated.

Well, that was... not the kind of joke I expected him to make.

As I blushed furiously, he walked past me to the darkness on the edge of the balcony. A large pot of flowers was nearly hidden within the obscurity of the darkness on the edge of the balcony. Wordlessly, he pulled a scarlet rose free and held it in his palm, bringing it to his nose for only a moment before turning back to me.

"I imagine that the magic will get more unruly the longer it's kept chained up and, therefore, more painful in its attempt to escape."

"I don't even know how I did it."

He held the rose out to me, flat on his palm between us. A thornless rose, pulled from the shadows and held between a Descendant of Zion and a Descendant of Hyrax, a silent invitation for me to unleash my murderous power once more.

"What were you feeling?" He asked me, his voice low.

I shrugged helplessly, not wanting to admit the truth behind the emotions that had inflamed my magic. It felt like a weakness, and I didn't want to admit to any of my weaknesses - not when I wasn't sure if I could trust him with them.

"Afraid," I whispered, eyes on the ground. "Afraid of him. Afraid of being stuck here while he makes decisions for me. I was angry too, though. It was this strange combination of the two, almost like an unwillingness to surrender to my fear. That must be why it's been so hard to tap into my powers. The emotion is too complex to replicate."

He didn't answer me, but his silence was answer enough. When I met his gaze, I knew what he was thinking without him having to say it aloud. We were all prisoners to the Dragon's wishes in some way or another.

With a deep breath, I turned my attention to the flower in his hand. Slowly it lifted, floating weightlessly in the air until it twirled in endless circles between us. Somehow, simply naming the emotion had made the magic click into place within me. Almost like I had pulled a plug that had been blocking it and now everything could flow uninhibitedly. The tingling within me was no longer overwhelming or frightening; it was a comfort, a friend waiting under the surface to support me. Calling it forth was as easy as calling my breath. Ryla had been right all along. It *was* as easy as moving an arm.

"I've felt like such a failure these past few weeks," I whispered. "And the entire time, this was right under the surface."

At some point, I'd begun to doubt whether this would even be possible. Everyone kept reminding me what I had done on the bridge, but I had started to convince myself that they were wrong. That I simply didn't have this kind of power within me.

Clay made a low sound deep in his throat, his eyes transfixed on the flower floating between us. Slowly, they lifted and through a curtain of full, dark lashes, he met my gaze.

"You've never been truly powerless, Thea."

No, I suppose I hadn't been. It had just taken a moment alone with the Crown Prince for me to realize it.

CHAPTER ELEVEN

We were in Clay's private chambers. That much was clear as I stepped back into the room, and he closed the terrace doors behind us. His bedroom was as grand as my own, but remarkably unkempt for a royal bedchamber. The blankets were thrown back across the bed haphazardly, with garments from the night before carelessly thrown over them. Papers and folders were scattered over the large desk under the window. And the books. Books covered the room. On the shelves, the end tables, and even stacked on the floor in the corners of the space.

I fingered through one gently, finding notes on warfare tactics and maneuvering.

"Do you ever take a day off from being a Prince?" I wondered aloud.

He leaned against the terrace doors, watching me explore with his arms crossed against his chest. Absentmindedly, I noted that we were breaking protocol. It was one of the few lessons I'd memorized on royal customs. Unmarried members of Council families were not to be left alone with potential suitors in their rooms, as if we were nothing more than unruly teenagers. Even in group settings, Rankor and Kent never strayed farther than the parlor of my own suite. It had to do with heirs. There could be no question about what bloodlines were running through my child, or Clay's future heir, for that matter.

I probably should have seen the arranged marriage plan coming from a mile away.

Clay would likely be married off, too, to a woman from Zion's bloodline, I realized. He would face the same pressures to produce an heir in a timely manner. I wondered how soon it would be for him. Based on how cluttered his bedroom was, it hardly looked like he regularly entertained company. Was it possible I was the only girl to have ever entered this room?

I mentally scolded myself for such a ridiculous thought.

"I suppose there are some," he answered me.

"Some?"

Some women?

He raised an eyebrow imperiously at me. "Some days off."

"Ah," I sighed. Of course.

He crossed the room slowly, approaching a small bar cart and pouring us both glasses of red wine. I started to refuse, but bit my tongue. After that dinner, I certainly needed a drink.

"Is your father always that pleasant?" I asked him as I smoothed my skirts and settled into a small armchair.

I was happily surprised to see a mystery novel sitting dog-eared on the end table. So, he wasn't all work and no play after all. Part of me wanted to pick it up and leaf through it, to see what kind of writing style my prince found to be intriguing, but I held myself back. It felt somewhat rude to go through someone's things. Especially considering Clay and I weren't necessarily friends.

He handed me a glass and took the chair across from me.

"Usually, he's much more so," he admitted a bit ruefully.

The wine was strong and bitter, and I fought the urge to grimace at my first taste. Still, I appreciated the slight burn in the back of my throat. Clay stared down at his, lost in thought.

"Can I ask you something?" I asked, surprised by the softness in my voice.

He raised that eyebrow again, a silent invitation.

"It's just that when you stood before me, it was like you expected him to hit me. Has he... hurt people like that before?"

Clay laughed darkly, downing his drink in a single quick gulp. He took my glass, also quickly finished, and refilled them both again. As he started talking, he kept his back to me. I suspected it was so that I wouldn't be able to see the expression on his face. That only made me want to look at him more, though.

"You truly do not understand what is acceptable to say to a Crown Prince."

"Perhaps not."

I suspected that even after years at court, one day, I would still find myself saying improper things.

"You remind me a little of my mother in that way," he told me.

As he returned and sat across from me once more, he kept his head down, eyes on the floor. I'd never heard Clay talk about his mother. I'd never heard *anyone* talk about her before. There were no portraits of her hung in the castle either. That had always struck me as odd.

"She often felt frustrated by the rules of it all too, like you. And she hated the gowns as much as you do. When I was younger, we would go out together to the mountains around the castle. She was much happier exploring the kingdom than at the big parties. Every time we would reach the top of an outlook, she would look at it momentarily and remind me: *never let the splendor of your castle cause you to forget the expanse of your full kingdom.*"

"That's good advice."

He nodded solemnly. "Her marriage to my father had been arranged, of course. He was initially supposed to marry her sister Elira, Iris' mother, but when he met the family to collect Elira, my father laid eyes on my mother and claimed her as his bride instead. Her parents were so honored at being welcomed into the royal family that they didn't care which daughter was wed off. So they struck the deal, and my parents were married when she was sixteen."

So young. Without meaning to, I shivered against the chill in the air and Clay, absentmindedly, grabbed an afghan off the corner of his bed and passed it to me. He didn't make eye contact as he did so, almost as if he had done it without even realizing. Silently, I wrapped it around myself while I waited for him to continue.

"My father was older, twenty-four, at the time of their marriage. I'm sure you can imagine the husband he was to her. In his eyes, she had become his property from the second he had taken her from her home. Her only purpose was to decorate his arm and bear his children. I was born three years after their wedding."

Clay cleared his throat, throwing back his second drink and leaning heavily into his seat.

"Around that time, the Great War was just beginning. My father was determined to produce a second heir should anything happen to me, but it didn't happen. So, as the years went by without another pregnancy, my father's treatment of my mother worsened. He was respectful in public, of course, but I would see healers leaving her room each morning."

I didn't move or even breathe as his story continued. Clay's eyes glazed over as he spoke. He was here, with me, but he was also there - in another time and place.

"I was seventeen when the Great Battle of Athenia happened. I'd been in the gardens with my Aunt Elira and Iris when we realized what was happening. It had started with the fog. Deep, heavy fog from the Water and Air Elementals working together, making sight nearly impossible. Elira gathered what was happening before most of the guards even did. She rushed us into the castle, straight to my mother's apartments. She was always protective of my mother in that way."

"He was with her?"

Clay nodded. "The halls were empty, all the guards beginning to mobilize. I remember hearing them shout as they were looking for my father. But as we entered the halls of my mother's rooms, we heard him yelling. It's funny; I sometimes hear it again in my dreams, but I can never pinpoint what he's saying. Elira started running. Iris and I followed. We were all too late. When Elira opened the door, he had my mother in his arms. He looked Elira right in the eyes before he threw her off the terrace."

That was.... well that was positively evil.

Since my arrival at court, I'd witnessed the Dragon's anger on several occasions, but I could never have predicted the extent of his cruelty went *that* far. How in all of creation had Clay continued his life day after day in this court after watching that?

I wanted to say something to comfort him, but what was there to say?

Nothing.

There was nothing I, or anyone, could ever say to Clay to erase that this had happened in front of him–to him.

Wordlessly and without thought, I leaned forward and touched my hand to his, squeezing softly in a silent show of support. The skin was warm to the touch, too warm, but I didn't flinch.

He sighed suddenly, staring at my hand on his. I wondered, numbly, how many others knew this story. How many times had Clay been allowed the space to give words to his trauma? Was that shudder he released from the relief of finally getting it off his chest?

Truthfully, I don't know why he trusted me with it. I seemed like the least likely person to serve as a confidante to him, but if I could at least give him the momentary relief of acknowledging his hurt then I would do that. Of course I would do that.

"What happened after that?" I whispered, urging him to continue.

He laughed bitterly, finally lifting his head to look at me. His eyes were golden.

"Nothing. He just walked out of the room. When the battle was over, everyone assumed she had died during it. Elira was devastated and blamed herself. She and my uncle left the country immediately after the peace treaty was signed. They've never returned. Two weeks after it happened, my father married Valentina, a Dragon from the Republic of Inanis, as a sign of the peace between our nations. He hasn't spoken of that day since."

Clay looked away, looking painfully haunted, and I allowed him a moment of privacy by going to refill his glass once more. As I gave it to him, I looked to his eyes, searching for the insight they would give me to his mood. They had faded to grey again.

I think we reached a silent understanding then, he and I. Neither of us was living the life we would have chosen for ourselves had we been allowed any other choice.

The silence seemed like it would stretch forever until the bedchamber door burst open, and Iris came stumbling in, calling for Clay. He ripped his gaze from mine, and I sat back suddenly, finishing my glass of wine in a rush. Iris focused in on us immediately, her eyes flickering back and forth. She smirked slightly, but quickly replaced it with one of her dazzling smiles as she hopped to perch on the arm of my chair.

"Oh good! You're both here!"

Clay's jaw clenched, and he looked like he wanted to smack her off his furniture, but she only winked at him. She began prattling on about something excitedly, but I could hardly make out the words. Not when I was so distracted by her clothing.

"Why in all of creation are you dressed like *that*?"

I was not one to turn my nose up to plain clothing, but this was Iris we were talking about. Iris loved the glamour of court life more than anyone else. She never left her rooms unless she was entirely done up in the most extravagant fashions. And yet, she sat in front of me in a simple beige gown with an apron tied around her waist. Had Iris ever even cooked something? Her hair, typically brightly colored and adorned in jewels, was hidden under a cloth that kept it out of her freshly washed face.

She looked quite similar to how she had looked last night when we snuck out of the castle.

But tonight we were sitting in front of the Crown Prince.

Surely she wasn't planning to escape the grounds right in front of him?

She grinned down at me conspiratorially and wiggled her eyebrows. I glanced at Clay, out of the corner of my eye, worried I was about to be in trouble. The Crown Prince only sighed and stood, though, shrugging out of his jacket and tossing it haphazardly across the room onto the pile of clothes on the bed.

"She wants to take you out," he told me.

Within just twenty minutes, Iris had changed us from two Descendants of royal families to ordinary townspeople. She had given me a shift gown, similar to the one she wore, and tied my hair away from my face with a handkerchief. Clay had removed his finery in favor of leather trousers and a simple cotton shirt. I couldn't help but awkwardly turn away from him to hide my flush when he came out of his dressing room wearing those pants. You'd have to be blind not to admit that the prince was incredibly well-built... in *all* areas.

"You're not using your magic on us?" I asked Iris.

"It's too much work to keep the illusion going all night. This will be fine."

She snuck us out the back of the Palace through a hidden chamber in Clay's rooms. There, in the gardens, a carriage was waiting for us with the blinds drawn.

"We're not exactly supposed to be doing this, I gather?" I asked as she shoved me into the carriage before she and Clay climbed in after me.

Iris snorted unattractively as she settled herself into her seat. "Please, the Dragon would have my head on a spike if he knew I was dragging his precious heir out to where the common folk entertain themselves."

Clay's eyes darkened and I felt my stomach toss unhappily. The memory of our conversation was still too fresh to find humour in Iris' words. Because now I knew, without a shadow of a doubt, that the Dragon truly was capable of harming her. He'd threatened me before with her safety, but part of me had doubted he could do anything to harm his own niece - even if she was just a niece by marriage.

He could and would, though. The Dragon's cruelty knew no bounds.

I sighed. "I can't imagine the festivities are worth the risk."

Clay glanced at me from across the carriage with a raised brow and what looked to be the beginning of a rare but genuine smile. "Now, I wouldn't say that."

As he turned away from me to peel back the blind and glance out the carriage window, I struggled to close my dangling jaw. It appeared our brooding prince really did like to have fun once in a while. Mystery books and a penchant for sneaking out of the castle. Clayton Vail was perhaps more human than I had initially given him credit for.

When the carriage finally pulled to a stop and we stepped out, my heart seemed to freeze. There were people everywhere. Dozens, if not hundreds, crowded the town square, shuffling to their homes, talking, trying to make the last sales of the day from their carts. Some had even begun to relax, bringing out guitars and instruments to play. Two women danced around each other, giggling. Looking around at the masses of them, I scoffed at our outfits. Surely, a simple shift dress and common white tunic would not be enough to hide us.

Wouldn't someone in this crowd recognize their own prince?

And yet, as we walked, not even one of the townspeople blinked twice at us. They had all stared at me as I made my grand declarations weeks ago, yet a simple change of clothes suddenly made me invisible.

"That feeling alone makes it worthwhile," Clay told me, placing a hand on the small of my back and pushing me forward through the wooden doors of a tavern. "The normalcy, I mean. It's only a temporary reprieve from the pressure to perform, but it's nice nonetheless."

"How do they not recognize *you*?" I asked him as we stepped into the tavern. The space was relatively empty and quiet, with only a few patrons sitting quietly at the countertop, nursing their drinks. They glanced at us mindlessly. We were both just faces passing through to them. Perhaps, if I tried to rationalize it, I could understand the people not recognizing me; I had only appeared a few short weeks ago and had only made one public appearance. Clay, however, had been in the public eye his whole life.

Still, only the bartender gave any inclination that he knew Clay by dipping his head slightly, a gesture that the prince returned to him.

"You'd be surprised how the finery of it all can hide the man underneath."

Iris brushed past him, grabbing my hand and pulling me with her up the stairs. "Would you two come on already? The fun is upstairs!"

I nearly tripped over my feet as she ripped me up the staircase, squealing the whole way. But as I found my footing and stepped into the top floor, I suddenly understood her urgency.

The quiet establishment downstairs had a whole other world on its upper floor. Candelabras on the walls offered only dim lighting, and people crowded in every corner, dancing and shouting over the music. I recognized Lorelai's bright red hair and Rankor's large form, from where they stood near the stage with Camilla. Music filled the room from the band, and yet the stairs and floor below had been entirely silent—Descendant magic at work, no doubt.

"Is that Kent?" I called out, pointing to what appeared to be our friend, belting out an upbeat song on stage. He was oblivious to our entrance, so lost in the music that he fell to his knees as he reached an incredible pitch. And while the action would have looked ridiculous on anyone else, Kent just looked... natural.

Iris glared at me. "Of course! He's a Siren."

I think she sometimes forgot how new this all was to me based on the way she spoke, as if the answers to my questions were obvious.

She escaped to get us drinks as we made our way to where our friends beckoned us from the corner of the room. They, too, had dressed down in ordinary clothes. Rankor looked as dashing as ever as he scooped me into a bear hug, and Lorelai, who never failed to look stunning, was still drop-dead gorgeous in an apron. Camilla was the only one who seemed uncomfortable with the simplicity of it all as she met my eyes.

"Oh, good, you're here," she grumbled sarcastically.

"Thanks for the warm welcome."

Her green eyes grazed over my body with disgust. "I think I've finally realized why you always look so out of place at court. Wearing dirty rags suits you so much better."

"Camilla," Lorelai chastised under her breath.

"What?" she sighed, heavily sipping on the amber liquid in her glass. "I'm not the one who invited the prisoner."

"She's not a prisoner," Clay corrected with irritation as he leaned against the wall and crossed his arms in front of his chest. "As of today, Theadora has free roam of the castle."

"She does?" They chorused around me.

But their shock was nothing compared to my own. I looked up at him suspiciously. "I do?"

Clay shrugged, taking his drink from an overly excited Iris. She had clearly known this special announcement was coming. Like earlier, he finished his drink in one gulp.

"I saw you use your powers," he explained. "There's no way you were faking the shock. You're not a threat, Thea, and it's not your fault you don't remember your past. The least we can do is make your future a bit more tolerable."

I didn't realize how badly I had needed to hear him say that until the words dangled in the air between us. He lifted his empty glass and nodded towards mine, and my stupid stomach railed against me once more. It hadn't settled all night. Allowing myself a moment to smile my thanks at him, I lifted my glass to him in return and sipped the burning liquor.

Rankor's head bounced excitedly between us before he threw his arms around us both.

"Well then, it looks like we're celebrating tonight! Let's have some fun!"

And we did have fun. There was something about this place that was positively magical. Kent's songs rolled effortlessly from one to the other and once in a while he would catch my eye and wink down at me. Lorelai taught me every dance she knew, and Iris floated about the room, flirting with every man and woman she saw. And boy, did they flirt back. She was infectious, drawing every eye in the room.

And yet, every so often, her gaze would linger on a tall girl with bright red hair—a girl who was all too willing to smile back at her. I suspected my two friends were getting closer than the others realized.

And secretly, I didn't mind that pairing.

Eventually, when the three of us dancing together became the two of them dancing together, I stepped aside to get another drink from the barkeep. As I waited for him to tend to me, I contentedly peered out over the room. Even now, hours into the night, it was still so alive with celebration. The dancefloor was as full as ever and several people crowded around the tables in the room's corner. Next to me, two women, an older lady with thick blonde hair and a younger teen, sat talking. I couldn't help but overhear their words.

"You're sure it will work?" The teen pressed her comrade.

The older woman sighed. "Of course it will work. If you want this boy to fall in love with you, The Alchemist will provide the potion for that. He has potions for everything."

The girl nodded. "I'll have to sneak away. I could go to him next month?"

"Very well," the woman agreed, and the teen hustled out of the tavern.

I gazed over at the woman. Her dress was quite nice, nicer than many of the others in the establishment, made in an iridescent fabric that reminded me of the one Iris and I had purchased in the market. The woman's eyes found mine, noticing my stare. I blushed furiously.

"I'm sorry," I apologized. "I couldn't help overhearing."

She grinned. "Don't suppose you're looking for a magic potion yourself?"

I laughed darkly, accepting my drink from the barkeep as he passed it to me. "Not unless you have something that can restore lost memories."

As I turned to leave, to return to my friends, the woman grasped onto my wrist. Her face was serious and a knowing smile danced on her lips.

"Of course he has something for that."

I froze. If potions like this existed, why hadn't the Dragon already provided me with one?

"How is that possible?"

She chuckled. "Lots of things are possible, girl. Just because the Descendants don't know about it doesn't mean that no other magic exists in this world."

Iris had dressed me in a high-neck gown, I realized suddenly, hiding my Mark from the world. I glanced at her out of the corner of my eye and realized she had worn a dress with long, tight sleeves so that the Mark on her wrist was also covered.

This establishment wasn't meant for Descendants.

I knew all too suddenly that I shouldn't be talking to this woman, that whatever *potions* she had to offer me wouldn't be looked upon fondly by the Dragon. But if it was true? If a potion truly existed that could restore my memories...

Wouldn't that be worth any risk?

A quick glance over my shoulder told me that no one was paying attention, so I stepped back to the bar and leaned against it so that I could look out at my friends and ensure they weren't watching.

"How could I find him?" I asked her softly.

Her eyes glanced over me. "I can take you to him. He prefers to keep his business discreet."

"How soon?"

She laughed. "That potions important to you, eh? I'm making a trip to him next week if you can come to me then."

Next week. I doubted Iris would help me escape from the palace for a second time, especially not if she learned it was for this. And there was no way I was about to scale the side of that wall for a second time, anyway. So I'd have to find another way out of the castle.

It wouldn't be easy, but it also wasn't impossible. There were hidden chambers in the prince's room, after all! Perhaps there were more I could find elsewhere in the palace. If not, I would just have to find out another way. And I could. I could do that.

I would do *anything* if it meant I would learn where I came from.

Slowly, I nodded at her.

She extended her hand to me. "I'm Mara. I'll meet you outside here at dusk in one weeks time."

I opened my mouth to introduce myself, but before I could, Rankor grasped onto my arm and demanded I come join him and Clay as they sat at a table playing cards with some of the townsfolk. Mara's eyes trailed after me until she too disappeared into the crowd.

"This isn't a game for novices," Camilla criticized me as I sat at the table, her eyes sharp and disapproving.

Frustration railed within me, fueled by the liquid courage I'd been drinking all night, the lingering rush of finally using my powers, and my overall distaste of the girl who had been nothing but snippy with me.

"And just why not, Camilla?" I shot back. "Are you so afraid the men might have someone else to look at?"

The table fell silent around us. Even with the band blaring behind him, Kent missed a beat of the song and struggled to pick up the melody. From the stilled table, Clay looked up from his cards, glancing between us expectantly. Camilla fumed, her shadowy eyes peering at me under those impossibly dark lashes.

"You can continue flirting with Clay if you want," I allowed her, picking up the stack of cards Rankor handed me. "I'm here to win the money on the table, not a husband. From what I've seen so far, he doesn't seem to return your affections, at least not any longer, but there is something to be said for persistence."

The music quieted as if everyone in the room now waited to hear how Camilla would respond. Even Clay, who was usually so quick to chastise me, now sat silently, brows raised, eyes bouncing between us. Camilla's cheeks flushed with quieted rage, and she opened her mouth to say something especially vicious, but Rankor's quick laughter cut her off.

"I knew I liked you!" He cried happily, patting me on the back. He quickly turned my attention to the cards, running me through the game-play rules, but I felt Camilla's hateful glare on me throughout the entire hand.

I ended up winning the game.

CHAPTER TWELVE

We talked and danced until the early morning hours, until the seven of us were the only ones left in the tavern. Rankor insisted I show off my newfound powers by floating silverware off the table. And while I didn't quite have the control I might have wished for, not yet at least, I was more than happy to oblige him.

Finding the emotional trigger for my powers had helped, as everyone promised it would. It was a challenge to gain the focus and strength to lift the small objects an inch or two off the table, but each minor success gave me a new sensation of accomplishment.

Maybe I wasn't such a failure of a Descendant after all.

Eventually, we all made our way back to the Palace, laughing and chatting in the halls before we went our separate ways, Clay and I heading to the east end of the Palace where the Royal chambers were while our friends went to their apartments in the west wing.

"So, what's the verdict? Did it end up being worth the risk?"

I laughed, remembering my doubts from earlier in the evening. "I can say the night ended much better than it began."

He insisted on escorting me to my rooms, and we made our way in a comfortable silence. As we came to a stop in front of my door, I sighed heavily. There were so many damn doors in this hallway. Doors to empty apartments with no one but me to fill them. And for the first time, I suddenly felt that responsibility, that duty, weighing upon me.

Was it my powers? Did the sudden emergence of my magical ties to Hyrax somehow make me feel more connected to him and his legacy?

"It's a great deal of pressure, you know," I thought aloud. "The responsibility of repopulating this hall."

He followed my gaze to the length of the chamber behind us. It was late, of course, but even so, the silence was overwhelming. There were no children here, no families, like in the other hallways of the palace. No one. No one but me. The section of the castle dedicated to Hyrax's Descendants was nothing more than a well-decorated ghost town.

"I can't imagine," he admitted. "We royals all have a degree of that responsibility, but not quite to the extent you do."

He paused suddenly, shifting his weight back and forth on the balls of his feet. He looked almost uncomfortable. And I couldn't recall when I'd seen him look quite so... awkward.

"Thea, bearing heirs is your duty," he continued. "It's mine as well. But they're still *our* lives. Ours to live and enjoy."

Clay's face was dark, and tendrils of blonde hair, damp with sweat from the night's festivities, crept towards his brow. His words were pretty and for a moment, I wanted to allow myself to believe in them. But I couldn't. They were so obviously untrue. What joy would I ever find in an arranged marriage and forced pregnancy?

Still, I smiled at him softly. Tonight had been wonderful, a singular night when we'd actually seemed to get along, where we had even managed to support each other in our respective hardships, and there was no need to ruin it now.

"Thank you for allowing me more freedom around the castle."

"Even I am limited in my power," he admitted, voice heavy. "I can't excuse you from the Council or your responsibilities, but if it would make things easier on you to be relocated away from the castle, perhaps another option may exist."

My heart skipped a beat. "Another option?"

"I'm sure there's an estate or property belonging to the House of Hyrax that we can look into obtaining for you. If you truly want to leave the castle, that is."

That was...

That was all I had wanted from the moment I learned I was going to be locked away in this palace. He was offering me the chance to walk out of these palace doors and not have to endure the whispers of the courts' people or the constant reminders of the Dragon's influence in my life. He was giving me as much of an escape as he could.

And yet, I found myself frozen as I stood there with him outside my suite. My mind locked, and while I opened my mouth, no sound escaped my throat.

"Well, it was certainly a memorable evening, Miss Moore."

"That it was Mr. Vail," I quipped, choosing his name rather than his formal title. His eyes flickered and one side of his lip tipped upward in response.

He lingered as I opened the door, almost as if he wanted to say something else, but I had already moved to step inside my suites. Nessira and Geia had left oils of lavender and vanilla burning - my favorite. As I took a deep breath, the sudden pull to sleep was so shocking that my knees shook. I was so caught by it that I didn't feel myself swaying until Clay's arms wrapped firmly around me to hold me up.

I frowned. I didn't think I'd drank nearly enough to knock me off my feet.

"Theadora?" He questioned, alarm prevalent in his tone. "You're bleeding."

Bleeding? Sure enough, I felt the wetness dripping from my nose and wiped at it, confused. My fingertips came away stained scarlet.

"Well, that's strange," I mused, staring at my fingers.

Things moved all at once. The world seemed to collapse entirely around me and I fell heavily into Clay. My chest heaved as a sudden coughing fit stole the air from my lungs. I coughed so violently that my vision blurred and my stomach cramped.

By the Gods, what was happening to me?

Clay sat me down, propping me against the door frame as he took my face in his hands and thoroughly looked over me. The light in his golden eyes was brighter than I'd ever seen it before. Without a word, he stood in a rush and stormed through the door into my suites. It wasn't until I saw that his hands, which had cupped my cheeks, were also stained red that I noticed my ears were bleeding, too.

Unable to stop it, I lost myself in coughing once more.

Pain lanced through me, sudden and sharp. The burn of it was nearly unbearable.

My blood was *everywhere*. It spilled out from my ears and nose and ran in tears down my cheeks. A fresh wave of fire filled my chest, and I clutched at myself desperately as I dissolved into another fit of coughing. Blood splatted onto the floor before me as I struggled to breathe through the agony.

"Clay?" I cried out urgently.

"Just stay with me!" He yelled back.

How could I? The edges of my vision were already blurring. I couldn't gasp in enough air through the blood that I choked on.

Was this the feeling of death?

Clay looked wildly throughout my rooms, ripping into the drawers on my dressers and end tables and pulling out the contents. He threw the chairs and tables over, destroying everything in his path. A feral snarl tore through the room as he stormed into the bathroom. One that sounded more like a beast than a man.

"Where the fuck is it?" He barked, returning to the bedroom.

I can't breathe, I thought wildly.

Clay's gaze flashed to me, eyes burning brilliant gold and wide with concern. His chest heaved, and I watched the skin on his hands darken.

"What's new here?" He demanded, coming back to me.

"Hmm?" I groaned. My head was aching. I couldn't think clearly through that throbbing pain.

"Look around, Thea!" He ripped at my chin, pulling my gaze forcefully to the destroyed apartment. "What in here is new or different?"

My chest constricted, the need for oxygen blurring out any other thoughts as I felt the blood dripping down the back of my throat. I choked on it, grasping the front of his tunic frantically. He clamped down on my back until I could suck in a short burst of air once more.

The suite, I reminded myself, *what's new in the suite?*

The furniture was all the same. Chairs in the parlor, a bar cart against the wall, my bed beyond that...

"There." I pointed, hands shaking. "The dresses."

He didn't hesitate. Clay moved in a blur. In one moment he was at my side and in the next he had lifted the package of dresses from where they had fallen to the ground. I tried not to flinch when I saw his fingernails extend into dark claws, but I didn't dare look away as he shredded through the fabrics.

"Got it!" He yelled as a small brown satchel fell loose from a tattered bodice.

I was dying.

The awareness of it was sudden and absolute. This was it. The past month of preparing to fit into this court had been pointless. My life was ending right here and now, long before they forced me into a marriage or onto the Council.

At least I would be free.

A black vignette clouded the corners of my vision, and slowly, the pain faded. Everything faded until all I could feel was the sensation of my body sinking.

I wondered if Hyrax would be waiting to greet me as I entered the Underworld.

Clay held the satchel in his palm, opened his mouth, and unleashed a torrent of scorching orange flames that filled the entire room with their sudden heat.

And then...

It was over, and I could breathe.

The relief was immediate. I slumped forward with it, shaking from head to toe. Slowly, too slowly, breathing got easier until the pain in my head subsided, and the burning in my chest calmed. I coughed the final bits of blood onto the floor before me before scraping the back of my palm across my mouth.

"What... was that?" I sputtered from where I sat in the puddle of my own blood.

The look on Clay's face was not one I would soon forget. With his eyes burning with golden fire and his fingers and arms black and scaled over, he looked down at me with a set jaw and furrowed brow. Sometimes, I forget the extent of animalistic rage that could exist under the surface of his princely decorum. I shivered, meeting his gaze. His shoulders trembled as he took a single, deep breath to calm himself.

"Someone just tried to kill you."

CHAPTER THIRTEEN

Clay and I talked little in the hour that followed the attack. His rage settled quickly, and he reverted to his role as a prince and responsible ruler. The night's festivities seemed a million miles away as he snapped into action, calling in guards and nurses within minutes. Gone was the man who had openly shared his childhood with me. All that remained was a future monarch with a threat to address.

The guards began investigating my suite while the nurses cared for me with tender touches and curious eyes. I had insisted I was fine when Clay first demanded the nurses come directly to my suites with haste, but he hardly even acknowledged me. I questioned whether he had even heard me at all. And so, the nurses looked me over, investigating my ears, nose, and mouth. I protested quietly but was more than relieved to be handed a goblet with hazy liquid, which soothed my raw throat.

"My lady," Dimitri greeted me, dipping into a low bow with a somber expression. "Is there anything I can do for you?"

Guilt clouded his eyes.

"Iris," I croaked, clasping my hands together close to my chest to hide how badly they were still shaking. "Can you get Iris?"

Dimitri nodded, exiting the suite promptly. There was no need for him to feel bad. I had been the one to go out to the tavern. If I had stayed where I belonged, he would have been able to keep a watchful eye on me, and perhaps none of this would have happened. I would need to remind him of that when I was finally thinking clearly and over the shock.

For now, though, my mind was scattered from exhaustion. In a matter of hours, I had signed away the rights to my marriage choices, learned that the kingdom's leader was an abusive murderer, identified the emotional trigger for my powers, impressed an entire tavern with my card skills, and nearly died. No, I hadn't just nearly died. I'd been nearly murdered.

Someone had tried to kill me.

Just when I thought I'd started to redeem myself from that day on the bridge, I wondered if I ever could. Had someone tried to kill me to seek revenge for that day? Or maybe a foreign enemy was eager to avoid a united Council in Athenia. Even the Dragon himself had told me he wanted me dead; perhaps my disrespect earlier in the night had been more than he would tolerate. And maybe there was no other reason than that I was the last living Descendant of a widely hated God.

Maybe people in this court didn't want the House of Hyrax to be resurrected.

"Oh, my Gods!" Iris cried, bursting into the room with all the dramatic flair I'd expect from her. She crouched before me on the floor, taking my hands into her own. Her cheeks were streaked black from where her tears had mixed with the kohl around her eyes.

Dimitri followed her in, holding the large door for the rest of our companions, still dressed for the tavern.

"You're all here?" I muttered, eyes wide as I processed the new flood of bodies. They were my friends. I trusted them, of course, but the growing number of people in the room was getting uncomfortable. I felt myself sinking back into the chair like I might melt away.

"We were all together in my suite when Dimitri came to get me," Iris explained.

"We all wanted to make sure you were okay." Kent clamped a hand down, supportively, over my shoulder, but I flinched from the suddenness of it.

It was all too much at once.

My reaction didn't go unnoticed. Iris's brow furrowed, and she sent a panicked expression to Clay as if silently asking how bad things had gotten. He still hid his feelings under a mask of cool calculation, eyes darting between us.

I felt Camilla's gaze on me before I turned to her, but sure enough, her dark eyes roamed over the sight of my bloodied dress and apron.

"Rough night?" She smirked mockingly.

Iris chastised her quickly, and Lorelai smoothed my hair, offering praises to the Gods that I was still okay, but their words hardly registered. They hadn't noticed it, of course, but I had. I'd seen the moment Clay's veins slowly darkened again when Camilla entered the room. That darkness stretched up his inner arms, neck, and jawline. His fists clenched as she leered down at me.

Perhaps it was the intimacy of him saving my life, but I suddenly felt wholly attuned to him. I felt his every movement, even from feet away, and I knew whatever was coming next wouldn't be good.

He turned to face the guards. "Dimitri, please stand post outside of Miss Moore's door this evening; the rest of you are dismissed. Go. Now."

His voice was sharp, domineering. Tension flooded the room as Kent and Rankor shared an anxious glance at each other over our heads. Gone was their childhood friend. This was their Crown Prince, and he was giving orders.

The guards bustled out of the room, each bowing to me in a silent procession until only Dimitri remained. He pledged his word that no more harm would come to me tonight, nodded to his prince, and closed the door tightly behind him. And then the only people remaining were those in the small circle of friends I had created in my time here and the prince, who was now more Dragon than man. I gulped unintentionally, adrenaline still coursing through my body, setting every nerve on edge.

"Iris, please help Miss Moore get cleaned up," Clay commanded.

She nodded wordlessly, pulling me up from my chair and leading me into the bathroom. She began rinsing washcloths and brushing them against my cheeks in rushed and sharp movements. And though she tended to me, her eyes remained locked on the other room.

Iris was afraid, I realized. And that realization was terrifying, because I'd never seen Iris scared before.

"I can do it," I told her, grasping the cloth and approaching the mirror.

I hardly recognized the woman who greeted me. The handkerchief had fallen from my hair, and now the curls were damp and matted down in sweat, the ends stained with blood. My white dress was now splattered in scarlet too as if someone had dumped paint onto me unceremoniously. Dried blood coated my cheeks, neck, and hands. The worst of it was my eyes though.

The blood vessels must have burst during the coughing fit, and now they were entirely red. I looked.... inhuman.

I certainly looked like a child born from Hyrax, one who had just narrowly escaped the confines of the Underworld.

No wonder Clay had wanted to keep this attack quiet. If the castle already doubted my intentions, seeing me like this would not likely win points in my favor.

The sudden urge to sob took me by surprise.

No.

I would not cry. I refused to do that.

I swallowed the knot in my throat and scrubbed violently at my face. Numbly, I was aware I might irritate the skin in a way that would leave marks for the next few days, but I didn't care. I was desperate to remove any sign of what had happened to me.

"Camilla, I will ask you this once." I heard Clay's voice from the other room. "How did a hex bag end up in the suites of a royal Descendant?"

Iris' eyes widened suddenly. Clay thought Camilla did this? Before I even consciously decided I wanted to, I pushed past Iris into the bedchamber so that I could see what was happening. I didn't care if Clay had just ordered me out. If they were going to talk about what happened to me, I needed to be there.

Camilla stood near the entryway as if she had taken a few steps back since I'd gone to the bathroom. Her shoulders slumped, and she kept her eyes averted from the weight of Clay's gaze. Kent and Rankor still exchanged glances of worry with each other, but neither interfered as Clay started towards her. Iris raced after me, reaching for Lorelai and pulling her away from the group and back towards where I hovered on the edges.

"Best to stay out of the way," Lorelai whispered, patting my free hand.

What in all of creation did she mean by that?

Camilla shook her head rapidly, utterly focused on Clay. "I know nothing about this!"

Clay's eyes were shrouded with the promise of violence as his lips tipped up in a vicious smile. He looked so different from the version of him that had coached me to use my powers and told me his secrets hours ago. This version of him was... deadly

"You don't?" He growled. "I find a Witch's hex bag in this room, and you, the only Witch to have been here, know nothing about it?"

"Trying to kill her would imply that I care about her!"

Clay moved quickly, shocking me once more with how fast he could be, and grabbed Camilla around the throat. In the same instant, he pushed her back against the door so hard her head slammed into the wood. Dark hair covered her face as she cried out. I stepped forward instinctively, but

Lorelai's grip on my hand was firm; she wasn't letting me move. As I looked down at our conjoined hands suspiciously, she shook her head in a gentle warning. She wasn't just gripping me in comfort, I realized; she was actively trying to prevent me from intervening.

"You might mind how you speak to your Crown Prince when he interrogates you on the attack of one of your Royals," Clay roared at her as an animalistic snarl rose out of his chest.

Camilla shuddered away from him, but the more she struggled, the tighter he grabbed her until her feet struggled to even touch the floor.

"I didn't do it," she cried, gasping for air and ripping at his fingers.

"She almost died Camilla. She was almost killed! I'll see to it that the party responsible is punished."

This was wrong. I didn't have a particularly fond impression of Camilla, but we had absolutely no evidence that she had anything to do with this! She didn't deserve to be harmed for a crime we couldn't prove she had committed.

And would she have even committed it? She had never been very kind to me personally, but the others swore that underneath her hard exterior was a good person. If Iris and Lorelai could vouch for her character, then I could trust that. Or at the very least, I could give her the benefit of the doubt.

Clay bashed her against the wall again, earning a scream that echoed through the otherwise quiet room.

"Do *not* lie to me!"

She whimpered, and it was that helpless sound that was enough to push me over the edge. I ripped my hand out of Lorelai's.

"Clayton, put her down!" I called.

The muscles in his back stiffened, but he hardly bothered to look over his shoulder at me.

"This is not your concern, Miss Moore."

This was my concern, though. It was *my* blood that puddled on the floor around his feet. This was *my* bedroom, and this was *my* damn life in question. It was every bit my concern. I wouldn't have this girl harmed on my behalf.

"Clay, put her down. *Please.*"

He let go of her in an instant, fingers splaying wide. She fell to the floor in a sobbing heap and crawled away from him as quickly as she could. For a moment, though I hated to admit it, it actually surprised me he had listened to me so easily. No one in the room dared to move as even Clay stared down at his hand suspiciously as if he, too, couldn't believe he had released her. Then, finally, he turned to face me. When he met my eyes, I felt the total weight of his fury now directed at me.

"You have no idea what is happening right now, Miss Moore," he reminded me, voice veiled with a threat. "I don't need your advice on how to handle my subjects."

Camilla looked up at me, her eyes wide and pleading, but everyone else averted their gazes. No one would come to Camilla's defense... or mine, for that matter. No one would challenge Clay on this.

I turned to Lorelai, who huddled helplessly with Iris.

"Is she telling the truth?" I snapped.

Perhaps if I could definitively prove Camilla wasn't involved, she would be spared any further harm tonight. Lorelai's eyes bounced between Clay and me, unsure of what to do. Of course, she wouldn't simply answer my question. I wasn't the one with the authority to ask it.

She was waiting for a command from him.

Finally, when he gave a slight, nearly imperceptible nod, she took a shaky breath and focused in on Camilla.

"I didn't put the bag in the room," Camilla whispered again.

It took some time, but eventually, she nodded, once to me and then more forcefully towards Clay. Camilla cried out in relief, letting Kent pull her to her feet and wrap an arm protectively around her.

"Get out, all of you," Clay ordered. "Miss Moore needs her rest."

They didn't hesitate. Iris and Lorelai rushed past me, stopping only briefly to ask me to get them if I needed anything. Kent held open the door to them, waving goodbye to me, and in an instant, they were gone. Rankor guided Camilla to the door as she desperately wiped the tears from her face, as if she was in a hurry to erase the fact that she had cried. She couldn't erase that fact, though.

None of us could erase what had happened here tonight.

"Camilla," Clay barked. "Thank your lady for her graciousness and mercy."

By the Gods, that was... humiliating.

I wanted to protest, to insist that forcing her to do that was demeaning and unnecessary, but even I could recognize that I'd pushed him too far. I would win no more battles against him tonight.

And right now Clay needed to remind Camilla that I was her better. Because even if she hadn't been the orchestrator of my attack, another Witch, one of her House was, and he couldn't tolerate that. An attack on one royal was an attack on us all.

She bit down on her lip, obviously irritated by the command, but dipped one foot behind the other and lowered herself into a curtsy. Her head bowed, eyes unable to meet my own. "Thank you, my lady."

"Just go." I sighed, tired.

She and Rankor left quickly, without another word. Clay followed them but, to my surprise, closed the door firmly after they exited, shutting me in my bedroom with my young prince. Twice tonight, we'd been alone in a bedroom together. Court customs be damned.

The air was thick with tension and unease as he turned back to face me from across the parlour. He raised an eyebrow and folded his hands behind his back, an unmistakable sign that a lecture was coming.

"I'm sorry if I spoke out of turn."

"I think it's pretty clear you spoke out of turn."

"Well, I've had an upsetting night. I hope you can understand."

A wave of exhaustion powered through me, burning my eyelids and weighing down my shoulders. I didn't have it in me to fight with him. Not after everything that had happened.

I turned on my heels to the closet, eager to change out of these bloody clothes. Clay growled and followed me, no doubt further enraged by the fact I had walked away from him, but after catching one glance of me beginning to untie my apron with little modesty, he scoffed and retreated.

"Are you out of your damn mind?" He huffed with exasperation. "You willfully disobey all decorum at every opportunity!"

I couldn't stop myself from rolling my eyes, feeling grateful he had turned away and could not see it. Decorum was hardly my first concern now. Without a response, I stepped into my nightgown and braided my hair behind my back. When I returned to the primary bedchamber, now fully clothed, Clay stood leaning against the wall with one foot kicked up and his arms crossed across his chest. It was a seemingly relaxed position, but I could see hints of black veins in his fingertips. His golden eyes burned into mine as I met his expression without fear.

"You're the one who's alone with me in *my* suites, Mr. Vail. Perhaps you should take your leave if my casual attire offends you?"

I tossed my braid over my shoulder as I stalked past him, eager to crawl into my bed and finally get some rest. His hand snaked out, wrapping around my wrist and pulling me suddenly towards him. I yelped softly in surprise and stumbled as he shifted past me. Clay tossed me against the wall and threw his arms on either side of my head until he had completely boxed me in. He was all I could see.

"*I am your Prince!*"

"You are," I agreed, keeping my voice soft. "And you were being cruel to her."

His skin rippled suddenly as scales started emerging. He rolled his neck and breathed deeply and I watched as he struggled to contain himself. Somewhere deep down, I knew I was tempting a beast. Enough people had warned me. I had seen with my own eyes that even Clay's best friends were afraid of him. And yet, here I stood, alone in my suite, pressed against him, unwilling to submit to him.

Clay's body was firm against mine, and I was mildly aware that I wore only a thin nightgown. Could he feel how hard my heart was beating?

We stood there for a moment, frozen and both trying to control our anger. My power danced at my fingertips, itching for a release, but I didn't dare move. Then Clay's eyes slowly darkened to their natural gray color, and his scales receded to wherever they had come from. Finally, he stepped back, releasing me, and I sighed in relief.

"Unless you want to see how cruel I can truly be, Miss Moore, I'd suggest you never use those powers on me again. I won't forgive it a second time."

He stormed out without another word and slammed the door heavily behind him. Breathless, I sagged back against the wall as his words sunk in.

Had I used my powers on him?

I thought back to his fingers wrapped around Camilla's throat. I'd pleaded with him to release her with all of my emotion leaking into the request, and sure enough, his fingers had splayed open, and she had fallen to the ground. It had surprised me he had actually done it. It surprised my friends that he had done it.

It surprised *him* he had done it.

Well, shit. Whether or not I meant to, I had just used my powers against the Crown Prince, and he hadn't been able to stop me. A weight sank in my stomach. I hadn't been at court long enough to know all the rules, but some were obvious. Using your powers on the Dragon or his heir certainly wasn't permitted. Nor would it be tolerated.

The tears I'd been putting off finally fell freely as I crawled into my bed and pulled the covers over my head. And even though I'd been awake for hours, dealing with more stress than one person should have to in one night, sleep didn't find me for a long time. I could only surrender myself to it once I had sobbed out the tears I'd been holding onto since I woke up that first day in the hospital.

CHAPTER FOURTEEN

"I s this really necessary?" I scoffed, holding the letter out to Iris, who sat on the edge of my bed.

She shrugged, taking it from my hands and folding it neatly. The letters had been delivered to every apartment in the palace that morning, declaring that the day was to be spent in quiet solitude and prayer to the Gods. Food was to be delivered to apartments rather than formal meals, and no one was permitted to exit their suites. In carefully crafted sentences, it laid out some explanation of wanting to praise the Gods on the eve of the Peace Ball and pray for continued harmony.

Bullshit. It was all bullshit.

It was nothing more than a fancifully written lie to keep people from knowing about the attack or the investigation into it.

"Until we know who was involved in the attack, no one can be trusted," Iris explained in a soft voice. "And with the Peace Ball so soon, the Dragon doesn't want to show any weaknesses in our kingdom."

"Well, he's nothing if not concerned about appearances."

Iris laughed and stood to tie my corset. Nessira and Geia had been banned from my service until the investigation was complete, so Iris had been sent to help me prepare for the emergency Council meeting that would be happening in the afternoon. She had been quiet all morning, obviously on edge from the evening prior, and I was hardly pursuing conversation myself. My attitude was sour after nightmares of underground tunnels and a three-headed dog had kept me tossing and turning all night.

Dimitri escorted us to the Council chambers wordlessly, and Iris squeezed my hand in a silent wish of luck before we went in. My letter had instructed me to join Clay in the center of the Council floor when I entered the Council chamber. Iris would sit in the nearly empty viewing area. That viewing area had been practically overflowing on my first trip to the Council room. Today, it was reserved for the few permitted to attend.

The room was cold and tense as we stepped in. Clay was mid-way through his testimony, recounting the evening and his identification of the hex bag in my room. The Council members sat in their booths with tight lips and worried eyes.

"Miss Moore, can you please provide your testimony of the attack?" The Dragon called down to me.

The next hour proceeded slowly. I first recounted what little details I could remember from the attack. My primary focus at the time had been breathing, not taking stock of my surroundings after all. Then I listed every moment of my day, every person I spoke to, and every place I went. I was truthful through it all, only leaving out the details of my private conversation with Clay in his room. When his dark eyes met mine as I spoke, I knew he appreciated that. Eventually, though, the Council heard what they needed from me, and sent me to sit in the viewing area with Iris.

Geia and Nessira gave testimonies next, under the pressure of a Truth-seeker. He was a slender man with a balding head and thick mustache that curled at the ends. His resemblance to Lorelai was undeniable, and I knew I was looking at Mr. Pelland, her father. He was gentle with them, asking them to report on the events of their day. Nessira had spent the morning gathering herbs and flowers from the garden before preparing me for dinner with the dragon. Geia had gone to visit Ruthie in the morning to check on the gowns, but swore that nothing seemed amiss. Then, after helping me before the dinner, she and Nessira had both retired to their rooms.

"And who delivered Lady Moore's gowns?" Mr. Pelland questioned.

"A kitchen boy," Nessira told him, her voice sure. "I had thought it was strange for a kitchen boy to bring them, but he assured me that Ruthie had personally asked him to deliver them. They looked like perfectly normal dresses, so I thought nothing more of it."

After that, they lined each of the kitchen staff up for Nessira and Geia to identify the young boy who delivered the dresses.

He's young. I noted, as he timidly stepped forward, tucking his shaking hands behind his back.

His clothes were plain, like those we had seen at the tavern in town just last night. Blonde hair crested the top of his head, and his face was dirty with soot and flour from the kitchen, but his eyes were bright and his cheeks full with youth. He couldn't have been over fourteen.

"Surely this isn't the mastermind behind the attack," I murmured to Iris. She only shrugged, focused entirely on the scene ahead of us.

The Dragon's eyes narrowed down at him in disgust, and with a nod at Dimitri, he commanded the room to be cleared. The kitchen staff exited, as did Nessira and Geia, until all that remained was the Council, Iris and I, and the boy with his interrogator. As he sat in the chair at the center of the Council floor, the boy shivered. He was terrified.

"Did Ruthie give you the dresses?" The Dragon asked him.

The boy answered without hesitation. "Yes, Ms. Ruthie gave them to me herself; she did. She asked me to take them straight to the Lady's room right away. She said I should set them in her suites personally and not take no for an answer. Lady Moore needed to get her gowns without delay."

Mr. Pelland cleared his throat, looking up at the Dragon and shaking his head slightly. The boy was lying. Frowning, I shifted in my seat, leaning forward and resting my elbows on my knees. What possible reason could this boy have to lie? He glanced up at me, just for a moment, eyes wide with terror. Wordlessly, I looked to Iris, who hadn't moved an inch since we entered the room. Her jaw was tight, and her hands clenched.

"Iris, what's the penalty for an attack on a Council member?"

She didn't meet my eyes. "Death. The penalty is death by fire."

Dragonfire, no doubt. I stood, resting my palms on the railing that separated me from the child. I had to do something. Even if this boy was involved, certainly he had been coerced somehow. I couldn't let the Dragon murder this child. Not on my behalf. Not for any reason.

"*Who gave you the dresses?*" Mr. Pelland asked, his voice low and rough.

His magic spread through the room, and I nearly stumbled against it. I had thought Lorelai was powerful, but her father was something else. As easily as her power had pulled the words from my throat during my interrogation, his power pushed them down now, silencing me and all others but his victim.

The boy whimpered. "I- Well- Ms. Ruthie gave them to me herself, she did. She asked me to take them straight to the Lady's room right away..."

He continued, repeating the same story. And yet, it wasn't his words that made us all shift, glancing at each other as silent questions spread amongst the room. It wasn't his words that made Clay raise an eyebrow and fold his hands into his pockets before anyone else could see the skin start to wrinkle and darken. No, it was the *way* he said the words with the same intonation, the same pauses, and the same head shake.

Mr. Pelland frowned, stepping forward and touching the boy's shoulder. "*Who gave you the dresses?*"

He shuddered, groaning. "Ms. Ruthie gave them to me herself; she did. She asked me to...."

The boy trailed off, dissolving into tears and screaming at the pain of the Truthseeker burrowing into his head, but Mr. Pelland continued still, placing both hands on his shoulders and yelling the question again. I struggled to move, to scream, to do *anything* to help the child whose small body dissolved into tremors, but Mr. Pelland's magic forced me down. The weight of it only grew stronger as I struggled.

It took the boy falling off the chair, unconscious, for the Dragon to clear his throat and allow Mr. Pelland to finally stop. My breath came quick as I felt the tendrils of his power retreat. I stepped forward, furious, but Iris gripped my hand tightly and pulled me down.

"You can't help him," she whispered forcefully. "Interfering will only end up putting you in more danger."

The Dragon shifted in his chair, leaning back and crossing his hands behind his head. His expression was tired and bored, but I could see the heat in his eyes. I could see the glimmering flecks of gold beginning to emerge. He was better at hiding his emotions than Clay, but I knew even he was shaken.

"Care to explain what just happened, Stephen?" He questioned.

Mr. Pelland shoved back away from the boy, losing his footing and falling flat on his bottom with wide eyes. He glanced wildly around the room.

"I- I've only ever read about it- I've never truly seen it..." he sputtered, unable to form a coherent sentence.

The Dragon cleared his throat expectantly once more, leaning forward in his pew. "I'm waiting!"

"Compulsion," Mr. Pelland finally whispered after a few moments of silence. The room stilled. Mr. Pelland stood and nodded his head firmly. "He was compelled."

Iris' hand tightened on my own. The Council members shared concerned glances, and even the Dragon's eyes widened ever so slightly. I don't think I'd ever seen the Dragon thrown off. I met Clay's gaze from across the room. His face was a hard mask, not sharing a minuscule amount of the thoughts in his head, but he didn't look away from me.

"What does that mean?" I whispered to Iris.

Her grip on my hand was almost painful.

"There are different kinds of magic," she explained. "Most of which involve manipulations. You manipulate things to move them. Faeries like me, Dragons, and Werewolves manipulate our bodies to transform into other beings. Sirens manipulate emotions or physiological states. Elementals manipulate water, fire, air, and earth."

"And?" I pushed her on even as the Dragon's booming voice declared the Council meeting was adjourned, and we were all to return to our suites immediately.

The Council members remained seated even as the room started emptying. Clearly, they planned to discuss things further in private. Their expressions were tight and stressed. Dimitri was by my side instantly, insisting we leave right away, but I stayed planted in my seat. I needed to hear what the Council was about to discuss. It was going to be important; I knew that. Something important was happening right now, even if I didn't understand it.

Clay came to me, grabbing my arm and forcing me to stand. His grip was unbreakable.

"Witches get their power by manipulating energy," Iris continued. "They can borrow energies from living things like plants or magical objects."

"Iris," Clay growled in warning, eyes fiery.

He maintained his grip on my forearm, pulling me out of the room with such speed that I nearly stumbled over my own feet. Still, Iris followed her voice, calling to me over my shoulder.

"She deserves to know!" Iris insisted.

"Know what?" I cried, struggling angrily against Clay's hand. "Let go of me!"

As we emerged back into the palace hall, he released my arm and placed a hand on the small of my back, pushing me towards my rooms. Dimitri strode in front of us, eyes scanning the area protectively.

"Some kinds of spells or charms require more energy than a living thing can offer while retaining its own life," Clay explained, head dipping towards my ears and keeping his voice low. "We call this blood magic."

"It's sacrificial?"

He nodded. "It was outlawed years ago. Any Witch found guilty of it is subject to power stripping, a punishment worse than death. A blood transfusion is conducted with mortal blood until your connection to your ancestor is severed and your Descendant's Mark fades. The effects are permanent."

"Compulsion. It's a spell that relies on blood magic?"

He nodded once more, jaw locked tight with tension.

"And if someone used compulsion to drop off the dresses..." I trailed off as my body froze against the sudden sensation of fear.

Clay's golden eyes bore into mine as we walked. "Then they're not just willing to kill you; they're willing to risk *everything* to see you dead."

I shivered involuntarily as a realization settled over me. If this person succeeded in their efforts, the empty rooms in my hallway would never again know joy or laughter. The family tree would never be filled with additional names.

I couldn't let that happen.

As much as I may have wanted to take Clay up on that offer to live away from the palace, now that someone was looking to kill me, I needed to stay here and do my part to make sure that person was found and dealt with. I owed that to the Descendants of Hyrax that came before me and those that would come after me. I owed it to Hyrax himself.

CHAPTER FIFTEEN

*S*omehow, I'd grown accustomed to the darkened shadows that lined the cavernous underground halls I'd been roaming through each night in my dreams. What had once been frightening now was familiar. As I moved through them, the darkness walked with me like an invisible guest joining me on my journey. And though the smell of fire and smoke was consistently in the air, it was always cold. I rubbed my hands over my arms to fight back against the chill.

I spent nearly every night in this place. Sometimes, I'd dream of the lake with hands reaching out to latch onto my ankles. Sometimes, I'd greet the three-headed beast who roared at me with ferocity but never actually attempted to harm me. Most times, though, I would simply wander. I'd walk through the maze of tunnels with dirt floors and rock walls. I didn't know where I was walking to, but I kept on until I woke in my bed at the palace, shivering from cold and gasping for air.

Tonight, though, was different. Tonight, for the first time, I heard something. There was music playing. It was dark and melodic, with minor chords drifting seductively around me. It called to me, and so I marched forward. Each step pulled me toward the sound until I finally walked to a sizeable two-paneled steel door. I ran my hands over the monsters and faces that sat stranded in the metal, as if frozen in an attempt to escape. As my fingertips *touched the icy surface, I was met with a rush of magic that made me gasp aloud. I wrapped my hand around the bone-shaped handle and pulled.*

The music surrounded me, loud and clear. The room was large and open, with a fire raging in the corner that fought away the chill in the air. A large throne made of skulls and bones sat raised on the rocks. A matching, smaller throne sat to its left. Across the room was a massive wooden table nearly twelve feet long. And there, at the end of the table, sat a man.

"I was wondering when you would finally find your way here." He smiled.

He was broad-shouldered, and even sitting, I could see he was tall from the length of his legs. He wore dark trousers and a loose grey tunic. His full, gray hair was long, curling around his ears and the back of his neck.

"Sit." He invited me to the chair on his left, running a hand over his closely trimmed beard.

I felt his magic wash over me in a gentle wave. It didn't push down on me or force me to sit as Mr. Pelland's had, but it touched my skin in a gentle greeting, and I felt my own power rise to my fingertips in response. A smile played on his lips as he watched me.

"Theadora." He drew out my name as if testing it on his tongue. "So that is the name you chose for yourself? It's beautiful."

"Thank you."

"Wine?" He asked, and a full glass appeared before me in a rush of smoke. I gasped, which only earned a soft chuckle from the stranger.

"Who are you?"

He huffed. "That's hardly important. I'm here to watch over you, that's all."

I reached out, taking the wineglass and twirling the stem within my fingers. It smelt of smoked spices. The aroma was so intense that I nearly came undone and drank the whole of it right there, but, with shaking fingers, I forced it back onto the table. There was no way I would gulp down some magic-infused wine given to me by a stranger. His eyes sparkled as I pushed the glass away from me. This was a game we were playing, him and I. I'd learned how to play these kinds of games though, I'd been playing them for months.

I leaned back, throwing my elbow over the back of my chair in a picture of comfort.

"What makes you think I need to be watched over?" I asked, cocking an eyebrow tauntingly as I'd seen Clay do a million times.

The stranger laughed, clapping his hands together. "You learn quickly! Look at how well you've mastered their political indifference."

My pulse quickened, but I kept my expression schooled, unwilling to express my thoughts, though they swam in questions. Who was this man? And why did he care so much about me?

"Don't you need a guardian?" He pushed, his voice now serious and concerned. "Not all are happy to have the line of Hyrax restored."

I glanced away, still too shaken from the attack to hide all of my fears, no matter how much I wanted to maintain that mask of indifference. "The Council will ensure the attacker is caught."

"Will they? Will that Dragon stand up to protect you in your hour of need?"

I shrugged. Sure, I hardly thought The Dragon was losing any sleep over my personally being in danger, but there were more people at court than just him. I'd made friends, connections. They wouldn't let me get hurt. Hell, even Clay, who looked at me disapprovingly more often than he looked at me with friendliness, had fought to save me when he could have watched me die.

I could trust them.

"You can't trust them," the stranger insisted, as if he had read my mind. "None of them. You're more powerful than them all, and you know that. They're starting to learn that. The Descendants and Mortals will always try to destroy those whose power frightens them."

"That's not true." I shook my head, though I wasn't entirely sure which part of the statement I was protesting.

I woke to the sound of my apartment doors being opened. Geia and Nessira rushed in, with additional ladies' maids behind them carrying bags filled with beauty products, shoe choices, and jewelry. Two small girls brought a large gown wrapped tightly in protective cloth between them. I nearly groaned upon seeing the size of it.

Nessira winked playfully at me. She was so rarely in a playful mood. That alone was enough to get me to pull aside my bed quilt and stand.

"Come now, my lady." She grinned knowingly. "Certainly, you must feel *thrilled* knowing that the Crown Prince personally gifted you your wardrobe for tonight's Peace Ball."

I shivered. "*Clay* picked this out?"

Nessira laughed softly to herself and grasped my hand, pulling me from the bed. The new ladies exchanged panicked expressions, not accustomed to my hatred for pompous palace fashions. Geia bit down on her lip to stop laughing as she pulled out dozens of glittering diamond hair clips from the bag.

"Well." Nessira shrugged. "The Dragon wanted to be sure that you look your finest when meeting your marriage prospects, so Prince Clayton insisted we dress you in this."

I faked a gag as she prepared my bath. Nessira and Geia had returned to my service the day after the Council meeting. For the first two days, I refused to leave the suites at all. I was far too shaken by the experience to face the outside world, so Nessira and Geia were the only people I saw during those days. They brought constant snacks from the kitchen and left me in my nightgowns all day. We sat, talked, and ate from sunrise to sunset until I finally dozed off in the evenings, and they excused themselves. Sleep had been hard to maintain. Constant nightmares of coughing blood and underground caverns kept me from waking up and feeling rested.

So now when I greeted myself in the mirror, I saw pale skin and dark circles under my eyes.

And while my ladies and friends might have understood my need for some isolation and recuperation, the court didn't share that concern. The Peace Ball was here, and the Dragon expected me to smile and wave to our foreign dignitaries. He insisted I attend and meet all of my apparently many marriage suitors. So while my stomach was in knots trying to envision the night that lay ahead of me, there was nothing for me to do but simply accept what the Dragon and his son declared I must do.

"What color is it?" I questioned, glancing suspiciously at the heap of a dress delicately draped across my bed.

A sudden image of that hideous black ballgown I'd worn to the court briefing flashed in my mind, and I shivered. Surely, this one was no better—another depressing thing to mark me as the lone Descendant of the God of the Underworld.

Geia's grin spread from ear to ear as she began combing through my wet hair. Clearly, she was excited to get to play dress up with me once more. "You'll be pleasantly surprised, I think."

"Hmph," I grunted, seriously doubting that.

Geia only giggled before beckoning in the other ladies. Together, they worked as a team of five. One dried my hair while the other smeared smoothing cream up and down my legs. I wouldn't allow any of my suitors close enough to judge the softness of my legs, but it wasn't worth protesting. Another girl attempted to hide the dark circles under my eyes while the next painted my lips red. I suppressed the urge to shrink away from the hand that poked and prodded at my hair. It felt like hours until they finally decreed I looked perfect, and it was time to dress.

I narrowed my eyes at the gown, still covered, eager to see how bad the damage was. Nessira whispered in my ear to close my eyes as she walked past me to lift the gown into her arms. I wanted to protest, but knew better than to deny Geia the joy of surprising me. The small girl was practically bouncing up and down in excitement.

It took quite some time for them to get me into the gown fully, but finally, they pushed me in front of the mirror and instructed me to open my eyes.

Geia was right, I realized with a gasp. I was, indeed, pleasantly surprised.

The gown was a shade of pale blue that brought out all the blonde hues in my hair. It fell neatly to the ground, fitting my hips perfectly and emphasizing my curves in a way that my typical loose-fitting gowns did not allow for. The entirety of it was covered in crystals that swirled elaborately over me in waves of shimmering light. The bodice was sheer, with the intricate beading serving as a second skin for modesty. A stiff piece of boned fabric weaved across my chest, offering one delicate sleeve that rested off my left shoulder. The crystals danced as I approached the mirror, sending light across the room.

"And here I expected a ballgown," I whispered, gently running my fingers over the bodice.

Geia giggled in excitement. "Well, who are we to disappoint?"

That's when I realized I still wasn't fully dressed. Geia held out a sweeping, solid blue, cape-style overskirt that clipped onto each of my hips and pleated neatly to the ground in falling waves. It wasn't too heavy of an addition, but it added just a simple elegance to an otherwise elaborate gown.

It was far more intricate than my usually preferred styles, but, as much as I hated to admit it, I didn't *loathe* this particular choice in fashion.

"At least it isn't black," I muttered.

The ladies had folded my hair into a delicate arrangement, with soft curls already beginning to fall around my face. Nessira approached me and tucked a sparkling diamond diadem of ivy leaves onto the crown of my head. I rolled my eyes at it but didn't bother to protest. After all, diamonds were already adorning my ears, wrists, and fingers.

I might have had nightmare after nightmare of warnings not to trust those at court, but tonight, I looked like the princess everyone claimed me to be. And maybe, for the first time, I saw myself as that princess too. I looked like their princess, but I still looked like myself. Perhaps I was truly adapting to my life here.

A knock at the door sounded, and Rankor stepped in, looking strapping in a grey overcoat, clasped together with silver buttons. He looked me over appreciatively, and for a moment, I expected his usual crude joke, but he only tucked his right arm at the waist and bowed. Then, when he righted himself, a few impossible moments later, he nodded to me.

"You look divine, my lady."

I rolled my eyes but felt my cheeks flush. "What are you doing here?"

Rankor shifted uncomfortably and averted his eyes. "Clay has asked me to monitor your guard team."

I lifted an eyebrow. "Guard *team*?"

As if on cue, I saw them line up outside my door. Dimitri stood front and center of a team of ten—*ten* palace guards.

No way. Not happening. I did not need to be paraded around this castle with an *army* surrounding me. I drew enough attention as it was.

Not to mention, I still had plans to sneak out of this damned castle to meet Mara in a few nights. That task had seemed impossible with Dimitri standing guard constantly. With a team of ten, it was unthinkable!

"I don't need a guard team!"

The ladies-in-waiting made some excuse about taking their leave, obviously uncomfortable, and Nessira squeezed my hand in support on the way out. Rankor sighed and raised both hands as if to say, *What can you do?*

"It's for your safety," he reminded me patiently.

I could tell from his pained expression that he had expected this kind of reaction from me, and though I knew better than to shoot the messenger, I couldn't stop myself.

I placed my hands on my hips with a stern expression. "You're an army general, Rankor, not some glorified babysitter!"

He sighed dramatically and came to stand behind me. After placing a hand on the small of my back, he pushed me gently in a silent but firm gesture to show I would not talk my way out of this. The guards parted like a sea for us, but did not hesitate to form two long lines on either side of me as we walked through the palace hall. They were practically ritualistic in their uniformed movements. It made me want to gag.

"He was worried about you," Rankor told me, his voice low. "You haven't left your rooms."

"Then he could have talked to me. He could have asked me if I thought this was necessary!"

Rankor smirked and rolled his eyes as if I was missing the punchline of a joke. "He's the Crown Prince, Thea. He's not accustomed to asking things of others, and no one tells him what is or isn't necessary."

It was my life. I should have gotten a say in how it was conducted.

And yet, it was his kingdom.

So I knew I wouldn't get a say.

I let the topic drop, knowing any of my arguments against the guard team would be unsuccessful. And besides, I could feel butterflies swirling in my stomach as I began to hear the commotion of the party. I could hardly meet the standards of my own king; I shivered at the thought of having to impress the rest of the nobles who awaited me in the ballroom. Clay's decision to commission a guard team without my consent wasn't my primary concern. It couldn't be, not when the Dragon and my suitors were all waiting for my arrival.

I had never seen so many colors in one room. The golden flag of Athenia hung proudly in the center of the far wall, high above the lofty thrones of the Dragon and his Queen. The flags of the other nations flanked the Athenian banner, each reflecting its heritage and unique color. Light blue for the ice lands of Gelumont, bold orange for the deserts of Tenebris, forest green for the mountainous Republic of Inanis, and elaborate swirls of purple and yellow for Promissa.

The most influential people in the world twirled effortlessly around the room, doing intricate dances and laughing merrily. Each dignitary was dripping with diamonds and pearls, both male and female alike. The women wore sweeping gowns with their hair pinned up elaborately, and their partners sported jewel-encrusted sashes and the finest tailored jackets.

Even the decorations were extraordinary. I'd seen the ballroom decorated before, of course, but for the Peace Ball, no expense had been spared. Ice sculptures sat glistening in the corners of the room. Floating candles hovered above the dancefloor, reflecting light against the giant sparkling crystal chandeliers. Food that seemed to double as artwork covered tables along the walls.

I smirked as I took it all in. I was simultaneously amazed by its beauty and ruefully impressed by the Dragon's display of power. This was a party to celebrate peace, but I could also recognize it as the performance that it was. This was the Dragon showing just how wealthy and powerful Athenia was.

I spied my friends across the room, laughing happily. My first instinct was to run to them, to lose myself in their company and pretend I wasn't a princess for an evening. But already, the Dragon had spied me and was making his way through the crowd. I wanted to turn and retreat, to flee from the towering man who no doubt would want me on his arm all evening, but even I knew when a battle was futile.

"Miss Moore," he greeted me, eyes scanning over me appreciatively. "If I didn't know any better, I'd say you actually look like the princess you're supposed to be tonight."

Of course, I did. He and his son had dressed me up like I was nothing more than a doll for them to play with. I was just another tool for him to show off Athenia's power.

Begrudgingly, I extended my hand to him and dipped into a deep curtsy. "Your majesty."

As he kissed my knuckles, I felt the stubble of his graying mustache and was grateful that my bowed head concealed my flinch.

"Looks can deceive, though, can't they?" He chuckled.

Looks *could* be deceiving. After all, someone could look like a dutiful king and loving father when he was actually nothing more than a psychopathic, abusive asshat who murdered the mother of his child.

And a long-lost princess could appear thrilled to be at the party of the year, meeting everyone who's anyone, even though every fiber of her being was screaming at her to flee.

The Dragon held onto my hand, wrapping it around his arm and declaring that I needed to meet some people. Unsurprisingly, he warned me to be on my best behavior, to smile and nod, lest my friend Iris pay the consequences. My eyes flickered to her instinctively, and the Dragon laughed, knowing his threat had landed.

He dragged me to the throne, where the Queen spoke quietly with the visiting dignitaries. She kept her eyes low, muttering only one or two-worded answers while the others prattled on around her.

"President Jonan, always a pleasure." The Dragon greeted the man speaking to the Queen with a stiff handshake.

Though not by much, the man was older than the Dragon, with hair that had long since turned white. He wore a gray jacket with the green sash of Inanis across his chest. He dipped his head politely at The Dragon, but his eyes glinted with hidden anger.

"It's my pleasure entirely. You know I love these opportunities to see my daughter," President Jonan replied curtly.

Only then did I notice the resemblance between him and the Queen. They had the same tilt of the eyes and hitch in the nose. Her lips were fuller, and her skin relatively paler, but their similarity was undeniable. No wonder President Jonan kept his shoulders tight with barely disguised rage. Anyone with eyes could see how mistreated the Queen must be. The Dragon only sneered as he proudly met the eyes of his father-in-law.

"I'm sure," he taunted. "As you know, Clara and I have sent our two daughters off to study at the finest school in Athenia, so I know well the pain of missing a child."

Clay had sisters? I made a mental note to ask Iris about that the next time I saw her.

President Jonan huffed in response, and the Dragon smiled toothily, before turning his attention to the couple who stood to President Jonan's left.

The man's hair was thick and golden, falling in well-trimmed waves, and adorned with a pompous diamond-encrusted crown. His purple sash trimmed in yellow marked him as the King of Promissa. His wife also wore the color of her nation proudly on a long velvet gown with a high neck and daringly low cut back. Diamond cuffs sparkled on each of her wrists. Like the Athenian Queen, she wore bracelets that stretched across the back of her hand, connecting to rings on each of her middle fingers. The only difference was that while my Queen wore golden carved dragons, the Promissan Queen's dragons were made of diamonds.

The Promissan King grasped my hand eagerly, bowing his head to kiss my knuckles as I quickly dipped into a rushed curtsy. I felt the Dragon stiffen behind me, undoubtedly irritated that his adversary had acknowledged me before him.

"My dear, I must admit I had heard tales of your beauty, but it is truly unparalleled," the Promissan King gushed.

I smiled softly. Apparently, political insincerity was consistent across cultures. He released my hand, and I stood, only to dip once more in respect to his Queen, who grinned happily at me.

"Quite true, Ledger," she agreed with her husband. "You look lovely, my dear."

The Dragon bristled beside me again, and I could feel the heat beginning to roll off his skin as his temper riled. Clearly, he had had enough of being ignored. My arm was still linked to his, but he released me suddenly, instead placing his palm on the small of my back and stepping closer. Uncomfortably closer. He hung against me as if an air of familiarity existed between us. An air of familiarity that insinuated things I did *not* want to be insinuated.

What in all of creation did he think he was doing?

"We are quite proud of our young Lady Moore," the Dragon cooed. "She's our very own blessing from the Gods. After all, how else could you explain the sudden reemergence of House Hyrax other than the Gods expressing their favor of my great nation?"

The Promissan King smiled with narrowed, calculating eyes. "How else, indeed? It is good to see you again, Vyncent."

I fought the urge to laugh in surprise, covering it with a cough. I'd never heard the Dragon's name before. No one in this kingdom would dare disrespect him by not addressing him by his formal title. And yet this foreign King had engaged my ruler into a battle of wills with just one word. One word I committed to memory.

As *Vyncent's* hand wrapped possessively around my waist, pulling me tighter to his hip, I pledged myself that one of these days, I'd find the perfect opportunity to call him by his name in the most disrespectful way possible.

"You as well, Ledger," the Dragon echoed, his voice sharp. "Although we hoped you'd bring a shipment of silks and cotton. We are still waiting for that."

"And you shall have it, of course!" The Promissan Queen promised. "But there is that matter of a fair price. Perhaps if Athenia cannot afford our request, you could supplement some costs with a shipment of steel weapons."

The Dragon bristled and narrowed his eyes at her before turning back to her husband as he continued the conversation. The fact he refused to engage with a woman on the matter of politics didn't necessarily surprise me, but it gave me yet another reason to hate him. He and the Promissan King continued prattling on about trade deals and foreign affairs as I scanned the room, eager to escape this mindless posturing.

Across the hall, my friends danced. Rankor twirled Lorelai throughout the room while Iris bounced from partner to partner merrily. Their joy was positively palpable. Even Camilla grinned and laughed as Kent dipped her low in the music's crux. Yearning hit me at once. I longed to join them, to drink away the stress of the evening and lose myself in the music that filled the room.

They weren't future Council members though. They didn't have the responsibilities I did.

As I sighed and turned my attention back to the conversation at hand, I briefly met eyes with Clay, who stood nursing a drink at a table across the hall with his attention entirely on his father and I. He raised an eyebrow questioningly as if he doubted my ability to continue playing this role successfully.

"Well, I, for one, have had enough politics for one evening. Wouldn't you agree, dear?" The Promissan Queen asked me.

So much for hoping I'd be able to spend the night simply smiling and keeping my mouth closed. My stomach flipped nervously. If I said the wrong thing, there would certainly be consequences from the Dragon. As if thinking the same thing, he looked down at me, almost daring me to speak out of turn as his grip on my waist tightened. I stood frozen as all three of the most powerful Descendants in the room waited for me to speak.

"I'm still learning so much about my future role as a Council member of Athenia," I told the Queen. "So, I'm grateful for the opportunity to shadow his majesty this evening as I prepare for my trials."

The Promissan King chuckled. "Well, of course, you are, as any good leader would be. But I must agree with my wife. This is a party, after all! So, tell me, Theadora, is it true that you know nothing of your origins?"

His voice was laced with hidden meaning, and I shivered against it. "That is true, your Majesty. I remember only waking in the infirmary. I hope that one day the grace of the Gods may return my memories, but for now, I can only work towards fulfilling my duty to the people of Athenia."

The Queen grinned as her eyes grazed over my chest, taking in the Mark of Hyrax, which was again displayed brazenly. Without asking, she took a step closer to investigate it, as if she doubted it was really on my skin. Her fingers were ice cold as they grazed my flesh.

"Marvelous," she mused. "A blessing from the Gods indeed, to Athenia and the world. I'm sure we will have many little Hyrax Descendants in no time. Did you know my father was a necromancer? He was one of the last few to live. He was hopeful of producing an heir, but of course, the blood of Zion was far too strong on my mother's side."

"You don't say." The Dragon chuckled as if he very well knew her lineage. I didn't doubt that he did. I suspected he had memorized the lineages of every person in this room.

The Promissan King nodded, a glint in his eyes. "We have been quite fortunate with heirs, six strong, healthy young dragons. I'm sure you would get along well with one of my sons."

His wife smiled widely and began clapping her hands as if this was the first time she had considered the idea. Which it clearly wasn't. It clearly wasn't the first time either of them had considered a potential match between one of their sons and the last Descendant of Hyrax.

"Oh, yes!" she exclaimed. "What a wonderful alliance between our two nations that would be. And, of course, you would have multiple heirs, children to sit on the Councils of both their parents' home nations."

The Dragon shifted, returning his arm to its raised position and waiting for me to retake hold of it. For once, I did not hesitate. You wouldn't have to ask me twice to leave a conversation about my unwanted arranged marriage and uterine politicization.

The Dragon bowed his head to each of them politely. "That is something to consider. But, of course, Lady Moore has many young suiters at her disposal, so we will need to be quite thoughtful with her future match."

"Of course," the Promissan King agreed under his breath as we left.

I breathed a sigh of relief once he had put a safe distance between the Promissans and us. There really was no way I would get out of this marriage thing, I realized painfully. I might be able to delay it until after I ascended to the Council, but to what end? I would only delay the inevitable. The Dragon would eventually find a match that made sense politically and genetically. And then, it was only a matter of time before I was posted up in some bed like nothing more than a breeding cow.

Isn't that what you did with an endangered species, anyway?

The Dragon kept me on his arm for hours, parading me through the room and introducing me to each senator, Duke, and King. I smiled and sang Athenia's praises as I needed to, but mostly I watched the giant wooden clock by the door as its ticking arm taunted me wherever I went. Eventually, the room began to clear out. The real power players stayed, continuing to prattle on about trades or marriages. They seemed locked in a competition with one another and the first person to leave lost the game. Some of the Lords and Ladies, though, those who had only come to enjoy the festivities, had drunk their fill of the evening and started filtering through the doors out of the ballroom.

"Clayton!" The Dragon boomed, looking away from his thrilling chat on the fertility of Athenia's wheat fields. He had long since introduced me to everyone worth knowing, but still kept me trapped on his arm. I'd spend most of the evening debating if his need to keep me close tonight had more to do with wanting the room to see a pretty young girl on his arm or with some perverse pleasure in knowing that I was unhappy. Probably both.

"Father," Clay greeted him, bowing low as he came to my side. "I was wondering if you might excuse Lady Moore for a dance."

The Dragon's eyes flickered gold, betraying that he did, in fact, mind. He placed a hand on my back possessively once more and I fought the urge to lean away from him towards Clay.

"I don't believe Lady Moore has learned the court dances," he replied, his voice upbeat and joyful but his eyes shining golden.

"Actually, your Majesty," I coughed, taking any excuse possible to step out of his grip. "I've taken quite a few lessons, and I think you'll find I'm a rather talented student."

"Well, why not let the princess show us?" cried one of my apparent suitors across the way. He was a grotesquely tall man with a balding head and a wart the size of my thumb on his chin. It would be just like the Dragon to choose him as a match one day.

Clay extended a hand, and I accepted it gratefully, not bothering to hide my urgent desire to flee. He pulled me away from his father until we stood in the center of the room. Wordlessly, he placed a hand delicately between my shoulder blades and tugged until I pressed my body against his. His cinnamon scent enveloped me. I looked up to his eyes, nearly a foot above my own, and felt my stomach somersault as I recognized the heat in them.

And then we danced. I followed his lead perfectly, albeit with a few glances toward my feet, to be sure I was doing the right thing.

"You've been practicing," he noted, with a poorly hidden smile.

"Told you," I quipped.

He narrowed his eyes at me, but the expression was oddly playful. "I think the words you're searching for are 'Thank you, my grace; I've been so terribly miserable all night that I forgot how to hide my frown until you came to save me.'"

I scoffed, as if I would ever admit to that. Even if I was terribly grateful to him for pulling me away.

"If you wanted your ego stroked, you should have pulled me away an hour ago. I'm all out of fake compliments."

He raised an eyebrow at me. "There are plenty of genuine ones you could give me. I'm dutiful, gallant, handsome..."

"Arrogant, controlling, aggressive." I interrupted.

Gold specks filled his eyes. At first, I hardly noticed them. I was so used to momentary flashes of his magic. It was typically here and then immediately gone, as he kept his emotions perfectly controlled. Tonight, though, he let that golden light spread until I looked fully into a dragon's eyes.

"I'm your Prince, Thea," he reminded me, voice suddenly serious and thick with a warning.

I wasn't sure what the final straw was that allowed me to speak freely to him at that moment. Perhaps it was the exhaustion from playing politics all night or the remnants of anger from our fight after the attack. Maybe it was the fact that, much to my own frustration, the feeling of his fingers against my back was terribly distracting. Either way, I met his eyes without fear.

"You're just a man, Clay. No more, no less."

He opened his mouth as if to spit back some fiery response, but at that moment, my two left feet got the better of me, and I stumbled backward, bumping into the older woman who danced gracefully with her partner behind me.

"Watch what you're doing!" She criticized, turning towards us. Her dark eyes scanned hungrily over Clay, and a sly smile spread across her lips. "Excuse me, your grace. I didn't realize you were providing a dance lesson."

She was a thin-framed woman with delicate features and worry lines, not much taller than me. Her gray hair was piled on her head, and her lips were painted a deep red. Her gray dress was modest, with long sleeves and a high collar. Despite its simplicity of style, the night sky's constellations had been hand-etched into her skirt, with tiny crystals representing each star. She hardly paid any mind to me as I appraised her, choosing instead to embrace Clay fondly and I couldn't help but note the way she pressed her breasts tightly against him as she hugged him. "It's so good to see you, my grace. It's been far too long!"

Clay's face was a portrait of irritation. "Alina, I didn't realize you would be here tonight."

"Why, of course, I would be! My granddaughter is still in need of a handsome husband, after all. Whatever happened between you and Camilla? You were the quaintest couple."

"We weren't a couple," Clay muttered, but I had already tuned out. My attention was on something far more interesting than Clay's romantic history.

"You're Camilla's grandmother?" I demanded.

I didn't expect my voice to be as firm as it was. And from Alina's reaction, neither did she. Even Clay, usually so stone-faced and unreadable, jerked his head towards me in surprise. Alina's hand flew to her chest as she finally looked at me as if I had offended her by addressing her so forcefully.

"Yes..." She drew out the word, her voice thick with contempt. "I'm Alina Maslov, the matriarch of House Hypatia. And you are?"

Alina knew precisely who I was. The Dragon had ensured that. So the fact that she was pretending otherwise told me everything I needed to know about her. I had played enough games for one night. I was uninterested in playing them with her.

"I believe you're very well aware that I'm Princess Theadora Moore of House Hyrax," I spit out. My magic soared under my fingertips, ready and waiting. "Do you care to tell me why Witches in this palace are conducting blood magic?"

Alina gasped, looking at Clay as if she expected him to defend her. But the Crown Prince only tucked his hands into his pockets and shrugged as if he, too, were waiting to hear her answer. The corners of his lips were just so slightly tipped up in what might have been an expression of pride.

"My dear, I cannot be expected to monitor every Witch in the kingdom."

"It's 'my lady,'" I corrected her. "And I believe monitoring the Witches of Athenia is exactly within your responsibilities as the Matriarch of your line. I merely asked you about the Witches here in the palace, which should be a fairly simple question. So are you incompetent, or are you willfully disrespecting a Descendant of a royal bloodline?"

My circle of friends was closing in, sensing my tension. I noticed Iris watching us unabashedly, with Rankor close behind her. Camilla stood at a table between Kent and Lorelai, and though she watched us interestedly, she didn't move towards us. Not that she would stop me now. With Alina in front of me and the shock of the attack still coursing through my veins, I wanted answers, and I wanted them now.

"I don't know who attacked you," Alina sneered, rolling her eyes dramatically.

"Then perhaps you would better serve your kingdom by returning to your family and identifying the threat than you do by spending your evening trying to arrange a royal marriage that we *all* know will never happen."

Alina gasped, mouth opening and closing like a fish as she struggled to decide what to say next. Her eyes flashed briefly between Clay and Camilla; from my peripheral, I could see Camilla's cheeks turning crimson. Finally, Alina turned back to me and bowed her head respectfully without seeing another way out of this situation.

"Yes, my lady. I'll see to that right away."

I watched the long train of her dress slither out of the hall.

Camilla followed after her, stopping in front of me with an expression of hate. "A bit hypocritical, don't you think?"

I narrowed my eyes. "I don't catch your meaning."

"Please," she snorted. "We all know you pretend to hate this lifestyle. Yet here you are, taking advantage of the power it offers you. Who's the real villain here?"

I suspect Clay might have tried to say something in my defense had Camilla not stormed out of the hall before either of us could think of a response. Instead, he simply nodded briefly towards Kent and our friend excused himself after her, likely to calm her down.

"Careful," he warned in my ear as our friends swarmed us. "You're sounding more and more like a Council member each day."

I didn't bother to meet his gaze. I recognized the truth in his words; I also recognized the truth in Camilla's.

"The only thing I'm doing is ensuring I live long enough to make a life here," I said, but I wasn't sure if I was reassuring him or myself.

CHAPTER SIXTEEN

I had promised my friends to officially re-emerge from my rooms again by the end of the Peace Ball. Rankor convinced me to upgrade our dancing lessons to combat training, and Lorelai insisted on getting me fitted for new gowns again since my last shipment had gone up in flames. Literally. I wasn't particularly eager to risk another death-by-dress situation, but it was truly inevitable. I couldn't very well keep wearing her borrowed gowns or the dresses Clay sent along for me.

When I woke in the morning to the sound of a card being slid under my door, though, I knew with a sudden certainty that I wouldn't be seeing my friends after all.

Bare-footed, I padded over to it and felt my stomach fall as I read its brief message.

I had a private summons to the Dragon's office.

"Miss Moore, do come in." He greeted me as I entered and automatically dipped in the customary curtsy.

The Dragon's private office stood in sharp contrast to the rest of the castle's light and golden design. Dark tapestries covered the windows so that the only light was the dim sparks of the fire torches hung on the walls. He sat behind an enormous mahogany desk, feet kicked up, a chilled glass of whiskey waiting at his side.

"Sit," he commanded, pointing to the velvet couch on the far side of the room. "Nice of you to dress up for the occasion."

I felt his eyes on my back as I crossed the room and sat, tucking my ankles politely. I expected he was used to women wearing their finest fashions to see him, with jewels dripping over handsomely exposed breasts. But I had purposely picked my most simple gown to wear today. A dress with a high enough neckline to hide the Mark on my chest that he so loved to see. His eyes narrowed over the space where it rested, and he smirked, likely guessing the reasoning for my choice.

"You made quite the splash last night," he commented, pulling up a stack of papers and perusing through them.

"Did I?"

I suspected I knew exactly why he had called for this little meeting.

He grunted, folding the papers and sitting them in front of himself on the desk. "Four marriage proposals already."

"And here I thought I would have been present for those."

The Dragon grinned, lifting an eyebrow. The movement made the resemblance between him and Clay uncomfortably obvious. "That's a formality, of course. But, I assure you, once I decide on the best match, we'll arrange for an extravagant public proposal."

Just the kind of thing I wouldn't enjoy. Just the sort of thing he *knew* I wouldn't want.

"And have you?" I asked hesitantly, voice betraying my fear. "Decided on a match, that is. I presume that's why I'm here."

He stood, crossing the room in three long strides to look at the world maps plastered across the wall. Then, as he folded his hands behind his back, he jerked his head silently for me to join him. Once I had, he placed his finger on the easternmost coast of the deserts of Tenebris.

"This is Fort Charu," he explained, pointing. "It was a stronghold for Tenebris during the Great War but has been largely unoccupied since. Until about four months ago, that is, when Emperor Long started moving some forces to it. Now, why might that be a concern to me?"

He turned to me with narrowed eyes. A test, then. Sighing, I looked over the maps once more. Tenebris wasn't a particularly powerful enemy of Athenia, but it was geographically the closest landmass to us, separated by only a slight stretch of ocean on our southern border. I pursed my lips, turning my attention to Fort Charu. The fort wasn't within attacking distance of Athenia, so that was an unlikely explanation for mobilization.

"Where's the rest of this map?" I asked.

The Dragon grinned, pulling out another sheet of paper from a desk drawer and hanging it to the right of the existing sheet. That's when it all made sense.

"Fort Charu is the closest base to Promissa," I observed, running my finger from the fort, across the water, to Promissa. "If they're gathering forces, it could be because Tenebris has allied with them. They could be preparing to house Promissan soldiers."

The Dragon nodded, apparently happy with my answer. Then, with a sweep of his arm, he ushered me back towards my seat on the couch. As I sank into it, the stench of burnt ash and pine needles enveloped me and I crinkled my nose against it. Rather than returning to his place at the desk, he sank next to me, crossing an ankle over his knee.

"Emperor Long is a fickle woman," he criticized with repugnance. "She goes where power is. Once she sees that Athenia is far too formidable to buckle, any alliance between Tenebris and Promissa will be squashed."

"Athenia's full Council," I guessed.

My earlier suspicions had been wrong. He hadn't decided to marry me off. Not yet, at least. This meeting was about the Council.

He nodded. "You're a clever girl, I admit. I'll send you on a coronation tour in Tenebris once you pass your trials before ascending to the Council. We'll wait to announce any engagement until after then to give them the hope of securing your heirs as their own."

I tried to hide my sigh of relief, but I feared it was all too obvious as I finally sunk back into the cushions. I might not have been able to claim my fate and marriage, but at least, it seemed in that moment, that I could delay it for a bit longer.

For once, it seemed like the politics were on my side.

"That seems like a reasonable plan of action."

"Glad you approve of my ruling, Miss Moore," he snorted. Then, slowly, purposefully, he edged closer to me, running his fingertips suggestively across my knee. My eyes focused in on the movement immediately. "I won't be marrying you to someone in Tenebris though."

My blood ran cold in a sudden rush and though the air in his office was warm, I shivered. I locked my attention on his hand on my leg, entirely unable to ignore the feeling of his body inching closer to me. A sense of precognition warned me that this meeting was about to take a turn in a direction I didn't want to follow it.

And yet, I was a girl alone in the office of her king. I felt powerless for the first time in a long time.

"Oh," I mumbled, unsure of what to do as those fingers slid higher up my thigh.

"You like it in Athenia, don't you? You've made friends."

Instinct pushed me to lean away from his touch, to scoot further down the couch in search of escape. But his grip became a vice as I did and his eyes danced. He knew he was making me uncomfortable. He wanted to.

With one hand still firmly planted on my thigh, his other reached to brush my hair back, away from my neck. Nausea pounded through my stomach.

"There are arrangements that could be made to ensure that no one ever takes you or your children out of this country," he whispered, as his hand locked around the back of my neck and held me firmly in place.

"Perhaps those are arrangements we could discuss at a Council meeting," I proposed through a locked jaw.

A Council meeting where other people would be present.

The Dragon only laughed, and I didn't stop my flinch as I felt his breath hot against the hollow of my throat.

"This is my kingdom," he reminded me. "I make the decisions. And no one, including you, can stop me. I'm. The. King."

He punctuated each word by pressing his searing mouth sloppily against my throat. To make his ultimate point, his teeth nicked the delicate skin, and I couldn't help but to cry out in a soft, helpless whimper. The sound only inflamed him on further and he bit down, hard. Magic rushed through me angrily, willing itself to be released, and I tore away from him, standing in a rush and grasping onto the flesh I knew would bruise.

Internally I clamped down on that power in me, knowing that losing control of it would only make this situation worse, but it sparked in protest against me. The feeling was surprisingly painful, and I slammed my jaw closed so tightly I was sure my teeth would crack.

He only laughed at my distress.

"See to your training," he ordered, giving me his back as he returned to his desk. "I want those trials completed sooner rather than later. Ryla reports that you're gaining a quick mastery of your powers. Be sure that you learn your history and combat skills just as quickly."

Every fiber of my being told me to run, to flee from this room and find someone, anyone, who would stand up for me and say that what had just happened was wrong.

But I didn't do that.

I only dipped to a curtsy before twisting on my heels and leaving the room with as much decorum as I could muster. As I left the Dragon's chambers, I couldn't stop the tears from falling down my cheeks, and yet, not a single member of my ten-man guard team tried to comfort or reassure me. Their gazes remained plastered ahead, avoiding me entirely.

No one asked what happened. No one even asked if I was okay. And it was so obvious that I wasn't. They wouldn't stop the Dragon from tormenting me. As he had reminded me, he was the king, and there was no one in the kingdom of Athenia who could protect me from him.

CHAPTER SEVENTEEN

Nothing was going to stop me from getting out of this castle, getting to Mara, and securing that memory potion. After my meeting with the Dragon, I felt even more urgency to understand where and who I came from. I couldn't know if that information would help me, but if there was any chance that I had someone in this world that cared for me, that wanted to *protect* me, then I needed to know. I needed to find them.

The tricky part would be getting out of the castle.

After spending the rest of my day pacing and turning over the possibilities, I had finally devised a plan.

It wasn't a particularly good one, but it was a plan.

So after my evening meal, after Nessira and Geia left me for the evening, I set to work. I donned a simple dress and tied a scarf around my neck to hide the reminder of what the Dragon had done. Then, I'd grunted my way through dragging one of the small ottomans from the parlor towards the window that faced the gardens before opening the panels to let in the chilly night air.

"This is a terrible idea," I muttered to myself before setting my sights on the ottoman.

It wasn't hard to summon my powers. I was, after all, afraid, but I was also determined. I was getting out of this castle and finding out the truth of my past, even if it killed me. My emotions raged, and the magic responded instantly, flying in sparks down my arms and fingers. As I lifted my left hand, the ottoman followed, floating gently off the floor and out the window, where it hung patiently in the sky.

"Okay, step one down."

I knew if I allowed myself any time to think through the next phase of this plan, I would never muster the courage to go through with it. So, without allowing myself time to panic, I climbed to the windowsill, threw one of my legs over the ottoman and shifted my weight onto it until I was sitting. For a moment, I marveled at my own accomplishment. I was seated on an ottoman that my powers were keeping afloat twenty feet above the ground.

"By the Gods," I whispered. It was working. It was actually working!

The last step of my plan involved me gathering enough control to slowly lower that ottoman, with me on it, to the ground where I could then sprint off the property and into town to meet Mara.

As I set my intentions on lowering the ottoman, my power soared in a sudden rush. I struggled desperately to pull it back to me, but my control slipped and I gripped onto the seat as my decline picked up speed. It took everything in me not to scream as I hurled through the air and bounced roughly onto the grass below. The ottoman made a sharp *thud*, and I flew from it, landing heavily on my knee and rolling. For a moment, I laid on the ground helplessly, nursing my wounds and thanking Hyrax I had even survived that.

But I had survived.

Which meant I needed to stand up off the ground and get back in motion before someone found me laying here.

I ran as fast as I could out of the palace gardens and onto the courtyard, ignoring the bite of pain each time I placed weight on my injured right knee. Thankfully, the square was filled with people, making it easier than expected to lose myself in the crowd without anyone realizing who I was.

By the time I reached the outside of the tavern, the sun was just beginning to make its descent and Mara stood patiently waiting for me. As she met my eyes, her lips turned upward.

"You made it."

I nodded, slightly out of breath. Her calculating eyes scanned over me slowly, and she jerked her head, urging me to follow her into a small house across the street. We entered a tiny kitchen, with a broken wooden table and black pot seated above the dwindling fire. The room smelled of musk and food that had gone rotten, but it didn't seem to bother Mara as she kicked off her boots and drank heavily from a jug on the table.

"You look awful," she criticized. "And you can't wear that. There's a bedroom upstairs with a gown waiting for you. We'll be joining the Alchemist for a masquerade ball."

A party? Mara had mentioned she was making a trip to see the Alchemist, but she had never indicated it was for a party. I didn't have *time* to go to a ball.

"How long will it take us to travel there?"

I needed to get there, get the potion, and get back to the castle before anyone noticed my absence.

"Does it matter?"

Did it?

"No, I suppose it doesn't."

With a sense of dread settling in my stomach, I went to the staircase. I needed that potion; I wasn't going back to the castle without it. I'd just have to hope I could get it quickly. Clay would kill me if he found out I had left.

The Dragon would do something worse.

After I dressed, Mara had ushered me into a carriage where I sat with two other young women on a bed of hay while we made our way to the Alchemist's estate. The blood-red gown she had instructed me to wear was hardly more than a scrap of cloth. While its halter neck rose high enough to cover my Descendants Mark, the back of it barely skinned the tops of my hips, leaving all of my spine and much of my sides completely bare. Two slits rose high across both of my thighs, ending at the tips of my pelvis. Any movement in the wrong direction would leave me entirely bared to the world. She insisted I complete the ensemble with a black mask that she had tied across my eyes.

The other women in the carriage were younger than me, but just as scantily dressed.

"Is this gown not a bit indecent?" One of the girls asked in a soft voice that reminded me a bit of Geia's.

Gods how old was she? She had to be barely over sixteen. Where were her parents?

"These dresses are very in fashion in the district we're going to." Mara promised. "You'll fit right in."

"Why aren't you wearing one, then?" I demanded.

Mara grinned, but didn't bother answering me. While the two other girls and I had large portions of our body on display, she had dressed in an oversized tunic and cotton leggings.

As the carriage pulled to a stop, after what felt like hours, two large men appeared to help us out. They grasped onto our hands as we climbed down and I leaned away from the smell of them. As inconspicuously as possible, I scraped my palm against my dress to wipe away the sweat that lingered on my skin from where they had touched me. They each took responsibility for the other women, while Mara grasped hold of my arm and began leading me towards the house.

The estate was a large brick-faced home with treacherous gargoyles hung above the stone stairs that led to the entrance. Sounds of festivities were already escaping from inside as a line formed to gain entry into the party. Many of the guests were men who chatted and smoked with each other as they waited to enter. They watched us as we walked past the line towards the entrance, their eyes lingering on the patches of exposed skin.

"Mara!" One called out to her.

He was a thick man with a swollen belly and overgrown beard. He stared at us – at me – with a grin while a cigar dangled from his mouth.

"How much for her?" He asked.

I bristled. *How much for me?*

Did this man think he could purchase me, as if I was no better than some common household object?

Wait. My thoughts swam suddenly with memories of the night Iris and I had escaped the castle.

Was this party meant for something else? Something *more,* like Madame Stefania's was meant for something more. My eyes trailed over the gown I was wearing once more. It certainly looked like some dresses I'd seen the ladies of Madame Stefania's wearing.

Good Gods, what kind of party had I come to...

"She's here for the Alchemist, not as a party guest," Mara explained as she tugged me along.

The man pursed his lips with a dramatic whimper while he held his right hand to his heart in mock injury. Mara only rolled her eyes at him and muttered something about greedy men.

"Where will we find the Alchemist?" I asked her when we crossed the threshold into the building.

"I will take you to him now," she assured me.

The estate was by far less grand than the castle, but still covered in dark marble and gilded bronze furnishings. Masked individuals crowded from corner to corner as they laughed and drank with each other. Across the space, a band played soft music while servers brought forth trays of appetizers.

But despite how refined the party seemed, there was an overwhelming metallic smell that strangely filled the air, leaving me on edge.

"That smell," I mused.

Mara laughed. "It's mortal blood. The Alchemist diffuses it into the air. It's not often that Descendants make their way here, they have little need for his services after all, but he prefers an even playing field. The blood in the air has the effect of temporarily numbing their powers."

That... wasn't ideal. I reached for my magic, longing for its comforting tingle, only to find *nothing*. There were no sparks, no electric awareness of it. I was as powerless as I had been those first few weeks at court, and that sensation was unbearable.

"That wouldn't be a problem for you, now would it?"

Her smile was venomous and her grip on my arm tightened until her nails dug into my flesh in small crescent-shaped stings of pain. I jerked my arm from her, but she held fast, picking up the pace of her steps as we moved through the party.

"You're hurting me," I growled.

"And what can you do about it to stop me?" Her eyes were knowing as she met my gaze and my heart fell through my stomach.

I was so stupid.

The sudden knowledge that I had made a mistake in trusting her overwhelmed me. "You know?"

Her laugh was vicious. "I suspected. You confirmed. Which God do you come from, girl?"

I bit down on my lip aggressively, drawing blood, thanking the Gods that my dress covered my Descendants Mark. My only saving grace in that moment was that they didn't seem to know exactly *who* I was. I could only imagine what they would do with me once they found out I was the precious last Descendant of Hyrax.

I was so foolish to have trusted a stranger in a tavern. I'd allowed my desperation for knowledge to blind me. And now, with Mara's nails digging into my arms, I suspected I was about to pay the price for that stupidity.

Clay was going to be furious when he eventually found my suites at the castle empty.

She led me away from the party and down a staircase into a dimly lit hallway. I stumbled on the bottom step and her hand slipped from my arm as I fell. Unwilling to waste the momentary advantage, I pulled from her, scrambling back and sprinting back up the staircase. I needed to get far away from here *before* I found out what these kinds of people did to Descendants.

I should have known running was futile the second her laughter began to echo around me.

At the top of the staircase, a brute of a man with dirty boots and a deadly sword stood with arms crossed against his chest. His shoulders were wide enough to fill the entire frame.

"Please try to run." He grinned. "Please give me the slightest excuse to put my hands on you."

Gasping, I stumbled back directly into Mara's arms once more.

Stupid. I was so stupid. They could engrave that on my tombstone when all this was over. Here lies Theadora Moore, the girl who stupidly put herself in danger and effectively ended the line of Hyrax forever.

"No one touches her!" Mara snapped, shoving me forward. "No one but the Alchemist."

"He's going to love this one," the man replied from behind me, a smile clear in his voice. "Think he'll keep her?"

Mara shrugged. "She's worth a pretty penny. The Alchemist enjoys making money."

"He enjoys fucking more."

Good Gods.

"Here we are!" Mara announced with a laugh, opening the door to an office and throwing me inside.

I flopped onto my bruised knees and cried out unintentionally against the stinging pain. Mara snickered again and for a moment, I was back in the Dragon's office while he laughed as I cried. My neck ached in reminder.

This office was nearly as large as his. Across from me, the Alchemist, I presumed, sat at an over-sized cherry-wood desk talking to a gentleman who sat with his back to me. The man didn't turn to face us as we entered. The Alchemist, though, met my eyes immediately and a sly grin spread across his lips. He was tall, obviously so even while seated, with dark hair and piercing green eyes.

"I thought I had asked not to be interrupted, no matter how pretty the interruption is."

"This is the girl I told you about," Mara explained. "It's as I suspected."

He nodded, twirling a small blade between his fingers. Then he truly smiled, a teeth-bared kind of smile that warned of pain and violence.

Shit.

I needed to get out of here. Now.

The pounding of my heart was audible, an increasingly frantic beat in my ears. In a panicked rush, I scrambled backwards on my hands and knees before struggling to my feet and attempting to run past Mara. I made it only a few steps before the man reached out suddenly, backhanding me so sharply that my body seemed weightless as I fell to the floor once more.

"What did I say?" Mara hissed.

He shrugged. "She gave me a reason."

He bent down to where I sprawled on the ground clutching my cheek. Without warning, his fingers laced through the hair on the back of my head and pulled sharply. The pain was intense, temporarily blinding me as he wretched me to my feet. I cried out once more, clawing at his fingers, but as his hand circled my throat and squeezed, my only thought became that of trying to continue breathing.

Desperate, I lifted my foot to stamp onto his, but he only increased the pull on my hair until only the tips of my feet could touch the ground.

"It's all right, Mara," the Alchemist calmed her. "I'm rather enjoying the show."

The Alchemist stood and approached us slowly, taking his time to look me over before finally tapping on the fingers around my throat. The grasp loosened enough for me to suck in a much needed gulp of air.

"What God do you come from?" The Alchemist asked me.

I glared, knowing better than to give away that secret. "Wouldn't you like to know?"

"I would actually." He grinned and his eyes trailed over me slowly. Gods, the look on his face was unnerving. "There are other more fun ways to get the answer to my question, though. Perhaps we should send our guests out and I can take my time finding where the Mark is etched on your skin."

Darkness rolled through me as my blood chilled in an icy fury. For a moment, I felt like a true embodiment of Hyrax's power, because if my magic had still been accessible, I would have unleashed it right then. My emotions were unhinged, my rage was palpable, and nothing would have stopped me from sending his soul to greet my ancestor in the Underworld.

"You even think about touching me and you'll spend eternity regretting it."

The entire room laughed. Was my threat that obviously empty? Gods, without my powers, I was nothing.

Not just powerless... I was utterly helpless.

"So you want a potion, do you?" The Alchemist taunted.

With impossible speed, he reached for me. His fingers wrapped around my chin, gripping my face and shoving a vial of stormy liquid into my mouth. It tasted of dirt and bitterness and I protested, doing everything within my power to tear my hair out of my captor's grasp, but as he plugged my nose and held my mouth shut, no amount of fighting could have kept the vile liquid from sliding down my throat.

"That's a good girl," the Alchemist praised, running his thumb across my lower lip. "Drink up."

Furious, I lashed out, capturing his finger in my mouth and biting down hard, ignoring the disgust that flooded me as his thick blood filled my mouth. The hand in my hair ripped me back sharply as the man sputtered a curse under his breath.

"Stupid bitch!" Mara hissed.

The Alchemist only chuckled, dipping his thumb into his own mouth to suck away the remaining droplets. He nodded to his henchman and the hand in my hair released suddenly. With a cry, I fell forward in a heavy heap.

"Now, now," the Alchemist chided, running his hand up the exposed skin of my leg. He left a trail of blood along my inner thigh that made me want to gag. "Mara should have warned you I like my women with a little fight in them. I take great pride in breaking those rebellious spirits."

"Burn in the Underworld," I spit at him, shoving him away as he reached up to knead my breast.

He laughed. "I'll be taking you there with me. Now be a good girl and enjoy your potion while I finish my meeting."

He patted my cheek two times before turning away and it was all I could do to not fall heavily back onto the floor. Whatever *potion* he had forced me to drink had an immediate effect. My head spun with it. My limbs were too light, too removed from me.

I was floating.

I was there, in that room, listening to them talk above me. I saw Mara and her henchman leave. I heard the door click shut behind them. And yet,

I couldn't move, couldn't speak, could hardly *think*. I was a body on the ground whose soul soared helplessly.

"Apologies for the interruption," the Alchemist said to the man at his desk. "Some matters of business cannot be delayed. Where were we?"

"Discussing percentages," the man replied. His voice was oddly familiar, but I couldn't seem to place it. It sounded nice, though. Deep and almost... sensual.

Gods the sound of it did something to me. Warmth traveled through me, lingering deep in my belly.

"Ah yes," the Alchemist intoned. "I can offer fifteen percent of my profits for the use of your ships."

"I think twenty might be more appropriate, given the level of risk involved."

"Twenty?" the Alchemist laughed. "That is perhaps a bit steep. How about we settle on fifteen and I can throw in one of my girls?"

There was a pause. In the silence, I marveled at the way the room began changing colors. Orbs of pink and blue danced across my vision. They carried sounds and extraordinary smells with them. The world around me changed. Where was I?

"How about we settle on fifteen and I take *her*?"

Another pause.

"She's worth more than five percent." The Alchemist's voice was low and laced with intensity.

"I'm *well* aware of that." The man sounded oddly exasperated. That voice flooded over me again, deep and comforting, coating my skin with a rush of warmth and heavy anticipation. My stomach pitched once more in need.

"I haven't yet decided if she's for sale."

"You're taking her as your own?" The man growled, irritation obvious.

"My last pet has lost her appeal," the Alchemist sighed. "They all do after some time. This girl, though? She is exquisite, don't you think?"

"You give me the girl and ten percent of the profits, and I'll offer a fifth ship for your disposal."

The Alchemist laughed. "Surely you're not that desperate for a woman's touch?"

There was a moment of silence.

"Like you said, she is exquisite."

Did I fall asleep after that? I didn't know for sure, but the next thing I was aware of was the shuffling sound of chairs being pushed back against the wooden floor. Then, hands swept under my back and knees and I was being lifted. The air danced across my unusually sensitive skin and it felt... nice. A long sigh escaped from my mouth.

The Alchemist laughed. "Looks like the potion has settled in. She should be especially pliable for you tonight."

"The ships will be available to you at the port in a fortnight."

"It's been as enjoyable as ever to do business with you, my friend."

We were moving quickly. The arms around me were strong, but gentle as we moved through the lower level of the estate, climbed a staircase, and stepped out into the cold night air. I shivered as the breeze rushed over me and he pulled me closer against his chest.

My eyelids were heavy, fluttering slightly as sleep called for me. I snuggled against the chest that held me.

"Stay awake, Thea," he growled. "You owe me an explanation before you fall asleep."

My heart stuttered as I finally recognized his voice.

CHAPTER EIGHTEEN

We walked for a long time. I couldn't be sure if it was minutes or hours. Time had somehow lost all meaning.

At some point, I must have fallen asleep in his arms despite his warnings. When I woke, he was carrying me up a dusty staircase and into a tiny bedroom. The air felt damp and cold, and the bed made a terrible creaking sound as he deposited me heavily onto it and shut the door behind himself.

"Where are we?" I asked, but the words came out in a slurred mess.

"An inn," Clay replied in a clipped tone.

He was angry. He was very angry.

"We are in the last shitty room in a shitty inn because the roads back to the castle are too dangerous to travel at night. And unlike me, you can't very well fly home."

The room was small. The bed took up too much of the space, leaving only a few feet on either side to walk. Without a fireplace, the air was frigid, made worse by the window with a clear crack across its center. There was no armoire for clothes, not even a hall or doorway to a bathing chamber. Just a bed with a single sheet and a small stool in the room's corner. We were a long way from the palace, indeed.

Numbly, I noticed that the single bed meant we would be sharing. It was a clear violation of court protocols, but I couldn't bring myself to care after everything that had happened. Obviously, I'd broken more than a few rules tonight.

As he looked down at me, his eyes caught alight, burning brilliantly and unabashedly golden. He stood, leaning against the door with arms crossed over his chest. His fury rolled off of him in waves and I felt myself sinking back into the bed. If the Gods were kind, they would have killed me right then and there rather than making me face him.

The Gods were not kind, though.

"How exactly *were* you planning to get back to the castle?" he demanded.

"I suppose I hadn't thought that far."

He scoffed, raising an eyebrow at me in a look of such utter disappointment that I suddenly felt like a child. "You have no idea how much danger you placed yourself in tonight! What in all of creation did you even go there looking for?"

"A memory potion."

"A memory potion?" He echoed me incredulously, as if he couldn't even comprehend the ridiculousness of the idea.

Irritation soared, breaking through to the surface despite the fog of what drug remained in my system. I sat up on my knees on the bed, not minding the way the slits of my dress opened wider against my thighs. Clay's eyes flickered unabashedly to my legs as I did, but his jaw only clenched tighter in anger.

"How can I trust that you or the Dragon will give me any of the answers I need?" I criticized with a raised voice. "You clearly don't care for my well-being."

Clay turned away from me suddenly. His hand twitched and for a moment I thought he might actually punch one of the thin walls of the room, but he ran it through his hair instead as he released a pained sigh.

"All I have done is try to keep you safe! Though I can't bring myself to understand why I care so much when you're willing to throw your life away over some fake promise of a potion that doesn't exist."

My anger at him met my frustration with myself and the situation overall. Of course, the potion hadn't been real. I'd realized that once I recognized Mara knew what I was. But still, hearing it said aloud stung.

I would never remember the life I had before I came to Athenia.

"He uses the potions to lure women to the estate," Clay explained, voice low and expression grim. "Then he doses them with that drug and moves them to a private estate. He keeps them there for a few months, *training* them, before he sells them off to the highest bidder."

"And what were *you* doing there?" I spit out through the tears that had welled in my eyes.

"He imports the drugs, Thea! For *two years*, I've been working to get close enough to him to identify the port they're coming from. Two years of work that I almost abandoned the second I smelt you on the property."

I found myself momentarily distracted by the apparent refinement of Clay's sense of smell. Was that because of his powers? What did I smell like?

"You bought me," I muttered, making sense of the conversation I'd overheard earlier. "What would you have done if he said no when you asked for me?"

Clay's eyes were piercing, unflinching in their intensity as he held my gaze. "I would have killed him."

He would have. He said it so seriously, with such resolution.

Clayton Vail would have abandoned his plan and killed the Alchemist if that was what it would have taken to get me out of there safely.

He would have protected me.

The realization left my chest fluttering for a moment... until I suddenly remembered *why* he would have done that.

These words about wanting to keep me safe were promises made to Hyrax, not to me. None of this was about me. It was about my bloodline.

Which left me feeling cheap and unimportant.

"You should sleep," Clay instructed with a tired sigh. "We need to leave early in the morning before my father realizes you were out of the castle."

Before I knew what he was doing, he reached over his shoulder, grabbed the neck of his cotton tunic, and pulled it over his head, tossing it to me. I sat frozen, eyes skimming over the expanse of him. Tan skin covered an impressively muscular torso. Just above the line of his dangerously low-hanging trousers, I could make out the shape of a dragon wing. His Descendants Mark. Without meaning to, my tongue darted out to wet dry lips as I wondered aimlessly about the *rest* of that tattoo.

"Quit ogling me," he ordered, snapping me out of my highly inappropriate thoughts.

The heat of a flush peppered my cheeks, but as I quickly returned my eyes to his face, I found only upturned lips and an expression of amusement.

"I have to go settle our bill. Change while I do so. That dress hardly looks comfortable."

"It's actually not that bad, you don't have to-"

"For me, Thea. That dress isn't making things *comfortable* for me."

Oh.

His lips curled unhappily against the word, and his eyes were heated as they roamed over my body, lingering at the flesh that sat exposed through the tops of the slits. Apparently his eyes didn't just shine golden when he was angry. Magic filled them when he felt... other things too. I shivered, feeling a slight comfort in knowing that I wasn't the only one entertaining inappropriate thoughts. The motion was enough to snap him out of whatever place his mind had traveled to, and he cleared his throat in a rush.

Without another word, he turned and left, leaving me alone and clutching his shirt to me.

Clay was gone for some time. While he was away, I'd discarded the dress in favor of his too-large tunic. It hung wide, falling over one shoulder and skimming the tops of my knees, but it was certainly more *comfortable*. And I didn't mind admitting that the smell of cinnamon and oak was somewhat comforting as it enveloped me.

Still, it did little to provide any warmth. As I tried to settle into the bed and sleep, I couldn't stop the shivers that terrorized my body. The patter of rain sounded outside and a brisk wind pounded against the window. I buried my face into the flat pillow as I waited for the air to still.

But it wasn't just the cold that kept me awake.

It was the way I seemed acutely aware of every place that fabric touched my skin. It was the growing tension in my core that screamed for some kind of release. I was cold *and* hot. I shivered while I trembled with need.

The door opened slowly and though my back was turned, I could hear Clay tentatively step inside as if he worried he might wake me. The floor creaked under his weight at first, but then the only sound was that of the rain falling on the pavement outside.

"You're cold," he observed, voice hardly more than a whisper.

The rational part of my brain told me I should pretend I was asleep. That part of me knew that continuing any conversation with him wouldn't end well, not when I was so desperate to be touched. But the other part of me *needed* to be touched.

I needed to feel safe.

And even if he had only protected me because of what I represented, I couldn't deny that Clay had made me feel safe tonight.

I needed him more than I needed rational thought.

So, I turned, and I met his gaze.

"May I?" he asked, pointing to the bed.

Afraid my voice would betray the fire in my blood, I only nodded, and he pulled aside the sheet and sank onto the bed next to me.

There wasn't enough space for the two of us, but I didn't mind. I wanted to feel him pressed against me. I wanted to explore his body like it was my own, to find out what the rest of his tattoo looked like from where it lay hidden by the belt of his pants.

"Dragons run warm," he explained, guiding me to lie back on my side once more. He wrapped an arm around my stomach and pulled me closer to him, while his other arm slipped under my neck to wrap around my chest. His skin was indeed hot to the touch. Waves of heat rolled off of him and enveloped me in warmth. Slowly, my shivering eased, and my thoughts all collided into one single demand.

I pressed myself against him, relishing in the small growl that escaped his throat as I ground my hips into his hardness.

"Thea," he warned. "I should have told you that the drug they gave you can have a bit of an arousing effect."

"I'd noticed that," I panted, somewhat surprised at how deprived I sounded.

He laughed softly and the sensation of his breath across my neck sent a fresh wave of anticipation down my body. It lingered at the crux of my thighs, demanding attention. I couldn't think of anything but that desire. I couldn't feel anything but his body against mine.

Briefly, my mind wandered back to Madame Stefania's for the second time that night. I thought of the woman who had sat perched atop a man who buried his hand between her thighs. I thought of the way her head had fallen back in pleasure.

What would Clay's hand feel like on my skin?

And while the drug may have spurred my need on, I certainly wasn't alone in it. I could hear the hitch of his breath as I ground my rear into him once more. I could feel the twitch of his fingers as he held himself back from grasping my breast. Greedily, I arched my back, attempting to push myself into that waiting hand, but his arms locked around me, holding me still.

"You're not thinking clearly," he reminded me.

"So help clear my thoughts."

I twisted desperately, trying to turn myself to face him, but he moved in an instant, gripping my chin and pulling my head so that I met his golden eyes over my shoulder. His grasp was tight, his body taut, his desire for me pressing firmly against my back. I gasped slightly.

"If you let me touch you tonight, you're going to wake up and regret it," he breathed. "I know you want it now, and Thea, please believe me when I say I want nothing more than to fuck you so thoroughly that you dream of my cock. But I will not be someone you regret."

I stilled, staring into his eyes and feeling the sincerity of his words settle over me. He released me slowly, and I pushed onto my elbow to turn and face him fully. It was somewhat unfair for someone born into such power to be blessed with such beauty as well. His face might have been carved by the Gods themselves. Sharp jawline, passionate eyes, full lips that were as masculine as they were delicate.

"Who's to say I would regret it?"

"Who's to say you wouldn't?"

I frowned. "I know what I want Clay. I *want* you to touch me. Are you going to tell me you don't want the same?"

"You haven't the slightest idea the things I want to do to you Thea. But I'm trying very hard to be a good man right now."

Everything in me wanted to protest more. I wanted to reach out, grab his hand, and place it exactly where I wanted it. That place where the curling tension was nearly unbearable. But Clay just patted the bed next to him, encouraging me to lay back once more.

"It should wear off soon. Just give it a minute."

I flopped unhappily onto my back, content to stare up at the ceiling in frustration. He chuckled softly. Eventually, the need began to fade, but still I glanced towards him from the corner of my eye. With his hand behind his head and his chest completely exposed, he was truly... beautiful.

Without warning or a real understanding of my own actions, I moved towards him. I pressed my lips against his in a gentle touch. The feeling was electric, setting my blood on fire once more, but I didn't push for more than just that touch.

His lips trembled slightly under mine in surprise, before finally offering me the slightest bit of pressure in return. His hand reached to cradle my head as I pulled away.

"Thank you for protecting me tonight," I whispered.

He hovered there, staring at me while we shared each other's breath, listening to the rain fall outside, before he finally swallowed and nodded. I moved to turn back to my side once more, content to settle myself into sleep, but his arms locked around me again, tight and restricting.

"Is that from tonight?" he questioned, golden eyes staring at my throat.

I frowned, unsure of his meaning until I remembered that in his loose shirt, the bruise from his father's bite was fully visible.

"No, but I'm fine." The words flew out in a suspicious rush that left him raising an eyebrow at me while I lifted a hand to hide the evidence of the Dragon's crime. "It's nothing."

"Who did that, Thea?" His voice was like death, or at least the promise of it.

I chewed on my lip, unable to bring life to the words. It wasn't for the Dragon's benefit that I kept my silence. I owed it to Clay. He had protected me from the Alchemist, so the least I could do was to protect him from yet another incident where his father had failed to do the right thing.

In the end, though, I didn't have to say anything. Clay already knew the kind of man his father was.

His eyes darkened as he continued staring at the bruise.

"I'll speak with him. He won't do that to you again."

I wanted to pull away, to insist that I was fine and that he shouldn't cause trouble on my behalf, but he pulled at me suddenly until he was on his back and I was draped over his chest. We sat like that for a long while. I lost myself in the sound of his breathing and the comforting way his fingers traced circles over my shoulder. As the effects of the drug began to waver and the reality of the world crushed back into me, I couldn't help where my thoughts lingered.

"Not even you can protect me from him, Clay."

CHAPTER NINETEEN

My trials for ascending to the Council would be threefold. First, I would take a written examination encompassing Descendent history and world geography. They would expect me to know details from the time when the Gods walked among us to the present day and be able to genealogically map each line of Descendants back to their original godly ancestor.

Once that was complete, I would face the physical examination. As a Council member, I would be well-guarded throughout my life, but I was still expected to be adept at defending myself in hand-to-hand combat should I ever need to enter a battlefield.

My last test would be a trial of my powers, custom-designed for me by the reigning Council members. No two trials were the same, each was specifically designed to challenge that person's unique strengths and weaknesses. To pass, I'd have to rely on my magic. Failure often meant severe injury or death.

My life lately seemed to be in jeopardy more often than not, though.

With the Peace Ball successfully concluded and Athenia no longer hosting visiting dignitaries, there was more pressure than ever to prepare for my trials. The Dragon had made his opinion on my timeline abundantly clear.

After we had returned to the castle, Clay and I had gone our separate ways. And since then, I spent my days in hours of tutoring and power training sessions. The date for my first trial had yet to be set, but I constantly felt its impending weight. Which meant studying and practicing magic wasn't enough. I needed to begin training physically.

Rankor had graciously volunteered to help me, though I suspected he was more than happy to take on the role. To prepare for actual fighting, I'd been required to spend time with him in the castle's training area, working to build strength and endurance. He would force me to stretch my legs and arms into ungodly positions before dropping into dozens of squats and lunges. When my legs burned with such ferocity that I was sure I couldn't push myself off the ground, he'd hand me a set of weighted stones and order me to lift from my arms.

He assured me he typically wouldn't force a full-body approach, but the timing of my trials required that I build muscle mass as soon as possible. While that was likely true, I suspected he just enjoyed seeing me squirm. The workouts often left my muscles screaming by the end of the day, but slowly, I had gotten stronger. And Rankor had noticed.

So, I had woken to a note under my door indicating it was finally time for my first lesson in hand-to-hand combat. I dressed in the same versatile garments I wore on the mountain with Ryla and braided my hair into two tight plaits. As I entered the training space, with guards trailing behind me, Rankor strode over to me with an appraising eye.

"I was worried you'd show up in a gown," he laughed, rubbing his hands together mischievously.

He wore loose trousers and left his chest bare. As he greeted me, he slung a towel over his shoulder. His overgrown hair was damp with sweat and already beginning to curl around his ears. As we began a warm-up to loosen our muscles before the lesson, the room filled. I had long since adjusted to being subjected to the prying eyes of the court, but at that moment, it wasn't just me they were looking at.

They peered at Iris too.

I had never doubted that Kent and Rankor, two esteemed members of the Athenian military, would be skilled fighters, but Iris was surprisingly adept as she sparred with Kent. She flittered around quickly, easily evading each punch and kick until finally, with one sure-footed step onto his thigh, she climbed him entirely, swinging her leg over his head and twisting until he fell to the floor. Then, without hesitation, she rolled, placing herself neatly atop him and wrapping her five delicate fingers around his throat.

"I win!"

Kent huffed as if he wasn't thrilled about the fight's result, but eventually, he nodded and yielded. She bounced off him with glee and offered a hand down for help.

"It's because she's a fairy," Rankor explained. "The air doesn't ground her as much as it does the rest of us, so she can move quicker. You saw her speed, right?"

I nodded.

"On your trial, you'll be barred from using your powers. Before the test, they'll give you a transfusion of mortal blood, which will dull your magic. The effects are only temporary, but effective nonetheless. So you'll need to learn to defend yourself without any magic."

I shivered against the memory of my night at the Alchemist's estate. Rankor might not know it, but I was intimately aware of the effects mortal blood could have on me, and that fact alone motivated me more than anything to take his lesson seriously.

If I was ever trapped without my powers again, I wanted to defend myself in the way I hadn't that night.

Rankor instructed me to practice punching, and I nodded. Using Iris' movements as a guide, I matched her stance and threw my weight into my right hand, determined to prove I could be good at this. Before I could make contact with his extended palm, though, he ducked out of the way with a disappointed frown.

"You throw shit like that, and you're going to break a hand," he criticized, grasping onto my wrist. "Here, like this."

Carefully, he untucked my thumb from within my fist and guided me through holding my wrist steady and where to ground my weight. The movement came naturally after a few practice rounds, and my trainer gave me approving nods in no time.

For the next hour, Rankor issued commands. After teaching me how to jab, he moved on to various forms of punches and kicks. Eventually, he moved to more complex maneuvers, like the one Iris had used to beat Kent.

I took the information in greedily. My magic lessons had become dull and too easy. My history lessons were dry and outdated. But *this?* Learning how to use my body after too many close calls of men trying to take advantage of it made me feel... powerful. I poured months of frustration and anger into each new combination he taught me, and I learned it all quickly, desperate to become proficient.

"I must say," he noted with raised brows. "You are surprisingly adept at this."

"Thanks," I grumbled, chest heaving with exertion.

While I might have some natural skill at combat, it was abundantly apparent that my cardiovascular health was still not up to snuff. Rankor noticed me clutching the cramp in my side and rolled his eyes before announcing that daily runs were in order.

"Ew," Lorelai groaned as she strode next to where I huffed by the pool of drinking water. "There's not enough gold in the kingdom to get me to go on daily runs."

I suppressed a laugh as I glanced at her, and Rankor sighed dramatically in disgust.

"You can't wear that!"

While most people wore simple training garments of thick trousers and form-fitting shirts, Lorelai wore a rose-colored dress, cut at her mid-thighs.

Her fiery red hair had been expertly twisted and knotted into an elaborate braid, giving her a fierce and still feminine mohawk-style updo. Even her shoes, the same leather boots we all wore, were recently shined. She chuckled as a mischievous smile danced on her lips.

"I'm only here because Clayton insists."

"We've been doing this for years, Lori," Rankor whined. "Maybe for once you could be a good sport."

She only shrugged half-heartedly and filled a glass with water as my eyes bounced between them.

"Years?" I asked.

"Since we were kids." Lorelai nodded. "Clayton had to train every day growing up before his trials, and at first, we just came because he was here. But then Kent and Rankor were tabbed for the military, and Iris was recruited as a spy. So, training became required for them all, and Clay refused to let me sit out."

Rankor rolled his eyes and launched into a rant about the importance of physical fitness and healthy practices. He eventually trailed off, throwing his hands up in exasperation once he realized he wouldn't get through to her.

Determined not to lose the interest of another mentee, he forced me to return my attention to the hanging sandbag to practice my newly learned skills. He prattled on to Lorelai, trying to get her to participate, but she simply stood sipping her water absentmindedly with a hand on her hip, and her eyes zeroed in on Iris, who was expertly flipping on and off high ropes.

"She's really something, huh?" She mused appreciatively to herself, her voice barely more than a whisper.

Iris caught her gaze and winked with a grin, and I couldn't help but mirror it as I glanced between them. Rankor demanded I 'get focused,' and

I returned my attention to my training, but a spark of glee at what I'd just overseen between the two of them still filled me.

Eventually, the locals seemed to have soaked their fill at seeing the Descendant of Hyrax train and they left. They all bowed their heads graciously as they went, even though I barely knew them. I flushed crimson every time someone said their goodbyes to me.

I would never adjust to all this notoriety.

And finally, after Rankor had drilled twelve different offensive maneuvers into my brain and I felt like my arms and legs would fall off at any moment, he announced that I'd done well and should get washed up for dinner.

Thank the Gods.

"Miss Moore!" called a familiarly angry voice, and I stiffened against the sound of it.

Clay strode in with an edge of irritation painted on his brow. Wearing a simple white shirt and gray trousers, he barked that the room was closed for the day, effectively dismissing the remaining lords, ladies and courts people until only he, I, and our frowning friends remained. His eyes twinkled golden, and I grit my teeth in frustration and anticipation of what would come next.

I could only assume this anger was lingering from the night I had snuck out to the Alchemist's estate. I hadn't spoken to him since we had returned from the inn, but it seemed our time apart had done nothing to calm him. The dragon in him had awoken, and it had marked me as its target.

"You'd be impressed," Rankor announced, clapping a hand down on Clay's shoulder as if he was oblivious to the barely contained wrath rolling off our prince. "Our little telekinetic here is quite the natural."

Clayton's eyes narrowed at me and the corner of his lip turned up devilishly. "I'll decide that."

"Oh?" I questioned, voice shaking as I suddenly remembered the last time he had looked at me like that.

It had been while he whispered how thoroughly he had wanted to fuck me. And then I'd practically begged him to do it.

Was he remembering the same thing? Was that why the skin at his fingertips was slowly blackening?

He inclined his head to the sparring arena where Kent and Iris were toweling themselves off.

"My father set your trial dates for four months from now," he announced. My friends exchanged worried glances, but Clay continued, attention solely on me. "Perhaps you might benefit from practicing with the person who's actually passed them before."

My adrenaline spiked. Clayton Vail, Crown Prince of Athenia, who had trained for battle his entire life, who looked like a God had personally carved every muscle in his body, wanted me, who had just learned how to throw a punch, to fight him.

I was going to die.

Camilla snorted as she strode into the room to join us. "Clearly I came just in time."

Kent, ever the mediator, was quick to notice the fear etched on my face and stepped close.

"Clay, don't you think that might be pushing her too fast?" He asked, his voice soft and reasonable.

"I don't recall asking for guidance from my subjects!" Clay barked, looking so much like his father that I shivered. What had gotten into him today? This anger couldn't all be from my sneaking out of the castle.

I didn't have time to ponder on it long though before his eyes were on mine again and my stomach was flipping in a nervous rush.

"What do you say, Princess?"

I felt the weight of all six sets of eyes bearing down on me. What did I say? No. I wanted to say no. I wanted to tell him I wasn't ready, and I knew deep down that if I said those words, he would let me decline. He would respect that.

And yet even as I opened my mouth to protest, the Mark on my chest warmed all too suddenly, as if the blood of Hyrax within me was all too unwilling to turn down this challenge. It was reckless to agree. I was wholly unprepared, after all.

But I was not created to back down.

With a fiercely determined tilt of my head, I spun on my heels without another word and walked to the sparring arena.

"Not so fast," Clay growled, reaching out and grabbing my arm. I barely had time to register what was in his hand before he stabbed the syringe into the sensitive flesh inside my elbow and injected me.

"What in all of creation was that?" I cried, ripping my arm out of his grasp.

"Mortal blood," he explained, tossing the syringe to Rankor, who caught it with a single hand. "If you're going to be tested without powers, then you'll train without them."

I bit down on my lip and the sudden urge to release a few choice words that weren't appropriate to say to your Crown Prince. Holding those in, I ripped my arm from his grasp and continued forward. If Clayton had wanted to piss me off, he could consider the mission accomplished.

I no longer cared if I was ridiculously out of my depth. If this man wanted to fight me, I would give it my all. I would fight hard and dirty if that's what it took to prove that the House of Hyrax was alive and prospering.

The effects of the mortal blood were instant. It was as if I could feel that power humming and grasping for me, but I couldn't quite take hold of it.

"Don't mess up my face," I demanded through my teeth as we took our stances.

He raised an eyebrow in surprise, and his golden eyes flickered momentarily before he shook his head and smirked. "Wouldn't dream of it. It is rather *exquisite* after all."

I was going to hurt him.

Before this was over, he was probably going to kick my ass, but at least once I was going to hurt him. That was a vow I could make to myself.

We circled for a while, each waiting for the other to make the first move. Rankor had instructed me to always play defensive at first, to wait for my opponent to strike first and use that as an opportunity to identify their weaknesses. So, I waited patiently for him to attack.

I was shorter than Clay and overall weaker, so as Rankor mentioned earlier, I needed to be faster. I also had the luxury of knowing Clay. Sometimes I felt like I knew him better than most. I knew that based on the shade of his eyes, the tension in his jaw, and the way his veins flickered black every so often that he was angry. So it was just a matter of time before his inner dragon got the best of him. That beast would draw him to take the first swing.

And maybe he would leave himself open. If I could be fast enough, I could land a hit.

So I waited, and sure enough, I saw his right-hand flex.

He punched out, and I spun to my right, kicking up my leg and drawing it down against his back in a move Rankor had taught me only moments ago. My teacher cried out happily from below us, but my attention was entirely focused on Clay.

He flinched for a minute before stepping back and punching out again. His left hand flexed, and I anticipated the jab as I did before. I raised my left arm to block, but he ducked below and swiped my gut. The pain was sharp, knocking my breath, and I huddled over, desperate to regain the air in my lungs.

Dear Gods, he was strong.

And he was not holding back.

"Clay," Iris warned from below, voice thick with concern while I contemplated the possibility if he had just broken my rib.

"Stop being so focused on my fingers," he said, voice low and meant only for me. "You're being obvious with where your attention is, making it too easy to psych you out."

He leaned down to where I hunched over as he lectured me, but my mind was only half listening to him and half preparing for my next attack. Struggling through the pain in my stomach, I gripped his shoulders and pushed his frame down to meet my rising knee before slinging that same leg behind his and kicking his feet out from under him. He fell forward, and the sound splintered throughout the room. The others gasped.

"Your grace," I wheezed. "I appreciate the advice, but perhaps now is not the time for conversation."

The gold in his eyes slowly faded as he rolled over to grin up at me while he wiped the splash of blood from his face. I was so momentarily consumed by my small victory that I didn't notice his leg quickly flying out and knocking me off my feet. I fell to the ground all too suddenly. My arms stung from my feeble attempts to catch myself, and I cried out involuntarily as my still-healing knee took the bulk of my weight.

"Maybe if you listened better, Miss Moore, you wouldn't have just lost the fight."

He moved all at once, twisting from where he laid next to me. I tried to react, rolling over and preparing to jump up, but I couldn't match his speed as hard as I tried. He was on top of me in a moment, straddling me and pinning my arms above my head with a firm, one-handed grip. His eyes had now retreated to their familiar gray color completely, and a taunting grin danced on his features.

"Tap out," he instructed, not bothering to hide his satisfaction.

For a moment, I lay there frozen. His grip on my arms was tight, pulling them to the point that my back arched. My breasts lifted toward him with each strained breath I took. His hips pressed down onto mine with distracting heat and his free hand rested on my midriff, delicately touching the skin that was exposed from where my shirt had lifted.

"Tap out," he whispered, his voice low and heavy. "Or do you just enjoy being underneath me?"

I knew I was blushing. I could feel the heat of it as Clay's gaze trailed down my body. Without meaning to, I arched once more, shifting my hips underneath him and feeling him stiffen above me. There was no drug in my system now to blame for my brazenness. I had only myself to blame for the way I responded to him.

"Are you going to deny that *you* enjoy being on top of me?"

"I see no sense in denying that." He chuckled, tongue darting out across his lips. "But if we stay here much longer, people will begin to talk, so admit you've lost."

People were already talking. In some corner of my mind, I was dimly aware of the sound of Kent whistling and Lorelai clearing her throat.

At some level, I knew continuing to fight him was pointless; Clay was a foot taller than me and nearly twice as broad. I couldn't possibly overpower him, especially not from this position. He had, in fact, beaten me.

But I couldn't give up.

"No," I insisted, surprised by the heat in my voice.

"You've lost, Thea. Just admit it."

I couldn't. I couldn't surrender this fight, just as I couldn't admit the truth of how much his body against mine was affecting me.

"Get *off!*" I cried out, and my magic roared to life suddenly, soaring past the invisible barrier within me, rushing to my fingers and pulsing out.

Clay's eyes widened as it hit him and carried him off me until he crashed into the wall. The thud echoed as he bounced onto the floor, sending me scurrying back in confusion.

That was not supposed to have happened.

The room was quiet and still until Rankor laughed excitedly. The others gave soft, nervous smiles and applause after him, but I stayed frozen on the floor.

"Guess you didn't dose her hard enough!" Rankor explained, clapping his hands together.

Clay's eyes flashed, clearly not thrilled at my using my powers against him for a second time, but he stood and offered a hand down to me. "You let your magic get the better of you. Even if the dose wasn't enough, you should always be in control of your powers. Not the other way around."

I nodded, relishing the familiar tingle of my power spreading throughout my fingers. "I'll take note of that."

"Well?" Kent asked, waving his arms wide. "What do you think?"

Clay shrugged, accepting a towel from Iris and brushing it over his face. He turned his attention to Rankor. "She has some natural skill, but it'll never be enough. She needs refinement. Her endurance is pathetic, and her punches barely carry strength. The trials will be dangerous, my father will ensure that. You can't be going easy on her."

"*She's* right here," I reminded them, feeling the burn of Camilla's gaze searing into my back.

Iris giggled and bounced forward to take my arm into hers as she began leading me away from the sparring arena. "That is the closest you could have gotten to a compliment, my dear! Which I think that calls for celebration, and I know just how. You see, there is a lake that's not far behind the palace, but very private. As teenagers, we had a tendency to steal the palace liquor and go swimming for hours."

Clay barked a laugh in a momentary show of normality that managed to steal my breath.

Gods what was wrong with me?

"It's a wonder we never got caught!" He grinned. "Could you imagine the gossip?"

Lorelai smiled softly. "As if that was the worst thing you were doing back in those days?"

My attention wandered suddenly to what kinds of trouble teenage Clay had found himself in as we made our way out the castle's doors toward the gardens. Camilla grinned over at him with a tauntingly knowing expression and I fought the urge to gag.

Suddenly, I decided I actually didn't want to know what kinds of trouble he engaged in.

"Thea just survived her first Dragon fight," Rankor reminded us. "I agree with Iris. I say it's high time for her to receive a proper induction into the group with a trip out to the old lake. What do you say?"

We all exchanged glances with each other. I shrugged my interest, a cheerful grin spreading across my features. Why not? A day away from the palace politics seemed like exactly what I needed.

Kent raised his eyebrows. "I don't know. It's been years."

Iris grinned, already beginning to beeline for the woods. "We will only be this young and beautiful for so long, my friends. It is now or never!"

We weren't far outside before I realized I had left my overcoat in the gym. Iris offered to come back with me to retrieve it, but I waved her off. They were having too much fun with each other at that moment for me to interrupt them. So, I encouraged them to continue without me and promised I would catch up. Clay's eyes swept over me, and I knew he wanted to protest that I needed protection, but I jogged away before he could say anything.

I would be gone for only a moment before I caught up with them again.

As I walked the stone path back to the palace, I noticed Geia and Nessira in the gardens, picking flowers for my room as I passed. I smiled and waved at them happily.

"Roses!" I called. "Get roses this time, please."

After my day of fighting and training, my arms and legs ached with each step toward the glass doors of the castle, but I kept on at an even speed. Each sting of soreness was a reminder that I was doing okay. Every day without an update about my past left me wondering if I would ever get the answers I desired, but I had finally started getting a grasp on my powers and building friendships that meant the world to me. I may not have known my past, but at least I was finally starting to feel a bit more confident in my future.

The training room was empty as I returned, the candles burning dimly. I hurried to my overcoat, where it sat on the table next to the water pool, eager to return to my friends before they disappeared into the woods behind the castle. As I began making towards the door, though, I stilled.

Something was wrong.

It was a feeling in my gut, a premonition of a sort. Perhaps it was the stillness in the air, the utter silence, or the scent of something burning. Whatever it was, my magic rushed over me in a sudden warning so strong that I nearly stumbled under the weight of it.

RUN! A voice in my head commanded.

Without knowing why, I sprinted, pushing my legs as hard as possible, but I simply wasn't fast enough.

I heard the explosion before I genuinely felt it wash over me. It was a deafening crack that echoed through my skull as I went catapulting through the air. I crashed into the wall, feeling the bone in my wrist snap clean as I screamed. My head smashed against the stone, and I felt consciousness fade for a moment.

The pain was unlike anything I'd ever felt before as I landed heavily on the ground. My stomach railed, threatening to reject this morning's breakfast and darkness danced on the edge of my vision. I grit my teeth as I clutched onto consciousness.

I was dead if I fainted.

Instinctively, I threw up my hands, throwing out magic tendrils as hard and recklessly as I could. As the flames of the blast rushed towards me, I braced myself and felt them slap sharply against the barrier that I had managed to create around me with my magic.

I held for a moment there, sweat beginning to bead on my brow as the air became too thick to breathe. I coughed and the motion sent spikes of pain shooting through my skull.

I couldn't hold this. Already, I was buckling under the force of the blast and the pain of my broken wrist. My arms shook as my shield faltered, and the burning tendrils reached toward me. One slipped past far enough to kiss the skin of my ankle, and I screamed once more, desperate to push it back away.

The pain in my head was practically unbearable.

Do not pass out. I told myself. *Do not pass out, or you will die.*

Tears fell loosely across my cheeks as my magic slowly began to fail me. I grasped onto it wildly, but it was sputtering and weakening. The smell of ash powered through the room, invading my nose and senses as the heat of the flames left me drenched in sweat.

I was going to lose control of my magic at any moment.

Desperately, I looked around me for some sort of physical protection. With the last of my strength, I launched the rest of the magic that coursed through my veins to drag the stone tables by the water pool to me. I grunted against the weight of them as I summoned them to me, propping one in front and one above me as a makeshift shelter.

There was a momentary relief as I let go of the weakening magic before the smoke invaded my lungs. I was coughing again. Huddled under my shelter, clutching my arm to my chest, I was coughing like I had been after the witch's hex bag had cursed me.

Whoever had done this may have failed in their first attempt, but they wouldn't on their second.

The shelter wasn't enough. Already, the flames were breaking through. They latched onto my ankle once more, and this time I didn't even have the strength to cry out.

I was going to die.

The knowledge was sudden and resolute.

"Thea?"

I blinked once, twice, pulling myself haphazardly back towards consciousness. Clay? My ears were ringing. I couldn't be sure of what I was hearing. Perhaps it was only my mind playing tricks on me. In the moments before death, perhaps we hear the promise of hope when it doesn't truly exist.

Clayton wasn't here. I was alone. I was going to burn, alone, here in the fire. Closing my eyes again, I gasped in a last breath of oxygen.

"Theadora!"

There he was again, his voice calling out to me, closer now.

His fingers wrapped around the table's edge above me and he threw it across the room as if it weighed nothing at all. Panic filled his golden eyes and I was in his arms within moments.

"I'm here," he whispered to me.

And he was. He was strong, and he carried me away from that place. He held me gently even as his legs kicked the broken furniture that blocked our path.

"The fire?" I asked, concern for him breaking through the pounding in my head.

"I breathe fire," he mumbled in explanation. "It can't burn me."

I laughed softly at that. Of course. Dragons don't burn.

As I laid my head on his shoulder, everything faded away.

CHAPTER TWENTY

The cool brush of fresh air against my tender skin was the first thing I noticed as the world came into focus again. I was lying on the grass outside, surrounded by friends, as one of the palace nurses tended to my wounds. Camilla leaned against Kent, who rubbed up and down her back. Rankor had thrown an arm around Iris, who chewed at her nails nervously while Lorelai clenched her other hand.

I tried to speak up, to tell them I was okay, but the smoke had left my throat tender and burnt. Somewhere in the distance, I could hear the Dragon barking orders to close the damaged wing of the palace until repairs could be made and an investigation completed.

The nurse was stoic as she examined my injuries, giving reports to Clay. "She's got some burns on her arms and will probably be bruised tomorrow. I've begun healing her broken wrist, but that will take some time."

"Your recommendation?" Clay questioned, his voice stern and commanding.

"She should stay in the hospital wing for a few nights. Just to be sure that healing goes well."

I coughed, desperate to find my voice once more. "No."

Someone had just tried to blow me up. The castle's southern wing was a shamble of blackened wood and still lingering embers. There was no way I was spending a night in an infirmary full of strangers. Not when the person responsible for all this was still a mystery.

I would sleep in my own bed.

"Thea," Clay warned, clearly uninterested in entertaining any of my protests.

"Clay," I echoed him. "I'm fine. It's just a headache, and my wrist already feels much better. Iris can stay and look out for me if you'd like, but I'm going to my rooms."

"You were just in an explosion," he reminded me. "Let me see to it that you're taken care of."

Needing to prove that I was okay, I pulled myself up and stood on shaking legs. Despite my determination, though, standing sent waves of pain up my hips and back from where I had crashed against the wall. Was she sure I hadn't injured myself worse than a few bruises?

I touched the tender skin and, as I winced against the sudden pain, I blinked and saw that room once more. I heard the voice urging me to run. I felt the wind brushing across my skin as I was blown back through the air.

"Clay," I whimpered as he grasped my waist to catch me from falling. "I'm not going to the infirmary, and unless you want the entire court to see us engage in an argument over it, then you'll announce that sleeping in my own bed will be good for me and help me to my rooms."

He arched that infuriating eyebrow at me and it was all I could do to sigh and attempt to keep myself standing. His arms tightened to take on more of my weight as I leaned heavily against him. I was close to tears, and I didn't want the others to see that.

"Please, Clay," I whispered, turning towards him and away from prying eyes. "Please, just take me home."

I wasn't quite sure when I'd started to think of it as home.

Our gazes tangled together. I saw his irritation with me, but also his worry and confusion. I wondered what he could see written on my face.

"On second thought," he finally sighed. "Perhaps Lady Moore would feel more comfortable in her own bed tonight. Iris will stay with her and Nurse Kira, you will check in on her again tomorrow morning while the Council discusses this matter. The rest of you can go home."

I squeezed his hand as a thank you, and he didn't hesitate to lift me into his arms once more. On any other day, I might have insisted that I walk on my own, but I didn't. I simply buried my face in his neck, breathed in the scent of him, and allowed him to take me through the gardens, into the palace, and down the hall of Hyrax. The ever-watching eyes all bowed their heads as we passed. Iris followed behind us silently, and eventually, the three of us crossed into the safety of my suites. Clay kicked the door closed behind him with a resounding thunk.

He didn't let go of me while he sat on the couch in the foyer.

He didn't let go of me while I reached for Iris' hand.

He didn't let go of me when I finally released the emotions I had held back and allowed my sobs to echo throughout the room.

CHAPTER TWENTY-ONE

*T*he stench of sulfur was overwhelming, burning my nose and gagging me. Struggling to ignore it, I pulled my cloak tighter and looked around me. I'd been here before so many times. I knew these rock caverns with their winding tunnels and icy chill as clearly as I knew the hall of Hyrax at the palace. As I twisted through the endless maze, I traced my hands along the stone walls, recounting my previous steps until I was back in that room with the throne of skulls. Somehow, even though I knew he would be here waiting for me, his presence caught my breath again.

"Back again so soon?" He asked, combing a hand through his gray hair with a mischievous and knowing smile. He lounged in his chair, the picture of relaxation, with one leg kicked over the other and his hands thrown proudly over the armrests.

"I suppose," I replied curtly, joining him at the table again.

That's where I was supposed to be. At least, I think that's where he wanted me to be.

He pushed forward a chalice of wine, and with a wave of his palm and a rush of magic, the same eerie music that filled the air during my first visit returned once more. He must have liked it to play it so much, but I didn't personally care for the melody. It raised the hairs on my arms and neck, leaving me uncomfortable and on edge.

"And why have you visited me tonight, my dear?"

"I didn't."

Why in all of creation would anyone choose to return to a nightmare?

He pursed his lips. A smile danced on his features. "No? You're here, aren't you? There must be something you need from me. Something those friends of yours can't provide. Not even that so-called Prince."

His voice had darkened, betraying his disdain, and I titled my head, questioning. "Clay?"

Anger flashed in his eyes as I said Clay's name, and the air chilled suddenly. Instinctively, I flinched away from him, but his rage was gone within a moment, as if I had imagined it entirely. The temperature warmed again, and the music picked up in tempo. He leaned back in his chair, playful once more, and crossed his arms behind his head. He grinned widely at me.

How strange.

"Yes, Clayton Vail, of House Zion." He tsked his tongue disapprovingly. "You two have gotten quite close."

"I suppose we are friends."

"Is friendship all you feel towards him?"

I frowned, partially because the question felt too personal to be coming from a stranger and partially because I wasn't sure if I knew the answer.

"Come now," he sighed. "You must know that a son of Zion will never love the daughter of Hyrax."

Frustrated, I looked anywhere but at him, ignoring his words.

Why was I here? Night after night, I dreamt of this place. Sometimes, I walked the caverns for what felt like hours with nothing of importance to remember. It mattered not whether I had a good day or a terrible one. Nothing I did in my waking life could keep me from this underground hell.

What was so special about this place, this man, that it would constantly invade my dreams?

"Who are you?" I mused, leaning forward and resting my elbows on the table before us.

"Who am I?" He laughed, slapping a hand against his chest in mock offense. "I'm the one person in all the realms who truly cares for you. Clayton won't, not as I can. You must understand that the Descendants of Zion will always stand in opposition to those of Hyrax. This is a fact that has prevailed since the Gods began having children."

"You make it sound as if we have no free will in this. As if we are nothing more than victims of the animosities of our ancestors."

"Perhaps you are not so far removed from Hyrax as you imagine. The Descendants are already intrigued by you. How long until that intrigue becomes fear? Hatred, even. They will turn on you as they turned on your God."

"No!" I cried, standing so suddenly that my magic launched out and threw my chair across the room. It splintered against the stone and fractured. The man stood as I did, his eyes gleaming with as much passion as I felt.

"You don't need them to be strong, Theadora! You were strong before they ever found you."

"I was trying to kill people when they found me!"

He laughed, the sound echoing across the cavern and creating a piercing pitch that surrounded me and had me covering my ears in desperation.

"There is still so much you have yet to understand. So much knowledge you are still holding yourself back from."

"That's not true!" I insisted, hating the fact that I sounded like a petulant child.

He looked over at me with exasperation before finally running a hand over his face, falling back into his seat, and summoning a new chair for me with a wave of his hand. As I stood motionless, he sighed and pointed towards it. Grinding my teeth, I sat.

"You don't believe me," he noted. "I understand why you don't. These people mean something to you. This Clayton means something to you. I had hoped you would trust me, that you wouldn't have to learn these lessons the hard way."

"What do you mean? Nothing you say makes any sense."

"It will in time, child. In time, the Descendants of Zion will show you their cruelty. They're all the same. They have destroyed everything the House of Hyrax has held dear throughout history. I don't want to watch them destroy you."

He lifted his wineglass, twirling the stem in his fingers as he stared at the scarlet liquid thoughtfully. For a moment, we sat in silence, each pondering over what the other had said.

"Clay won't hurt me," I insisted, finally.

I knew that in my soul. Clay had shown me time and time again that he would keep me safe. Even if his dedication to me was because of nothing more than my bloodline, he had proven that I could trust him.

"I know you believe that." The man breathed. "I believe otherwise. As I said before, a son of Zion will never love the daughter of Hyrax. You are headstrong though, you will need to see their barbarity for yourself. I wish that wasn't the case, but I hope when you do see it, you will finally trust my advice."

"And what is your advice?"

"Stay away from Clayton Vail."

CHAPTER TWENTY-TWO

I woke from the nightmare suddenly, damp with sweat and scratching absentmindedly at the Mark on my chest. Were these nightmares some kind of manifestation of guilt over what had happened that day on the bridge? If so, what would it take to rid myself of them? They had plagued me for weeks and left me waking up shivering, terrified, and confused. I wasn't sure how much longer I could take them. Perhaps an infirmary nurse might be able to offer something to help me sleep...

I glanced towards the foyer where candlelight was still dimly visible and I could make out the sounds of Clay and Iris speaking softly. I must not have been asleep for long. I shifted in the bed, preparing to join them, but stilled as I heard my name.

"Are we going to talk about Thea?" Iris asked with a sharpness that I was unaccustomed to hearing from her.

Clay sighed heavily. "Iris, I love you dearly, but not tonight."

And even though I couldn't see into the room enough to actually see them, I could picture them so clearly in my head. Iris stood, one hip popped out, and her arms crossed over her chest. Clay, exhausted from the stress of the day, sank into the velveteen chair. He pinched the bridge of his nose between his forefinger and thumb as his shoulders slumped.

Iris snorted. "Oh, yes tonight. I will not pretend I didn't see that petrified look on your face when you carried her out of the blast!"

"Of course I was scared!" He replied, voice raised.

For a moment, there was silence while they waited to see if they had woken me. My better sense told me I should stand and alert them to the fact that I was, in fact, awake. It simply wasn't appropriate for me to eavesdrop on them.

And yet, I did not stand.

"You didn't see her in there," Clay continued, voice softer. "She held back a wall of fire with her magic alone, Iris. She barely had the time to pull a barricade over herself before collapsing. And when I finally got to her, she passed out before we even made it out of the building. By the Gods, I didn't know if she had just died right then and there in my arms."

I'd never heard Clay sound quite so... unsteady. I waited, listening only to my breathing and my blood pumping in my ears. Until finally, after what felt like an eternity, Iris sighed.

"Anyone would have been afraid, Clayton. I'm not saying you shouldn't have been. But that's not my point."

"Then what is?" He demanded.

"You know what my point is, Clay! I'm asking if you were afraid because she's a royal bloodline or because of something else?"

"You don't know what you're talking about."

"I don't? Who knows you better than I do? I see the way you look at her, Clay! And it's only a matter of time before she figures it out, too. Do you truly think your father isn't aware of it? How do you think he will respond?"

"I am abundantly aware of my father's... *fascination* with her."

Iris didn't respond. It was quiet for some time.

His *fascination* with me? What did that mean?

"My father has been insufferable since she arrived. He talks of her non-stop. You can't even imagine the things he says, Iris, the things he wants to do to her. It's taking everything in me to keep the two of them apart. It doesn't matter though. She knows how dangerous he can be, and she's entirely unafraid of him."

I shivered. It's not that I was unafraid of the Dragon. I would have to be an idiot not to realize what he was capable of. But respect couldn't be earned through creating fear. The Dragon didn't have my respect, I wouldn't pretend that he did.

"She's so recklessly brave," Clay continued, voice thick with emotion. "Did I tell you I found her at the Alchemist's party? I swear to the Gods I wasn't sure if I was more infuriated by her lack of self-regard or impressed by her determination. I'm so fucking grateful he didn't find out about that. You know what he would have done."

"I do," Iris whispered.

"And it's not just that bravery that manages to amaze me. It's the fact that against all odds, she's created a home for herself here. You all love her. The dignitaries loved her. By the Gods, the entire kingdom is ready to worship at her feet, and she couldn't care less. I don't even think she realizes how completely enamored everyone is with her. She has no interest in the power or fame that comes with her title and only gives respect to those she feels have earned it.

"I have lived my entire life in this castle surrounded by people who will do or say anything to win my favor. I have watched them try to manipulate me or manipulate my father through me in order to win status. But Thea isn't like that. I'm not accustomed to the way she treats me."

I stilled. Clay rarely spoke this openly and honestly. The only other time I'd ever seen him let down his guard so wholly was when he told me the story of his mother's death. This was a version of the Prince he rarely let others see.

It was a version that he allowed Iris to see because she was his family.

It was a version that he had allowed me to see.

When I arrived in Athenia, Clay had been abrasive. He'd told me so clearly that he didn't care about my wishes and only wanted me to play my role. He had sounded so much like his father in those early days. Just like the Dragon, he had demanded respect for a position he'd been born into and hadn't seemed to earn, and part of me hated him for that.

I didn't hate him for it anymore, though.

At some point, I'd realized Clay *did* deserve my respect.

He wasn't his father. He was a man who cared for others more than himself and he'd allowed me the rare privilege of seeing the man under the crown. It was true that he could be demanding and controlling, but it was also true that he thought that was the best way to keep his loved ones safe.

Shared respect wasn't the only thing that had changed between us, though. We'd exchanged looks across ballrooms where we'd communicated silently with each other. We'd shared secrets and confessions while locked away in a bedroom we never should have been alone in together. We'd slept peacefully in each other's arms.

No, I didn't hate Clayton Vail anymore.

But I could never be anything more than his friend.

Iris was right in saying that we had other responsibilities. Clay and I would end up married to other people. He was a Prince from House Zion and I was the matriarch of House Hyrax. We were leaders of the houses of two Gods at complete odds with each other.

A son of Zion will never love the daughter of Hyrax.

Chewing on my lower lip, I pulled the covers to my neck and turned away from their voices. My head was still pounding, and overhearing this conversation left me with even more questions about my status at the palace. As I faded out of consciousness once more, I could just make out their voices, ending the conversation.

"If I'd known you had such a thing for blondes, I could have set you up with Sheila Waters while we were completing our studies," Iris quipped.

Clay chuckled darkly. "Sheila Waters was bitchy and high-maintenance."

"Most mermaids are."

CHAPTER TWENTY-THREE

I slept late into the morning the next day, and when I finally woke, Iris was still happily resting next to me, leaving me to wonder how long they had stayed awake talking after I had fallen back asleep. I didn't check to see if Clay was still in my foyer; in my gut, I knew he was. So, instead, I took the brief moment of privacy to draw myself a warm bath. I took my time scrubbing off the marks of yesterday's attack until my skin was red and raw and my fingertips were pruning. I didn't want to see a single reminder of what had happened.

After what felt like an eternity of scrubbing, I combed through my hair and folded myself into a thick midnight blue robe that Nessira had hung on the door. But although my body was clean, my thoughts were still terribly muddy.

Would I ever be safe in this castle? Clearly, whoever wanted me dead was willing to go to extraordinary lengths to ensure it.

The rest of our circle had arrived while I bathed, bringing breakfast treats. The smell of bacon was overwhelming as I stepped into my foyer and greeted each of them with gentle hugs. As I gazed over the cart stacked tall with an arrangement of fruits, cakes, and breakfast meats, I almost dissolved into tears once more. Usually, I'd protest the special treatment, but my growling stomach prevented me from being too stubborn, and I took the plate that Kent handed me gratefully.

"How are you feeling?" He asked as he stacked a steaming pile of pancakes high on my plate for me. I smiled my thanks as I folded into the couch next to Lorelai and avoided eye contact with Clay.

"After the attack or after Rankor's workout?"

The room chuckled, and Rankor winked at me from where he sat folded with his elbows on his knees. "Just wait until the next one. Now that you can handle your own with a Dragon, I know I need to step things up."

"She cheated," Clay grumbled.

My back went rigid at the sound of his voice, but I kept my focus on the plate in front of me as they chatted about the palace repairs and made jokes to lighten the mood. I appreciated their efforts, but there were only two places my mind was willing to be today, and I wasn't interested in spiraling over Clay and what I may or may not feel for him.

"So what's next?" I asked, sharply. "This is the second attack by a Witch. Surely, that won't go unpunished."

Camilla, who sat perched on an armrest of a chair next to Kent, rolled her eyes dramatically. "You have no proof a Witch is responsible for this latest attack."

Clay frowned, his jaw working to contain his frustration, though for once it didn't seem directed at Camilla. I suspected he felt angered by still not being able to identify the attacker. Finally, he sighed, folded one leg over his knee, and resignedly raised a hand. "She's right. An explosion like that could very well be from a Detonator of House Arto."

Iris sighed as she met my eyes. "Two attacks on a Royal Family cannot be overlooked. It'll reflect weakness in the ability of the Dragon to protect his own castle. He'll be firmer in his investigation moving forward."

The air thickened with tension, and I noticed Rankor's eyes flicker worriedly to Camilla. She had averted her gaze, focusing instead on her cuticles, but her posture spoke volumes. It was strange to see her like that when I was so used to her haughty attitude and air of self-importance. Her hunched shoulders now told me all I needed to know about what a 'firmer investigation' meant. The Dragon would get information however he needed to, starting with another interrogation of the palace Witches.

"The court has already been assembled," Clay informed me, standing and smoothing out his clothes from where they had wrinkled in his sleep. "You'll need to speak this morning to show the world that this attack has failed and you are stronger than ever."

I suppressed the urge to laugh. I didn't feel stronger than ever. With my body aching and my heart leaping anytime Clay's tenor voice rang through the room, I felt more like a scared teenager than I did a paragon of strength. Still, I nodded in agreement. I'd been expecting the Dragon would want a statement to be made, and I knew better than to think I could fight against his wishes.

"I assume this means I'll need to wear another one of those ridiculous gowns."

His lips pursed as he fought the urge to smirk. He failed, and those full lips turned up ever so slightly, causing my stomach to somersault. "I had something delivered while you bathed."

"I'm sure you did."

And in that moment, there was only him and I.

Eventually, the others began to clear out, and Clay instructed Iris to help me dress. Surely, I would need her help and expertise to paint away the purple bruises on my arms and shoulders from the blast. She nodded to him that she would care for me just fine and rushed him out of the room. As she shut the door behind him and locked it up, I sighed a breath of relief and threw my head back against the plush velvet of the settee.

I expected her to be comforting, to ask me if I was okay or pull me into a hug, and yet when I peeked open one of my eyes to glance at her, I found her glaring down at me with a raised eyebrow and arms crossed over the fabric of her orange tulle gown.

She always dressed in such elaborately detailed clothes, with flamboyant hairstyles. Seeing her like this, in just a simple gown with her hair in its natural brown coils and no paint highlighting the peak of her cheekbones or fullness of her lips, was a startling reminder of how serious last night had been. Her gaze was unforgiving as she tapped her foot impatiently, waiting for me to say something.

"What?" I asked, attempting to sound ignorant of her meaning.

She scoffed, rolling her eyes dramatically. "Don't be coy. You're a terrible actress."

Well, yes. I was. But if only she knew that her very life often depended on my ability to perform well enough when the Dragon demanded it.

"I assure you, I do not know what you mean," I sighed, rubbing the bridge of my nose as my headache from the night before began threatening to return.

Her eyes narrowed. "I'm an Athenian Spy, Thea. My job is quite literally to tell when people are hiding things."

I stiffened immediately, then mentally chastised myself. Of course, I hadn't hidden it well. I'd clearly shown how tense I was as I looked anywhere in the room but at Clay. It didn't take any particular intelligence to figure out what had made me uncomfortable, and Iris was no fool. Kicking myself for not being more subtle and desperate to escape her inquisition, I stood and made my way to my closet, where Clay's dress hung. Perhaps if I could rush myself into it, I could end this conversation before it started.

"Well?" she demanded as she followed me through my suite, arms firm on her hips.

"Someone tried to kill me last night," I reminded her. "I'm allowed to seem a little off this morning."

Iris chuckled, and for a brief, glorious moment, I thought she might let the conversation go, but she didn't shy away from my gaze as she crossed her arms over her chest.

"I know you heard us last night."

I turned away from her, desperate to avoid the conversation, only to finally glimpse the gown Clay had chosen for me.

"Oh," I gasped.

Clay's choice of gown had surprised me once more; this time, he had left me utterly breathless.

It was stunning. The full sleeves were made of a sheer fabric that would drape off my shoulders. The tight white bodice was constructed of the most delicate lace, which met the swell of a full tulle shirt. I turned it in my hands, running my fingers over the long cape that extended from where the dress would meet my shoulder blades. It was impossibly long, and I was sure it would extend for a few feet behind me as I walked. The capes' edges had been fitted with lace and tiny, barely noticeable crystals. The Mark on my chest would be visible to all, so the Dragon would be happy. And it was elaborate enough that it would reflect my status as a royal family member, but it was far more simplistic than the formal gowns I had previously been gifted.

He had obviously considered my tastes when picking it for me.

And the thought of Clay carefully thinking over which dress I would most like to wear made me feel things I wasn't ready to give voice to.

I sighed as I ran my fingers over the soft fabric. I couldn't avoid this conversation. Not when Clay's affections for me were so clear in this choice of dress.

"Well, I hardly think you can blame me for the fact that neither of you is very good at whispering."

Wiggling her finger at me playfully, she pulled the dress off its hanger and gestured for me to disrobe so she could slip it over my head. It slid on perfectly, fitting every part of me immaculately. My shoulders straightened as she pulled the laces at my back, and I could only imagine how I looked.

"The bruises?" I asked, noticing where they were visible through the sheer fabric.

"Let them see," Iris practically growled. "Show the world it'll take more than that to knock you down."

We were quiet then as she laced the gown tightly and began twisting my hair out of my face. Finally, she wrapped a diamond diadem onto my head and gently smoothed a sparkling powder onto my collar bones. It brought your eye directly to my Descendant's Mark and the bruises surrounding it. I knew that wasn't a coincidence. She remained focused on her work, and I didn't dare interrupt. What was left to even say?

After she finished she retreated to my bed-chamber, where she fell into the sheets of my bed. Seeing the dark circles under her eyes was easier without her regular extravagancies. She was exhausted. Iris was like her cousin in that way, always hiding her true feelings behind a mask. Where he took on the role of a somber diplomat, she hid behind her boisterous fashions and makeup. I wondered if we were all hiding behind something.

"You know, Dragons have taken mistresses before," she whispered, as I laid back beside her.

"With other Council members?"

The idea of being anyone's mistress didn't particularly thrill me, but I doubted it was even possible for me. Clay's duties weren't the only ones in question here. I had responsibilities of my own. I doubted I could serve as a mistress outside of my eventual marriage and have children with questionable parentage. No, there could be no doubt as to the bloodline of my children. So, while it may be okay for a male king to take another lover, it would never be acceptable for me.

She frowned. "Well, Theadora, just you being here, years after the extinction of House Hyrax, is already accomplishing the impossible. Who's to say you can't or won't continue to establish new norms?"

"And *that's* the groundbreaking change I want to accomplish? Serving as a king's common whore?"

She flinched at my words, and for the first time since I arrived in Athenia I felt a mask settle over *me*.

I couldn't just be Thea. Not anymore. Not after everything that had happened. I needed to be the leader of my House.

"This is not up for discussion, Iris. And I would appreciate if you were not to repeat what we have said here."

Her brow furrowed with what almost looked like disappointment as she took in my tone. After a moment, she bowed her head respectfully. "Very well, my lady."

For a moment, I felt the sting of bitter regret. What was I doing? It wasn't like me to talk down to my friends simply because I had the status to do so. Wasn't the fact that I avoided doing that one of the things Clay liked about me?

Wasn't that one of the things I liked about myself?

A knock sounded then, pulling me from any of those thoughts, and Iris wordlessly collected her things as I went to open the heavy wooden door with shaking hands.

My breath caught as I met Clay's eyes. He had dressed formally in a grey jacket with the purple sash of Athenia draped across his chest, marking his importance. A silver crown perched on his golden hair. It was the first time I'd actually seen him in a crown; I noted. It's one thing to know someone's a future monarch, but it's another entirely to see them decorated as one.

And though it somewhat pained me to admit it, it did suit him. As he stood tall at my door, Clay looked like the great ruler he would one day become.

Something came over me as I stood staring at him. Perhaps it was the knowledge of what I had overheard, or the gentleness with which he had carried me the night before, or that he simply looked positively breathtaking. Whatever the reason, I fell into a low curtsy and bowed my head, greeting him, for the first time, the way tradition dictated I should. His eyes flickered with surprise and some other unnamed emotion, but after a momentary pause, he, too, bowed his head respectfully to me.

"You look beautiful," he complimented, his voice clipped and formal.

"Thank you for the gown."

He nodded and extended an arm to me. "It was an investment I do not regret, Lady Moore."

So formal. The knowledge that we were both tasked with playing roles that evening overtook me. There was no time for us to banter or hover on the edge of inappropriate thoughts and feelings towards one another. There was no time for me to regret stepping into this role that I had fought for so long.

We needed to be royals.

And with that in mind, we left the safety of my suite, and I lifted my chin high. I would not let this castle see the raging storm of emotions that threatened to overtake me. I would not let them see how confused I was about Clay, how afraid I was of another attack, or how angry I was about the positions they constantly forced me into.

I was a Descendant of House Hyrax. I was *the* Descendant of House Hyrax. And if someone was determined to end my line once and for all, I would not make it easy for them.

CHAPTER TWENTY-FOUR

The Dragon spoke for quite some time before the court, while we stood formally behind him. And while I pretended to be utterly captivated by him, I found myself losing focus as he spoke. I couldn't bear to listen to him for too long as he prattled on about the disrespect of these attacks and the audacity of someone to assume they could injure the Athenian castle.

As he spoke, I stood next to Clay, wholly surrounded by my guards. I doubted another attack would happen so quickly after the last, or so publicly, but Dimitri constantly scanned the area, keeping one hand firm on his weapon. I could feel another guard close at my back, ready to grab me and pull me out of danger if necessary. The knowledge all at once left me on edge and somewhat comforted.

"I want to assure my people that the Athenian Council is stronger than ever, and we will protect our own! We will not let your princess of House Hyrax falter!" The Dragon called out strongly.

The people cheered, first softly and respectfully, but then more powerfully. I gasped as the hum of their voices unified into a single word.

My name.

"Theadora!" they chanted repeatedly, throwing roses onto the balcony at my feet.

Clay had mentioned my popularity in his conversation with Iris last night, but I hadn't paid it much mind. It had been a fleeting comment in a conversation that had stirred up a wave of emotion in me. I had nearly forgotten it entirely.

But Clay had been right. At some point, the people of Athenia began to love me. And yet, Clay had also been wrong.

They didn't love *me*.

These people had only ever seen the version of me that the Dragon wanted them to see, the version he had forced me to show them. They loved the *idea* of a long-lost princess but did not realize that the princess standing before them, accepting their cheers and roses, had only ever spoken to them with pre-scripted words drafted by the Dragon. Today, the Dragon had not even given me words to say. The palace guard team had determined it was too dangerous for me to step into the front of the terrace to speak.

I was to stand in the back, silent and under guard.

Just as I was to silently accept the Dragon's unwanted advancements on me or whatever else he wanted to do because of his *fascination*.

Just as I was to ascend to the Council, bear this kingdom's children, and silently accept that I could never be with the one person I might actually want.

I was tired of being silent.

I had been silent as I accepted all the rules of this court and although I had played along with every demand, I was still in danger. Did standing quietly in the back protect me or only paint me as a docile victim? Easily manipulated and easily controlled. They had brought me into this court to be a figurehead on their Council. But these people, the people of Athenia, didn't see me as a puppet. They saw a powerful woman. They saw an inspiration. They saw the promise of a resurrected House.

A sudden resolution fell over me. It was time to show everyone, including and especially the Dragon, that House Hyrax was strong. That I was strong. And that if they insisted on making me a Council member and subjecting me to the stipulations that came with that responsibility, then I *would* speak for my House.

The Dragon made his closing remarks and stepped backward to the palace, waving emphatically at the people, some of whom had already turned away to return to their homes.

It was now or never.

Clay grabbed my arm immediately as I tried to step forward, his grip firm and pressing into my bruises. And though it hurt, I met his fiery eyes with my own heat, and I did not flinch.

"What in all of creation do you think you're doing?" He demanded, voice low and angry.

"I'm going to speak to my people," I told him, not bothering to quiet my voice.

The Dragon glanced at us, and he turned his back to the crowd, shielding us so they could not see Clay's grasp on me. His eyes were flaming golden as he looked down at us.

"Miss Moore, excuse yourself back into the palace," the Dragon demanded.

Grounding my feet, I peered over his shoulder at the crowd awaiting me. He tried to shield me from them, but they could see something happening between us three. *Theadora. Theadora. Theadora.* They chanted my name over and over. They wanted to hear from *me.* The Dragon might want to stop me, he might even want to punish me for my disrespect, but he certainly couldn't do it before them, so I couldn't waste this opportunity.

"With all due respect, your majesty," I spit out sarcastically. "It's quite apparent that I'm the sweetheart of Athenia. And I doubt your people would be too fond of you or your son stopping me from greeting them."

Clay's grip on me tightened, to the point of causing significant pain, and I bit down on the inside of my cheek, refusing to falter as his fingers pressed in on the tender flesh. His father looked down at me with murder in his eyes, and it felt like an eternity that we three stood locked there, each weighing out our next moves. For a moment, a small part of me worried if I had gone too far in tempting the beast. But finally, the Dragon stepped aside.

"By all means," he growled, waving his arm and beckoning me to step forward.

I approached the podium slowly, greeting the eyes of as many people as I could. I identified a few as patrons of the tavern we had visited, but I doubted they would recognize me now in all my finery. As I reached the front, I locked my feet, bearing down my weight into the delicate heels of my shoes, and, after taking a breath to steady myself and my nerves, I spoke.

"I understand my story has not been the typical one and that there are still far more questions than answers regarding my origins. I'm sure that some part of you chants my name simply because of the intrigue of that mystery. I assure you, I long for the answers as much as any of you. But if there is one thing I know, it's that I'm an Athenian, just like all of you. Someone out there seeks to harm me. And I don't know if they want to harm me because of my lineage or the uncertainty within which I entered this castle, but harm to one Athenian, regardless of whether they are a Council member, is harm to us all and cannot be tolerated.

"I am no more special than any of you just because I have this Mark on my chest, and yet because of it, I have been gifted a home in this palace, these fine clothes, and true friends. Truthfully, I don't know why the Gods have blessed me in these ways; I can only hope to earn my place here and among you all.

"Should I allow myself to become a victim to these plots, then I will fail in my mission to earn your respect. And something you should all know about me is that I am far too stubborn to accept that. So, my vow to you is that I will not let this plot come to pass. I will not accept death at the hands of this criminal because I refuse to be taken away from any of you. I may not know my past, and I honestly know very little about what to expect in my future, but I do know my duty is to you. I know my responsibility is to protect and represent your interests and serve *you*. And I can promise you, I will. Not. Falter."

There was a moment of silence when the world was still.

And then the crowd erupted around us. I stumbled back as the echoes of their cheers reverberated through the kingdom. Women cried, and men clapped fiercely above their heads. They chanted my name once more, and I found myself smiling with them because, at least for today, they were actually cheering for the real *me*.

Then, slowly, purposefully, I dipped one foot behind the ankle of the other and I bowed low. I was breaking custom; I knew that. As a princess of House Hyrax, I wasn't to bow to anyone but the Dragon and the Crown Prince. But I did it then. I bowed to my people.

Because who is it that truly rules a land, if not the people within it?

With sweeping arms, the Dragon ushered me back to my guards while the crowd continued its cheers. Clay instantly grabbed my hand, stepping between his father and I.

"Clayton, take Miss Moore to my office and wait for me there," the Dragon growled, smoke pouring from his nostrils. His eyes scanned the guards. "The rest of you are to wait outside. I do not wish to be disturbed as we debrief."

He turned on his heels and then returned to his place at the podium to, presumably, conclude the ceremony. Clay wasted no time pulling me inside and rushing us through the castle halls to his father's office. I struggled to keep up with his pace and had to gather my skirts in my hand to keep from tripping as he pulled me on. The guards followed us, my constant shadows, but did as they were told and took posts outside the door as Clay pushed me in and slammed the door behind him.

"What the fuck, Theadora!" He boomed, tossing his crown onto the nearby couch and ripping a hand haphazardly through his hair.

I sighed, stalking away from him and sinking into the settee. The Dragon's office was exactly as I recalled from my last unwanted visit. Just as dark and gloomy as ever. At least his decor matched his general mood.

"They needed to hear from me," I insisted, voice firm.

"That's not up to you to decide!"

"And who is it up to then, Clay?" I yelled back at him, standing in an angry rush. "Your father? I didn't think I'd have to remind *you* that man's judgment isn't always sound!"

Clay flinched, making me immediately regret my choice of words. It wasn't fair of me to use that secret he trusted me with against him. But it was the truth. This was Clay's kingdom as much as it was mine, and he should care just as much as I did about ensuring that his people were treated fairly. The veins of his neck darkened, and he turned away from me in a rush, resting his hands on his hips and beginning to pace the room to calm himself.

"You don't understand, Theadora." Clay's voice was low, measured... panicked. "You openly defied him! He won't accept that."

"I sent a necessary message to someone trying to kill me, Clay. I showed them and the world that I would stand up for myself and my people. So, I'll accept whatever lecture I need as punishment for that crime."

Clay froze and met my eyes. His gaze was golden. I'd only ever seen his eyes *that* bright in moments of anger, yet nothing about him seemed frustrated now. He only looked defeated from his hunched shoulders, wide eyes, and set mouth.

"You don't understand," he told me softly. "I would fight the world to keep you safe, but even I can't protect you from this."

My blood froze as he repeated the words I had said to him that night in the inn.

"I made my choice, Clay, and I'll stand by it. It's not your responsibility to shield me from the consequences."

"But I-"

"Enough." I raised my hand to stop him. "Whatever's about to happen right now isn't your fault. And you need to let it happen. I'll be okay."

The door creaked suddenly as the Dragon stepped inside. Clay turned away as if he couldn't bear to look at me. As the Dragon shut the door behind him, I noticed the skin on his hands had completely scaled over. He was more beast than man, yet he seemed entirely calm.

"She doesn't understand," he agreed with his son. "But she's about to."

Wordlessly, the Dragon went to the top drawer of his desk and pulled out a thin chain. Clay rushed forward, grasping me by the waist and pushing me behind him.

"Father, allow me to see to her discipline," he pleaded.

The Dragon only looked up at us with boredom. "I can't trust that you will do what's necessary."

"Please," Clay asked again. "Father, please reconsider. There must be another way for Miss Moore to make amends."

Ice rolled over my skin as I realized there was yet another side to Clay. There was my friend, there was the Crown Prince, and there was also this childlike fearful version of himself. This was the boy who'd watched his mother's murder.

"Arton!" The Dragon called to the guard outside, who opened the door promptly. "Escort my son to his rooms. Ensure that he stays there."

"No!" Clay insisted, but the team of guards was already moving in.

He fought back. Clay fought with everything he had, even opening his mouth to release bursts of dragonfire to hold them back, but there's only so much even he could do when he was so terribly outnumbered. Numbly,

I watched as a team of six held him in their arms and pulled him from the room. His eyes locked on mine in terror as they swept away with him.

Calmly, the Dragon closed the door once more and slowly flicked the lock into place. My legs were frozen and my arms overly heavy as he approached me and began twisting the chain around my wrists.

I didn't regret my choices, but I knew with an overwhelming certainty that I had finally gone too far.

CHAPTER TWENTY-FIVE

T aking his time, the Dragon stripped off his coat and rolled up the sleeves of his tunic before slowly approaching me. Unafraid of breaching my personal space, he stood close and ran his fingers across the diamond diadem on my head.

"This is a lovely piece," he complimented.

I kept my head high, and mouth closed. I would not give him the satisfaction of seeing my fear.

"I wonder, though, if you confused these diamonds for a crown of your own?" The Dragon mused, following the links of the diadem to where they folded into my hair. "No words for me now? Perhaps this crown of yours is a bit too tight."

His movements were sudden as his fingers grasped onto the chains of the diadem and pulled hard, ripping it against my skin and pulling my head back violently. I bit down hard on my lip, metallic blood exploding through my mouth. Within a second, he pushed me just as hard as he had pulled, and I fell forward, landing first on my knees in a loud snap that sounded across the room and then, with my bound hands unable to catch my fall, onto my face.

My guards were just outside. The men who had sworn to protect me were gone now. I was alone with a beast, and no one would help. How many others had met this same fate?

"I let you go for far too long," the Dragon continued. "Clayton assured me you were learning our ways, doing well in your studies. He told me allowing you some minor hiccups in adjusting to our customs was an opportunity to show my grace."

The Dragon pulled me up by the chain on my wrists. His skin was burning, sending fiery pain everywhere it met mine. He dragged me to his desk, pushing aside the papers and clipping my bindings to a metal clasp at the corner. This was not his first time doing this to someone. Surely, there had to have been screams and injuries. How many in this court were complicit in allowing this man's cruelty?

"You've had long enough to learn," he growled, coming behind me and beginning to untie my gown. I wanted to pull away, to fight against this invasion, but he stood too close behind me. I was trapped between him and the desk.

"I should have known better than to allow my son to council *me.*"

Fingers turned to talons, and he slashed the sleeves that held up my gown around me. It fell to my ankles in a heap, leaving me completely bare. A flush of humiliation peppered my pale skin and once more I bit onto my lip. I would not cry. I would not allow him that.

"You went against me out there," he reminded me, trailing to the front of the desk to look down at my exposed body.

I met his eyes, and I did not look away. My pride was the only thing I had left, and I would not let him see my fear. I would not let him make me another thing he dominated. So I allowed him to look at me and hoped the image of the Mark of Hyrax on my bare skin would haunt his nightmares.

"I hope you know I can't have that. It would create discord in our kingdom. It's not good for the people. And it makes it more difficult for me to keep all of you safe. I'm doing this for your own good."

He opened the bottom drawer of his desk and pulled out a black leather riding crop. My stomach dropped with the full realization of what was about to happen to me. A burst of terror overwhelmed me suddenly before my temper flared.

He was a monster, and he deserved to burn in the Underworld.

"Yes, I'm sure you do this solely for *my* benefit."

A wicked smile danced on his lips as his arm flew out. The slap cracked across my face with such power that I saw stars for a few moments. I spat my blood at him as he came to stand behind me.

"I think fifteen lashes should do the trick," he sighed, and I could sense the excitement in his voice.

My magic rushed suddenly to my fingers, refusing to accept this treatment. Acting of its own accord, it pushed out of me, making the papers on his desk dance. The Dragon laughed as if I had somehow embarrassed myself with its display.

"I wouldn't do that," he warned. "You see, part of this exercise is proving that you can show control. For every time you lose that control, your ladies-in-wait shall receive ten lashes as well."

I stilled, pulling my powers back to my core in a rush. *No.* No one else would suffer for me. Not Nessira, and certainly not little Geia. Grounding my feet beneath me and my hands on the table before me, I stood tall. I would survive this. House Hyrax would survive this.

And one day, I would watch the Dragon die.

I envisioned that moment over and over in my head as he announced it was time to begin.

I heard the crop flying through the air before I felt the sting of it against my back. The pain was like lightning being struck directly through me. My knees buckled under it, and though I tried not to, I fell. The electricity of my magic surged through every fiber of my skin, and it took all my might to keep it contained. That was a second punishment in itself, I realized.

As Descendants, we relied on our power to protect ourselves. Being forced to stand here, powerless, was yet another moment of humiliation.

No.

This beast didn't desrve my shame.

I had done nothing wrong. I had done nothing to deserve this treatment.

I would feel no shame for this.

I steadied one foot under me, then the other, and stood tall again.

The Dragon chuckled. "I will make you scream for me, Miss Moore."

It took four lashings before I finally made a sound. He laughed.

By the eighth, the pain was unlike anything I could have possibly imagined, and I was sweating under the exertion of containing my powers. He told me I looked even more beautiful when blood decorated my skin.

By the fourteenth, I couldn't hold up my weight any longer and the world began fading in and out of view.

"When I fuck my Queen tonight, I'll be thinking of you like this, bare and crumpled before me," he declared, as the crop slapped down onto my fractured skin for a fourteenth time.

And, finally, I screamed.

I screamed at the top of my lungs as he finished his *punishment*.

He let out a long exhale as I cried, and I felt the air shift as he came to stand behind me. I felt his hands under my arms and he pulled me to my feet. The feeling of his tunic against the raw and bleeding flesh of my back left me screaming once more, and he wrapped an arm around my waist, both to prop me up and pull me tighter against him.

"That's it," he crooned, wrapping a meaty hand around my throat and pulling my chin towards him. "Cry for me."

I had suffered my way through the pain. I wasn't sure how I'd done it, but I had kept the thought of Nessira and Geia close to me each time that magical power pulsed in frustration. Through all of it, I had fought to keep them safe.

But when his mouth dipped towards my throat and his hand traveled possessively down my body, I couldn't control it any longer.

"*No!*" I cried, and the tendrils of my power escaped, pushing him back several feet from me.

In the silence that followed, my stomach catapulted.

He was grinning when I finally lifted my eyes to meet his gaze. He pulled his tunic, stained with my blood, over his head, and opened the door, beckoning in a guard.

"Get her dressed and return her to her room," he commanded. "When you're done, bring me her ladies."

"No!" I shrieked, fighting against the guard that unlatched my wrists and lifted me. "Leave them alone. It was me! Punish me!"

CHAPTER TWENTY-SIX

By the time the guards deposited me back in my suite, healers were already waiting. I had fought to leave, to return to that office and defend Nessira and Geia, but the nurses had forced me to drink a potion that left my body heavy and calm. Then, they mended my injuries, fused the cut skin back together once more, and gave me something for the pain. It would scar me, they warned, but I already knew that. No amount of magical healing would fix what had happened. Not all scars were visible after all.

So they would serve as a reminder of the retribution that waited for me.

"I hate him," I finally whispered, unsure if I was talking to Clay or myself.

Like the nurses, he, too, had been waiting for me. His clothes were rustled from his own fight to get back to that office, and I didn't know how he had got from his room to mine, but I was grateful he was there. His skin was paler, a shade I hadn't quite seen him wear before, and his eyes, though still glowing gold, were haunted. It reminded me of the night in his rooms when he told me of his mother.

"I'm so sorry, Thea," he whispered again.

I struggled to sit up from where I had been laid gently on my belly, hissing in protest as the tight, still healing skin pulled. He was at my side instantly, gently touching my shoulder and urging me back down.

"Don't," he breathed. "You should rest."

"It's not your fault," I told him, my voice so hollow it was nearly unrecognizable.

Clay grunted but said nothing as he softly pulled my hair aside from where it had fallen across my back. The nurses had pulled it out from its curls and removed the diamond chains that had cut into my forehead. They'd dressed me in a thin shift, cut low across the back so the fabric wouldn't bother the tender skin. Clay had ordered them out when they'd finished their work, and I was grateful for it. It was wrong of us to be here together, especially with my being in such little clothing, but I doubted Zion himself could convince Clay to leave me now, and truthfully, I too would fight back against Hyrax if he demanded my prince to go.

"Will they be okay?" I whispered, unable to think of anything but the image of Nessira and Geia in that room.

Clay sighed. "I believe this is not the first time he has summoned Nessira to him."

My blood boiled.

"He'll likely focus more of his attentions on her since Geia is young."

Was that better? No. There was no version of possibilities that ended well for either of my ladies. And that was my fault. I'd condemned them to this fate. If I had fought harder to control my powers, if I'd just let him do whatever he needed to, I could have kept them safe.

"It's not your fault either," Clay told me, sensing the direction of my thoughts.

"How is it that no one has done anything to stop this, to stop him?"

Clay shifted and ran his fingers in small, comforting circles over my shoulder. "Kings aren't so easy to control."

"Kings can be removed from power," I insisted, as magic swarmed angrily throughout me.

Clay's eyes were distant. "You're right. They can be. Sometimes they should be."

We sat like that for a while in silence. I waited for my ladies, as I wordlessly debated what we could do to overthrow the Dragon. Surely that thought alone was treasonous. But could anyone blame me in this circumstance? Was treason always wrong when the ruler was corrupt?

Still, though, what could I do? I was from a royal family, sure, but I wasn't even a Council member yet. I was still so new to court. I couldn't possibly forcibly take down a king. Not by myself. Not now.

I would have to wait. I would have to do what Clay had done in the years since his mother's murder. We would bide our time and wait until the right moment.

And then, I knew with a certainty that came deep from within my gut that I would watch the Dragon die.

Clay's fingers continued tracing those circles on my shoulder while I was lost in thought, and eventually I allowed myself to focus on that sensation and relax. I could do that with him next to me. His presence was... calming.

As the sun began to set, though, it was clear he couldn't stay with me much longer. We weren't allowed to be in here together, and now wasn't the time to break any more rules. The bed shifted under him as he slowly stood, careful not to jostle me too much. The pain had faded some time ago, though, as the healing medicines took effect. So as he stood, I too worked to sit up. His eyes flashed to my back, to the scars I knew he saw there, but neither of us mentioned them.

"Can I take you somewhere tomorrow?" He stopped to ask before leaving my bedroom, turning towards me with an oddly hopeful expression, given the day's events.

I wanted to question where in all of creation he wanted to take me. I wanted to warn him that the Council wouldn't like it, and the court would talk about how many customs we were breaking by constantly being alone together. I wanted to remind him that our relationship could ultimately go nowhere, despite how he might feel for me.

I wanted to tell him what I felt for him.

But I didn't fully understand that myself. So, instead, I only nodded.

I knew where I was going because I knew why I was here.

To see him.

He waited for me at the table like always, but tonight, the table had been set with a meal for two. Tonight, he smiled pleasantly. That shouldn't surprise me. Our conversations weren't always quite so contentious. Some nights, he merely spoke to me of my day. We talked of my developing powers, and he even helped me gain better control over them. He was certainly opinionated about Clay and whatever budding relationship I had with him, but regardless, I'd come to see the stranger as somewhat of a mentor.

"I still don't know your name," I reminded him as I sat across from him and eagerly pulled the glass of wine to me. After a day like today, the bitter taste was almost necessary.

"Names are meaningless," he scoffed, waving a hand dismissively. "They're nothing more than titles given to you by other people."

"Not mine," I reminded him somewhat playfully, thinking back to the day in the hospital when I had spit out the name of a nurse when I'd been unable to recall my own.

He grinned. "Yes, Theodora. I suppose you chose your own title. At least that one."

"Have I others?" I frowned.

"Don't we all?"

He stood suddenly, rounding the table to stand behind me. Without a word, he pulled my hair aside so my back in the low-cut shift was visible. He looked over it quietly, running a finger across one of the marks there and huffing in disgust.

"I shouldn't be surprised a descendent of Zion could show such violence towards you."

"It has nothing to do with his bloodline and everything to do with who he is as a man."

He scoffed, letting my hair fall free once more before he resumed his seat at the table.

"Perhaps. Or perhaps it is a matter of both. Perhaps biases and hatred are passed down just as easily as the color of your hair or the nature of your magic."

"So what did I inherit from my ancestor, hmm?"

The man's eyes danced as he chuckled. "A great many things, I suspect. Although, apparently not his instinctual aversion to House Zion."

Taking a deep breath, I shrugged. Sure, a Descendant of Zion had done this to me, but that didn't mean the entire line was out to get me. I had to believe that each person had the power to control their fate and actions.

"You're trusting," he noted. "There's nothing wrong with that. But you must consider who deserves your trust if you're going to keep yourself safe. There is someone who wants you dead, Theadora. And now, a descendent of Zion, the leader of his house, has outwardly moved against you. He has brought this pain down upon you. In the days when the Gods walked freely between the realms, that would not be allowed to go unanswered."

I shivered, imagining those days. How would Hyrax have responded to a son of Zion doing this to a daughter of Hyrax? Would it have mattered to him? Or would it have mattered so much that it started yet another war between the houses?

"The Gods have left us," I reminded him. "They do not rule the Mortal Realm. I have to handle this on my own."

He sighed, taking a sip of his wine pensively. "It's possible that you are wiser than I am. It is also possible that I am right, though, and every Descendant of Zion is an enemy of every Descendant of Hyrax."

His voice dripped with double meaning, and I thought back to our previous conversations. To his prior warnings.

"Clay would never hurt me."

"I know you believe that." His voice was soft, concerned. "But I don't."

CHAPTER TWENTY-SEVEN

I didn't see Nessira and Geia until the following day, when they woke me early after the sun had risen in the East. I clung to their hands, pulling them into the bed with me as tears came freely.

"I'm so sorry," I sobbed. "Are you okay?"

Nessira patted my hand supportively. "Do not fret on this, my Lady. You are not responsible for another's cruelty."

"I am."

She shook her head. "You are not. Blaming yourself will only hurt me more. Stand tall, you inspire me when you do. Today I can use some inspiration."

I nodded, wiping away my tears, and she stood to begin her tasks for the day. She beckoned Geia to follow her, and I watched as the young girl spun away from me with heated eyes and a grim expression. Nessira might be forgiving of my actions, but it was clear I had betrayed the trust of Geia. That was something I could never forgive myself for.

Part of me wondered what exactly had happened to them as a result of my actions.

Another part of me didn't want to know.

They filled the bath with warm water and hints of lavender oils, letting me soak a little longer than usual. I dressed in thick cloth pants and a loose tunic made of a delicate material that didn't irritate my skin. Geia fastened me into high leather boots as Nessira wrapped my hair into braids at the nape of my neck. The heavy woolen cloak draped across the foot of my bed told me we would travel outside the castle, but not even my ladies knew where Clay planned to take me.

As I dressed, anxious thoughts raced through my mind in a rushed fury. My subconscious had to be trying to tell me something through these near-constant nightmares that warned me away from Clay. Were these dreams just a manifestation of our ancestral feud? Was the man in my dreams right in warning me that Clay and I were destined to be at odds regardless of all else?

I didn't want to believe that. If it were true, then that meant we were nothing more than the product of those who came before us and I didn't want to–I *couldn't*–believe that Clay was anything like his father. But as much as I refused to believe that in my waking life, my dreams said otherwise. And didn't those manifestations of my subconscious warrant some consideration?

After all, Clay *had* been unkind to me when we first met. He'd never shown the kind of psychotic joy in cruelty that his father did, but did that make any of his initial treatment of me excusable? Perhaps my dreams spoke the truth. Maybe that initial hatred we had felt for each other was our blood recognizing the enemy in the other.

But were we then powerless to fight against that? Or were we, as individuals, strong enough to make our own choices despite the animosity between the Gods we descended from?

I was still musing over these thoughts as I walked out of the palace to greet him. My guards were at my side, but none dared to speak. Either they could tell I was lost in my own head or they were worried about breaking protocol after the events of the day before. Whatever their motivation was, I didn't mind their silence. My nightmares and anxieties had left me in a sour mood, one I would need to snap out of before spending the entirety of my day alone with my prince.

He waited for me by the stables, tending to a white mare who seemed positively enamored by him. She nuzzled him as he brushed through her mane and offered sweet treats from his pockets. He was nearly unrecognizable without his usual finery. But truth be told, as dashing as he was in a crown, I preferred him without all the pomp. Standing alone with the horse, he might have been mistaken for any other stable hand in his leather trousers and simple white tunic. His hair was due for a trim, and he'd skipped his usual shave, but, for once, he looked at ease. He looked happy. A rare sight indeed. And one I committed to memory as I stood staring.

He grinned when he finally turned and saw me, dropping the brush and dusting his hands off.

"Good, they made sure you dressed for riding," he noted as his eyes scanned over me. With a curt nod, he dismissed the guards, and they didn't hesitate to take their leave.

"This is Netta," he announced, waving me towards the mare. "She's typically very good with strangers, but tends to be a bit stubborn at times. I figured you two would get on famously."

I rolled my eyes as I extended my palms toward Netta. When she bowed her head, I ran my fingers over her nose and smiled when she huffed appreciatively. We'd be famous friends indeed.

"How long is the ride?" I asked as he disappeared into the stables.

Clay led out a tall stallion that seemed more suited to charge into war than head off on a mid-day ride through the countryside, but he threw himself onto the horse's back with an ease that suggested they'd been riding partners for some time. After several more quick pets, I followed his lead and hoisted myself upon Netta.

"We're headed about forty-five minutes south of the castle. Try to keep up."

And with that, he was gone, leaving me wide mouthed and frozen in surprise as the sound of his laughter enveloped me. I had seen Clay serious. I had seen Clay regal. That, however, was the first time I had ever seen Clay playful.

"C'mon," I whispered to Netta as I ran my fingers affectionately through her mane. "We can't let the boys get away with that now, can we?"

She stomped her hoof in agreement, and then we were off.

Netta followed my every command and ran at top speeds to catch up to them and pass them easily. Clay's horse may have been built for war, but Netta was made to *fly*. She was just a few wings shy of being a pegasus sent to me directly from the Gods, and she knew it. She didn't quiver or shake and hardly seemed to tire as I pushed her harder. The wind ripped through my hair, sending tendrils flying behind me, and for the first time since I'd arrived in Athenia, I felt blissfully free.

When I was sure we had made our point, I finally pulled gently on her reins to allow Clay to join us. He grinned suddenly as he reached my side and took the reins from my hands.

"What are you smiling over?"

"That was cheating!" He accused.

"How was that possibly cheating?"

"How is using your magic not cheating?" He shook his head incredulously.

I stiffened, thinking back over our run. "I didn't use magic."

Clay raised an eyebrow as he met my gaze above our horses. "No? So Netta was able to lift herself into the air and fly through the sky?"

I blanked. Netta had been *actually* flying? A wave of guilt rushed over me, and my hand sought to scratch the back of her ears apologetically. I'd been moving her through the air without even realizing it. That seemed... wrong.

"I didn't even realize," I whispered. "I didn't know I could do that."

Clay sighed, darkness flashing briefly across his features. "There's probably a lot you still don't know that you can do. I don't think Netta minded too much, though. You probably made her job quite a bit easier."

I smiled ruefully as she leaned her head into my touch. He was right; at least, I hoped he was.

We rode in a comfortable silence then, and I basked in the feeling of the sun on my skin. A breeze filled the air, brushing more tendrils of blonde hair loose from my braid, but I didn't mind. I was far too fascinated by my surroundings to care much about my appearance.

Athenia really was quite beautiful.

Everywhere was green, even though the air had developed a chill that warned winter wasn't too far off. The tips of some trees had painted themselves shades of sun-kissed yellow and bright red, but you could almost pretend it was still a comfortable summer day when you let your gaze wander over the rolling fields. I could see the beginning stretches of the woods in the distance with the crested tops of mountains lingering behind them, and every part of my soul wanted to push Netta to conquer the distance and show me what waited on the other side of the mountainous range that bordered the outskirts of the castle.

Clay navigated us away from the main roads to avoid any towns where we might be recognized. As much as I enjoyed spending the day without the constant shadow of my guard team, I wasn't naïve to the fact that the Crown Prince and the last living member of House Hyrax shouldn't be caught unawares. And I didn't mind roaming off the path, especially not when the views of the kingdom were this magnificent.

As we reached the top of a peak, our destination, the manor ahead of us, came into view, and my attention focused intently on it.

My blood felt like it was singing. My magic danced just beneath my skin.

It was a sweeping property with large tinted bay windows and dark shutters. Pointed spires stretched towards the sky, threatening to pierce the clouds. The bricks were a pale grey in complexion, appearing worn and dated. Two black gargoyles of winged demons sat on each side of the marble staircase, threatening away all those who dared to enter. And despite the overwhelmingly ominous appearance of the estate, I still pushed Netta closer to it. It called to me in a way I didn't quite understand. As if it were somehow alive, the house reached out to me, pulling me towards it one step at a time, and I was all too willing to oblige.

This place felt like...

"Welcome home, Thea," Clay said beside me. "Welcome to Hyrax Manor."

"Each line has its own estate," Clay explained as we entered through the heavy doors. "Some have multiple homes that are passed down among the family, of course, but there's always one primary residence that the head of the House maintains. Council families tend to have estates that are a bit more extravagant than others, but typically, they are a place for the bloodline to convene about issues, gather for celebrations, or store important artifacts."

We entered a large foyer, which was home to two large Cinderella staircases that kissed each other on the overlooking balcony. Ornate black rugs danced down the stairs, and steel chandeliers hung from the ceiling, offering dim candlelight. I ran my fingers across the etchings on the stone wall, admiringly.

The metal furnishings and dark colors contrasted the pristine marble and gold palace decor that I'd grown accustomed to. Everything about this place stood in opposition to the Dragon's home. Clay's eyes scanned the room as he frowned, unable to keep his distaste for the decor private. I might have been offended if my whole body wasn't still humming with the aura of this place—my *home.*

I traced my fingers across the dusty walls as Clay led me through the manor, pointing out the sitting rooms, kitchens, and bathing rooms. It all might have seemed depressingly dreary to anyone else, but I had never felt more at ease. It was possibly the most comfortable I'd felt since waking up in the infirmary those weeks ago. The doubts that had plagued me all morning finally quieted, and that was partially because of the house and partially because of *him.*

Clay was a Descendant of Zion, that was true, but by bringing me here, he had given me the greatest gift I had ever known. We had to be more than just two warring bloodlines.

"This is what I really wanted to show you," Clay informed me, stopping before one of the doors. "The Hyrax Archives."

With a sweeping gesture, he beckoned me forward, allowing me to take the lead and push into the room. The smell hit me before I could even let my eyes adjust to the darkness. It smelt *old.* It was more than the overwhelming smell of dust that startled me, though. There was a wash of pure and ancient power that danced over my skin as soon as my foot crossed the threshold. I shivered against it as Clay set to work, lighting the candles and illuminating the small space. He seemed completely oblivious to it.

Books lined the four walls, tomes that looked far too timeworn to risk running my fingers across them. Blades and weapons, combs, jewelry, jars, and more sat encased in glass containers protected from the air. Stacked along the far wall was portrait after portrait, each progressively older than the last, with fashions that seemed more and more outdated.

But despite all the treasures hidden throughout the room for me to spy upon, only one truly caught my attention.

"That couldn't possibly be the-"

"The Bident of Hyrax," Clay confirmed, following my gaze to where the tall, black, two-pronged spear hung in a glass case across the wall. "I wasn't sure you would recognize it."

How could I not? It was tattooed permanently across my chest. I shook my head, shocked that such a powerful object sat so carelessly in this empty estate. My mythology lessons had only just started. We'd barely covered Crolun and the rise of the High Gods, but I'd skipped a few chapters ahead one night when I couldn't sleep and read about the Tokens of the Gods–instruments of power governed by each God and controllable by them alone.

"How is it here?" I questioned, frowning. I still had much to learn about the Gods, but I couldn't imagine the King of Underworld was happy about being parted with the magical instrument that amplified his power.

Clay shrugged. "Legend says that when Zion banished Hyrax to the Underworld, after the Second War of the Gods, he worried about Hyrax being able to escape with his power of the bident. So the ruling Dragon at the time, Caldrius, risked his life getting it for Zion while Hyrax slept. Zion banished Hyrax and gifted the bident to Caldrius as a reward for his faithfulness. For years, Caldrius attempted to use it to magnify his own power, but as a Descendant of Zion, the magic of Hyrax was toxic to him and ultimately poisoned his mind. He grew cold and murderous, eliminating anyone he viewed as a threat, and he saw nearly everyone as a threat. Eventually, he directed his suspicions towards his younger brother Ennoss, who was widely respected in the country.

"Hundreds stood behind Ennoss, ready to lay down their lives in defense of him, but Ennoss already had witnessed the death of too many of his people. So, instead, he gathered those who feared Caldrius or simply no longer wanted to live under his rule and fled across the sea to an unexplored land. He prayed to the Gods every day while they traveled for the wisdom to lead his people without forcing them into a war with his brother, and when they landed on the shores of their new home, he named it after the Goddess of Wisdom hoping she had heard his prayers."

"Athene," I whispered, recalling the name of the Goddess. "*That* is how Athenia was established?"

Clay nodded, turning away from me to the shelves of books along the wall and gazing over them, looking for one in particular. I knew I should follow him, but I found myself still drawn to the bident, as if its magic and my own were inexplicably attracted to each other with the force of magnets brought too close together.

"So, how did the bident get here?" I wondered.

"Ennoss took it from his brother when they fled. He returned it to House Hyrax, trusting the magic wouldn't poison their minds as it had his brother."

"Wasn't he worried they would use its power against him?"

"They couldn't." Clay shrugged. "Many have tried throughout the years, but just because we carry the blood of Gods doesn't mean we are godly. No one has ever harnessed the magic in it. Only Hyrax himself would be able to."

My fingers lifted, drawn to the cold steel handle of the bident. I needed to touch it. I needed to feel it. And it wanted me to. I could sense that. The spear wished to connect with me as much as I needed to hold it. Was this what Caldrius had felt, or was this the effect of Hyrax's blood in my body pushing me to connect with my ancestor?

The sound of Clay dropping a heavy book onto the table in the center of the room was enough to snap me out of the trance and turn back towards him. He flipped through the pages quickly, pausing when he found what he wanted and turning it towards me.

"Look," he commanded.

I strode to his side, and his fingers gently slid over the tome to me. The pages were lined with name after name, ending suddenly with one final signature. *Zacharia Moore*-the man presumed to be my father. And the man who had once been presumed to have been the end of the Hyrax line.

Until me.

Clay pushed something into my hand: a quill.

"I believe this page is missing something," he whispered.

My breath caught. We still didn't know where I had come from, or even if Zachariah *was* my father, but I had obviously come from Hyrax and that made the names on this list my family. Even if I couldn't remember them, by adding my name to this list, I could claim them.

Steadying my hand, I dipped the quill into the ink jar Clay held for me before officially signing my name into the family tree of Hyrax. Just like that, a book that had been put away on a shelf forever was given a second chance at life. And a girl who still carried the burden of lost memories was able to reclaim some semblance of family.

"Thank you," I whispered, acutely aware of how close he stood to me and the heat that radiated from his body towards mine. "Thank you for bringing me here."

He shrugged, cheeks reddening slightly. "I know you've felt alone and are desperate to know your past. I wish we had found more information for you, and I swear to you I am still looking, but I thought knowing this place existed, knowing your family's history is here, might help you."

I nodded, trying to breathe through the sudden emergence of a lump in my throat. "It does help."

There was a stillness in the air, a tension that grew thicker with each breath I struggled to achieve.

"I hope you know you're not alone, though," he continued. "You're an Athenian citizen and that makes you my responsibility technically, but you're more than just that. You've become more than that to all of us."

His fingers brushed over my cheek, wiping away the tears that had dared to escape. And for that moment, I simply forgot.

I forgot everything that had happened until we stood pressed together in the Hyrax Archives.

I forgot about all the nightmares and subconscious warnings.

I forgot about the Dragon's cruelty and the responsibilities Clay and I both had to our people.

I forgot about everything and everyone until all I was aware of was how his shining gold eyes seemed to stare right through me. All I could think of was how this man saw *me*. Clay saw me as a woman, not just a pawn or a princess. He saw me and he embraced who I was instead of what I represented.

His arm wrapped gently around my waist, pressing into the small of my back, and I turned to him. I met his eyes, and I didn't look away. I didn't want to. Who moved first was unclear, but in the silence of Hyrax estate, Clay's lips finally pressed into mine.

He was gentle at first, questioning. He left that question in the air, inviting me to tell him whether this was okay.

Looking back, I should have taken a moment to allow my rational mind to consider what I was doing, but I let my body and the desires it had suppressed for months take over entirely.

Yes, I wanted to fulfill my duty to my people.

I wanted to remember the life I had before this kingdom.

I wanted so much, but above all, I wanted him.

And I was realizing that I had wanted him for longer than I had allowed myself to see.

"*Yes*," I whispered.

I stepped forward, pressing myself into him more fully and reaching up to rest my hands on his hips. His tongue pressed against my bottom lip, and I opened for him, reveling in his taking ownership of my mouth so entirely. He reached for my chin with his left hand while his right lost itself in my hair, pulling out my braids until the golden locks rushed over my shoulders.

"Gods this hair." His mouth left mine so his gaze could crest over its waves. "I should have known you would ruin me the first time you wore it down so freely."

"And have I-" My breath caught. "Ruined you?"

Those heated eyes traveled from my hair to my lips. The way he looked at me... it was like a man in awe. He worshipped me with his eyes alone. And suddenly, the overwhelming need for him to worship me with *more* than his eyes nearly took me off my feet.

"Not yet, princess. But you might be the only one in the kingdom with the power to do so."

I couldn't fight my grin as I pulled him to me once more. I would accept that challenge happily.

His touch was a flame, setting my skin alight wherever his fingers brushed my skin. *Yes.* I had needed this. For so long I had needed him without realizing it, and now with his mouth on mine I couldn't think of anything more perfect than the way Clayton Vail kissed me. I pressed myself to him hungrily, needing more, demanding more from him. An unfamiliar ache in my core overwhelmed me as I tangled my fingers in his sandy hair.

And yet for as desperately as he clearly wanted me, he still held himself back. I could feel it in the tension of his shoulders and the softness of his hand sliding down my back. Clay was still waiting for me to stop this.

But I didn't want to stop. I only wanted him.

As I pulled his bottom lip between my teeth, a breathy moan managed to escape me and his restraint *finally* shattered.

He pushed me back, never breaking our kiss, and guided me towards the wall. My back crashed against the glass case containing the bident of Hyrax with such force that I was grateful it hadn't shattered. I doubted I would have even noticed if it had. Nothing existed outside of he and I and the place we met. My knees weakened as he nipped at my lower lip, and he strung his arm around my waist, lifting me so that I could lock my legs around him. I pulled on the wavy strands of his hair, delighted at the softness between my fingertips. As he broke our kiss I whimpered in frustration, but my cries turned to those of need as he trailed his lips across my throat, finding the sensitive flesh that made me arch against him.

The world began and ended with him.

"I've never..."

His eyes pulled back, meeting mine. "Should I stop?"

The idea of his warmth leaving me was almost too terrible to imagine. "Please don't."

"Gods, Thea," he whispered my name like a prayer. "I don't have the strength to be gentle with you right now, especially not if you're going to say *please*."

That was good because I didn't want him to be gentle. I didn't want him to be a proper, dutiful, *gentle* prince right now. Clay had seen me, and now I wanted to see him. I wanted the man under the crown. Pulling back, I took his face in my hands and forced him to look me in the eyes once more. I knew very well the heat he would see there. I knew it mirrored his own.

"I want you Clay. *Please*."

"Fuck," he groaned, burying his face against my throat as his fingers dug into my ass. We brought our lips together once more. Months of forbidden passion had left us starving for each other. He was all I could think of, all I could feel around me. I was positively burning alive for him.

"You're so beautiful," he whispered, piercing me with his eyes as his hand began reaching for my inner thighs. "You're the most beautiful thing in this entire fucking kingdom. Do you know that? You must."

His fingers reached that delicate spot between my legs and it was all I could do not to scream out. That felt... well, that was indescribable. He trailed kisses down my throat as his thumb continued tracing circles over *that spot* and by the Gods I started to move with him. My body knew what it needed even if my mind didn't.

Clay watched me, unblinking, as I struggled to chase the tension that was building within me. As his free hand reached under my tunic to grasp my breast and pinch at the subtle peak, his golden eyes were more aflame than I'd ever seen them before. I whimpered when his tongue slowly darted out to wet his lower lip and the sound earned me a small grin. That grin nearly pushed me over the edge.

"We gotta get you out of these pants, princess."

I wanted to agree, but words escaped me. I was hot. Too hot to think clearly. My skin was scorched and tiny beads of sweat began pebbling my forehead. It was all too much. The heat was impossible, both in my core and between my shoulder blades. It spread over my back until it encompassed me entirely and flowed freely through my veins into my fingers and toes, warming every part of me. The feeling was indescribable, only comparable to the sensation of my own magic rushing in me before it exploded.

Magic.

There was only a moment after I realized the heat at my back *was* magic, pulsing from the bident into me and mingling with my own, before it finally erupted out of me in a vicious rush. It pushed into Clay sharply, snapping his head away from me.

"What? What happened?" He questioned, frozen.

Power pounded in my body, more potent than anything I'd ever manifested before, and sent tingles across my skin. Silently, I pushed his shoulders, removing him from me and stepping away. The bident behind me was entirely unchanged. There was no glow, no cracks in the glass, no visible sign of any magic emanating from it. That spear was nothing more than an antique on the wall.

And yet, I had *felt* it. I was sure of it.

"Did you feel that?" I whispered.

"Feel what?"

It made little sense that I would have been able to feel the bidents power. Clayton had just told me that only Hyrax himself could use that weapon. I doubted the God was able to lash out with it from the Underworld.

So it must have been... me.

It must have been my own magic.

That was the only option.

I had pushed Clay away, because somewhere in my subconscious, I must have actually believed in my nightmares. Maybe my blood was truly unwilling to accept him.

A son of Zion will never love the daughter of Hyrax.

Clay's hands wrapped around my shoulder, giving a gentle squeeze. "Thea, what's wrong?"

"We shouldn't be doing this," I breathed, finally, after a moment of silence.

I turned from the bident suddenly, unable to look at it anymore. I couldn't beat the sight of it, not when it reminded me so clearly that I couldn't have the person I wanted. Not now, not ever.

"Did I do something wrong?" He questioned, eyes wide and cheeks still flushed from the moment.

His expression nearly broke my resolve right there. This was Clay at his most vulnerable. This was the version of him that so few people had been allowed to see.

And I had just pushed him away.

He had been so gentle at first. He had tried to prepare himself for my rejection and I had encouraged him to continue, only to push him away after all. Gods, what must he be thinking of me?

For a moment, it took all of my self-control not to run back into his arms like I wanted to deep down, but I steeled myself and did what I'd seen him do so many times. I put on a mask. I became who I needed to be at that moment: Lady Theodora Moore of House Hyrax.

"This is wrong for several reasons," I reminded him, voice hard. "Thank you for bringing me here. It was kind. But it's not... proper for us to be here alone. And as I'm sure you have many responsibilities to attend to, perhaps we should return to the castle."

He flinched as if I had physically slapped him, which I might as well have for how harsh I sounded.

"Since when have you ever cared about what's proper?" He frowned, his expression betraying his feelings. I couldn't care about his hurt feelings, though. Not when my own sadness was threatening to drown me.

"Since when have you stopped reminding me I should?" I spit back.

He flinched once more, and I watched as he hardened, as the emotions drained from his eyes until all that was left was steely indifference. My heart ached, a sensation so palpable it came with an actual physical pain. I suspected that would be the last time Clayton Vail let down his walls for me. I had just lost him, and that knowledge cut me deeper than I ever expected it would.

In just a few moments, I had experienced the most intense joy and the most crushing heartbreak. I had no one to blame for that but myself.

He straightened, closing the book and returning it to the shelf swiftly.

"Very well, Miss Moore. Let us not waste any more time."

I led the way out of the house silently, through the dark halls and sweeping doors that had felt like home only moments ago. Now, they just felt cold. Or I felt cold. I wasn't sure I knew the difference at that moment.

He followed me and helped me onto Netta but averted his gaze completely, even when I couldn't help but seek his eyes. We were silent as we rode back to the castle stables. There were no races or jokes between us now. Now there was a divide I wasn't sure we could ever recover from. He stayed a few paces ahead of me until we arrived. As grey clouds began rolling in to ruin the otherwise beautiful day, I wondered if the Gods had been watching us. Had their moods soured, too?

Dimitri was there waiting for us with the rest of my guard, and he helped me off Netta silently, shooting curious glances between Clay and I. The prince ordered that I be returned to my room, and Dimitri only nodded. And then he was off. Clay set a brisk pace back towards the castle, and I knew that was the last I would see of him for a long time.

And that didn't sit right with me.

My legs were moving before I realized it, running after him. Some part of me heard the guards attempting to grab me, only to have Dimitri grasp onto them to provide me this moment. This one moment where I could allow myself to regret the words I'd said to him. I reached for Clay, pulling his arm to stop him.

"Clay, wait," I demanded.

His expression was so hard I might have mistaken it for cruelty if I didn't know better. "For what, Miss Moore? What exactly should I be waiting for?"

I sputtered, unsure what I could even say to explain the conflict that was raging within me. "I don't know, I just-"

"No, you don't know. You don't know a damn thing," he fired out, exasperated. "You don't have the slightest idea how to perform your duty. A duty that one moment you rebel against and the next you use as an *excuse*."

"It wasn't an excuse, Clay."

"That wasn't really the point, Thea."

Anger rushed over me, and I bit my lip so hard I tasted blood. I allowed the rage to overtake my senses because anger was easier to feel than the sadness that was bubbling underneath the surface. I knew what point he was prepared to make; I didn't want to listen to it. But that's the thing about people like Clay. They say the things you don't want to hear, especially when they think those are the things you *need* to hear.

"You don't know what you want, Thea. You never have. But somehow, you now have it in your head that you've accepted all this. And you know what, if that *is* what you want, then fine.

If you've decided you want to be a proper councilwoman, then do that. But you don't get to keep pulling me around while you struggle to maintain your chosen path. So, now the choice is out of your hands. Just do your job, Miss Moore. That's all I need from you."

Unable to help myself, I met his fire with my own. "And is that all you want from me?"

Clay pulled back, removing his arm from my grasp. He looked towards Dimitri sharply, issuing a final silent command. This conversation was over.

"It is now," he declared.

I sensed Dimitri's presence before I felt his gentle touch on my shoulder. Clay left instantly, storming towards the castle without a second glance back at me. I shivered involuntarily as I watched him go. As the stable hands approached me from behind, I was dimly aware of them preparing to take Netta back to her stable. At some point, two other guards joined Dimitri, and they all walked me back to my suites. He tried to make small talk as we went, a sign that I must be wearing my emotions visibly. After all, Dimitri wasn't likely to break protocol and talk colloquially with me unless he felt he needed to. Ultimately though, I only muttered one-syllabic words back at him.

I had nothing to say when I could still feel the echo of that overwhelming power in the Hyrax Archives rushing over me like a memory that refused to fade.

When we finally reached my rooms, I was ready to collapse into my bed and never come out. I walked through the door quickly, not even bothering to say goodbye to the guards who had walked with me.

"Lady Moore?" Dimitri called, standing hesitantly at my door.

"Yes?"

He sighed heavily. "I must let you know that we've just received word from Prince Vail. He has a message for you."

My already injured heart dropped once more.

"He wants you to know that he has reevaluated your security," Dimitri continued. "Until they have neutralized the threat against you, he has ordered that you stay within your rooms under guard."

I could only nod my understanding as Dimitri turned and shut the door after him. He might as well have locked me in. I was a prisoner once more.

CHAPTER TWENTY-EIGHT

"Tell me again, girl," Hansel snapped at me, drawing my attention back to the room.

My thoughts had been a million miles away all day, and the Royal Tutor had grown tired of reminding me to focus on my studies. But paying attention to anything other than the memories of Clay's body on mine and the heartache of seeing him walk away from me seemed utterly impossible.

"I'm sorry, where were we?" I sighed, running a hand over my face. Gods, I was tired. Sleep had been hard to find of late.

"Where did Zion get his dragon?" Hansel barked.

My tutor was rarely in a good mood and never failed to remind me that most of his pupils were half my age and twice as knowledgeable. Our mythology lessons often felt rushed as he tried to get me to memorize as much information as possible ahead of my impending trials. Try as he might, though, he couldn't inspire the curiosity and passion in me that he found in his younger students. But then, his younger students didn't have half the responsibilities or stressors I did, so could he really hold that against me?

I pinched the bridge of my nose, annoyed at having to repeat the story. "After Zion and Hyrax joined forces with the other High Gods, they overthrew their father Crolun. Zion took power over the Upperworld and Hyrax took the Underworld. Shortly after the First War of the Gods, when Hyrax tried to claim rule of the Mortal Realm, a group of lesser Gods, known as Triad, rebelled against them. Zion gathered allies by freeing his aunt Ciclopia, who Crolun had imprisoned, and allowed Hyrax to return to the Upperworld. Together, she, Zion, and Hyrax all banished Triad to the Underworld."

"Get to the point."

I bit my lip in frustration. "Ciclopia, otherwise known as the mother of beasts, took a hair each from Zion and Hyrax and from them she created a dragon for Zion and a three-headed hound for Hyrax."

"Good," Hansel complimented. "I think you've finally got that part down."

He removed the text from the table before me and moved to return it to the library shelf. The palace library was one of the few places I could go to since Clay had locked me up again. And I could only be here for the sole purpose of my mythology lessons, and then my guards were always sure to swiftly escort me back to my suite.

I hadn't spoken to any of my friends about what happened between Clay and me at Hyrax Estate, but somehow, the others had realized we weren't exactly on speaking terms. Iris had taken one look at my tear-streaked face after I returned from the stables and been able to put two and two together. She had sighed, shook her head, and announced, 'Well, at least you now know one way or the other.'

And that was true, at least. I did now know. I knew that Clay and I would never work. I knew that now that I had accepted my future as a Council member, I needed to prioritize the resurrection of my House above any feelings I may or may not have for him. I just didn't understand why I felt so damn conflicted by that.

My emotions had been a mess since that argument with Clay. I was a volcano of anger and frustration, ready to erupt at any unforeseen moment. I knew I'd been worrying my friends. Iris and Lorelai checked in on me daily. One afternoon, after my power burst out of me and I tossed furniture upside down, they convinced Clay to let me leave - under supervision–to continue my preparations for my trials. So, I had returned to daily lessons in the library with Hansel, physical training sessions with Rankor in the newly restored gym, and power exercises with Ryla on the mountain. And every afternoon on that mountain, once I was safely away from the castle and others, I allowed my power to finally escape me and shake everything around it.

I was getting stronger.

No one really knew why or how. Most brushed it off as my being a natural, but I could tell there was something more to it than that. They would send nervous glances at each other while noting that they'd never seen someone learn hand-to-hand combat as quickly and efficiently as I had. Ryla would clear her throat with pursed lips as I toppled a tree in the woods without even breaking a sweat. They couldn't understand how quickly my powers and strength were growing.

I could feel their unease pressing down on me, and it was that awareness of their suspicion that kept me from being completely honest with them.

I still didn't feel like I was tapping into my full potential.

Something deep within me told me I had a well of magic that was untouched but constantly swirling, ready to escape. I knew without a doubt that I could do *more*. And that feeling scared me as much as I knew it would disturb others. So I kept my mouth shut and kept the lid on the raging storm of magic that felt like it was constantly building in my veins.

"I still don't understand, though," I told Hansel, frowning as he pulled a new book to study.

"What's not to understand?"

"Well, I don't have a hound on my chest. The Mark of Hyrax is a bident. Where did his weapon come from?"

Hansel's eyes twinkled in the way they did to show me I had asked the correct question. I had learned in our first few lessons that Hansel liked questions. He appreciated when you asked questions about missing information or storylines that contradicted themselves – and there were very many contradicting stories I had learned.

That's what happens when you have Descendants of so many different bloodlines all writing histories of their ancestors. Sometimes, the same stories are told differently, and the same characters are shown in a different or more flattering light. And you're left wondering if the story that's been accepted as historically accurate is actually the truth of what happened.

"Hyrax has been said to be a rather jealous God," Hansel explained, sitting across from me. "There have been conflicting reports of what happened to Ciclopia after the battle. The most common myth we have is that she entered 'eternal rest.' Some debate whether that means sleep or death, but that is neither here nor there. The point is that when the Gods celebrated the defeat of Triad, they celebrated Zion and Hyrax only. The twins were gifted several items from the Gods of the Upperworld. Arto, the God of Violence, gifted them weapons."

"The bident?"

Hansel shook his head. "Not quite. He gifted Zion a most powerful sword and gifted Hyrax a bangle that granted invisibility to its wearer."

I snorted involuntarily, then sputtered when Hansel leveled me with a glare that would make Clay proud.

"It's just that hardly seems like a weapon."

"You are not far removed from your ancestors' thinking. Hyrax insisted Arto should give him a better weapon, and Zion was enraged by his ungratefulness. And so the King of the Gods commanded Hyrax to the Underworld once more. Hyrax went willingly, having already devised a plan to steal the Mortal Realm from his brother. You see, before entering eternal sleep, Ciclopia birthed two new monsters–Tyran and Eckna."

I had read about the beasts recently. Tyran was known to be extremely poisonous. He'd had four heads and each of his teeth delivered a deadly venom. But how was any of this relevant to the question I had asked, or those that had since risen to mind?

"What happened to the invisibility bangle?" I questioned.

Hansel's eyes darkened as he scowled at me. Hansel liked questions, but he only wanted the questions he deemed to be necessary. And apparently, I had asked something irrelevant.

"I imagine it's in the Underworld still."

Stopping myself from groaning my frustration with the old man, I changed tactics. "Okay, so how does any of this relate to the bident?"

"Stop rushing me, girl!" He criticized. "To defeat Tyran, Zion decimated a mountain and pinned Tyran under it, effectively burying the beast. Hyrax knew this. He also knew that as the God of the Underworld, the beast would one day enter his domain. So, he waited. Some say he waited hundreds of years for the beast to finally die. But when it did, he took a bone from the carcass and fashioned it into a bident, a weapon he felt was more appropriate for his power."

He stood and placed a second book in front of me. Impatiently, he motioned for me to open it and begin taking notes. Our lessons always ended with me taking notes on the texts he expected me to study overnight. He didn't allow me to take books from the library. I suspected he didn't trust me not to harm them. And considering that whole furniture explosion in my suite days prior, I couldn't really blame him.

"What happened next?"

Hansel rolled his eyes. "There is still much to cover before we get there, girl."

Sighing, I frowned up at him. There were dozens, if not *hundreds,* of myths and legends to learn and memorize before my trials, but could he really blame a girl for being curious about her own history? Hyrax was my ancestor, after all. Didn't I deserve to know his story? Wasn't it somehow part of my own?

Hansel scratched a hand through his beard as if he, too, were debating that same question. Finally, he sat back down and nodded.

"Then, Hyrax rose to the Mortal Realm, bringing his beasts of the Underworld with him. He claimed a throne for himself and demanded the mortals submit to him. Of course, Zion and the Gods of the Upperworld fought back, but they knew they would need to make a sacrifice to banish Hyrax back to the Underworld fully. I'm afraid no one truly knows how they managed it. The reports are inconsistent, but to end the Second War of the Gods, they created the Veil."

"The Veil?"

Hansel nodded. "When Hyrax announced to his kingdom that he would return briefly to the Underworld to retrieve his bride Pasnia, the Goddess of Madness, and bring her to the Mortal Realm, the Descendants of Zion alerted him to Hyrax's plan. Zion instructed Caldrius to steal the bident while Hyrax was away. Then, the Gods created the magical veil between the worlds. A gate, if you will, that answers to no God or Goddess. Once it was created, traveling between the realms was impossible, locking Hyrax and Pasnia permanently in the Underworld and keeping all other Gods in Upperworld."

I sighed, chewing on my lip and questioning again what it meant to descend from the God labeled an enemy to all. Everything I'd read of Hyrax so far painted him as a jealous, gloomy man with no other desire than to conquer an entire realm of mortals and Descendants. Who knew what he would attempt to do if he ever fully got dominion over the mortal realm?

"No wonder people don't trust me," I mumbled.

Hansel scoffed. "If there is one thing I have learned by studying these histories, girl, it is that the only people who can tell you the truth of what happened are the Gods themselves. And besides, we are our own people, are we not? Do we not make our own choices?"

Well, wasn't that just the question that motivated all my anxieties?

Were Clay and I destined to be enemies, or could we choose to be something else?

And if we *could* enact that kind of choice within our own lives, how could I choose Clay over restoring the name of my House on the Athenian Council and ensuring that heirs would be born to continue it?

Perhaps Hansel was right, and these stories were nothing more than history being told by the victors. Perhaps Hyrax was not the villain he was so often portrayed as. But didn't that make it more critical than ever that I stand tall in the name of my House and prove to Athenia and the world that House Hyrax could be more than just the Descendants of an evil God?

I lifted my quill and began taking notes on the tome before me, more determined than ever to ensure I passed the trials. After all, none of my pining for Clay meant anything now, not when he had made it abundantly clear that the only thing *he* wanted from *me* was to fulfill my duties.

CHAPTER TWENTY-NINE

"I must send out my most gracious thanks to all of you for joining us on this special night." The Dragon's booming voice seemed to echo throughout the great hall. "Please, grab your drinks and join me in raising a glass to honor my son's twenty-third birthnight celebration. Clayton, son, you are a pillar of strength that would make your forefathers proud. Happy birthday, son."

I downed my glass, avoiding the false spectacle the Dragon was putting on. I doubted his majesty wanted to be here any more than I did. It had been exactly three weeks since the doors to my suites were shut behind me, and there hadn't been a single update from Clayton about when I could expect to be allowed to leave.

There hadn't been a single update from Clayton about anything, in fact.

The Crown Prince was obviously avoiding me. And though I knew I didn't have any reason to begrudge him for that - I was the one who rejected him after all - I still grew more irritated each day that passed without him.

I wasn't entirely sure when it had happened, but Clayton Vail had become my addiction, and the more time that passed without him, the more I wanted to see him. And the more I wanted to see him, the more I hated him.

For three weeks, Clayton had avoided me. There had been no visits, no communication through my guards, nothing until a small invitation arrived at my door. Apparently, the Royal Birth Night celebration was an occasion that demanded my presence.

I suspected the invitation had come from the Dragon and not my prince. And it likely had more to do with my many suitors in the room than it did with anyone actually desiring my presence at this party. I remembered some of the marriage hopefuls from the last ball, but most of their faces were nothing more than a blur. Each one faded into the next as men from across the kingdom - and beyond - offered me drinks and dances. I suffered silently as best I could, offering timid smiles and polite dances, unable to stop remembering how the last time this had happened it had been Clay who had rescued me from it all.

Most of the suiters were kind enough, except for Lord Ducay, who promptly reached for my rear end once he pulled me to him for a dance. Much to his chagrin, though, Lord Ducay mysteriously had his drink fall from his own hand onto the top of his head. It was almost like magic. Fortunately, he hadn't been seen since.

As Nessira and Geia dressed me for the party earlier, I'd been filled with nerves. I'd changed three times before finally settling on a pale yellow dress with cap sleeves. I couldn't sit still long enough for Nessira to do anything elaborate with my hair, so she'd twisted the front pieces away from my face and held them back with pearl clips. Neither questioned my anxieties, and I suspected they already knew the cause. Coming to the princes' birthnight celebration meant I would finally have to come face to face with him again. And that made me uneasy at best and nauseous at worst.

Clay *had* been right that day, though. I did need to stand by the path I had chosen for myself. And I had decided to embrace my role in this court the second I had stepped forth to speak for myself that day on the terrace. So I had vowed to myself that all anyone would see when they looked at me tonight was a respectable future Council member with a pleasant smile and a gracious attitude.

That attitude was getting difficult to maintain as the night went on, though.

"I'll take one of those," I called, reaching out for a glass of sparkling wine as a servant passed by. He bowed stiffly, extending the tray towards me. I took the glass silently, fighting the urge to roll my eyes at the ridiculousness of this man bowing before me. I hardly deserved that, nor did I really want it.

Lorelai folded her arm into mine as she took a glass herself. "Best not to drink too fast."

I raised an eyebrow at her as she giggled.

"We have to come to this party every year with all the fancy old dignitaries, but we've been known to continue things afterward. You've got a long night of fun ahead of you."

I doubted that.

"No one parties quite like a Prince on his birthday," Rankor agreed.

I doubted that would be fun for me at all.

"I think I'll pass on the afterparty," I replied stiffly.

"Because you have such better plans, Miss Moore?"

His voice had an immediate effect on me, sending tremors throughout my body and, though I hated to admit it, warmth between my legs. My jaw locked, and my back stiffened. My core was molten lava, and my heart fell into my stomach. By the Gods, what kind of man can do that with his damn voice alone before I've even laid eyes on him?

Clayton Vail could.

Clay briefly kissed Iris on the cheek before hugging Camilla and Lorelai and bumping fists with Rankor and Kent. All I got was an icy stare, but I met it without flinching. My stomach might be toppling with butterflies, but there was no way I would let him see that.

"A night spent evading Hyrax's hound would be preferable to an evening spent with you, Mr. Vail." I smiled.

Rankor covered his laugh with an aggressive cough while Kent whistled appreciatively, leaning back on his heels and tucking his hands into the pockets of his breeches. Clay glared at them both, an expression that would have sent anyone else fleeing.

"I'm only appreciating that our future Council member has been studying her mythology," Kent explained.

Clay sighed, beckoning a servant to bring a tray of particularly small drinks to the table. Rankor winked at me as he passed one out to each of us. It smelled vile, which likely meant it was precisely the kind of drink I needed in a moment like this.

"You would think," Clay scolded, "that someone who has been so diligent in her preparations for her trials would know how to respect her future king."

Lorelai slid her hand out from under my elbow as she went to stand by Iris. The two clasped hands and exchanged worried glances as the tension between Clay and me became palpable. Still, I didn't back down. I was too furious.

I was furious at him. I was furious that we both needed to prioritize our future marriages and children above our current desires. And I was furious at myself for not just acting on that desire that day in Hyrax Estate, if only to have experienced just once - because that desire had been burning me alive ever since.

But if I was going to burn... I was going to take him down with me.

I rested my elbows on the table in front of us, pressing my breasts together as I peered up at him through hooded eyes. "And here I thought you might want to act like a real boy on your birthday."

"I seem to recall I'm not the only one who struggles to set aside their title to have some fun," Clay reminded me, that damn eyebrow perched mockingly. "And you and I both know I'm far from a *boy*."

My breath caught. The memory of his body, his manhood, pressed against me was sudden and overpowering. My cheeks burned, and I knew they were visibly reddening. Still, I stood tall, and I didn't miss when his gaze dropped to the low cut of my gown. That cut had been the exact reason I chose this gown above the others. Grinning wickedly, I lifted the tiny glass towards him in a toast.

"Happy birthday, your grace," I whispered.

Our friends drank rapidly, losing themselves in laughter, but Clay and I held each other's gaze for a moment that was excessively long, both unwilling to surrender to the other.

The party lasted utterly too long. Most people seemed to enjoy themselves. I just wasn't in the mood for dancing or socializing. Still, I could admit it was a proper celebration, more so than any I'd experienced in the palace thus far. The food had been divine, the twelve-foot ivory cream cake had been the sweetest thing I'd ever tasted, and the music was contagious, filling your soul and pushing you towards your feet whether you intended to or not. Those damn sirens certainly made it hard to stay in a bad mood.

And Clay was genuinely happy. It was rare to see him like that, entirely relaxed and content, but people had traveled far to be here with him. He treated every person he saw like a long-lost friend, joking with the men and dancing with *all* the girls. And by the Gods, did they all swoon over him.

Which isn't to say he wasn't swoon-worthy. I could at least admit that. There was nothing wrong with admitting that he was handsome. Anyone with eyes could agree with that. Especially tonight, when his golden jacket made his sandy hair seem particularly bright. I hadn't always noticed the hints of red in his hair, but tonight, they were there for all to see. And his smile, the one he so rarely unleashed upon the world, made me positively weak in the knees. And those damn leather pants...

When had I become so hopelessly enamored by him?

It was impossible to deny the reaction I had to him, but it was nothing more than a physical attraction. Physical attractions were completely natural. Nothing more than hormones at work. Well, that and the effects of three glasses of champagne and constant flashbacks of what it felt like to have his tongue down my throat and his hand between my legs.

I shook my head as if to dislodge that memory from my consciousness.

The after-party was the talk of the room. Lorelai had made it seem like an exclusive event, but nearly everyone under sixty was planning to be there. There was to be a large fire by the lake on the outskirts of the palace grounds. There would be singing and dancing, and I'm sure Rankor would end up throwing people into that water after a few more drinks. He'd been eyeing up people all night, no doubt trying to devise the order of his victims.

"You don't want to come," Lorelai noted, coming to stand by me on the edges of the ballroom. "To the lake."

"How'd you guess?"

"I'm a Truthseeker. It's my job to know things."

She nudged me playfully, and I rested my head on her shoulder, watching Clay take some beautiful, tall woman for her third dance of the evening. She was a Dragon. I wasn't sure how I knew, but I could tell. Perhaps it was how fitting they looked together. Both were tall and lean, with striking eyes and lush hair. They'd make perfect little babies. Perfect little heirs to Zion that I could never provide.

I wondered if his future wife would be a Dragon or a lightning wielder, the other form of Descendant that originated from Zion. Did it matter? Or was the only qualification for breeding that they simply needed to be descended from Zion one way or another? If you really stopped to think about all these rules about marriages and children, it all started to seem a bit incestuous.

"I don't want to go," I confirmed.

"What happened with you two?" Lorelai asked, nudging her head towards Clay. "He's been extra moody lately."

He didn't look extra moody. He seemed quite happy with that girl wrapped around him. I watched his hand as it slid slowly down her back until it rested on her waist—a little too low on her waist. Magic rushed to my fingertips and so help me if he grabbed her ass right in front of me... I wasn't sure I could contain it from lashing out at the pair of them.

But that was ridiculous.

This had been *my* choice. I was the one who rejected him. I had no right to be jealous. We were never even in a relationship in the first place.

Sighing, I allowed Lorelai to wrap her arm around mine as she guided me to sit at a table by the window overlooking the gardens.

"Nothing really," I explained. "I think for a moment, we forgot that nothing could ever happen between us. We don't have the luxury of making those choices for ourselves. And then, all at once, we both realized our responsibilities. And I think we realized that neither of us wants something to happen in the first place."

She snorted in an entirely un-ladylike way, and I gasped. I had never heard Lorelai make a noise like that before. Lorelai was always so prim, so put together, but here she was looking at me like a child who had just been caught stealing deserts before dinner.

"Sorry." She laughed. "But like I said, I'm a Truthseeker. I know when I'm being lied to and that my friend was a very big lie."

I could only sigh and shrug, partially because *I* didn't even know which part of that was a lie. I suppose I could have asked her what the lie had been. And while that might help to clarify my thoughts, it certainly would have left me embarrassed for the next century. So, I kept quiet.

Clay was right; I didn't know a damn thing.

Well, actually, I knew *one* thing. And that was that I'd had enough of this party.

And I'd certainly had enough of watching that woman lean on Clay and dip her mouth close to the lobe of his ear while she spoke. Her feet stumbled slightly on the corner of a rug that seemed to have moved two feet from where it had been positioned earlier in the day. Clay's eyes found mine suddenly, a glare darkening his features. I turned away from him and clenched my fists, pulling that magical power back into me.

"You're a good friend, Lorelai," I told her. "But I think it's time for me to say goodnight."

She squeezed my hand as I stood and offered a supportive smile. "It'll all work out, Thea. We'll figure out who your attacker is, you'll ascend to the Council, and you and Clay will figure out a way to be around each other. Just give it time. Trust me, it all works out in time."

I smiled my thanks at her and grabbed my shawl from where I had left it on a table by the door, waving my goodbyes to Iris and the others. They barely noticed me in the merriment, and I didn't mind. They all deserved some fun, even the Crown Prince himself, I supposed.

Clay was *finally* finishing his dance. He swooped her low and pressed his lips to the hollow in her neck before they both stood and laughed. I ignored the ping in my stomach as he grabbed onto her hand and they left the dance floor together in search of refreshment.

That's it! I thought to myself. *I have got to get out of here right now.*

Every glance in Clay's direction had my stomach lurching and my power swirling. I'd already used it spitefully once. If I spent another second in this room, I'd either say something I would regret, or this magic would burst out of me entirely and the night would end in a catastrophe.

"Oh," I cried, barely catching myself before barreling directly into a servant as he closed the doors to the ballroom. "Excuse me; I was just leaving."

"Sorry, Miss," he sputtered, his high-pitched voice betraying how young he was and the lack of a title betraying that he didn't recognize me. "M'afraid you can't be going quite yet."

CHAPTER THIRTY

The boy stood about four feet tall. His uniform was as polished as all the others, but obviously too big for him. Undoubtedly, he had been sent to guard the door and prevent guests from leaving before an extravagant surprise for Clay's birthday. Perhaps the Dragon had gotten him a new crown or jewel-inlaid sword. I didn't need to stay for whatever was planned to close the evening.

"Oh, that's fine. No one here will miss me. If you'll just excuse me?"

He steeled himself against the door, planting his feet and folding his arms. It was silly to see this boy, barely twelve years old, trying so hard to stand tall and defiant.

"M'afraid you can't be going quite yet," he repeated.

I laughed softly. "Listen, I hate to play the future Council member card, but I'm Theadora Moore of House Hyrax, and I would like to return to my suite now. So if you'll just step aside?"

The boy stood frozen. He didn't move; he didn't blink, he barely even seemed to breathe. There was something strange about him. It wasn't just that he seemed too young to work as palace staff.

The hair on the back of my neck rose all too suddenly.

"Why can't I leave?" I questioned him.

"Sorry, Miss, m'afraid you can't be going quite yet," he repeated, in the same intonation and pitch as before. That type of speech pattern was... familiar.

The sound of it sent my magic sweeping from my core into my fingertips and this time I didn't fight to repress it. I kept it there, controlled but at the ready.

Gently, I made a move to push past him.

"Sorry, Miss, m'afraid you can't be going quite yet."

The boy was impossibly quick, pushing me away from the door and brandishing a blade. At first, it seemed as if he planned to use it against me, but he pressed it to his own throat.

"I'm to stop anyone who tries to leave, Miss. I'm to pierce this blade into my throat if they try."

The realization hit me with the force of the Gods themselves stepping back down upon the Mortal Realm. I stumbled back a few feet, but he didn't react. He stood like a statue, unmovable and unphased. I was in danger. We were *all* in danger.

I knew why this was so familiar to me.

I fled from him in such a rush that my heel caught on the back of my dress, and I stumbled, falling to a heap on the floor, which earned me a few suspicious glances. Unwilling to waste any time, I scrambled up, hiking my skirts above my knees as I sought his blonde hair and broad shoulders. Muttered complaints met me when I bumped into people on the dancefloor as I sprinted to him.

"Clay!" I cried out, latching onto his arms as I threw myself at him.

His dance partner spit out complaints, but Clay steadied me, shoulders tightening in annoyance. His lips turned down in a frown, no doubt ready to bark a complaint at me, but he froze when he saw the fear in my eyes. I felt his grip on my arms tighten.

"What is it?"

"The servant." I panted, pointing at the boy on the wall. "He's being compelled."

As we met each other's eyes, there was only a minute for us to prepare each other for what was about to happen. He looked over my head to the room around me, to the people filling it, as the ground began to shake. And then he pulled me to him, wrapping an arm over my head to shield me as the explosions started sounding around us.

The world faded around me and somehow I was back in the moment I sat on the ground, fighting off a wall of fire and struggling to breathe. The memory was alive around me, suffocating in its intensity and entirely paralyzing. Only Clay's grip on me kept me from tipping over. Could he hear my heart? Surely it pounded loudly enough for him to hear. Clay spoke, but the roaring of terror in my head kept me from hearing anything.

Breathe. I commanded myself, forcing air in and out of my lungs.

The candles in the hall were all extinguished, and screams filled the air. In a frenzied rush, people moved to seek cover and attempt to aid those who were injured in the blast. And by the Gods, there were *so many* who were already wounded. Numbly, I noticed the streak of blood on my dress. A piece of debris had hit the arm Clay had used to cover my head, slicing the skin open.

I grabbed at his arm, as if the only thing that mattered in that moment was making sure he was okay. The shard had ripped the skin open, but the cut didn't look deep. At least, I didn't think it was. I wasn't a nurse. Clay needed to see a nurse. Someone needed to check that he was okay.

Gently, he sat his hand over mine and nodded that he was alright. I wanted to protest, but his hand wrapped around the back of my neck, forcing me to look at him.

"They're locking us in here," Clay told me, voice tense.

"How can you tell?"

"Look." He pointed to the walls, and sure enough, posted at each door was another servant with arms crossed over their chest and feet planted.

I squinted as my eyes adjusted to the darkness, frantically trying to determine what was happening. The room was a tangle of bodies, more and more falling dead and injured by the minute. The servants were attacking, each brandishing all forms of swords, knives, and magic. And while the guests were starting to fight back, it had taken far too long for them to realize what was happening. It had already been a massacre.

Clay snapped into action immediately. Grasping hold of my hand, he pulled me back to a corner of the room by the empty throne, which the Dragon and Queen vacated hours ago when they retired for the evening. He roughly shoved me under a table without hesitation, shouting for Rankor to stand guard.

"No!" I screamed, latching onto his wrist so tight I felt my nails break the skin.

"They're here for you, Thea!" He reminded me, eyes flashing around the room as he calculated his next move.

I knew they were here for me. Gods, I knew that. And I felt the weight of every lifeless body on the floor pressing into my heart. Before this night was over, more would lose their lives because of me. So Hyrax help me, I wouldn't sit here and hide while innocent blood was shed on my behalf.

"I can help!" I declared, voice firm. "Let me help, Clay. I won't let these people die for me while I do nothing."

"You're a liability," he barked, reaching behind the back of the Dragon's throne and pulling out a chest of weapons. Did they always store weapons there? Were there weapons hidden in every room of the castle?

Clay started tossing them out to those in need. "I can't protect you."

His golden eyes were desperate, pleading, and his voice had lowered to a tenor just meant for me. I understood suddenly that his desire to keep me safe extended past the fact that I was of a royal house. His desire to keep me safe likely came from the same place that made me stop thinking about anything but a cut on his arm.

That was just another reason Clay and I couldn't allow ourselves to go there, though.

We both had jobs to do and people to protect right now. We needed to focus on them and not on each other.

"I don't need your protection."

I ripped a sword from his grasp. It was short and light, perfect for my minimal skill set. I'd gotten quite good at hand-to-hand combat, but had barely begun my weapons training. I would have to make do. Before Clay could stop me, I took off at a sprint and launched myself into the chaos.

The dim lighting made it challenging to understand what was happening fully, but the screams made it clear that people were being hurt. A child cowered in the center of the room, curled into a ball and screaming. My legs were moving before my mind had conceptualized a plan and that well of untouched power in my belly swarmed.

A servant stepped into my path, swinging a blade toward my head at an impossible speed. I ducked quickly, grabbing his shoulder and pushing him into my knee. I stomped down on the back of his thigh and twisted as another servant reached to pull my hair. I gasped at the blinding tug. Perhaps wearing my hair in the pinned up fashions that were more in style was something I should start considering.

I spun, trying to ignore the sting of chunks of hair being ripped from head. My sword sliced through the air, tearing at the delicate skin of the man's throat. He fell.

By the Gods, I had just...

I had just killed him.

I'd never killed a man before.

My stomach lurched as I stared down at his body and I swallowed down a retch of disgust and guilt. There was no time for those feelings now.

I reached out to the child, who still sat cowering, and pulled her into my grasp. She wrapped her little arms around my neck and squeezed, crying viciously. I wondered if she recognized me.

"It's okay," I told her, smoothing her hair and pulling her hands from my throat. I hoped she recognized me. I hoped she knew enough to trust that I was one of the good guys. "You're going to be okay, but I need you to be brave and close your eyes right now. Can you do that?"

Her little brown eyes widened initially, but eventually, she gave a small hiccup and nodded. She blinked twice, then closed her eyes, and I didn't waste another moment. I imagined my power flowing out of me and wrapping around her. I pictured it enfolding her in a stiff cocoon, lifting her through the air, and landing her safely in Clay's arms across the room. He caught her easily, having noticed her flight. With surprised and remarkably impressed eyes, he nodded at me and tucked her safely behind the throne.

I had only a second to breathe a sigh of relief before a rush of acute pain flooded my senses. One of the servants had sliced their blade down my forearm. I cried out, grasping at it foolishly, and the servant only laughed.

I really hated when people laughed at my pain.

"Such a scary girl, but you cry so easily," the servant taunted.

She was tall, well over a foot higher than me, with dark hair tied back neatly at the nape of her neck. Her uniform was bloody, stained with her misdeeds. Effortlessly, she twisted a knife through her fingers as she paced around me, with her face contorted in disgust. Silently, she squeezed her fist, and the air was torn from my lungs, leaving me gasping on my knees. Fucking air elemental.

She chuckled again, pulling my head up by the hair so that I could meet her gaze. "Tonight, I'm finally ending this."

I ripped at her wrist with my right hand, not strong enough to break it, but enough to get it out of my hair. As three more servants ran toward us,

I threw out my left hand, blasting them across the room, where they fell unconscious.

"I will gut you, demon." She roared, stabbing at me.

Dear gods, I scrambled away from her madness, but wasn't nearly fast enough. Her blade sliced through my hip, a surface wound but deep enough to leave me screaming.

"I've waited so long for this."

"You?" I sputtered as she attempted to suck the air from me once more. "You're the one behind all of this?"

She rolled her eyes, and her boot connected with my stomach. The pain was blinding as I felt one of my ribs crack under the pressure. My scream only joined as an echo to the chaos around me. The woman lowered to her knees before me, tracing my cheek with her knife.

"I am but one," she whispered.

She moved to slice my throat and even got a nick in before I wrapped my fingers firmly around her wrist. "You're no one anymore."

Power rippled out of me, and I threw her through the air. She slammed into one of the iron rod chandeliers. A spire pierced her through, so deeply that she remained suspended, hung, there upon it. I could only watch the life fade from her as I clutched at my side.

All I could do for a moment was sit and struggle to catch my breath as the pandemonium continued. I'd never seen so many Descendants using their powers in one place. People were moving at inhuman speeds. Fire, lightning, and water erupted into the air, and small explosions constantly sounded. I used my powers to push back servants who rushed at me as I struggled back to my feet and immediately was grateful for having such an offensive power.

There were plenty of Descendants whose magic was useless in combat. The Whisperers of House Herea, for example, whose gift was communicating with animals. Or the empaths of House Harmonia. Or the Truth-seekers of...

Lorelai.

I scanned the room for her wild red hair in an anxious rush.

Rankor and Kent had trained as members of the Athenian military. Iris was a fast and calculated fighter. Camilla was likely ruthless in battle, given her typical attitude. Lorelai, though, her power would be useless here, and I had never actually seen her fight. I was sure she had been trained; Iris said they were all required to train, but *I'd never seen her fight*. I had no idea if she could defend herself in this.

A servant launched at me, and I slammed my elbow into his nose, feeling it break against my skin. He fought on, jutting his blade toward me, but I stepped aside, driving my sword under his ribcage. He roared in pain as I ripped it back out. His body fell onto me, knocking me to the ground, and I groaned against the pain of my still-open hip wound. I rolled out from under him with a magically assisted shove and struggled to my feet.

I needed to find Lorelai.

I caught sight of Iris in the corner, fighting three larger men with unnatural speed. She seemed to be holding her own, but the fight was requiring her full attention. As she briefly found my eyes, her face was a picture of fear, not for herself but for the woman she loved.

Lorelai! She mouthed to me, ducking under a swinging sword.

Iris couldn't go to protect her. She was trusting me to do it. I nodded my understanding.

With a quick glance at the throne to ensure my prince was still standing and fighting, I darted through the crowd, swerving away from stray lightning bolts and miniature storms.

Where was she?

Suddenly, a Detonator sent a table next to me, bursting into a massive explosion that sent me flying backward. I tucked my shoulder, rolling into the fall as I skidded across the floor. My backside hit the wall, and my head bounced against the stone so forcefully that it was all I could do to stop myself from vomiting right then and there as the world spun around me.

I sat on my hands and knees, struggling to catch my breath, when I finally saw her. I'd recognize that hair anywhere. Lorelai was only a few feet from me, caught on the ground. A massive man with dirty brown hair and clothes soaked through with blood wrapped his hands around her throat. Instinctively, I threw out my palms, attacking with magic and pushing him across the room, but he didn't go as far as I intended.

My power was waning. I'd been using it sporadically all day, even before the battle. And now? Well, I had only ever used it in practice settings. This was the first time I'd actually had to use it in controlled, repetitive strikes. I wasn't used to that. I wasn't strong enough for it. Exhaustion was pressing on the edges of my consciousness.

Still, I pushed onto my feet, limping to where Lorelai coughed on her hands and knees. Gripping onto her, I pulled her to her feet.

"Thea?" Tears streaked her face. "What's happening?"

"I don't know right now. But we need to get you somewhere safe. Come on, let's go behind the throne. Clay's there."

I pulled her toward safety, only to lock eyes with the man who had been trying to kill her. He stood tall now, well over six feet. Sometimes, I thought Rankor had to be the strongest man in the Kingdom, but this man's bicep alone seemed twice the size of my head. By the Gods, he would murder me.

"The daughter of Hyrax," he called to me, grinning toothily as a cut from his forehead leaked blood down the side of his cheek. "We've been looking for you all night."

That unknown part of my magic roared angrily in my stomach forcefully and it took me a moment to gain enough control to push it down. A moment was all he needed.

He backhanded me so sharply that I fell violently to the floor, clutching my face. By the time I spun back around to face him, his blade had already struck through Lorelai's chest.

A moment was all he had needed.

"No!" I screamed.

Things moved slowly, like a series of events I watched more than I actively took part in.

He dropped Lorelai and walked to me.

His fingers wrapped around my throat, lifting me off the ground as she fell.

Lorelai sputtered, gasping for air and clutching the wound.

"Such a shame a pretty girl like that had to die for you," he growled.

I clawed at his fingers, desperate to breathe, desperate to fight, desperate to do *something* to save my friend. She couldn't die for me. Too many people had already died for me. Not her. Please, not her.

And yet, I saw the moment the light left her eyes. I could have sworn I *felt* her soul leaving its body and beginning its descent to the Underworld.

Lorelai was dead.

Lorelai had died because of me.

Lorelai had died because they came here for me and I wasn't fast enough to save her from them.

Lorelai, who had always been kind to me, who had loaned me countless dresses, who had comforted me only hours ago... *was dead.*

And finally, the well of power in my stomach refused to stay suppressed any longer.

A raw scream ripped through me, and power erupted from every nerve in my body. It touched everyone and everything and then suddenly I could *feel* them all.

I could feel Kent as he sang, knocking as many people unconscious as he could. I could feel Camilla as she sliced through her attacker without remorse. I could feel Rankor as he wrapped his arms around the head of a smaller man and snapped his neck. I could feel Clay as he unleashed a torrent of dragonfire on a group of attackers.

I felt *everyone*.

Their life forces around me were palpable. I could feel their hearts beating, their lungs inflating and deflating, their blood moving through their extremities. Grasping onto each of the attackers was remarkably easy.

The man holding me felt it when my magic wrapped around him. He looked at me, eyes widening with shock and what might have been fear, and with a brush of my will, his heart stopped beating. He fell. The attackers all fell. One by one, I took them, and as I had felt Lorelai's death, I also felt when their souls left their bodies.

The ballroom stilled.

Eyes landed on me.

From across the room, Clay's gaze met mine, eyes wild and afraid. I held his attention until a tremor fell over me. The weight of exhaustion hit me suddenly, and then I too fell.

CHAPTER THIRTY-ONE

I wasn't sure what I expected to see when I opened my eyes, but it surprised me to find Clay waiting at my bedside. We were back in the infirmary. I was laying in the same room we had first met in all those months ago.

But our worlds had both changed so much since then.

His hands were crossed on the bed before me, fingers still stained with blood, and his head hung low. That blonde hair that usually was so well-kept was dirty and out of place. His shoulders slumped as if pressed down by a weight I couldn't begin to imagine. And yet, though I knew he had other places to be and things to do, he sat here with me.

"You're alone," I noted, my voice hoarse and dry. Internally, I kicked myself for saying something so stupid.

When he looked up at me, I didn't miss the flash of relief on his face. I also noticed the red and sunken rims of his eyes, as if he had been crying. Numbly, I noted he was still in his party clothes.

He ran a hand roughly over his face as if to shake himself back into alertness. "The guards are just outside. Every Council member is being attended, myself included."

"A lot of good that does for us now."

He chuckled darkly, and I felt the heat of his eyes scanning quickly over me. "Does anything hurt? The nurses gave you something for the pain."

Everything hurt. My broken ribs ached, and my head pounded from where it had hit the wall. The worst of it was the exhaustion, though. I'd never felt quite that tired before. My entire body screamed at me in protest, my limbs were heavier than normal, and my eyes burned as I struggled to keep them open.

"How long was I asleep?" I asked, evading his question.

"Almost two days."

I frowned. Two whole days, and I still felt so entirely wiped. What in all of creation was that power I unleased? It had been unlike anything I had ever felt before. It was *intoxicating*. Beautiful and natural, but also deadly. It had taken more energy than I had expected.

"The servants?" I whispered, already sensing the answer to that question.

They were dead.

That intoxicating, beautiful power had killed them all. And I had felt when it happened. I had felt it when my magic wrapped around their hearts and squeezed. I had felt it when they fell. I had felt it when they left this world.

Clay sighed, looking away as his shoulders tensed. When he finally responded, his voice was low, barely more than a whisper. "A few escaped when they realized what you were doing and are in custody now. You killed the rest."

"I-" Words failed me.

How could I possibly have stopped the hearts of over two dozen people with my magic alone?

"Have you ever heard of a Descendant being able to do something like that?"

He was still for a moment, but then his fingers wrapped around mine and his eyes scanned over my face. There was no anger in his gaze. I couldn't quite place the emotion I saw there, though.

"No, Thea. I've never read or heard anything suggesting something like that is possible. No Descendant has ever had the power to kill an entire room in one fell swoop like that."

No Descendant until me.

The room was warm, too warm, but I shivered.

"I tried to save her, Clay," I whispered. "I wasn't fast enough."

His grip on my hand tightened. He took a ragged breath. "You did everything you could, Thea. We all did."

I unleashed my tears silently. "Iris is going to hate me."

He said nothing. He only stood, gently adjusted me so that he could sit in the bed with me and pulled me to him. As my tears turned to sobs, I buried my face in his chest and he pressed his lips to my forehead. And though I knew I shouldn't, I found comfort in his embrace.

It wasn't long after the nurses cleared me to leave before I demanded Clay take me to the Council. His surprise was clear, but I knew it was where I was needed. I knew there would already be investigations about the attack underway. The Dragon wouldn't let this go unanswered for long. Clay assured me that no one expected me to be there, but their expectations didn't matter. I wasn't doing this because I thought I had to. I was doing this because I wanted to be there when they punished those responsible for the attack.

I needed to know who was responsible for Lorelai's death.

This unnamed villain had killed dozens in a misguided attempt to target *me*. They'd killed my friend in the process. So, I would go to that Council meeting and I would show them all that I was alive and well. Whoever was behind this would see the promise of revenge in my eyes.

The castle was silent as Clay and I moved through it, our guards close on our heels. It was all a bit eerie. I had grown accustomed to the court people moving through the halls with jittering voices as they delivered the latest gossip to one another. But today was silent. And remarkably empty. I hoped that was because many had stayed in their rooms, but somewhere deep down, I knew it was because so many had lost their lives.

As we entered the Council's chamber, we greeted faces shrouded in rage and grief. The Council sat in their usual balcony seats, as usual, but the Dragon had abandoned his seat.

"Tell me who orchestrated this!" he shouted from the center of the Council floor.

Not all the servants who had attacked us had been compelled. I felt that when my power had connected us all. I had eliminated those who had killed of their own volition, but the young boys who had been compelled to guard the doors had been the ones who survived me. The compulsion must have broken by now, and the seven of them sat before the Dragon cowering.

"I cannot," one sobbed. "Don't remember, Your Majesty. Don't remember nothing."

The Dragon moved in a blink, lashing out with his right hand and backhanding the boy so hard his head snapped back. Absently, I ran my fingers across my cheek. I'd been hit so many times in the same way over the past months. At the Alchemists, in the Dragons chambers, at the attack. Rage bubbled in my gut and I swallowed it down.

I didn't want to accept that anymore.

I was *so* done with people trying to hurt me.

"They were compelled to forget your Majesty," Councilor Clara reminded him.

Clara was an older lady, but the night's events had aged her even more. I wondered if she had lost anyone she loved in the attack. Had the other Council members? Were they in mourning like I was?

Did I have a right to mourn Lorelai when I could have prevented her death?

Clay sighed next to me, and I knew why. The boys were unlikely to tell us anything. They couldn't. The compulsion had taken the memory and moved it so far behind mental walls that not even a Truthseeker could pull it out.

I froze.

The compulsion had moved the memory.

Wasn't that my very power? To move things? Iris had once explained to me that all magic involved manipulations. We had always assumed I could manipulate physical things in the world, but just hours ago, I had moved souls from this life to the next. Was it possible that my abilities extended far past the physical world? Who's to say that when I tapped into that well of power inside me, I couldn't just as easily manipulate a person's body or consciousness as easily as I could now move apples on mountains?

Perhaps I could just *move* the memory back to where the boy could access it?

"I can get the name," I announced as every eye turned to me.

The Dragon didn't bother to hide his disdain for me or my suggestion as he looked me over. I suspected my display of power in the Grand Hall had put him on edge. He had distrusted me long before he knew I could kill with nothing more than a magical whim. Perhaps he was afraid of me now.

Perhaps he should be.

But if I was the only one that could do this, he would have to learn to trust me. And if he couldn't, I would invite him to stop me.

"How?" Councilor Gregory questioned.

I stepped forward, aware of Clay tensing beside me.

"Truthseekers force us to bring memories to the front of our minds. These boys' memories are stuck behind a wall *they* can't pass. But perhaps I can move it for them."

"You better be sure," the Dragon warned, voice low. "Are you aware that when Truthseekers attempt to push past compulsions, the victim dies?"

My heart thumped heavily, and I couldn't help but glance towards the boys. I *hadn't* known that. There had already been so much death, either through my hand or because of me. Was I willing to risk even more?

The boy on the end, likely the oldest, sat up straighter and nodded at me. He was perhaps seventeen or eighteen, with copper hair and the shadow of a beard just beginning to show.

"Do it, m'lady," he commanded. "If I must risk death to keep my kingdom safe, then that is a small price to pay."

The Dragon rolled his eyes but waved his hand at me, inviting me to move forward.

"It's too soon," Clay protested, grasping onto my hand and pulling me back. "You're not strong enough to use magic again yet. You still need time to rest, Thea."

I felt the eyes of the room on us, on our connected hands. I felt their curiosity and suspicion wash over us and wondered if Clay felt it, too. Did he even care? Or had Clayton Vail finally found something he would sacrifice his princely responsibilities for?

My stomach soared as I stared into his grey eyes. His jaw was tight, brows furrowed, and his grip on my hand was tight. He was worried for me. And that made me feel... well, I didn't know how to describe what that made me feel. But I tugged on my hand, regardless.

"I want answers to this as much as anyone, Clay, and I know I can get them. This isn't just my life at risk anymore. It's my duty to do whatever I can to protect my people. I hope you can understand that."

He was silent and while his fingers twitched, as if he was ready to let go, his shoulders still inclined towards me. For months, I'd hated Clay for his devotion to duty above all else, but now I was asking him to prioritize it above me. I was begging him to prioritize his duty – *our* duty – over me and whatever he may feel for me.

And though it looked like it pained him, he released my hand.

I wanted to ignore how hard that had been for him.

I wanted to thank him for it.

I wanted to turn away from him.

I wanted to run into his arms.

Truthfully, I simply wanted the things I couldn't have.

My steps were slow and timid as I approached the boy. Without thinking, I bent down and kissed each of his cheeks in a silent show of gratitude. I may not understand everything about my powers, but I knew, without doubt, that this would hurt him, and for that, I was sorry. But not sorry enough to stop myself from doing it.

With a deep breath, I closed my eyes, grasped the boy's shoulders, and let loose the tether on my powers. I let its electricity rush over me, feeling it first in my belly until it climbed over my chest and poured into my arms and legs. It traveled into the very ends of my fingers and toes until I questioned whether those around me could see the shimmering energy that swarmed me. And though I was about to hurt a young boy and give everyone in this kingdom another reason to distrust how dangerous my powers could be, that didn't stop me from marveling at how alive it all made me feel.

The only time I truly felt comfortable with myself was when I let this mass of magical energy rush over me so completely.

This power may be dangerous and unheard of, but I was born to use it.

I pushed it towards the boy until I felt it wrap around him, connecting me to him as easily as it had connected me to all those servants in the Grand

Hall. I was only slightly aware of his shudder as I explored him and finally coiled my magic like an iron-fist around his mind.

The resistance came all too suddenly. I stumbled backward as I hit it, feeling its fortitude like a stone wall. Someone caught my weight and helped steady me on my feet. It might have been Clay, but I lost myself too completely in the boy's mind to see the world around me.

For a moment, I thought I would lose myself in there, in the sensations of thoughts and memories flowing easily over my consciousness. Emotions that weren't mine, anger, determination… fear.

"Breathe, Thea," Clay whispered in my ear. "Control the magic."

The familiar advice sent a shiver down my spine. That was what he had told me that day on the terrace when I first summoned my powers. He'd been there for me then and he was here for me now.

I could do this.

Breathe.

The gasp of air I sucked into me tasted of cinnamon and oak. I sank into that scent and focused on the memory I wanted from the boy, envisioning it like a golden orb inside his mind. I imagined that orb floating towards me through the darkness. It struggled as if some unseen force was pulling it back, but I clutched at it tighter. He started to whimper, and then he started to scream. The boy cried out in howls of pain that left my toes curling. Dimly, I noticed my nose had started to bleed. I swiped at it quickly, unwilling to give up.

"That's enough," Clay cried. "She's going to kill him."

"As long as she gets the answer, I don't care," the Dragon growled in response.

They might have spoken more. I couldn't hear them over the ringing in my ears. I couldn't focus on anything but the power rushing through me.

I was so close. I could do this. They needed to let me do this.

Arms wrapped around my waist, pulling me away.

"She's going to kill herself!" Clay insisted, voice filled with panic.

I just needed to pull a bit harder...

The boy and I collapsed simultaneously as the memory crashed through the magical wall. Clay's arms around my waist were the only thing keeping me standing as we watched the boy's eyes flash with understanding.

"Camilla." He panted. "Camilla of House Hypatia compelled me. She compelled us all."

CHAPTER THIRTY-TWO

She was gone. By the time the guards had run from the Council chamber to her rooms, Camilla had already disappeared. In her suites they'd found everything they needed to confirm that she had been casting black magic spells. There were forbidden grimoires, weapons, and what appeared to be several large blood stains. I shivered to think what or *who* had to die for her to compel so many people.

She was more intelligent than anyone had given her credit for. She'd done just enough, delegated just enough, so that she could make it by Truthseeker interrogation without actually having to lie. And I had helped her do it myself. After that first attack I'd insisted Lorelai use her powers to confirm that Camilla was telling the truth. And she had been. After all, she'd only said *she* didn't place it there. She never denied having orchestrated it. No one had suspected her again after that.

I had given her the perfect alibi.

And now Lorelai's death was doubly my fault.

The Dragon had wasted no time bringing her grandmother in for interrogation, but Alina swore she didn't know where Camilla was or what she was planning, and the Truthseekers had confirmed it. Though, I questioned whether we could trust that after all that had happened. The Dragon subjected every Witch in the castle to Truthseeker interrogation, but found no additional leads.

He and Clay both got more irritable each day that went by without finding Camilla, so much so that both had showed their scales on more than one occasion. Clay seemed more and more like the controlling and domineering version of himself that he'd been when we first met. Which also meant that while Camilla was being hunted down, he had commanded me to stay locked away in my rooms once again.

I felt as banished as Hyrax was, sentenced to live alone with nothing but my guilt for company.

Lorelai was dead.

I couldn't move past her death, or my own culpability in it. I saw her face when I closed my eyes or flashes of red hair when I turned corners too quickly. She was everywhere, and she was nowhere.

She was dead because of me.

Nessira and Geia tried to assure me it wasn't my fault, but their words were lies. Pretty lies perhaps, but untrue. I couldn't bear to hear their comforts. Eventually, I sent them away. With no reason to leave my room, I didn't need their help in dressing, and I certainly didn't need or want their friendship. I didn't deserve it.

And so, most days, I sat on the bench by my windowsill overlooking the garden, bouncing between emotions. There were moments when I was so angry I was sure I would shake the castle to shambles around me. There were moments when I succumbed to my grief and cried for hours. There were moments when my terror grew so intense I could only lie frozen on the floor and live through the memories of that battle.

After a week of complete solitude, a knock at my door finally sounded. The sudden sound in the silence I had grown accustomed to was jarring and left me jumping uncomfortably. My hair was unkempt, falling loosely in knots down my back, and I wore nothing but an oversized silk tunic and cotton leggings. It was hardly the attire for entertaining guests, but I was past the point of caring. I waved my hand at the door, using my power to yank it open from across the room.

Kent entered first, followed by Rankor, with Iris tucked between them. Rankor and Kent looked so tired, the dark circles under their eyes and slumped shoulders caught my attention first, but when my gaze finally landed on the small girl between them, my stomach sank. I hadn't seen Iris since the attack, and no one had spoken to me of her.

They'd refused to talk to me about her.

Clay hadn't acknowledged whether she was angry with me over Lorelai's death, but his silence had been answer enough. As was the venom in her gaze as she met my eyes. Her expression was sharp and vicious. I'd never seen Iris look at anyone that way, let alone *me*.

I hardly recognized her. Her hair, usually vibrant and elaborately dressed, was straight and dark. She wore no fancy gown with bright embellishments and instead donned a simple tunic and riding pants, both black. And she must have lost nearly ten pounds. She had already been so thin I wouldn't have thought she had an extra ten pounds of fat to lose. But now, her arms and fingers were bone-like. And yet it wasn't the clothes, or hair, or weight-loss that truly sank my stomach. It was her eyes. Hollow, dark circles swelled and surrounded her usually bright and teasing eyes. She'd been crying. She looked as if she'd been crying for a long time.

I struggled to gasp in a breath through the clenching of my heart.

From behind her, Rankor shifted slightly, pushing gently on her shoulder until she started to walk into the foyer. She ripped her intense gaze from mine as she sat. Rankor and Kent were silent as they watched her go, and it was only after she seated herself that I felt the pressure of their gazes scanning over me as if they were trying to predict which of us would need the most support next. I nodded my head to the parlor. Iris. Iris deserved their attention.

"We thought it might be nice for us to see each other," Kent explained, shutting the door behind him. "We won't stay long if you'd prefer to be alone."

"Please, sit." I hurried to follow them. "How are you?"

He nodded, pulling me to his side and squeezing my shoulder as his head dipped briefly to press a kiss to my forehead. "It's been a hard week. I'm sure for you, too."

The emotion clogging my throat prevented any words from escaping in response, so I simply squeezed him back and let him go to Iris. As I went to join them though, Rankor stepped into my path and gathered me in his arms, squeezing harder than usual.

"I'm glad you're okay. I didn't get to see you afterward, but you made me proud that night."

My stomach somersaulted slightly at the compliment, both in joy and disgust. Fighting in the battle had felt natural. I wasn't trained for a battle of that size, but my body knew what it needed to do. That swirling feeling in my stomach had guided me.

And yet, for as fast and deadly as I had been, I hadn't been able to do enough.

Rankor squeezed my shoulder, pulling my attention back to the room, and he nodded to where Iris sat, picking at her fingernails.

"I've never seen her like this," he confided. "We're worried."

"Do you think seeing me right now is good for her? She blames me."

He sighed, not denying my assertion. "You're her best friend, Thea. Whether she's willing to admit that right now or not, she may not want you, but she needs you. She needs all of us."

"Where's Clay?"

"In town. He took a small team and they're searching houses."

I frowned. "Do they have reason to suspect anyone is hiding Camilla?"

Rankor sighed and shook his head. I suspected he was worried about the same thing I was. Why should the people be subjected to having their homes invaded when we had no evidence to motivate the intrusion?

"She needs to be found," Rankor finally murmured.

He took my hand and pulled me to join Iris and Kent in the foyer, bringing my attention back to the issue at hand. Gently, I sat on the couch across from Iris, feeling more awkward and nervous than I had since the moment I woke up in the infirmary wing.

"Iris?" I asked, feeling stupid as the words came out of my mouth. "How are you?"

The room was silent for a few moments, the only sound being our shallow breaths in and out. Finally, her weight shifted, and her dead eyes met mine. There was so much anger and pain hidden in them; it was all I could do not to turn away from her as a chill slid down my spine.

"How am I?" she questioned, as if she was musing over it herself. "Well, I'm... I'm simply stunned. You see, a year ago, my life was grand. I was living in this beautiful castle with all my friends and had a crush on this amazing woman. But then, suddenly, some stranger from a dead house shows up, and everything changes. Suddenly, one of my best friends - someone I've known since we were girls - has been conducting forbidden magic. She's been *murdering* people behind our backs."

Kent shifted uncomfortably, running a tired hand over his face. And though it was morning, Rankor excused himself to my bar cart to pour himself a drink. Part of me wanted to join him.

"And you know what the hardest part is?" Iris continued. "It's that I don't really understand it."

"I don't think we can understand what she was thinking, Iris," Kent whispered.

She laughed darkly. "No? No, you're right. Without talking to her, we won't know why this person we *all* loved and trusted decided she needed to kill Thea so desperately that she was willing to go to those lengths."

I jumped at the sound of shattering glass. Rankor had thrown his drink across the room. For a moment, we all sat frozen as we watched the amber liquid streak down the walls.

"This isn't her fault, Iris," he warned, voice low and irritated, as if it wasn't the first time he'd had to remind her of that fact.

"And what if I think it is?" She yelled. "We know nothing about her, Rankor! She just showed up, creating absolute chaos, and we were dumb enough to accept her into our lives. We don't know where she comes from or how she got here. We don't even know her real name!"

"I don't need to know any of that," he spit back, turning so suddenly that I flinched. "Who people are is based on more than their name. "

Iris laughed darkly, leaning back in her seat, and I felt her gaze drift over the Mark on my chest.

"Is it based on more than their blood line too? Because that's the other thing that changed this year. The House of Hyrax returned. Praise Gods."

Her voice dripped in sarcasm and I sunk heavily into the cushions of the armchair I had seated myself in. I couldn't even defend myself against her. Maybe part of me felt like I deserved her hatred. No one else would speak to me this way. No one would dare disrespect me this way because I was a future Council member.

And wasn't that Iris' entire point?

The entire kingdom had trusted me enough to give me the power and respect that I hadn't earned. And look what had happened as a result.

"It didn't even surprise me to watch you kill all those people in the ballroom. Maybe deep down I'd already realized you are nothing more than the evil child of an evil God."

"I didn't want this, Iris," I whispered, surprised by how empty and frail my own voice sounded.

"Oh, we all know that! You didn't *want* these rooms, the gowns, your place on the Council. But you took it all, didn't you? You accepted our friendship, let people wait on you, and danced at all the parties while proclaiming everything you thought was wrong with our customs. You denied our way of life until the moment Clay fell in love with you and then you used it all as a crutch to escape having to face him."

Iris' face flushed as she stood in a rush. Kent followed her lead, standing between us as if he was prepared to have to stop her from hurting me. Would Iris really go that far? Would I blame her if she did?

"And what did we get for embracing you? We all lost Camilla, and I lost Lorelai. I lost the love of my life because of *you*. So you know what Thea, I'm tired of feeling bad for you. I'm tired of pitying you for being locked away in these rooms. Now, I hope you never come out. I hope the Dragon keeps you locked in here for the rest of your pitiful life and when you go to sleep at night, I hope you rest easy knowing that you're a future Council member whose citizens have died for her. A sacrifice that probably wasn't worth it."

Her words slapped against my skin, hurting more than any physical blow ever could. I flinched against them and bit down on my lip forcefully as the lump in my throat grew so large that my eyes misted. I would not cry. I would not allow myself to cry in front of her.

"Do you mean that?" I whispered.

I don't know what I expected to see from her. Perhaps some softness, some sign that my friend-my *best* friend-still cared for me despite her grief.

"Are you going to convince me I shouldn't?"

I remained silent. Even I knew when I was on the precipice of a battle I would lose. And it was clear from the set of her clenched jaw and furrowed brow that she meant every word she had said to me.

We stared at each other until she scoffed at my lack of response and barreled out of the room with the kind of speed only a faerie could master. Kent threw his head back and breathed deeply, as if trying to muster the resolve to go after her.

"I'm sorry, Thea," he muttered. "What she said wasn't fair, but I need to make sure she's okay."

Kent's departure didn't surprise me. He was always willing to play the mediator. He was always the one who went after Camilla after she stormed away from me. Apparently, Iris had taken on the role of my enemy now, too. So he followed after her now.

I sat frozen as the door slammed behind them and the crash of it echoed throughout the room. My chest heaved, and I threw my face into my hands as a vicious sob escaped. The salty tears I tried to hold back managed to escape and rolled down my face in heated streaks.

"She didn't mean that." Rankor sighed, coming to sit beside me and rub a hand over my back in a comforting gesture. "She's just grieving."

"She's right."

Rankor began to protest, and I held up a hand to stop him. I didn't need him to tell me she was wrong, and she didn't mean those words. I needed the space to finally have *my* chance to give voice to the regrets that had been plaguing my mind for the past week.

"None of this would have happened if I never showed up on that bridge. I just appeared dealing out death and destruction and you all welcomed me into a life I didn't deserve. The people who showed me kindness are now dead or brokenhearted. I was so indecisive about joining the Council that I became careless with Clay's feelings. I was so focused on the battle being my fault that I wasn't fast enough to save Lorelai. All I have been doing since leaving the infirmary is causing harm to people. I've been so desperate to prove House Hyrax can be good that maybe I was just refusing to admit how evil the blood that flows through me is."

Rankor stood as I spoke, sighing heavily as he paced the expanse of the room in front of me. His fingers twitched before clenching and unclenching at his sides. The sound of a loud crack as he rolled his neck was all that filled the silence between us as the words finished rushing out of me.

Finally, he sat once more, resting his elbows on his knees and crossing his fingers together tightly. The past week hadn't been easy for him, either. Now far too overgrown, his hair had been haphazardly tied back at the nape of his neck and his shoulders sagged from exhaustion. It looked like it had been several days since he'd had a good night's sleep or committed to shaving.

"Now you listen to me," he commanded, his tone leaving no room for protest. "I have spent my entire life around nobility - Council members and their family who expect the world to be handed to them on a silver platter. They treat everyone around them as less than. And I've gathered that I don't need to lecture you on the extent of the Dragon's cruelty?"

My resulting flinch was answer enough. How many people knew about what had happened between he and I?

"Even Clay, for all his strengths, is a Prince first and a friend second. He demands respect and obedience above all else. After a while, you just get used to it, Thea. You adapt to that feeling of not being as worthy as them. You get used to them barking orders at you or snickering behind your back."

He sat apart from me, eyes focused on the fraying carpet at our feet. I hated that Rankor had been made to feel this way. I hated that any part of him thought he wasn't deserving of the upmost consideration. Rankor was good and caring. He was a better person than half this court. It wasn't *right* that he was treated differently than me because of our bloodlines.

"But you, Thea, you've never made us feel like we were any different from you. You have never acted above us because of your lineage. Your heart is *kind*. And if you ask me, that means a hell of a lot more than the Mark on your chest."

I sniffled. "Kindness doesn't excuse inaction. If I'd just been a little quicker, I could have saved her."

"You're right," he agreed, voice firm and I couldn't help but to flinch. "You probably could have. And the Gods know I've faced that same guilt in my life. When it comes to war, not everyone survives. But you're forgetting one important detail."

"And what's that?"

Rankor reached across the couch and pulled at my hand, gripping it tightly as his thumb stroked affectionally over the racing pulse in my wrist.

"This war isn't over."

Rankor left shortly thereafter, declaring he needed to go check on Iris too, leaving me alone once more.

And though my emotions were as strong as ever, after my talk with him, I felt something above my sadness and fear.

I felt determination.

Rankor was right. This wasn't over. This wasn't even close to over. Camilla was still out there. And while I couldn't bring Lorelai back, I could certainly stop Camilla from hurting anyone else in her mission to get me.

I was gifted a beautiful life here. It may not have been a life I wanted at first, but I wanted it *now*. It was my life now, and I loved it. I would go to the Underworld kicking and screaming before I let anyone take that from me.

So no, I didn't know why Camilla wanted me dead so badly, but I knew I would not make it easy on her.

I was going to finish this.

CHAPTER THIRTY-THREE

As the setting sun began sending hues of yellow and gold across the fields, I sent word to Nessira and Geia, asking them to dine with me. If my night went according to plan, it may or may not end with my death. And If I was going to die tonight, I wanted to enjoy my last meal with the two women who had spent so much time and effort caring for me. They brought a stew and bread from the kitchen, and we sat together, eating on the floor and laughing.

Between bites, I looked up at each of them, marveling at the rush of appreciation I felt for each girl.

"I wanted to thank you both for your friendship," I told them, taking each of their hands in mine. "I know it's your job to care for me, but I hope you both know you mean so much more to me than just that. I consider you both friends."

Geia had smiled warmly, a tender blush spreading across her cheeks. It had taken her some time to soften to me once more after the Dragon's punishment, but I was grateful she finally had. And Nessira, though she seemed suspicious that I had suddenly changed my mind and summoned them back to me, squeezed my hand.

"It *is* our job to care for you, my lady," Nessira reminded me. "But I wouldn't want to serve anyone else. You are strong, Lady Moore. And you should let no one make you forget that."

"We should have a toast!" Geia cried, clapping her hands together. She stood and retreated to the bar cart in the foyer. A few moments later, she brought me a glass of sweet wine, then returned to fetch two drinks for herself and Nessira.

"To Lady Moore," she cheered, raising her glass high. "I could have never imagined I'd be assigned to work with the daughter of Hyrax, but you have taught me to be brave. You have taught me to follow my intuition, even if everyone else in court says it's wrong. After these past months with you, I know I can do whatever must be done in the future."

I grinned, drinking deeply. Such faith they both had in me. I hoped to one day deserve it.

Darkness had already fallen by the time they left me. As the door closed behind them, the silence echoed and the nervous rush of anticipation settled over me. The time had come. I took a single deep breath to steady myself and got to work.

Tonight, I was going hunting.

I marched into my dressing room, searching for the fighting leathers that were tucked away ages ago. They'd been delivered to my suite earlier in my time in the castle. They were of thick protective material, only necessary for an actual war. Geia had joked that I would never need such things when she folded them away and instead set about displaying the endless racks of gowns and jewelry in my closet.

Part of me wished she had been right, but another part had always known I would one day need these clothes.

I slipped into the leather breeches and folded the thick corset over my tunic, ripping the cords tight over my chest. Some time ago, Rankor had sent me an assortment of blades as a gift, and I set about strapping them onto my person - one strapped to each thigh, one in my right boot, one to my left wrist, and one attached to my hip. Unused to dressing my own hair, I tied it in a single braid down my back before tucking it under the hood of a sleeveless black cloak, long enough to hide my weaponry. This plan hinged on my not getting caught.

Absentmindedly, I mused that this occasion called for an invisibility bangle. The very weapon Hyrax had once scoffed at. I wondered how things may have been different if he had appreciated that gift more. Would the Gods still be locked behind the veil? Would I still be under attack because of my heritage?

I shook my head to clear it of the unhelpful, wandering thoughts. Thinking of Hyrax did me no good. He wasn't here to help me.

I had to do this alone.

My plan was simple. I couldn't risk injuring myself from another fall out my window, so I needed another way out of the castle. From my room, I would send my power out in waves, shaking the castle like a quake of the Earth. Most of my guards would go to investigate, leaving Dimitri alone. Then, I would stop the blood flow to his brain, just long enough for him to pass out, but not enough to cause actual damage.

After that, once I was free of my guards, I would go through the castle, hoping no one would see me under the hood of my cloak. Clay would still be in town if the Gods were on my side, leaving his rooms empty. I would only need to get into his suite and use that back chamber to escape into the gardens, with no one noticing. I would get Netta from the stables and make my way to Hyrax Estate, where, away from the masses of people at the castle, I would finally call Camilla to me.

That was the part of the plan that made me most uneasy.

I had never tried to move my thoughts into someone else's consciousness, but I suspected I could. It couldn't be that different from burrowing into a mind to pull out memories through compulsions. So, tonight I would move my thoughts into Camilla's mind. I would focus all my magic on bringing her to meet me at Hyrax Estate. And when she and I were finally alone, I would finish this.

After getting dressed and armed, I knew it was time to put the plan into motion. Sitting cross-legged on the floor, I closed my eyes and picturing the Grand Hall. I imagined the thrones, the crystal chandeliers, the oil portraits hung high in golden frames. I imagined them quivering, ever so slightly at first, but then so much so that the portraits fell and the crystals shattered. The feeling of the vibration was subtle against my body at first, but as it grew, I heard the unmistakable shouts of Dimitri giving orders and the sound of boots on the floor as the guards ran to the threat.

Phase one was complete.

I stood quickly, preparing to make my way to the door, but a sudden rush of dizziness sent me stumbling. I reached out, bracing myself on the wall.

That was odd.

Groaning, I worked to push myself off the wall only to struggle through my next steps as a sudden pain reverberated through my skull.

I stumbled to the foyer, waiting for the head rush to pass, but my legs grew heavier with each step. The room spun abruptly around me, and I fell heavily, grasping onto the bar cart to catch myself. The glasses we'd been drinking from fell to the ground in a clattering mess. Gasping, I attempted to center myself and stop the wave of nausea.

Something was very, *very* wrong.

It took all my strength to lift my head as the door to my suite opened and shut swiftly.

"Oh good, the poison is working. I was worried it would take too long to set in."

I choked on my own breath as I met her eyes and gasped.

After Lorelai had died, I was sure my heart couldn't break any further. But I felt everything in me shatter as I stared at Geia's slight frame as she picked up the wineglass from the ground and returned it to the cart. That was the very wine glass she had served me not so long ago. She had brought it to me alone, then returned to get drinks for herself and Nessira.

Geia, the small young girl I had always considered my friend, had betrayed me.

"Why?" I cried.

She took hold of me, guiding me to the couch in the foyer, where I slumped heavily. I fought against the fog pressing in on my consciousness.

"I'm truly sorry, Lady Moore, but it's for the best."

She even had the audacity to sound sad about it.

"You were helping her all along," I realized. "It was *you* who put the hex bag in here and you saw me going back into the castle alone right before the explosion. All this time, I thought you were my friend, and you were trying to kill me?"

Geia smoothed my hair and hushed me. "I'm sorry it had to be this way. But when Camilla explained why it was necessary, I knew I had to do it. This is the only way to protect us all. Now, rest, Lady Moore. The others will be here soon, and you'll be back in the Underworld where you belong."

Exhaustion pressed in on me. Shoving her away from me, I pushed myself onto my feet towards the door. And when I fell once more, I crawled. But in the end, the poison was too strong and my eyes closed.

"*Are you ready?" The old man asked from his throne.*

"*For what?" I questioned, holding my pounding head between my hands. The pain had followed me here.*

He grinned knowingly, with a raised brow and a happy smirk. Around us, the room warmed as the fires in each lamp post flared without warning. In the distance, a beast roared in a victory call.

"*For them to all finally see what you are.*"

I frowned. "And what is that?"

His dark laughter echoed around me as his blue eyes scanned over me. It was like he could peer into my very soul. Like he knew me better than I would ever know myself.

"*Don't you know yet?" He snickered.*

CHAPTER THIRTY-FOUR

I woke with a start, shivering against the cold and groaning against the ache in my head. My swollen tongue felt too heavy for my mouth, dry and nearly choking me. As I came to slowly, I struggled against the binds that pinned my wrists sharply together behind my back. The world was too dark and the feeling of hay scratched against the exposed skin of my cheek. Gods, it stunk.

Or was that me?

Based on the bumping sensation of movement under me, I suspected I was in a moving carriage or cart of some kind.

"I thought you said she would sleep the whole way there!" A voice scoffed.

"She was supposed to," answered a second, deeper voice.

"I'll take care of her."

A wave of starlight flooded over me as a blanket that had been covering me, hiding me, was ripped off and I met the eyes of one of my captors.

He was so dirty. That was the first thing I noticed about him. He was tall, broad, and absolutely covered in blood, muck, and dirt. That *smell*. I fought the urge to wretch as it invaded my senses. That smell was definitely not me.

There was no kindness in his dark eyes as they scanned over me, lingering at the rise of my chest and swells of my hips. His tongue darted over his bottom lip.

All the bravery I had summoned when I had been naïve enough to think I could fight Camilla on my own terms dissipated as he hoisted himself into the cart and lunged towards me.

At that moment, it didn't matter that I was a powerful Descendant. It didn't matter that I had been trained to defend myself or that I could kill with only a brush of my will.

At that moment, I screamed.

"Shut her up!" hissed the voice from the front.

"Working on it," the man snapped, removing a cloth from the pocket of his breeches and jamming it into my mouth.

I ripped my head back away from him, struggling as best as I could despite the lack of access to my hands. Still, his meaty paw wrapped against the back of my head as he continued shoving the gag into my mouth.

"Time to go back to sleep, princess."

He smirked, an expression that I was positive would haunt my nightmares, and then with an unbelievable force, he pounded my head against the floor of the cart, and I slipped away once more.

The first thing I noticed when I woke was the overwhelming nausea that flooded me. Then I was suddenly aware of the stillness of my body. The cart was no longer moving. We'd arrived at wherever they were planning to bring me, which couldn't be good. I swallowed down my fear.

My captor once again ripped the blanket off of me, but this time his hands wrapped around my ankles and pulled. A strangled cry escaped through my gag as he yanked me towards him. He wrapped his fingers around my waist and ripped me up until his sweaty body was flush against mine.

"Camilla should be here soon," his accomplice said. That man was smaller and somewhat cleaner, but still appeared to lack any expression of kindness.

We were in a small clearing in an otherwise heavy section of forest. The second man perched against a tree, carving a small wooden block in his hand and peering at me under bushy red brows.

"Good," the man holding onto me replied, grinning toothily. His breath against my cheek was rancid, and I turned my face away from him, ignoring the kink of protest in my neck. "That means I can have some fun with her first."

My stomach dropped at the tenor of his words and the way his hand grabbed onto the flesh of my ass possessively.

"Do what you will, Henrick, just be quick about it. I'm going to go take a piss."

I wasn't necessarily counting on the second captor to help me, but as he left me alone with this man, Henrick, I couldn't escape the shiver of terror that made its way down my spine. His hand trailed down my thigh, lingering on the blade that was sheathed there.

"Oh look," he purred. "We missed one."

He ripped the blade out and for a second I almost questioned if he was going to use it to kill me right there, but he only dipped it to the binds on my ankles and sliced through them. Seeing it for the opportunity it was, I didn't waste any time in trying to lift my right leg and gain the momentum to kick out, but he gripped my calf to stop me with an unbreakable grasp.

"Here I was worried you would take this easily. Half the fun is the fight."

As his fingers grasped tightly around my forearm, I cried out in pain, which only earned me another vicious laugh. I knew I needed to fight back, needed to stop this, but as he yanked on that arm, I fell forward heavily. Gods, I flashed back suddenly to the Dragon's office. My hands had been bound then, too.

I fell to the ground and he was on top of me instantly, grasping at my waist and flipping me over. Magic soured through me, angrily, but remained trapped in the hands behind me. He must have sensed the frustration in my grunt because he laughed at me as his fingers trailed over the waistband of my leather breeches and reached for their ties.

No.

As his left hand began fumbling with those ties, his right reached up to knead greedily at my breast.

No.

I had yet to let a man abuse me in this way, and I would not let this disgusting creature claim that victory.

"*No!*" I screamed, managing to spit out the gag as he bit down on the fabric above my nipple. Magic exploded, even without my hands free to control it. I blasted Henrick off of me and sent him crashing into the cart. The splintering of the wood was sharp as it echoed around us, but I could hardly hear it over the sound of my own blood pumping.

His gaze was venomous as he rushed back to me. "You little Hyraxian bitch. You'll pay for that."

One thick hand wrapped around my throat, cutting off my air so fully I worried he might crush my windpipe, while his other grappled with the ties on my pants once more. I bucked my hips, reaching for my magic again.

"Enough Henrick!" A familiar voice called out. "Knock her out. We have work to do."

He sighed angrily but increased the pressure on my throat. I continued struggling, trying to grasp onto the sparks of power in my fingers, but even my magic seemed too frightened to function properly and it wasn't long before the lack of oxygen left me falling away once more.

"Hold her still!"

Henrick and his accomplice were on each side of me, clutching onto my forearms with such force that I cried out. I was in pain. I was *burning.* It was everywhere. Every part of my body felt scorched, like flaming razors were pushing their way through my veins. I reached for my magic, desperate to escape my captors, but froze all too suddenly.

There was no electricity. Not a single spark.

I reached for it, but no familiar tingle rose to greet me.

And it hadn't retreated in fear, because even in that deepest part of me, in that well of magic I rarely allowed myself to touch, there was simply *nothing.* The rushing darkness of pure, godly power that lived deep in me was quiet for the first time.

Powerless.

It had been quite some time since I'd felt that way, but I recognized the feeling

"My magic?" I gasped, struggling again.

Camilla's laughter rang out, cold and vicious. "I'm afraid that's gone now."

My skin sliced open, and Henrick ripped out a needle that had been folded into my arm. He threw the attached bag to the ground, and as it ripped open blood, *my* blood, splattered around us and soaked the grass until it stained the ground maroon. I stared at it numbly, unwilling to accept the truth in front of me.

I'd thought before that Camilla was more intelligent than we'd initially given her credit for.

It seemed like I was still underestimating her, because she had just sentenced me to a fate worse than death.

"What have you done?" I whispered.

She grinned, stepping forward. Silently, she touched my chest, pulling my tunic aside until I could see the faint outlines of my Mark of Hyrax as it slowly faded and disappeared from existence forever.

"I did what had to be done," she answered simply.

CHAPTER THIRTY-FIVE

When I'd first learned of power stripping, admittedly, I thought little of it. So much else had been going on at the time that I hadn't stopped to think about the severity of it. I hadn't realized how awful it would be to know that enough of your blood had been traded for that of a mortal that the connection to your God would be completely severed.

While in the castle, I'd met some rather religious Descendants. I'd met the High Priests who held weekly vigils in the palace temples. I knew that many in the castle prayed to their ancestors regularly. I'd just never personally taken the time to connect with Hyrax or pray to him. While I'd become determined to restore my family's good name, I often felt conflicted about my relationship with the God. Was he as evil as the stories said, or had he been misrepresented all along?

One day, perhaps when my trials were done, and my attacker had been caught, I always intended to learn more about him. It had always seemed like there would eventually be time to come to terms with who he was. And on that day, when I'd *fully* accepted my birthright, I would have prayed to him.

And now it was too late. I felt his absence in every fiber of my being.

I had grown so accustomed to the tingling sensation of power in my blood that without it, everything felt wrong. Too still. My body felt weighed down, my thoughts slower. Without the connection to Hyrax burnt into my chest, the loneliness was overwhelming. The hands on my arms released me, and I fell, unable to stop the scream of pure anguish. It was a sob of physical and emotional pain—the vicious cry of a woman who had just lost everything.

Power stripping was truly a fate worse than death.

Camilla and the others only laughed.

"You know," she mused, twirling one of my blades between her fingers. "This isn't exactly how I saw all this playing out. But then again, who could have imagined you'd be able to break compulsions and reveal me to everyone?"

I struggled to focus, half listening to her and half trying to process what had just happened. Consciously, I knew that my magic was gone, but I still searched for it haphazardly, scanning my body for any remaining shreds. It couldn't all be gone. I couldn't be powerless, not after all of this.

"You probably thought you were so smart by doing that," Camilla continued. "You probably thought you'd ended this by identifying me and forcing me on the run. But you never suspected little Geia! Why would you? You expect everyone to worship the ground you walk on, so much so that you never would have thought such a bright-eyed little girl could have been working against you."

Pull yourself together, I screamed at myself, forcing myself to breathe through the burning pain in my veins.

My magic may be... gone, but the threat wasn't. Camilla was making that very clear. And without the assistance of my powers, I was more in danger than I'd ever been in before. I needed to focus if I had any hope of making it out of this alive. I was at a disadvantage, but I wasn't dead yet. After all, I had spent months training with Rankor to fight without my powers, to not rely on them in moments of crisis.

It was time to put all that training to use.

I scanned over the scene around me. Camilla paced before me, and a group of twelve, maybe thirteen, was behind her. I didn't recognize any of them. Most were older men and women, though some teenagers stood scattered amongst them. Not a single man or woman looked at me with any sympathy. I'd find no compassion here.

I was a powerless mortal against fourteen Witches. It wasn't necessarily my favorite odds.

"How did I get here?" I croaked, throat raw from my screams. I needed to keep her talking long enough to come up with a solid plan.

Camilla raised an eyebrow at me as if she suspected my thoughts and doubted their feasibility. "I brought you here."

Her grin was positively demented.

She raised her hands before her, and the ground shook. Clouds pushed through the sky, and rain fell upon us in heavy, unnatural sheets. The air chilled, and goosebumps rose on my flesh. And then... the darkness came upon us.

The trees rustled under the force of hundreds of shadows, moving like living creatures, made their way to encase her in a dark embrace. They danced through her fingers, and her eyes transformed into black shells.

By the Gods, she looked like a creature straight from the mythology books Hansel forced me to memorize.

The attack, I realized. She had used all the deaths from Clay's birthnight celebration as sacrifices, and now she was high with the power of all that blood. How many times would I underestimate her? She'd proven to be smarter than I initially thought and far more cruel. Now, she stood before me more powerful than any other Descendant I'd ever met. Had she become as powerful as the Gods themselves?

I didn't stand a chance.

"Why are you doing this?" I questioned, hating myself for crying.

She threw her arms down and was in front of me instantly, ripping at my face until my eyes locked with hers. Hatred burned in her gaze and her eyes were completely black. The dark magic had taken her over entirely. In hindsight, I realized that I probably had never met the *true* Camilla, the one my friends had grown up with. Whoever she was then, she wasn't now.

"Are you going to sit here and pretend you don't know?"

Ripping my face from her grasp, I scrambled away on my hands and knees. "I don't know Camilla!"

I instantly felt the whip of her shadow power cracking against my cheek. The pain was shocking, worse than any blow I'd been dealt before. When I touched my cheek and felt my fingers covered in blood, it came as no surprise that the skin was torn apart.

"You don't need to do this," I tried to reason with her. "The black magic clouds your judgment, but we can help you. You have friends, Camilla. Iris, Rankor, Kent, even Clay. They're all worried about you."

With a scream of rage, she thrust a hand towards me. The shadows shot out of her fingertips, bursting through the sky in my direction with such ferocious speed that I had only seconds to throw up my arms and block my face as they hit me. Each was like a tiny beast, nipping at my skin until they covered me in a million tiny cuts. They held me for a moment in their gut-wrenching embrace before they dropped me, and I slumped forward, gasping in pain.

"Get up." She sneered, her voice devoid of any feeling. "You're not the victim here."

She barked something at the others, but I was too delirious with pain to recognize the words. They gathered behind her, shaping themselves into a circle and pointing their faces to the black night sky.

"The history books will paint me as the hero of this story," she promised.

Running was futile; somewhere deep down, I knew that. But I had three options. I could run, I could fight, or I could just let her kill me. Fighting was out of the question without magic, and I wouldn't willingly make the trip to the Underworld. So when she turned her back to me to join hands with the rest of the circle, I was on my feet and running before I had even registered what I was doing.

I felt the sting of every cut on my body as I sprinted through the woods, but I ignored it. I ignored the blinding pain in my throbbing head and the overwhelming nausea in my stomach. My feet slammed down, one after the other, until I was panting and my lungs were ready to burst. I needed to find my way out of these woods, but my brain was too scattered, too broken from the loss of my magic. I slumped against a tree, gasping for air and clutching the cramp in my side.

They could still find me. I needed to get up. Surely, someone had noticed my escape. They had to be chasing me by now.

Clutching onto the tree's bark, I pulled myself to my feet, determined to keep going, but I had only just managed to stand when I heard her laughter surrounding me. I spun, desperate to find her, but only saw trees and shadows. Until that darkness took shape.

"Going somewhere?" the shadows whispered to me, their voice thick and inhuman.

I screamed as they latched onto my ankles, ripping me through the sky and carrying me through the forest. As they dropped me back in the clearing, my head bounced against the ground, and stars danced in my vision.

"Keep her there," Camilla commanded, and the shadows locked around me, pressing down on my body and jamming themselves down my throat until I was nearly suffocating on the bitter taste of them. Then, when I was all but ready to give up fighting, they would retreat, allow me to catch my breath, and begin the entire process again.

I was being tortured and Camilla's laughter echoed through all of it.

Unsatisfied with simply stealing my breath, the shadows nipped at my ankles, slicing the flesh and tasting me. The pain was all-consuming. I couldn't think. I couldn't breathe.

Was this what dying felt like?

My last thought before I lost myself to it was of Clay, of his comforting scent, of the firmness of his touch when he touched my cheek or buried his hand in my hair. Gods, I so terribly regretted pushing him away when he had kissed me.

If I was back in the caverns again, I must have eventually passed out. Still, the pain followed me here. There was no reprieve from it as I doubled over, coughing up blood. Was it possible that mortals felt more pain than Descendants? I'd been hit before, nearly blown up a time or two, and nothing compared to the slicing pain of those vicious shadow teeth.

"Drink," he commanded.

A glass slid itself down the long table before me. I hobbled over to it, pleasantly surprised to find water and not wine. He always drank wine. I doubted I would ever trust a glass of the stuff again.

"You should tell me your name," I told him, flopping into a seat.

He turned his head from me, but I still noticed the way he dramatically rolled his eyes. I irritated him. That was odd. Usually, he was playful and taunting; I'd never seen him annoyed. What did he have to be angry about? It's not like his best friends abandoned or betrayed him. I doubted he had gone through a power stripping today.

"And why is that?" He sighed.

"If I'm to die tonight, shouldn't I know the name of the man who haunts my dreams?"

"Theadora, you know my name!" He huffed, standing quickly from his throne. That was odd, too. He always sat at the table, never the throne. "I do not know why you insist on this feigned ignorance."

I cringed, though I wasn't sure why. Perhaps it was because he'd always been kind to me. Even in these dark caverns resembling the scenery of a terrible nightmare, he'd only ever offered me friendship and mentorship. Perhaps I needed that friendship now, and his harshness only added insult to my injuries.

"You're not going to die tonight." He scoffed. "And you know that too."

"She took my powers," I reminded him petulantly. What good was I without my magic?

"Did she? Are you powerless or just accepting the rules of a society you never belonged to?"

"**S**he passed out again," a man criticized in disgust.

"Good, her screams were insufferable." Camilla sighed.

I opened my eyes briefly to see her flipping through a grimoire with irritation.

"Why can't we just kill her already?" A woman beside her demanded.

Camilla's shadows wrapped around the woman's throat, squeezing.

"We kill her when I'm ready!"

He wasn't making sense. I had watched the Mark of Hyrax fade from my skin. I felt the wall build itself up and separate me from every tendril of power that had once flowed so freely through me. That power was gone now. I couldn't reach it anymore. I didn't want to accept that, but it was reality. What choice did I have in the matter?

"You know what you're capable of," he continued, voice softening. "You've always known."

"I don't!" I protested, though I wasn't sure why.

"You did on the bridge. You did at the party."

"I had powers!"

"You have powers now!" He yelled back. "How many times do I need to remind you that you are stronger than all of them, Theadora? They cannot take from you that which you were born with. All this time, you have been trying to fit yourself into the role they've created for you, and you've known it isn't where you belong!"

He was wrong.

At least, that's what any logical person would think. Any logical person would know the effects of a power stripping. I was no different from any other Descendant who experienced one. The absence of my Descendants Mark was proof of that.

And yet... when had anything about my existence been logical?

From the day I had arrived at the Athenian castle, inexplicably, without any memories, I knew I didn't belong there. I knew I wasn't born to sit on their Council, suffer through an arranged marriage, or bow to a king who didn't deserve my respect. I wasn't born to bow to a king that wasn't nearly as powerful as I was.

And I was more powerful than the Dragon.

But I'd found my place in Athenia. I'd made friends, and I didn't want to lose that. So, I'd allowed myself to play their role. I'd allowed myself to be the princess they wanted me to be, even when all along I'd known deep down that I could be... more.

"She's cost me too much!" Camilla screamed. "I've lost everything because of her. So her blood will be *my* power. She will die so that I may be strong enough to take the entire fucking kingdom."

The shadows lifted me and carried my body through the air towards her. I didn't even have the strength to flinch as she sliced the blade across my chest. Warm blood poured over my skin, and she grinned.

"*Let's say I believe you,*" *I granted him. "I tried using my power, and it didn't work. So how am I supposed to access my magic if it doesn't want to work?*"

He laughed. "What is it that trainer of yours used to say?"

I froze. Of course.

All magic is tied to emotion.

This wasn't the first time my magic had sat dormant and out of reach. This wasn't the first time I couldn't feel its electricity.

"What are you feeling right now, Theadora?"

"I 'm afraid," I whispered, from where my body lay as a bloody lump on the ground. I was in my body, and yet I was somewhere else. Awake, and not. Here and there.

I was afraid, that much was certain. I didn't want to die, and I feared what awaited me on the other side of the veil. Would Hyrax forgive me for failing to resurrect our House? I feared how Clay would react when he found my room empty. I feared that Iris would hate me even more than she already did when she realized I had died anyway, and all of this had been for nothing.

I was afraid of it all.

The memory of Ryla's blade flying through the air was sudden and sharp. Fear wasn't enough to trigger my powers. It never had been.

I needed another emotion. An emotion too complicated to replicate unless I authentically felt it.

In my mind, I pictured Clay's hands on mine. I pictured him extending a rose and telling me to move it. He'd identified my emotional trigger that night, and I'd grown so accustomed to how easily magic came to me that I'd somehow forgot I needed to allow myself to feel that emotion.

It wasn't enough to be afraid.

It wasn't enough to be determined.

I needed an unwillingness to succumb to my fears.

I drew my attention back to the cavern, and to the man seated on the throne of skulls and bones. His eyes sparkled when he realized that I finally understood. I knew what I needed to do.

"I need to go back," I told him.

"So, go."

I didn't stop to look if the Mark had returned to my skin. I knew it hadn't, just as I knew I didn't need it. Not anymore.

Digging my fingers into the grass beneath me, I forced my legs to move, to push up on shaking muscles until I stood before her. My teeth mashed forcefully together as I pushed against that wall inside me, the wall that blocked me from my power - my birthright - with all my might. It held fast and strong, and I groaned against it.

Camilla turned from her place in the circle, and her lifeless eyes met mine. Icy fear lingered in my veins and I shivered against it. That terror grew as her shadows slowly began scrounging through the grass towards my legs and began their assault once more.

But I did not cower.

"What exactly do you think you're doing?" She teased, laughing at me.

I spit my blood on the ground before me and wiped my mouth with the back of my hand. The scarlet droplets no longer scared me. They were the reminder of who I was. She couldn't take that from me. No one could.

"I'm fighting back, bitch."

The wall shattered, and the rush of electricity, familiar and natural, was so overwhelming it nearly drove me to my knees and brought tears of relief to my eyes. For once, I didn't temper it down. I didn't shy away from that pit in my stomach. That much power may be abnormal and make others suspicious of me, but it was part of *me*. It was who I was and, by the Gods, I was done hiding it and hoping those around me would trust me despite it.

I was the last Descendant of Hyrax, and they were about to feel my wrath.

CHAPTER THIRTY-SIX

Letting go of that power was effortless. It exploded out of me, crashing into Camilla and sending her flying haphazardly through the air. The other Witches gasped in shock, falling over themselves as they tried to get away from me, eyes wide with fear. They should be afraid. They wouldn't be able to escape me now.

"That's not possible!" Camilla screeched, voice filled with hatred and anger. "I power-stripped you!"

I wanted to prove to her just how wrong she was, but at that moment, a monstrous roar sounded through the skies, shaking the surrounding trees. The Witches clutched at their ears, glancing up worriedly around them, and I felt my stomach somersault. Not in fear but in anticipation, the way it did for only one person in the world.

"What was that?" One teen screamed, grasping at a woman who must have been his mother.

I didn't need to look up at the sky to know what was coming for us, but I did so anyway. Because even though I could feel *him,* I wanted to see him with my own eyes. And I grinned like a child when I saw the enormous golden dragon fly over the tree cover. By the Gods, he was nearly as large as the entire palace gardens. His enormous jaw opened, revealing rows of deadly teeth, and a plume of fire filled the sky. He was terrifying in the most beautiful way. Deadly and utterly breathtaking.

I had never been more enamored by him.

"What's the matter?" I laughed, meeting the eyes of my attackers. "Don't you recognize your Crown Prince?"

The armies of Athenia were coming for me. They were leagues away still, but I could *feel* them. I could feel the movement in the air as they pounded towards us. Rankor was leading the charge, Kent beside him. They were all coming. And my power extended so far that I could feel their hearts miles away.

I was with them, even when I wasn't.

That godly power connected me to them all, and I was everywhere.

Camilla stood and summoned the shadows to her. They swirled dangerously around her feet and hands, climbing up her limbs slowly.

"Brothers and sisters," she called. "I need your help."

The Witches traded looks amongst each other and fell to their knees within an instant. The awareness of what was coming was sudden, too sudden for me to stop them.

"No!" I screamed, as they lifted the blades to their throats.

None hesitated, not even the teens. As they took their dying breaths, the bodies heaved, shaking as shadows escaped their eyes and mouths and flowed easily into Camilla. Her breathy moans turned my stomach as she welcomed the power into her and the ground trembled.

"I wasn't strong enough to fight you by myself when you first came to Athenia," she hissed. "But I am now."

She flung her head back and shadows flew from every pore on her body, leaking out until day momentarily became night. Until the darkness took shape. Wide eyed, I shivered as her shadow-army rose. Some assumed the form of a human, while others were larger and far more disastrous. Some took to the skies, while others slithered on the ground.

And they felt... *wrong.*

The air stilled, and an icy chill settled over me. The shadows smelt of... death. I didn't connect with them the way I did with others. I couldn't *feel* them the way I felt Clay above or my friends who pushed their steeds to run faster to reach me.

The kind of magic that created these beasts was not meant for this realm.

When Rankor and his soldiers finally crossed through the trees, they met the shadow army immediately and, because my power still connected me to each of them, I *felt* the moment their blades connected. The creatures attacked without fear or compassion. I *felt* as their touch alone sliced through armor, fabric, even skin. It was a bloodbath.

The Athenian blades and weapons had little effect on the beasts. Magic coated the air as the soldiers resorted to their powers to fight back the shadows. Fire erupted viciously in the sky above me, and I ducked, only sparing a moment to glance at Clay, in his Dragon form, fighting his own enemies. Iris once told me that only the most powerful Dragons could completely change their shape into a total beast. I'd never stopped to ask if Clay was one of those few. Deep down, I'd already known the answer to that question.

"Thea!" Rankor approached me at full speed, grabbing my arm and spinning me out of the way of an approaching shadow blade. He pulled me into the cover of the forest, and his eyes scanned over me quickly.

"I'm fine."

It was a lie, of course. My head throbbed from where it had hit the ground, and I was sure my cheek was already black from where Camilla had lashed out at me earlier. But the feeling of my full, untapped power was still rushing through me and fighting off any sensations of pain. For now, at least.

Rankor nodded and glanced back at the fight. I knew he was trying to create a battle plan and struggling to find one. How could we fight against an enemy who was impervious to our weapons?

Simple.

Strike the heart.

"Camilla." I grasped onto his arm, forcing him to meet my eyes. "She's doing this, and I need to stop her."

He shook his head. "It's too dangerous, and you're injured. You can't die tonight, Thea."

I knew that. The logical thing was to return to the castle and preserve my bloodline. I knew that if I died tonight, the line of Hyrax would die with me, and Camilla would get everything she wanted.

When had I ever been logical, though?

I was not running from this fight, not after all this time. Not after everything Camilla had done to me, done *because* of me.

"She's mine," I growled through a locked jaw. "I can do this."

Rankor met my eyes. I wasn't sure what he saw there, but it must have been enough to convince him. He pulled me towards him and kissed the top of my head.

"Be safe, my lady," he whispered. "And make her fucking pay."

I took off at a sprint, ignoring the screams in the air. I tried to, at least until one inhuman bellow of pain tore my gaze to the sky. A shadow beast with bat-like wings and three heads had lodged a tail of spikes into Clay's flank.

No!

The battle faded around me until all I could see, all I could hear, was Clay as he screeched in pain. The sound echoed through the air. I didn't realize a noise could pierce a heart until I'd heard Clay's yipes. He somersaulted, shaking the beast's tail off of him, but the shadow was persistent, chasing him through the sky at impossible speed. Clay twisted, releasing a torrent of dragonfire aimed at the shadow and for a moment I thought he might have defeated the creature.

But the beast flew through the fire and sank his teeth into the scales below Clay's neck.

"Clay!" I screamed.

Without stopping to think, I lifted my left hand into the sky, grasping onto the monster with my powers and wrenching it toward the ground. The shock of the attack must have momentarily stunned him because Clay too began to fall, and my heart fell with him, but after a moment his wings beat strongly and he regained his place in the sky. His reptilian eyes looked down on me from above, and he roared angrily at me.

"You're welcome," I muttered.

I knew the intention behind that glare. Clay would rather I focus on keeping myself safe than interfering in his fight, but I wouldn't let anyone else die for me. Especially not him. Never him.

Camilla was battling a fire elemental when I found her in the chaos. He rushed at her, hands ablaze, and she quickly tossed him aside with a burst of shadows. His head landed at an impossible angle, and shadows from his body poured into her. I ignored the rush of nausea at the sight, and the *feel* of his soul leaving it's body—so much death for her stupid vendetta against me.

"I'd rather fight you anyway," she told me, spitting blood.

"Ditto."

She didn't hesitate to throw her shadows at me. They exploded forward, but this time I ran *towards* them, waiting until the last second to tap into my magic and push myself off the ground until I was soaring over them entirely. Camilla grunted in frustration as I landed behind her and rammed my elbow into her kidney. Her knees buckled, and she fell, cursing the Gods as she did.

"Someone's been practicing some new tricks."

"You have no idea what I can do," I replied.

"I know *exactly* what you can do."

Her shadows ripped across my chest, pulling at the open wounds. I kicked out at her, desperate to get them off of me, and she latched onto my ankle, twisting it until I felt the mind-altering pain of the bone snapping.

I fell heavily, screaming, and blind to anything around me. All too suddenly, she crawled over me, wrapping her fingers around my throat. Her shadows latched onto my wrists and ankles, pinning me to the ground beneath her.

"You must die!" She screamed.

Above, Clay cried out once more.

For a moment, I lost myself to the pain of it all - the head injury, the broken ankle, the cuts and slashes that covered me from head to toe. I let myself feel every one of my wounds.

Until a shadow beast bit into Clay's tail above me, stealing my full attention. Clay howled in pain, the sound raw and animalistic. He jerked, spinning wildly as he tried to remove the monster, but it only used its momentum to slide its claws through Clay's torso while remaining latched onto his tail. Clay yipped once more before his wings faltered.

The ground trembled as the two creatures crashed down into it, and my blood turned to ice.

Please don't be dead.

I blasted Camilla off of me and crawled towards where Clay had landed. Blood coated every inch of his reptillian form, but I could still feel *him*. He was okay; he was going to be-

The shadow beast stalked towards him and plunged a midnight-black horn into the soft belly where Clay's scales were less formidable.

When he cried out, it was more of a whimper than a roar.

"Clayton, get up right now!" I demanded.

His head whipped towards me, and our eyes met. We were hundreds of feet away from each other but I still felt his concern for me as Camilla ripped me back by my hair. He snarled at her, clashing his teeth together as he ripped himself away from the beast and struggled towards me.

The beast followed him, smashing a thorny tail into his hide once.

Clay stumbled.

The beast hit him a second time.

Clay roared.

The beast hit him a third time.

Clay fell.

"Don't you fucking die!" I screamed to him, desperately.

I threw my head back, connecting with Camilla's nose and feeling it crack under the pressure. As I struggled to my feet, I sent my first prayer to Hyrax.

You may not have him! Do you hear me? You want me to restore your House - your name? He is mine *and you will not take him from me.*

Hyrax wasn't here to help me, though. If I wanted to save Clay, I needed to do something.

Camilla's eyes were so black, so inhuman. She was fueling an entire battle with magic stolen from the life force of human souls. And each person who fell fed her power even more. She was only growing stronger and crazier by the moment while Clay, Rankor and Kent - my family - were being killed.

I needed to stop this. *Now.*

An inhuman growl escaped from the depths of my chest as I tapped into the well of magic in my stomach and connected with her, allowing myself to *feel* her. I felt for her heart, her lungs, even the movement of her blood. And just when I was about to squeeze her heart and end this, end her, I froze.

I could feel them inside of her, the shadows. They filled every part of her, and they were... evil. They whispered to her of death and destruction. They were poisoning her with hate and violence. She may have chosen to invite this darkness into her initially, but there was no choice in this. She was consumed by them.

The shadows themselves were the enemy.

I realized suddenly that I didn't have to be ashamed of being a Descendant of Hyrax. Even if Hyrax was as evil of a God as the history books foretold, we *had* to be more than just our bloodlines. Because I could feel the existence of true evil inside of her and that... it wasn't me.

I wasn't a monster simply because I was a daughter of Hyrax.

There had to be more to our existence than just our ancestors. We were the ones who got to decide whether we were good or evil, regardless of where we came from.

Camilla had chosen to accept this evil. She chose to kill in the name of power.

I didn't have to make that same choice.

"You must die," she whispered again, diving to strangle me once more.

"No, Camilla." I gasped, struggling against her fingers around my throat. "I will not die tonight, and neither will you."

It took every ounce of strength in me, but I saw her eyes widen when she realized what I was doing. She didn't expect it; no one did. No one expected I would be strong enough to surround each member of the shadow army with my electric power, but I did, and I *pulled*. I tore them from the battle until they catapulted through the sky toward us.

"No!" she screamed, wincing as they hit her one by one, sinking themselves back into her flesh.

With each shadow returning home to her, she quivered until the power was too much for her body to contain. Camilla wasn't a goddess. She lived in a mortal body and had been gifted the ability to wield a fraction of a Gods power. She'd tried to take more than she could handle, and now her human body couldn't support it.

Her eyes bled, her screams echoed, her veins darkened. We watched, every eye on the battlefield, attuned to her, as she lifted from the ground, screeching in agony.

The power eventually overwhelmed her completely, and finally, her cries quieted. She must have fallen at that point, but my attention was on the massive golden Dragon lying impossibly still across the field. I tried to crawl to him, but with my magic sufficiently drained and my wounds becoming more painful than I could bear, I slipped off into unconsciousness once more with his name on my lips.

CHAPTER THIRTY-SEVEN

When I finally woke, I had woken back in that damn infirmary room, screaming and causing chaos with unchecked power. The nurses calmed me as best they could, but I had spent that day receiving minor details about what had happened between sleeping potions.

Camilla had, in fact, lived through the power surge as I hoped she would and had been taken to the palace dungeons to detox from the black magic. The power was addictive, and the shadows would fight to stay in her system. They weren't sure if she would live through the process. I wasn't sure how I felt about that.

Geia was gone. They'd determined she was Camilla's half-sister, born from Camilla's mortal mother. No one in the castle even knew Camilla's mother was alive, let alone that she'd had another child. We weren't entirely sure how Camilla and Geia had first come to know each other, but it didn't matter. Geia had left the palace, and while they had sent a team to look for her, part of me hoped they wouldn't find her. I wasn't sure I could bear to see her again. I couldn't even begin to think of what I would say to the young girl I had befriended who had ultimately betrayed me.

The nurses were diligent in tending to my wounds. Most of the cuts were simple enough to heal. The broken ankle had needed to be set before they could heal it, which had been... uncomfortable. But thank the Gods for magical tonics that healed most of the injuries in just a few days.

The one thing that hadn't seemed to heal was the Mark of Hyrax. No one was quite sure how I had stayed connected to my magic after the power stripping. They all assured me it was impossible, and the missing tattoo on my chest seemed to confirm that the tie to Hyrax had been severed. And yet, I felt more connected to that electricity than ever before. The only explanation anyone had brainstormed was that Camilla hadn't completed the blood transfusion to the extent she needed to. She had given me just enough mortal blood to suppress my powers for an extended time, and apparently remove my mark, but not enough to remove my magic permanently.

It was hardly the loss of a tattoo that pained me most, though. There had been plenty of casualties on the field that day. They'd had a memorial service while I was in the infirmary. The nurses had offered to summarize the Dragon's speech for me, but I refused. I'd been at the battle. The faces of the dead weren't ones I was likely to forget.

And yet, I couldn't bring myself to really care about Camilla, Geia, the Dragon, or anyone else, for that matter. There was only one person I truly cared to hear about in those days when I was locked away in my hospital bed.

During the first few days, they had been strict about not allowing me out of bed. They insisted I needed time to heal, but once it was clear that I was on the mend, the nurses let me know I was free to leave and I wasted no time doing so. I dressed in the tunic and cotton pants Nessira had brought me the day before and tied my hair back. Dimitri waited for me on the other side of the door, but thankfully, the rest of the guard team was finally gone. The threat had passed, which meant my days traveling with a group of ten were over.

Clay had been badly injured. That was all they would tell me. Each time I asked about him, they repeated the same story. That he had fought bravely, been severely wounded, and that they were doing everything they could. My stomach dropped when the nurse had first whispered those words to me, and it hadn't steadied itself since.

"Shall I escort you to your suites, my lady?" Dimitri asked, bowing respectfully as I finally stepped into the hall.

I shook my head firmly. "No. Take me to him."

"My lady," a nurse called, overhearing. "I cannot allow that. The Prince needs his rest. His father will surely keep the Council updated on his health."

"I don't care about the *Prince's* health," I insisted, words clipped and tense. My concern wasn't for the Crown Prince or the fate of the Council. I cared only for the man underneath the title. "Take me to see Clayton."

"My lady, please-"

"I'm not asking."

The nurse sighed but nodded nonetheless and led us through the hall. Each step seemed to take longer than the last as we approached him. The air pressed in on me until it was nearly suffocating me. He had to be okay. He *had* to.

There were guards posted outside his door. They looked at me suspiciously as I approached, but something in my expression must have told them that my entering the room was not up for debate. They stepped aside, and as Dimitri pulled open the door for me, I couldn't help but hold my breath.

I held up a hand, instructing them to wait outside as I took my first few shaking steps inside. Clay was sleeping, and for that, I was glad because I couldn't contain the raw emotion I felt looking at him. Even now, days after the battle and after several healing rituals, Clay's wounds still looked fresh. He must have landed on his left when he fell; he had a broken left leg and bruises covered his left cheek and arms. He was shirtless, his torso wrapped in layers of gauze, but even with the bandages, I could see fresh blood leaking through.

"My Gods," I whispered, unashamed that the Guards and nurses could see me beginning to cry. They would talk. They would question why the future Council member from House Hyrax showed such high regard for the Crown Prince.

"I know it looks frightening, my Lady, but we believe the Prince is healing at an expected pace," a nurse told me from the door.

"Has he... has he been like this since the battle?"

"The Crown Prince has not yet woken."

"My lady?" Dimitri called, his voice soft and tender. "Would you like to stay with the Prince for a little?"

I sniffled, pulling myself together and wiping away the tears. Clay was so damn good at donning his mask when necessary. I could don mine for him. I could play the role of Council member for now.

"Yes, I think I will. Please bring in a chair for me."

Dimitri nodded and waved toward the nurse, who left instantly to fetch it.

"Is there anything else I can get for you, Thea?" He asked.

I met his knowing eyes and took a deep breath. Dimitri had been with me since my first day in this castle; he knew exactly what I felt for Clay, even if I hadn't been brave enough to voice it yet. Dimitri's compassion in that moment was something I would always appreciate.

"Could you perhaps arrange for a pillow and blanket? I should like to stay until the Prince awakens."

He smiled and nodded.

I stayed with Clay for two more days, watching him, waiting for him to wake. Sometimes, I would look out the windows at the front steps of the palace and watch the townspeople leave flowers and tokens to the Gods in memory of those who had died. In the moments when exhaustion could not be ignored any longer, I would sleep fitfully in the chair. I woke every hour in a cold fear that he needed me.

And yet, when he finally did wake, it was on one of those occasions that I had finally closed my eyes.

I woke to him squeezing my hand. I must have latched onto him in my sleep.

"You're drooling," he informed me, voice hoarse and weak.

"You're awake!"

"It would appear so."

"How do you feel?"

"I feel like..." he groaned. "I feel like I was thrown out of the sky by a surprisingly strong shadow."

I winced and stood rapidly, announcing that I was getting a nurse at once to check on him.

"Thea, wait."

I paused, hands on the doorknob.

"Will you- will you just sit with me first?"

Frozen, I hesitated at the door. Intuition told me I should ignore him like always and get the nurse. This was the first time he had woken in *days*. He should get looked at immediately. Not to mention that he was the Crown Prince, after all. I had a responsibility to protect his well-being.

But he was more than that to me.

So when Clay asked me to sit with him, I returned to my seat without protest.

"Are *you* okay?" He asked, reaching for my hand again.

I laughed darkly, entwining my fingers with his. "I'm not the one in the hospital bed."

I swear my heart stopped when he raised an eyebrow at me. I'd never been so happy to see him looking disapprovingly at me.

"Physically, I'm fine. Otherwise, I'm not sure. We have a lot to catch up on."

His eyes grazed over the bare skin of my chest, and even in his weakened state, I could see the wheels in his head turning to understand what that unmarked flesh meant.

"I can see that." He nodded, then winced as if the movement caused a rush of pain.

"Sit still!" I chastised, reaching up to smooth down his unkempt hair and adjust the pillow under his head.

"You've been here the whole time?" he asked, glancing at the chair I had made into my temporary bed. "Why?"

I tried not to flinch from the harshness in his voice. I didn't know why I was there, in truth. Nothing had changed, not really. We were still from conflicting houses; we each had a duty to produce heirs and couldn't do that with each other. There was no future for the Crown Prince and the Council member of House Hyrax.

But in these days at his bedside, I hadn't felt like the future Council member. I felt like nothing more than a girl who could do nothing but pray to the Gods that he would be okay.

And when I saw him fall on the battlefield, the emotion I had felt for him was too great to put into words. It was the emotion that superseded Houses and responsibilities.

But that kind of emotion was confusing.

I didn't know how to handle it.

I did, however, know why I was there. I may not want to admit that, because I had a habit of lying to myself when the truth seemed too difficult to face. But I knew why I was there.

Everyone knew why I was there.

It's why Iris had been so harsh with me. It's why Rankor had reminded me that my heart was more important than my duty to the Council. It's why Dimitri had known I would sleep in this room until he woke up.

I was in love with Clayton Vail, Crown Prince of House Zion.

"How did you know where to find me?" I whispered, changing the topic.

He rolled his eyes at my choice to ignore his question, but a smile danced on his lips, regardless. "You called to me. I heard your voice in my head as clearly as if you were right next to me. You called my name, and I knew you needed me. I followed the pull of your magic right to you."

I frowned. That moment. There had been that moment, right before the shadows had started the torturous assault that had brought me in and out of consciousness, that I had thought of him. Had I called to him then?

That had been before I broke through to my powers, though. If I had called to him then, that meant that the mortal blood hadn't temporarily dulled them, as we suspected. That meant that I'd never truly been separated from my magic at all. The mortal blood had not affected me.

And that... that wasn't possible.

"She power-stripped you after that?" He mused, fingers brushing over my unmarked collarbone.

I took his hand and squeezed. "She tried. But you, of all people, know I don't like to back down that easily."

He laughed and finally let me call a nurse to look over him. Everyone was ecstatic to see he was awake, and the nurses proudly announced that he officially seemed to be on the mend. It would take some time for him to return to normal, but she was pleased. Which meant I was thrilled.

I stayed with him the rest of the day, talking about all manner of things. I filled him in on what had happened to Camilla, how I'd reignited my powers, and how the army had come at just the right time. We tried to brainstorm what it meant that my mark was gone, but couldn't make heads or tails of it.

When the sun set and we'd exhausted all topics of conversation, we sat quietly, and I watched as he dozed in and out of sleep, his hand locked in mine.

"Clay?" I whispered during a brief moment when I couldn't tell if he was awake or not.

"Mmm?"

"I think I know how I called out to you."

"Yeah?"

"I had just hit my head pretty badly. I couldn't use my powers, and the shadows were crawling up my skin. The pain was unbelievable. I was just about out of my mind with it. But I remember thinking about you. I remember thinking that I was sad that I would die without having the chance to kiss you again."

He grinned sleepily. "The next time I kiss you, I'll make it worth the pain."

Clay slept through the night peacefully. He kept assuring me he was fine and I could return to my rooms, but I knew I needed just one more night at his side. The world would return to normal the second I left this room. There would be expectations and responsibilities. There would be rules about who I could be with.

So I spent the night wide awake, watching him sleep and thanking every God I could think of for sparing his life. When the sun rose high in the sky, and I knew I could no longer avoid it, I folded the blanket neatly and laid it in the seat behind me. I didn't bother waking him to say goodbye; he needed rest, and I needed to do something he would disapprove of.

I ran a hand tiredly over my face as I closed the door quietly behind me and prepared to face the world. "Okay, Dimitri, I'd say it's time I go home-"

I froze.

Dimitri wasn't the one waiting for me.

"I thought we should talk," the Dragon announced, stepping forward from where he leaned against the wall.

The rest of the hallway was empty, not a guard or nurse in sight.

"Very well."

He nodded his head and began walking away. The command was clear, and I followed the Dragon through the halls of the infirmary wing. I didn't know where our destination was, but I didn't dare ask. The Dragon didn't like me on a good day and this week had been filled with bad ones.

He cleared his throat and tucked his hands together behind his back. "The nurses tell me you've been staying with him."

"Yes, your Majesty."

There was no use in denying that.

He sighed heavily, and for a few moments, we walked in silence. We stepped into the grand foyer of the palace with its sweeping arches and golden murals. He steered us toward the East Wing, back to the suites of the Council members. He was walking me home.

"Miss Moore, I must be frank with you. It's become quite clear that my son is rather infatuated with you. I wasn't particularly happy with this when I realized it myself, but at the time, it seemed that you could at least do one thing right by turning away his advances. Apparently, I've misjudged you yet again."

The Dragon stopped walking suddenly, focusing his attention on me entirely. "My son has responsibilities to this realm. He will be a king, my girl. And you will never be his queen."

"I'm very aware of my position in this court," I reminded him. "I'm well aware of both of our responsibilities."

"I'm sure you are. But let me remind you, your usefulness is in your womb. Plenty of fine suitors overseas would be more than happy to have their wife sharing their home."

I sucked in a breath. Surely he wouldn't do that. The Dragon wanted a complete Council. If he shipped me off as some mail-order bride, that would mean giving me to another kingdom entirely. He wouldn't do that.

Unless he really thought Clay and I's relationship was that risky.

"Love." He scoffed. "A useless notion for people like you and I, don't you think?"

Biting my lip and any retort that rose to it, I nodded. "I suppose."

"Stay away from my son, Theadora. I don't intend to have this conversation twice."

He began to stride away, and I wanted to let him. I wanted to let him go so I could fully embrace the feeling of my heart-shattering, but I knew there was still one thing I needed to do before this day was over. And he was the only person who could make it happen.

"Your majesty?"

He turned, raising an eyebrow. He looked so much like Clay at that moment that it was truly painful.

"I'd like to speak with Camilla."

The silence echoed around us briefly before his hollow laugh filled the air around us. "Absolutely not."

"I need to see her."

"For what purpose? Do you know how many of my people died trying to save you in that field? Now, you want to throw yourself directly into her path *again*? Just how unintelligent are you?"

I grit my teeth, ignoring the urge to let loose some magic in my frustration. I knew I was more powerful than the Dragon. He likely knew that too at this point. But magic wasn't the only form of power in this world. And if I wanted to stay in this castle with the friends I'd come to love, I needed to play his game.

Well, I needed to continue playing his game.

I had been playing it since the moment I stepped onto that bridge so many months ago.

I chose my words carefully, knowing this sentence would make or break his decision. "She put my life and the lives of my fellow Athenians at risk. The people she murdered weren't just yours, but mine, too. She needs to see that I am alive, that I am powerful, and that I will ascend to the Athenian Council despite her. She needs to sit with that knowledge."

His eyes widened as a slow grin spread across his face. I had chosen the right words. He nodded slightly before turning and leaving, but that was all I needed. I would visit Camilla this afternoon, and no one would get in my way.

The palace dungeons weren't a place I'd ever wanted to see again. And yet, I walked through these halls under a very different circumstance than my last visit. Today, I walked them with my head held high.

I'd allowed Nessira and Rei, my new lady-in-waiting, to dress me in a sparkling rust-orange ballgown with a shimmering golden belt. Since all of my gowns were specifically designed to display the Mark of Hyrax on my collarbone, they now all painfully revealed my bare skin, but that was no matter. I had them twist my hair into an elaborate allotment of braids and curls with golden jewels entwined throughout. They adorned my fingers and wrists with stunning diamond and pearl jewels.

Nessira had watched me warily throughout the process. She knew I hated the typical grandeur of court fashions and that I'd only wear them willingly if I was doing it for a calculated reason.

Which I was.

I insisted the Guards wait for me at the entrance of the dungeon. Dimitri protested vehemently, but I added such authority to my voice that they finally submitted and let me go alone.

I didn't want anyone else to hear this conversation.

Camilla's retching echoed through the chambers long before I set my eyes on her. And what a sight she was. Her usually shining black hair was stuck to her face in sweat. Every vein in her body was visibly black through her skin. She hovered over a wastebasket, body heaving but unable to spew anything else.

"Oh, good." She groaned as pushed herself onto her elbows to look up at me. "You're here."

"You look like shit."

She chuckled softly. "I feel worse."

"It's not as if you don't deserve it."

Camilla flinched. With effort, she pulled herself up to slump against the wall of the cell. She wiped her mouth with the sleeve of her tunic.

"I know that. It's not an excuse, but the shadows cloud your judgment. When I came off of it, I realized all the things I'd done... the people I'd hurt."

"Like Lorelai?" I spit.

Tears welled in her eyes. "That was an accident."

"Murder is never an accident, Camilla."

She nodded, and for a second, I wondered if this was the first time I was actually speaking to the real Camilla? Was this the girl that Iris and my friends had grown up knowing and loving?

"Is that what you came here to say?"

"No." I sighed and folded my arms in front of me. "I actually came here to ask you something."

"What in all of creation could you have to ask me?"

"Do you-" I stuttered, partially unwilling to ask the question. "Do you know what I am?"

CHAPTER THIRTY-EIGHT

Camilla laughed darkly, and the sound of it echoed around us. Ice prickled across my skin as I looked down at her and for a second I wavered in my resolve to ask this of her. Camilla had spent a year trying to kill me, and now I was asking for her help - her insight? She was the last person I should be trusting with this.

And yet, she might be the only person who had the answer.

I had spent the past week reflecting over all that had happened in the last year, and had come to one conclusion. I could do things that shouldn't be possible.

My power was stronger than anyone had an explanation for. I'd learned to fight like a trained soldier in less than two weeks. Magic still rippled in my veins despite the fact that the Mark of Hyrax was absent from my skin. So, what was it about me that made the impossible reality?

"You really don't know?" She questioned.

"Would I be here if I did?"

Camilla was quiet, and the rush of regret I had felt quickly turned to irritation. I should have known better than to hope she could help me.

"A few summers back," Camilla said suddenly. "I was cleaning out the old Hypatia Estate for my grandmother. Clay had just broken up with me, and she was pissed that I hadn't gotten him to fall in love with me. She's always been so obsessed with marrying into that family."

"Get to the point."

"Some Witches, powerful ones, have seen into the future and while I was cleaning out the old junk, I came across our collection of old prophecies. Hundreds of them, and everything I read in them had already come true. I didn't think much of it, so I set them aside, but then I found the prophecy about you."

Magic sparked in my fingertips, as if drawn to her words, and I clasped my shaking fingers together behind my back.

"It was old, carved on stone. I didn't even think much of it at the time; it hardly made any sense, but then you showed up and wrecked the bridge. That's when I realized it was true. I know it won't mean much to you, but you should know that none of this was ever personal, Thea. I was doing what I thought I had to in order to protect everyone."

Could she hear my heart racing? I could hear it like a pounding beat echoing throughout my head, like an ominous warning of what was to come.

"What was the prophecy?"

She frowned and leaned her head back against the wall. Through hooded eyes, she met my gaze and didn't blink as she recited the words that had changed both of our lives.

"*The daughter of Hyrax will shake the veil, and the King of Damnation will rise once more to rule over the children of the Gods. She will create a new death in the mortal realm and will stand at his side as his armies usher in the new age. Prepare for the Final War of the Gods.*" She chuckled to herself. "It seemed stupid when I first read it. There were no children of Hyrax remaining until-"

"Until me," I whispered.

That's what she had meant when she said the history books would paint her as the victor. She had truly thought that by killing me she would be saving the world because, according to this prophecy...

I was destined to unleash Hyrax from the Underworld and start a third War of the Gods.

"I can't do that," I told her, not sure who I was trying to convince. "The veil isn't even under the control of the Gods themselves. How could I possibly do anything to lower it?"

Camilla shrugged. "There are many things you've done that others can't."

No. Not that. Even if I could, I *wouldn't.* Because while it may be true that the victors write history, and while it may be true that Hyrax isn't the violent, vicious, jealous God he's portrayed as, I wouldn't take that risk.

Because even if Hyrax *wasn't* the villain in this story, unleashing him from the Underworld, lowering the veil and allowing the Gods to walk amongst us once more, would most likely start a war. Zion and Hyrax had done nothing but fight with each other since they took control of the realms. Their sibling rivalry would claim thousands if not millions of Descendant and mortal lives if it escalated to another war.

"I won't do that," I whispered.

Her brow furrowed, not in confusion but in pity. "I think you believe that, but no one can fight their destiny. So, if you care about these people at all, you'll finish what I started yourself."

I wanted to run. Anxiety bloomed in my muscles, pushing me to walk faster and faster through the halls of the palace.

Camilla's words haunted me as I traveled, hanging over me like a foreboding cloud. It couldn't be true. And yet, it wasn't just the prophecy that was leaving me on edge.

It was the question that now lingered in my mind. The question that had been burning in the corners of my consciousness for far too long.

Dimitri seemed surprised when I asked him to ready a horse immediately. He had likely assumed I would want to return to Clay's side or join the other nobles in a dinner honoring the fallen soldiers. I belonged at that dinner. As the matriarch of House Hyrax, my attendance would be expected by the Dragon and other Council members, but this simply couldn't wait.

We rode hard and fast. Netta took my every command without complaint. The distance wasn't far, but I felt bad for the way I pushed her. As I threw my leg off towards the ground, I ran my hand through her mane affectionately.

"I'll get you an extra sugar cube when we return to the castle," I promised her.

The sun had already set over Hyrax estate leaving shadows as the only guests. Looking over the manor left me feeling oddly conflicted.

This was my home. It was the only place I'd been that truly felt like it was *mine*, but it wasn't. This manor belonged more to Hyrax than it did to me.

The God of the Underworld.

The God who hadn't accepted that realm as enough.

The God who'd started wars because of his desire to rule the Mortal Realm.

And according to that prophecy, he wasn't finished in his quest to gain control of this realm. And *I* was the one who would free him. *I* was the one who was going to stand by him as he brought death to the people who lived here.

Without glancing back, I commanded Dimitri to wait outside for me as I lifted my skirts and ran into the house and made my way to the door Clay had pointed out as leading to the library. Floor-to-ceiling shelves of books stood nearly ten feet tall and sported literature of all forms. Sighing, I chewed on my lip as I glanced over the space. There had to be hundreds of books in here.

"Mythology," I whispered to myself. I needed the mythology books.

I found them in the back corner, five shelves up. Grunting, I pulled the ladder across the room and hiked up my skirts again to climb. I wrapped one arm through the ladder for balance and started tearing off the books one by one, flipping through the pages.

There.

I crawled off the ladder slowly, unable to tear my eyes away even as I felt my heart beating in an uneven rhythm. A soft sob escaped as I sank to the floor and ran my fingers helplessly across the worn page before me.

I had once asked Hansel why there were no illustrations of Hyrax in the palace. I had partially wondered if I looked like him at all. Hyrax was absent from any murals and paintings at the castle, though, and not even the history and mythology texts depicted his likeness. Hansel had said that years ago, the Descendants of Zion had burned away any image of him as a punishment for his crimes.

But Hansel hadn't been here. He hadn't been to this temple of a house built by Hyrax's Descendants.

Turns out, we had kept our pictures.

And in the center of this book was a single illustration of Hyrax, King of the Underworld, seated on his throne of bones in the caverns of the underworld. In his right hand, he lifted a chalice of red wine in a silent toast to the painter.

A painter that, from the angle, had to have been seated at a long dining table.

I knew because I'd sat at that table myself many times. I'd joined him in that toast. I'd witnessed him sit on that throne.

I'd sat in that very position in my dreams.

The dreams that had started as nightmares and had somehow, over recent months, turned into the guidance I had needed most. Dreams that provided me the insight I needed on that battlefield that had saved my life. Dreams in which I had spoken to a man who referred to himself as my friend but who refused to share his name.

He insisted I had already known who he was. Maybe at some level, I had always suspected the truth and refused to acknowledge it.

I could deny it no longer, though.

Since the moment I had awoken in this Gods-forsaken palace, I'd been unknowingly convening with Hyrax in my dreams.

CHAPTER THIRTY-NINE

CAMILLA

Camilla had never known agony like this. She was no stranger to pain. She'd taken plenty of beatings in the years since her father had died in the war and she'd gone to live with her grandmother. And there was, of course, the summer she'd turned nineteen when The Dragon had made her his own personal plaything. She'd never told anyone about that; she doubted she ever would, but needless to say, the physical pain of withdrawal wasn't necessarily worse than anything she'd felt before.

But the emotional pain was something else.

The shadows had a way of climbing into your skull, warping everything you were into what they wanted you to be. It was like she had been wholly possessed, unable to stop herself from shedding more blood in their name. The grimoires had warned her that the shadows gained their power from the Underworld. She should have known how dark it would all become.

If she could go back, she would have done things differently.

If she could go back and do things differently, Lorelai would still be alive.

Iris would never forgive her; she knew that. None of them would. That hardly mattered, though. The Dragon would have her publicly executed. He would make her a demonstration of the power of the Athenian government and what would happen to anyone who tried to disrupt it. She likely only had days left in this realm.

She knew she wouldn't see any of her friends again. In truth, she didn't mind that fact though, because she didn't think she could handle the shame of apologizing for all the awful things she had done.

Thinking about Lorelai was hard. That wasn't supposed to have happened. After she started recruiting others to join her mission, she'd noticed she had a few zealots on the team - people who simply wanted to kill anyone in the castle. Part of her knew they were a liability, but Shadow Camilla hardly cared about a little extra blood being spilled.

I'm going to be sick again, she thought before leaning over the toilet.

She couldn't even keep down water. Her body wouldn't handle it. The shakes came as soon as she finished retching. Those were the worst. The tremors shook her entire body from head to toe. Sometimes, she shook so violently she would bang her head against the cell wall and knock herself unconscious.

"My," a feminine voice called to her. "What an awful smell."

Camilla used all her strength to steady her body before turning to meet her grandmother's gaze.

Alina stood tall, nose wrinkled in disgust as she peered down at her. She wore her usual simple gown, her gray hair tied back at the nape. To anyone else, she might look like she had kind eyes, but Camilla knew better. She had grown up dealing with her grandmother's temper, unrealistic expectations, and unfailing manipulations.

Nothing she'd done in life was ever good enough to impress her grandmother.

Which meant all Camilla had ever done was disappoint the woman, which in turn simply incited her wrath.

"What do you want?" Camilla breathed, voice hoarse.

Alina gave a close-mouthed smile as she batted away a fly. "Oh, I came to thank you, my dear. You played your part absolutely wonderfully."

Camilla frowned, stomach churning uncomfortably. Her grandmother had never once thanked her in all her life. Why would she be doing it now, when Camilla had failed so profoundly?

Alina had been the first person Camilla had told about the prophecy. There was no love or trust in their relationship, but Alina was the matriarch of House Hypatia; who else was Camilla supposed to go to? To her surprise, it had seemed to be something that bonded them finally. Alina was sure it was Camilla's destiny to find that prophecy. She was convinced Camilla had to be the one to stop Thea.

For the first time in her life, her grandmother looked at her like she was worthy.

Or at least... she had looked at her like she was valuable for something *other* than marrying Clayton Vail.

She hadn't wanted to use black magic, not at first. She knew the laws, and the dangers associated with it. But Alina hadn't even given her a choice. She'd dragged Camilla to the Hypatia Estate and forced her to make her first sacrifice - a small barn kitten. Then it was a deer. Then a horse. Then, a kitchen servant.

Camilla felt each death, like small dark marks on her soul, until she didn't. Eventually, the shadows corrupted her so entirely that the death stopped bothering her. She only cared about getting more power.

"Thea is alive," Camilla reminded her. "That's hardly a success."

Alina's lips quirked in a venomous smile as she slowly reached into the pouch at her side and pulled out a small glass vial. Camilla's senses reached out towards it immediately. Her skin crawled, her stomach clenched, and the pain in her head reached an impossible peak. There was blood in that vial.

"Oh, but my girl," she mused, not looking away from the glass in her hands. "You got me this. And that was all I *really* needed you for. That and to stir a little distrust in the commoners."

"Is that-"

"Theadora's? Of course!"

Camilla frowned, trying desperately to calm the magic in her that was reaching towards that vial. "I don't understand, Grandmother."

"It always surprises me how stupid you all are," Alina laughed, finally meeting Camilla's gaze.

Her eyes.

Her grandmother had always had dull hazel eyes that had lacked any light, but now they were positively luminous.

And vibrantly *green.*

The elder woman reached up and pulled the pin out of her hair. It grew in length as it fell around her shoulders, morphing from the pin-straight gray Camilla was accustomed to into a wild mane of vibrant red curls. The wrinkles around her eyes and mouth smoothed themselves, and her facial features shifted until everything that was her grandmother was gone, and in her place stood a young woman. She was tall and thinly boned, with porcelain skill and a wild edge to her expression.

Camilla stumbled back instantly, at first in fear, before falling to her knees. Even as her mind struggled to function through the haze of withdrawal, she knew to bow her head to the Goddess in front of her.

"Now that's more like it!" Pasnia clapped giddily. "The look on your face is just delightful."

"How-" Camilla bit her lip to stop herself from speaking out of turn.

She was in the presence of a *Goddess.* An actual Goddess. It had been a millennium since a God had walked the Mortal Realm. And standing before Pasnia made one thing abundantly clear, Camilla may be descended from a God but her magic was so miniscule in comparison. No Descendant could ever think to compare themselves to the being in front of her.

Pasnia's pale skin was positively incandescent, shining so brightly that Camilla had to avert her gaze. Her green eyes sparkled with flashes of unchecked power. And that power was... overwhelming. Camilla could feel it all around her. It pressed down on her like the force of standing directly next to the sun. With her body already so weak, Camilla was sure Pasnia could simply disintegrate her with one look.

"None of you pray as often as you used to," Pasnia claimed, running her fingers across the cell's glass. "You abuse *our* power as it runs through your veins. You use it to accomplish your silly goals and rule your ridiculous little countries. All the while, you forget it is *ours*. That *we* are the Gods!"

Pasnia laughed suddenly, pitching over and clutching her side. Just as quickly, she righted herself, staring deep into Camilla's eyes without levity. The speed of her mood changes left Camilla's thoughts spinning.

"Alina never prayed a day in her life until the old bat started worshipping at Mama's temple," the Goddess explained. "She was so desperate for a baby in your womb. I don't understand why she cared so much, a baby would hardly have solved your problems."

Camilla swallowed thickly. Pasnia may not have understood her grandmother's motivations, but Camilla did. It was the same reason Alina had urged her to stop taking the fertility suppressant while luring Clay to her bed as hormone-overrun teenagers. Alina had wanted power. A royal child was a way of guaranteeing that.

Camilla hadn't known she'd started praying to the Goddess Delia, Pasnia's mother, for that pregnancy to be granted.

That's why Camilla never prayed lightly.

Sometimes the Gods answer.

"Your lives are so meaningless to us," Pasnia growled. "Mama didn't even bother to answer her. But I could always see the beauty in things

Mama ignored. Mama can't see how beautiful *desperation* is. Alina was so incredibly desperate. She would do *anything*. In the end, it didn't even take much to convince her. All I had to do was say I would advocate on your behalf to Mama, and the old crone slit her wrists right open."

Camilla gasped. "She sacrificed herself to you?"

Human sacrifices to the Gods were forbidden… for obvious reasons.

Pasnia grinned. "She *gave* me this mortal body to borrow. How sweet, don't you think? It's been a millennium since Zion and the others raised the veil. An entire millennium that I've been trapped in that torturous darkness of the Underworld. But because of you, I was finally able to escape! And my, your Mortal Realm has grown since I was last here. It really is something to see."

Pasnia clapped her hands gleefully as she spun to face Camilla. Her wide emerald eyes flashed wickedly. Slowly, the goddess tilted her head as her lips opened into a toothy smile. In that moment, there was no doubt that Camilla bowed before the Goddess of Madness.

How could she have spent *years* interacting with Pasnia without realizing it?

"Anyway, you were just magnificent in all of this!" Pasnia complimented. "Hyrax wasn't sure it would work at first. He so hates to put his trust in you creatures. I'm sure you can imagine why. But I always knew it was a good plan. I scribbled down one fake prophecy, and you just ran with it! It hardly took any convincing to get you to dip your toe in black magic. And that party! I mean, it's just magnificent. Truly impressive work. Bravo."

The shakes were starting again. Camilla's body was trembling with enough force that she could no longer hold herself up. Her mind raged with questions and fears until it was all she could do to gasp in air. She couldn't tell if she was suffering from the withdrawals or the effects of Pasnia's insane magic.

The Goddess was pacing once more, hardly even looking at her.

"Hyrax is so pleased with you, child. Did you know the shadow magic is his? Hypatia abandoned you the second you killed that cat. The irony of it! You tried to destroy the daughter of Hyrax using *his* power! I hope you know you have been truly instrumental in our plan to lower the veil once and for all."

Camilla retreated away, cowering against the wall as Pasnia's insane eyes perused over her.

"You've been an absolute doll, but I still have some work to do, so I best be going. Good luck to you with the execution and all. I'm sure I'll see you again soon in the Underworld."

She was gone in an instant. One moment, she stood outside the cell with her laughter echoing around Camilla, and the next, there was nothing. She was alone once again. Alone with nothing but her regrets.

The prophecy was never real.

All of this had been for nothing.

Theadora Moore would not release the King of the Underworld. She was never destined to release Hyrax, and yet it would still happen because the *Queen* of the Underworld had found a way to walk the Mortal Realm and wouldn't rest until her husband joined her.

"I need to speak to Theadora Moore!" Camilla was screaming before she even knew what to say.

She only knew that she needed to warn them. She needed to warn them all.

"Please! Someone! I need to speak to Thea."

If anyone heard her, they ignored her. She screamed until her voice ran out, and her body collapsed onto the floor in exhaustion. When her voice finally returned, she cried for the guards again.

But no one ever came.

AUTHOR'S NOTE

Holy cow! We did it!

If you've gotten this far, then I have to thank you from the very bottom of my heart. Thank you for taking your time to spend with me in the world of Athenia. I hope you've come to love Thea and the gang as much as I have.

This book has been a labor of love. I've spent nearly six years dreaming of this book, writing it, rewriting it, editing it, rewriting it again... Needless to say, the fact that it is out in the open world is absolutely surreal to me.

I want to take a moment to thank the friends and family who have supported me in this process and believed in me, especially my parents who have listened to me talk about this dream since I was 11 years old. Look guys, I finally wrote that book!

I also owe a HUGE thank you to my beta team, whose thoughtful consideration of this draft helped shape it into the story you just read. The time you gave me has not only helped bring Thea's story to life, it has made me a much better writer. Thank you to my ARC readers for the time they have spent in reading, reviewing and sharing.

And lastly, at the risk of sounding repetitive, thank YOU. Thank you, reader, for choosing my book out of the millions in this world. Thank you for investing in it and thereby in me. I hope you absolutely loved it and stick with me throughout the remainder of this journey, because Thea's story is not over just yet!

If you did love this book, I have a few requests for you! Please join my online community by following me on all social media platforms (@arcadiarayne). There you'll get all the latest updates on my books. I request that you also take a moment to write a brief review if possible. As an indie author, reviews are incredibly important for my success and are vital for connecting with new readers. Thank you in advance for any support you can give!

Finally, if this book has touched you in any way or if you have related to these characters as they've faced struggles such as grief, PTSD, addiction, and more please know that you are not alone and support exists. As an author, I strive to tell stories that allow us to face things that may be difficult to bear in the real world. Some of the struggles in this book are personal to me and some are not, but they are very real for many people in this world. Remember, you were not created to back down and you have *never* truly been powerless!

THEA'S STORY CONTINUES IN...

THE CROWN OF THE DARK PRINCE

Check out this exclusive sneak peak of The Crown of the Dark Prince, book two in the House of Hyrax series.

THE CROWN OF THE DARK PRINCE

CHAPTER ONE

The Dragon must have decided he finally wanted to kill me. That was the only explanation I could think of for why my combat trial consisted of me in a gladiator-style ring fighting members of the Athenian royal guard. Surely, he intended for me to die on this battlefield.

For a little over a year, I had been preparing for the trials that I would need to pass in order to ascend to the Athenian Royal Council, where I would represent House Hyrax, the descendants of the God of the Dead. It wasn't necessarily a position I had initially wanted, but over time, I'd finally accepted that serving in that role was my responsibility as the last living Descendant of Hyrax. More than that, even. It was my birthright.

So, I had dedicated myself to my studies of ancient mythology, world history, modern politics, Descendant lineages, hand-to-hand combat, weaponry use and, of course, magic use. And while combat had come surprisingly easy for me, impossibly easy even, there was no way that in a single year I had built up enough skill to take on Athenian guards who had spent their entire lives training to defeat others in battle.

I was going to get the shit kicked out of me. Which likely was exactly what the Dragon wanted to have happen.

I'd been surprised when I even managed to take down the first guard with a blade pressed to his carotid artery, but my victory had been short-lived. Before the crowd even stopped cheering, a door had opened on the other side of the arena and another guard strode forward.

He ran at a furious pace, intent on tackling me. I jumped sharply to my left and watched as he spun on his heels to face me. By the Gods, he was fast, wasting no time in recovering and launching a quick jab towards me. In my haze to deflect it, I didn't even notice his arm reaching for my wrist. He pressed down on the tendons there and I unwillingly released the blade, grunting as it fell to the sand at our feet.

He's bigger than you, you have to be faster. I heard Rankor's voice in my head.

My friend and trainer had given me that advice so many times in our preparations for this trial that I swore I could hear him reciting it to me while I brushed my teeth in the morning.

As the guard released my wrist, I went for speed... and surprise.

I ducked to the ground, crawling between his widespread legs.

The crowd gasped in shock, but the maneuver earned me a moment of hesitation, which was enough for me to throw my leg back into the guard's rear end and send him stumbling forward. Rolling, I launched myself back to my feet and set my sights on him once more.

This would be so much easier with my magic. As a Descendant of Hyrax, I had the unique ability of telepathy. Typically, Descendants of Hyrax had abilities related to... well, death. Abilities like necromancy or being able to talk to those who have passed on. To our knowledge, I was the first to move things with my mind.

And every part of me wanted to use that power in me to blast the guard across the arena, but use of magic during the hand-to-hand combat trial was strictly prohibited. They had even dosed me with mortal blood to prevent me from accessing my powers.

Little did anyone know that the mortal blood had no effect on me or my powers and that it was only my sheer will that stopped me from tapping into them.

It was another thing that made me different.

Like the fact I was a Descendant who had lived through a power-stripping and still had powers.

And like the fact that I was a Descendant who didn't bear the mark of her ancestor like a permanent tattoo across the skin.

There was so much that made me different...

A crushing punch to my stomach broke me free of my thoughts and had me gasping for air. I stumbled away from the guard, desperate to catch my breath as a flush of embarrassment colored my cheeks. I could almost feel Rankor's eyes on me from the audience, criticizing me for not staying focused. I should know better. My anxiety spiral could wait until *after* I lived through this.

As the guard unsheathed the sword across his back, I reached for the dagger that I had strapped to my thigh. They'd given me the option between a sword or knives and while I didn't *hate* using swords, the weight of knives was easier to manage and I could maneuver them more quickly. And as Rankor liked to remind me, most people were bigger than me, so I needed to be faster.

The guard stalked towards me, and I again opted for surprise. Might as well give the people in the stands a show. Turning on my heels, I sprinted away from him towards the opposite end of the arena. After a beat of hesitation, I could hear him following me. The heavy beat of his steps in the sand increased in frequency until he was just behind me. My side clenched with a searing cramp that I pushed through. I just needed to make it a little farther.

Just as he reached to grasp the end of my braid, I threw myself towards the wall, kicking and spinning, throwing the blade as I hovered momentarily in the air. It was a bit of a shot in the dark, not allowing me time to aim, but Rankor had made me practice this move a million times, using the sound of footsteps behind me as a judge of distance. And the practice paid off. The blade bounced off the center of his forehead.

I was glad they gave us toy weapons for this. I would have chosen not to carry anything into battle with me if they had insisted I use real steel.

The weight of enough death already pressed upon me.

I landed in a heavy crouch that sent pain radiating up my arms and legs, but I had successfully bested him. The roar of the crowd was deafening as the guard bowed and exited the arena... only for *another* one to take his place.

How many are they going to make me fight? I wondered, as I pulled the next blade out of the sheath on my wrist and launched myself towards him.

I fought as hard as I could, ignoring both the protest in my fatiguing muscles and the noise from the crowd that threatened to distract me. I hadn't expected a crowd to be here. Prior to the trial, I'd been given very little information about what to expect, but my first trial had been so private I expected this to be the same.

My written examination covering mythology and other important subjects had taken nearly four hours in its entirety to complete, but overall hadn't been too much of a challenge. The Royal Tutor, Hansel, had provided me all the information I needed ahead of time and I had been diligent in my studies, both those that I completed in the castle library and those completed by candlelight in the library of Hyrax Estate. I'd spent quite a bit of time in that library lately, but now wasn't the time to think of that either.

I beat the third guard with a blade pressed against his kidney and the fourth by managing to unarm him and use his own sword against him. By the time the fifth guard entered the arena, I was filled with equal parts of exhaustion and rage. The Dragon, our king, had once told me these trials would be more of a formality than anything in my case. Every Council member had to pass the trials in order to qualify for their seat, but since I was the last Descendant of Hyrax, there was no one else who could take my place on the Council. And the Dragon wanted a complete Council, filled with representatives from the Houses descended from the High Gods, more than anything. So, while I would technically have to complete the trials, it was pretty much a guarantee that I would pass them.

Even so, this felt like more than a formality. This felt like The Dragon wanted to see me bleed.

I suspected he did. The Gods knew that vicious man would get off on the sight of it. He and I had never particularly gotten along, and our relationship had grown tenser in recent months. He'd been overly confrontational since an attack at the palace that had ended when I killed every assailant with a simple thought and extension of my power.

It wasn't hard to realize why he didn't like me.

The Dragon knew I was more powerful than he was.

By the end of my fight with the fifth guard, though, he finally got his wish. I was, in fact, bleeding from a broken nose, but I had won with a blade pressed directly above his heart.

There was a pause.

No more doors opened. Was that it? Was the trial finally over?

Turning on my heels, I looked up to the crowd, and the perched box where the Dragon and the other members of the Council sat watching the show. Carefully, I avoided the gaze of Clayton Vail, our Crown Prince. I'd been avoiding Clay for some time now.

Clay had been one of the first people I'd met when I'd shown up at the palace a year ago without memories of my prior life. He'd been cold then and aggressive, much like his father. But I learned that while the Dragon was truly just an evil man, Clay's hostility was often just for show. Deep down, Clay *cared*. He cared for his family, his friends, his citizens... and he cared for me.

There was no room for either of us to have those feelings for each other, though. Council members had arranged marriages in order to ensure there would be heirs to our Houses. Clay and I would both be married off to others, likely sometime soon.

Our complicated relationship wasn't the only reason I was avoiding him now, though. I was terrified if I truly spent any time with him that he would be able to tell I was keeping something from him.

That I was keeping something from everyone.

The Dragon met my gaze without flinching. Slowly, he raised a bushy eyebrow at me and smiled. And that's when I knew this wasn't over.

Both doors on either side of the arena opened. From the left came a guard I hadn't met before. From the right came Dimitri, the head of my personal guard team.

Oh, come on now.

I glared at the Dragon, tossing my blade to my left hand while I reached to pull a second from my right thigh.

"I am sorry for this, my lady." Dimitri sighed as he approached.

Groaning silently, I wiped away the blood from my broken nose with my forearm and took my fighting stance.

"Let's just get this over with."

The last fight was a blur of flying arms and weapons. My muscles screamed in protest and my head swam as exhaustion threatened to take me under. But still I carried on. Dimitri grabbed my wrist and twisted, pulling the muscles there so tightly that I couldn't help but to scream out. He flinched as I did, but still we carried on. There would be time later to care about the strained muscles and broken bones. The palace healers would take care of all of that once this was over. I just needed to finish it.

I defeated the sixth guard with a blade across the throat and I bested Dimitri with a blade to the back. Dirty fighting for sure, but successful.

Music filled the arena as the band began playing the Athenian anthem. The heavy beat of the pounding drum seemed like it was set to match my heart as the crowd erupted around me, chanting my name. Slowly, the Dragon raised his hands and slowly clapped.

I had done it. I had passed the combat trial. I was officially two-thirds of the way to taking my place on the Council.

"You fucking did it!" Rankor cheered happily, sweeping me into a bear hug that lifted me from the ground and knocked the breath from my lungs.

"Did you doubt me?"

Rankor was a brawn from House Arto, making his strength magically fueled. He seemed to remember this, and that he could literally kill me from hugging me too tightly, all too suddenly, and sat me on my feet in a rush as his lips quirked in a bashful smile..

"No!" he replied too quickly, before sighing when I raised my brows at him in disbelief. "I believe in you, of course. I've always known that when you're at your best, you can handle anything that's thrown at you."

"But?"

"But you haven't been at your best." His hand cupped my face affectionately, thumb stroking the skin under my eyes that I knew was hollow and dark from lack of sleep. "You've been so exhausted lately. I've been worried."

Yes, well, I *had* been feeling exhausted lately. Exhaustion was the unhappy consequence of not sleeping. And I hadn't been sleeping in weeks. Since I'd discovered that I'd somehow been communicating with my ancestor, Hyrax, in my dreams, I'd been terrified to return to that place - the dark caverns that must be the Underworld.

Hyrax had lied to me. He'd never necessarily pretended to be someone else, but he hadn't admitted who he was either. For months, he had taught me how to use my magic and counseled me on how to navigate politics and relationships in the mortal realm, all while hiding his true identity. And a lie by omission was still a lie.

And if the God of the Dead was lying to me, then he had to have a reason. What did he want from me?

"You care to tell me what's been going on with you?" Rankor pressed, pulling my focus once more.

I sighed, overly dramatic. "Oh, I don't know Rankor. There is the fact that one of my friends secretly tried to kill me for months and only ended up killing Lorelai instead."

We rarely spoke about Camilla, or that she had fooled us all into thinking she was our friend, while she secretly got addicted to forbidden magic in her attempt to kill me. In her addiction-fueled rage, she had planned an attack during a palace party. The attack had been the first time I'd had to battle during a real-life threat, and I hadn't been good enough. I wasn't fast enough to stop an assassin from killing Lorelai, the fiery-haired Truthseeker who had been one of the first to befriend me.

Camilla's betrayal had shocked everyone in the kingdom. No one had deciphered *why* she had lost herself in blood magic. No one but me that is.

I knew the truth behind her motivations. In the immediate days after Camilla had been captured, I had visited her in the palace dungeons and she had told me of a prophecy she had once found. A prophecy written about me...

The daughter of Hyrax will shake the veil, and the King of Damnation will rise once more to rule over the children of the Gods. She will create a new death in the mortal realm and will stand at his side as his armies usher in the new age. Prepare for the Final War of the Gods.

That prophecy was yet another secret I was keeping. The last thing I needed was people in this palace thinking I would destroy the world. And it didn't matter anyway, because I didn't care what some stupid prophecy from hundreds of years ago said. I would not shake the veil between worlds. I *couldn't* shake the veil, not even the Gods themselves could move it.

So, giving voice to the delusional concerns of a dark witch was entirely unnecessary.

"Go bathe." Rankor commanded, flopping onto the settee in the parlor of my apartment suites and reaching for my bar cart. "The party in your honour begins in about an hour, which doesn't give us much time to get fashionably drunk beforehand."

I rolled my eyes, but did as I was told, eager to wash the sweat and blood off of me. They had pulled me from the arena straight into the infirmary where the nurses had set my broken nose and healed all other injuries until all that was left behind were bruises and small red welts.

From there, I'd found Emeryn, my new chief-of-staff, waiting in the hall. As my ascension to the council became more imminent, the Dragon had decided I would need someone on my staff to help manage my schedule, engagements, and public image. And so Emeryn had been hired and she had been my constant shadow ever since.

She was a stern woman, constantly dressed in simple black gowns with her hair pulled back into a tight knot. She would occasionally offer small smiles when she was pleased with me, but mostly she remained focused, taking her job far too seriously.

And so, I had no doubt that she would be knocking on the door to escort me to the celebration in exactly one hour.

Nessira, my lady-in-waiting, had prepared a steaming bath with lavender oils and left several bottles of soap and fresh towels for me, one of the many reasons she was one of my favorite people.

"We should discuss the young women who have applied for the opening within your staff, my lady," she breathed as she began twisting my long blonde hair into an elaborate knot at the back of my neck.

I didn't miss the way Rankor flinched at the mention that I needed a new lady-in-waiting. The second spot had been recently vacated after my initial lady, a cheery young girl named Geia, had betrayed me and helped Camilla kidnap me away from the palace. Temporary ladies were passing in and out of my services, but Nessira was growing more insistent in her reminders that we needed a more permanent solution.

I took the glass of wine Rankor offered me and downed it in a single sitting.

"Perhaps I do not need a replacement," I whispered. "You manage just fine."

Nessira raised a brow at me disapprovingly. "Surely I do not deserve more work because you are hesitant to admit that the girl was never the friend you wanted her to be."

I bit down on my lip.

"That's a bit harsh, Nessira" Rankor chastised.

Nessira shrugged. "My lady used to like when we spoke honestly to her."

She was right. I had always encouraged her to speak to me as an equal. I had embraced the advice and companionship of my ladies-in-waiting. Look where that had gotten me.

Still, Nessira was also right in asserting that she didn't deserve more work because I was too afraid to move on with my life. So I nodded my agreement and promised to look over the recommendations that she had left for me in the morning.

She dressed me in a floor-length gown the color of blood. Its boned bodice hugged my torso, emphasizing the curve of my breasts and swell of my hips before falling effortlessly to my feet. Two long capes of tulle hung over my back, secured by the sparkling golden aplicae that hung over my chest and shoulders. She painted my lips dark and lined my eyes in kohl.

"You look magnificent," Rankor complimented.

"I look like the daughter of Hyrax," I mumbled, staring at myself in the mirror as Nessira tucked a matching golden crown into my hair.

Rankor chuckled. "You are a daughter of Hyrax."

Didn't mean I had to be happy about it.

"There is one last thing, my lady," Nessira sighed, and approached me with the black ink.

Every fiber of my being wanted to protest as she set about painting on the Mark of Hyrax on my chest, but I ground my teeth until I was sure they would crack and allowed it, nonetheless. The Dragon had decided it would be better for the general public to not know about my missing mark. He believed it raised too many questions that could make my standing in society too precarious. In other words, he needed me to be unquestionably a Descendant of Hyrax and that came with a descendants mark.

But I liked the look of my bare skin without that bident on my chest. I liked not having a reminder of Hyrax or his lies and the prophecy so blatantly in my face.

"Come on," Rankor drawled, linking my arm through his. "Your adoring fans are waiting."

Emeryn was waiting outside for us, hand poised to knock on the door just as we stepped out. She looked over at me appraisingly and nodded, as if to say this look would work, before dipping her head respectfully and motioning for us to follow her.

"We expect full attendance for this evening's festivities, my lady." She announced, wasting no time in getting to business. Rankor rolled his eyes as she continued on. "The Dragon will announce you and give the celebratory toast to begin the evening. Dinner will take place at seven sharp and you will be seated at the head table with members of the Council and their families. Dignitaries vising from Tennebris and the Republic of Inanis are also in attendance this evening and will be eager for an audience with you."

They'll be eager to convince the Dragon and I to align with them through my marriage, she meant.

"Are you sure we have to go to this?" I whispered to Rankor under my breath.

"Yes," Emeryn barked, not even bothering to look back at us. "Now that Camilla has been apprehended, it's time to focus on your ascension to the Council and your overall role in society. This is your duty, my lady. You cannot delay it any longer."

I felt the truth of those words in every fiber of my being.

www.ingramcontent.com/pod-product-compliance
Lightning Source LLC
Chambersburg PA
CBHW021335310726
48971CB00001B/134